Bran forced me to ~~~~~~~ participation in our activities. He continually tested the barriers in my mind between real and manufactured consent. One morning, I must choose which whip he would use, but was allowed no say in the number of strokes. He would bring me to the point of orgasm, then stop short, no matter how I begged him to continue. The next morning, he would arrive with but one whip, and remind me how I had begged him to continue the day before. His strokes would drive me to and beyond orgasm after orgasm, until I collapsed in exhaustion.

Then, one morning, I awoke to find him sitting on the edge of my bed. Instead of a whip, he carried a tape recorder. When I opened my eyes, he pressed the button on the recorder and I heard first his voice and then my own responding. "Mostly side to side, sometimes in a circle at the end." The tape was of our conversation the second night, just after I signed the contract. I was describing the mechanics of masturbation. He pressed the stop button.

"Show me, Chantal...."

Also by CAROLE REMY:
Beauty of the Beast

Fantasy Impromptu

CAROLE REMY

MASQUERADE BOOKS, INC.
801 SECOND AVENUE
NEW YORK, N.Y. 10017

First Masquerade Edition 1997
First Printing March 1997
ISBN 1-56333-513-1

First Top Shelf Edition March 1997
ISBN 1-56333-897-1

Manufactured in the United States of America
Published by Masquerade Books, Inc.
801 Second Avenue
New York, N.Y. 10017

for
Keith Edward Ditto
1947–1991

allegro agitato
Fast and Furious

sforzando–subito piano
With Force, Then Softly

I shall try, as Lewis Carroll suggests, to begin at the beginning. I was an Alice in some ways, eager but hardly pliant. I had skipped and slid from path to path, led by a fading Cheshire-cat grin. Last September, when this tale begins, I was forty-three and living by myself for the first time. But let's back up a few years.

When my children were young, I needed money. The marriage that produced them outlasted the birth of the youngest by only a few months. My ex is an aspiring rock singer, one of the legion who slip unnoticed into ever-seedier bars. The first time he went into drug rehab, I forgave him. Five months later, I caught him shooting up, and I left.

I wanted to stay home with my daughters, so I took

in day-care children and refinished furniture on the side. I moved into a smaller house and through several boyfriends, none much better than my ex. I never let my children meet them, which should have told me something if only I'd been paying attention.

As the girls grew up, I began taking night-school and then university correspondence courses. By the time they entered high school, I was the proud owner of a degree in English literature, and I hadn't had a boyfriend in two years. I was making progress.

I still wanted a job that would keep me at home. With my degree had come a desire to write. I tried a romance novel, but couldn't attract an agent. Then I wrote a mystery and got an agent, but no publisher. When the agent gave up on me, I pretty much gave up on myself, too. I got another disastrous boyfriend, my former English professor. My best friend hated him for the way he treated me. She gave me the book *How to Overcome Low Self-Esteem and Achieve True Growth.* We had a good laugh. Then, after she left, I had a good cry.

When the professor dropped me, I was furious, and I wrote a revenge novel. I imagined our relationship as SM, with me as the *S* this time. It turned out erotic but not harsh, more erotica-lite. I sent it off to a sleazy publisher—no more agents for me. The editor rejected it because it was too conventional. Hah. As I went more upscale, the rejections got more enthusiastic and eventually I struck a deal with a small but prestigious press.

In three years I cranked out five novels. I wasn't particularly happy writing about penises and vaginas. I would say to myself, "I'm a practical woman. That's why I write erotica." Irony was my refuge. The money wasn't great, barely enough to keep the kids in saxophone lessons and Levi's, but we made it. I told everyone that now that I had my degree, I marked correspondence courses for a living.

My youngest turned twenty in May and moved into an apartment with her older sister. My story begins that September, when I thought my erotica days were over. With my children grown, my life would now have the peace and order I'd longed for. I could finally write something…good.

Then, on September 17, at about 6:30, he appeared. Poof, like a genie. I had bought an armload of groceries and was headed home in time for *Jeopardy*. As always, the garage was full of forgotten-but-not-discarded effluvia and I parked in the driveway. I climbed out of my car and walked up the three steps to the front door. One hand fumbled around in my purse for the house keys; I always keep them on a separate key chain. I figured a burglar could steal my car or my furniture, but not both. I didn't sense his presence until he put a hand over my mouth. He looped his other arm around my waist and carted me off the porch to the side of the yard—just like that.

To tell the truth, I hardly even fought him. I was too surprised, and his arm around my waist cut off my oxygen. I could barely breathe, let alone kick and scream. I cursed the giant rhododendron that blocks the view of my entryway from the road. Too late now to cut it back so the neighbors could see the front door.

By the time we got to the side of the house, I recovered enough wits to be afraid. Instinct took over. I squirmed and kicked and tried to bite his hand. He pinned my face under his armpit, twisting my hands behind my back. From that position I could kick his legs, and I did. He must have had shins of steel because he never flinched. He tied my hands, then let my face out long enough to slap a piece of tape over my mouth.

Now that I was trussed up, he put his hands on my shoulders and held me away from his body and looked at me. I kicked and wriggled and shouted muffled threats. Something about the amused and slightly patronizing look in his eye made me feel like a recalcitrant child— one who wouldn't play by the rules, so she wasn't having fun with the other kids. I stopped struggling and stared right back at him.

He was younger than I, perhaps thirty-five to my forty-three. He was much taller than I am, about six-foot-three. His face was broad, with strong bones under muscular cheeks. His forehead rose high above almost-bushy eyebrows. He had curly nut-brown hair and eyes and no facial hair, not even a shadow. He wore thick Clark Kent glasses and a Gucci watch. His $500 suit molded to a sturdy yet graceful torso and was hardly rumpled by our tussle.

I tried to ask him what he wanted, but all that came out was a mumble through the tape. He shook his head at me and stared some more. I waited for him to say something, anything. Finally, he shook me gently by the shoulders like a rag doll. The gesture felt final. I thought, Whew, I guess that's it. He'll go away, and I'll go inside and have a stiff drink.

Wrong.

He shook me again, a little harder. Then he began to pull me toward my front door. I did *not* want him inside my house so I dug in my heels, quite literally, and fought to keep from being dragged along. He stopped right away and I thought, "At least he can be reasoned with, sort of." He shook me again, hard enough that I stumbled, then pulled me again. When I resisted, he picked me up and threw me over his shoulder like a sack of corn.

When that happens in novels, it sounds romantic, but it's actually damn uncomfortable. With my hands tied behind my back, I had no way to cushion myself bobbing along on his shoulder, which dug into my stomach with every step. He kept his arms wrapped around my legs, so there was no way I could kick myself free. I began to wish I hadn't fought him so hard; I could have been walking instead of gagging.

He carried me right by the front door and over to my car. My driveway is visible to the neighbor across the street and I began to hope for rescue. Evidently, she wasn't looking out her window, for I learned later that I had vanished without a trace. The kidnapper found the car keys in the bottom of my purse faster than I ever do and opened the passenger door. He buckled me into the seat belt, which effectively cut off any chance to escape. Sitting strapped into the seat of a car with your hands tied behind your back is not comfortable; but then, nothing about this evening was comfortable. He climbed into the driver's seat and drove us away.

There I sat, in my own car, kidnapped by a nutcase in a Ralph Lauren suit and a Gucci watch. The car purred along, as well it should. I had just spent $120 getting it tuned up. I had sputtered through the summer in a jumpy, bumpy car, and now the kidnapper got a smooth ride. The irony rankled.

My first thought was to attract attention. I searched through the window for someone who might notice my plight. The kidnapper stayed in the right hand lane, so my window was never close to another car. We passed a lone pedestrian and I waved my gagged head frantically, trying to catch his attention. We passed so quickly, I doubt he saw more than a blur. It was almost a relief when the kidnapper finally spoke.

"Why don't you relax?" he asked, in a deep, melodious voice. He had one of those voices women swoon over, with a faint European accent. Think Richard Burton, and you'll get the general idea.

I tried to communicate by nods and with my eyes that he should remove the gag so I could answer him. Several blocks later, he reached across and pulled the strip of tape from my mouth. The adhesive stuck to my skin, and my face stung as if I'd been slapped. The pain startled me for a second; then I opened my lungs and screamed as loudly as I could. He turned on the radio, changed to a classical station, and cranked up the volume. So we traveled for several miles, music blaring and me yelling. When I quit screaming, he turned the volume down, and we cruised along listening to one of Beethoven's symphonies, like any middle-aged couple out for an evening drive.

"Could you please tell me what's going on?" I thought the question reasonable. He didn't answer.

"I know you're not mute," I cajoled. "Why don't we talk? I'm sure we can work something out."

I don't know what I expected. I knew the victim was supposed to keep the kidnapper talking. I also knew that once you got into a kidnapper's car, you were 90 percent dead. Strangely, I wasn't particularly afraid, but I most definitely wanted to get away.

"We'll talk after we arrive." Perversely, his voice reassured me.

"Where are we going?" I persisted.

He just shook his head and I couldn't get another word from him. I settled in to follow our route closely so I could get back home when I escaped.

I lived in a medium-sized town in the Pacific Northwest. The good side of town hugs the coastline, and I had sometimes daydreamed about living in one of the waterfront mansions. I suppose every town has a few mystery houses, giant homes that excite awe and a twinge of jealousy. When we turned into the driveway of one of those homes, I admit I felt a whiff of curiosity.

The driveway meandered through a manicured garden; a bit formal for my taste, but beautiful if you like that sort of thing. A bank of near-faded roses tilted down a slope beneath a carefully groomed weeping willow. Precise beds of asters flanked neat rows of boxwood. The drive wandered on, past peonies and artfully grouped evergreens, massed heather giving way to lush ferns, but still no house appeared. After at least a quarter of a mile we came to a raised drawbridge. The man got out of the car and pressed some numbers on a keypad and the center section of the bridge lowered into place.

For the first time, I felt a stab of real fear. I didn't like the idea of being on an island with this man, an island I hadn't even known existed.

"I would rather not go over the bridge," I stated calmly when the kidnapper returned to the car. He chuckled.

"Seriously, why don't we talk now?" I continued to try to reason as the car rolled forward. We neared the center section, and my stomach turned over. I started to beg. "Please, I don't know who you are, but why don't you just let me go? I won't say anything to anyone."

But he ignored my pleading. When we passed the center section, I began to cry. I'm not a graceful crier, and my sobs came in great gulps. By the time we reached the far end of the bridge, my nose was running. The kidnapper held a handkerchief for me and I blew. Then he got out of the car and punched numbers into another pad. When the drawbridge began to rise, I started to shake. Have you ever had a dream where you want to say something—you absolutely must say something—but no words will come out of your mouth? I felt like that. As he drove my car down another long driveway, I sat mute and shaking.

I came to know that driveway intimately over the

next several months, but that night I noticed nothing. I didn't see the towering old-growth trees I came to love, or the teeming West Coast undergrowth. I never saw the clear cool pond or the meadow that filled with bursts of wild color in the spring. That night, I sat and shivered, fear clamping a tight band around my chest so that I could barely breathe.

At last we came to a house. It appeared gradually as we rounded a corner several hundred yards away. It was a substantial older home, recalling a more-graceful century. Under different circumstances, I would have enjoyed a guided tour. We stopped under a sturdy porte cochere and the man turned off the car. He got out and came around to open my door.

"Will you walk?" His ironic smile reminded me that should I choose not to cooperate, he would fling me back over his shoulder. I nodded my assent. He unbuckled the seat belt, then held my elbow to help me out.

"Could you please untie my arms?" I asked. "My shoulders are cramped."

"Will you try to run away?"

"To where?" I sighed, exhaustion overtaking me.

He didn't respond, but led me inside, still tied. The main floor was about twenty feet tall and stretched without walls from the entry to the back of the house, at least the length of a tennis court. Arches separated areas for dining and sitting. The gleaming white expanse should have looked sterile, but instead the marble floors and gleaming walls and ceilings invited the visitor to enter and relax. Huge palms and orange trees and a rubber plant rose to the ceiling and their greenery softened the austerity. Statues waited silently in their niches, inviting a closer inspection. Far to the right and left, for the house was twice as wide as it was deep, broad staircases curved upward.

The effect was overwhelming. I breathed in the beauty and elegance that surrounded me. Though I couldn't forget that I stood bound, the captive of a madman, the house calmed me. My captor seemed to sense my relaxation, for at last he untied my arms. I fought not to cry as the circulation returned; my shoulder blades burned like banked coals.

"Come into the library," the deep voice invited. "I'll massage your shoulders."

"No, thanks." My voice was bitter, but I did follow him. We entered a room to the right of the entry, through a door I hadn't noticed. The library ceiling was lower—ten feet, perhaps—and the room was dark and cozy compared to the central portion of the main floor. Gleaming wood paneled those walls not covered by books. A fire burned in a large marble and oak fireplace. French doors led to a small terrace. I walked to the doors and tried the handle. It was open. The man moved to stand beside me.

"I don't want you to wander out and get lost in the dark," he explained.

"Do you mean I can leave when I wish?"

"The house, yes," he chuckled in a deep baritone. "But you can leave the island only when I decide you're ready."

18

I drew in a deep breath. If I tried to run now, he would catch me easily. I would have to wait for privacy to escape. I decided to learn all I could about my captor, so that I could describe him to the sheriff. I walked to a large leather-upholstered chair near the fire. He sat several feet away behind a massive walnut desk, the top inlaid with marble.

"You wanted to ask me some questions?" he prompted.

"Yes." I gathered my thoughts. I wouldn't allow his mellow voice or the sumptuous surroundings to seduce me. I began with my first thought. "Who are you?"

"A fan," he replied. His answer worried me. My erotic writing was secret from all but my own children. He must have seen the apprehension in my eyes. "Yes, Chantal, I have read every word you have published."

Chantal is my pseudonym, Chantal Renaud. I cut to the heart of my fears.

"Why am I here?"

"You're a brave woman, Chantal." Throughout our months together, he only called me by my pseudonym, until I began finally to believe it was my true identity. But that comes later. He continued, his deep voice rumbling with authority, "Few people are willing to be so direct with me."

"I'm not brave." I shook my head.

"You are here because you don't know what you're writing about."

"What do you mean?" I bristled. I consider myself a good writer; though I write erotic novels, they're well-written erotic novels.

He continued as if I hadn't spoken. "That annoys me. You write beautiful sentences, but you don't write truth. You waste your talent."

"My novels have nothing to do with my talent." The sentence sounded odd even to me, but in a strange way, it was true. "The books I write as Chantal are just for money. That's not really me."

"You can't divorce yourself from your writing, Chantal. Every word you write is really you."

"Well, the erotica isn't," I insisted. "I have no interest, desire, willingness, ability…"

My words petered out. He raised an eyebrow, inviting me to explain myself further. I tried again.

"Look at me," I demanded, standing up and holding out my arms. I turned to show him my five-feet-three inches of middle age. "My skirt comes below my knees and I perm my hair."

"At least it's still brown," he teased.

I blushed to my gray roots, but persevered.

"Do I look erotic? I am not the heroine of my novels. I don't write about myself. The fantasies aren't mine. I read books about sex, then I turn what I read into fiction. It makes me money to live on—that's all."

"That's what I was afraid of," he replied, shaking his head. "As I said before, you don't know what you're writing about."

"And I intend to keep it that way." My ranting had reestablished my sense of dignity and I sat down feeling resolute and strong. The kidnapper's next words froze me to my chair.

"I think not," he began, and I stared at him in disbelief. "We will enact the scenes of your books."

"Not a chance!" I shook my head and started to laugh.

"Stand up," he ordered me.

"No." I still couldn't believe this was happening.

"Do you remember the opening of *The Liar*, Chantal?" he asked. I nodded, gulping. "I think that will be a good beginning to your education."

"Who the hell are you?"

"The Master disciplines the young woman," he reminded me, ignoring my question. "He claims he wants her to know how the punishment feels, so that she will obey him in the future."

Shit! I thought. Was he serious?

"Look," I interrupted again. His frown warned me to be silent. I began to feel an urgent need to urinate; I never mentioned peeing in my books, I realized. Fear brings the call of nature bellowing. As I squirmed, he continued.

"You miss the reality of the fantasy entirely," he explained patiently. "She needs to be led past her barriers, for her own growth. Did you know that spanking releases endorphins?"

My God, he was talking about endorphins, and all I wanted was a bathroom. I tried to answer him reasonably; the longer we talked, the less likely anything would happen, or so I hoped.

"That's very interesting," I attempted to smile. "Could you please tell me where I can find a bathroom?"

He nodded as if he expected the question. "Through that doorway."

I went through the opening he pointed out, which led to a cubicle with a toilet and sink. The sink was marble and the light a crystal chandelier, but the room lacked one major amenity: a door. My need was urgent; hoping he would stay behind the desk, I answered nature's call.

"Better?" he asked, as I walked back into the room. God, I thought. He talks to me as if we were old friends, and then he says he's going to whip me. If this was a fantasy, it was unlike any I had ever written. Before I reached my chair, he started issuing orders again.

"Come to the desk."

I stopped and stared at him. Was he serious? If I defied him, what would happen? He answered my thought.

"If you do as I say, you will find the experience rewarding. Otherwise…"

The situation still didn't feel real to me. I wondered when I would wake up and find myself back at my own home. Again he read my thought.

"It's real," he stated, his deep voice taking on for the first time a hint of impatience. "I'm real. Deal with it. Come to the desk."

The sharp edge of his voice stabbed through my dream. He did mean what he said. He would make me live out a section of my book, and I knew exactly what he meant to do. I started to cry.

"Do you remember what the Master says to the girl

when she doesn't obey him?" he asked me, his voice stern.

I nodded.

"Tell me."

"He says that if she comes willingly he will only whip her half as many times as if he has to drag her." I gulped, and lifted my head. "But it's only fiction! I wrote it; it doesn't mean anything."

"Come to the desk."

I could tell by his voice that he wouldn't ask again and I walked forward, my stomach churning. As I got closer, I recognized certain features of the desk from my novel. Embedded in the top were two rings with leather straps, which would bind the woman's hands. My stomach heaved.

He swung the first ring up into position and held out his hand for mine. I couldn't lift it. I didn't care what he might do to me; I absolutely could not lift my hand. He seemed to sense the problem, for he stood and walked around the desk to my side. He lifted my icy fingers and held them between his two hot palms. Then he placed my hand on the desk beside the ring and threaded a leather thong around my wrist and through the metal loop. I began to shake and cry. My knees wobbled so badly I thought I would fall down.

He moved to my other side and took my left hand between his. His voice was soothing and calm.

"I see I was right," he began. "You need this experience."

His words goaded me. I wrenched my hand from his

grasp and shouted, "No, I don't. You're sick! Did you ever hear of consent? I don't consent! Do you hear me, I don't consent!"

"Your fear overpowers your reason, Chantal."

"Don't call me that name!" I screamed.

"But you *are* Chantal," he continued, still calm. "I will show you that your fear far outstrips reality, and then we'll talk of consent."

He recaptured my hand and tied it to the second metal ring.

"It didn't go this way in my book," I pleaded.

"You begin to see my point, Chantal. Your fantasy has no reality," he chuckled. "And this reality is no fantasy."

He moved back behind the desk and pulled a long white whip from the top drawer. I recognized it. I have a signature whip, white leather like this one, which appears in all my novels. The handle is a white leather phallus. The only difference between the whip in my novels and this one was that the real handle was more robust than my imagined one. Perversely, the sight of the whip excited me. I hated what he was doing to me, yet I felt my panties grow moist as I looked at the whip.

His words brought me back to earth with a jolt. "I'll stroke you ten times if you don't fight me, twenty or more if you do."

"Jesus!" I swore. "You don't really mean to do this, do you?"

"We're up to twelve strokes now."

"What?" I cried.

"Fourteen. Don't argue."

I stifled the protest that rose to my throat, and only glared. He moved behind me. My buttocks tensed as I waited for his next move. I wondered how closely he meant to follow my novel. He grabbed my hips and moved my feet back about three feet behind the desk. When I pulled my backside in tight, so that I stood straight but leaning into the desk, he laughed.

"Bend your waist," he ordered. "And present your bottom to me. I'll add strokes if you don't obey me."

I thought for a few seconds, then obeyed. I had on a wool skirt which he flipped up over my back, leaving my pantyhose exposed. He stepped back and I wondered why. Surely he was not admiring my slightly plump rear end. The first blow took me entirely by surprise. I had thought he would remove my hose and panties and strike bare skin. I arched my back instinctively and pulled away.

"Present your ass!" he bellowed.

I obeyed without thinking. The second blow came swiftly. This time I didn't pull back. I felt little pain, only a heavy thudding, for my hose and cotton panties cushioned the blow. I sighed in relief. Perhaps he was right and my anticipation was worse than the actual experience. With relief came a surge of anger. After the fourth blow, a corner of my brain reflected that he wielded the whip with only a fraction of his strength. My anger ebbed in confusion.

"I've given you a break with the extra strokes, Chantal, since you're new to the game."

I couldn't think what he meant. Then I felt his hot

hands on either side of my waist. He pulled the panty-hose down over my hips to my knees, where he left them, binding my legs together. My panties followed the same path. Fear and acute embarrassment returned. A rational part of my brain remembered his withheld strength and hoped his restraint would continue. The more primitive, emotive part of my brain sent tears down my cheeks and set my legs shaking.

"We'll talk as we continue, Chantal." He paused, waiting for me to respond.

"All right," I whispered, hoping to win restraint by my cooperation.

"This whip design is not very effective. I'll show you why." As he spoke, he stroked the leather thongs across my backside. Then he stepped back and flicked them sharply.

"Ow!" I responded, for the leather tips stung when they landed. Then the fire faded almost before it began.

"Precisely," he agreed. "They produce an 'ow,' where one hopes for a moan. However, repetition will improve the sensation."

He flicked the whip. The tips stung my flesh again. Before the pricks could fade, he struck again. I caught my breath. He flicked again, and again, and I felt the heat build in my buttocks.

"Stop!" I cried, and he stopped.

"Do you do this to all your lovers?" he laughed. "You'll never reach an orgasm if you call 'Stop.' I'll have to add back on the extra strokes. Don't call for me to stop again."

Still chuckling, he swung the whip, a bit harder this time. The tips stung more fiercely, and the heat deepened more quickly. He flicked the whip again rapidly and the smart from the second stroke augmented the first. He struck again and again, until my buttocks throbbed with an aching glow. I was torn between my desire to call "stop," hoping he would again obey me, and my knowledge that he would begin again, perhaps harder. Mixed with my indecision was a growing desire to feel what came next.

At first I tried to count the blows, though I didn't know whether he meant to stop at ten or fourteen. As the heat built, I lost count and only breathed in a steady rhythm with each stroke. Like a massage which torments even as it penetrates deep into tight muscles, the heat from the blows reached down into my buttocks and warmed the tension from my body. I relaxed into the heat, and a pool of arousal grew between my legs. When he stopped, then at last I moaned.

His hot hand felt cool when he laid it gently against the steaming flesh of my bottom. After a moment, he lifted my left foot and removed my shoe. He did the same with my right, then slid panties and hose off my legs. Unconstrained, I stepped back toward the desk and stood upright.

"We need to talk," I began, still breathless, but with returning mind.

"Not tonight."

"Yes, tonight." I tried to sound firm.

"I'll give you a choice." He sounded weary. "You can

argue with me and remain tied to the desk for the night, or you can agree that we won't talk tonight and I'll take you to a bedchamber."

"The bed." I didn't want to spend the night strapped to the desk. I didn't want to be in his house at all, but I pushed the thought to the back of my mind and opted for the simpler choice. I repeated, "The bed."

The man—I still didn't know his name—untied my hands and led me from the library. We ascended the broad staircase to the left of the entry. He opened the door to the first room at the top of the stairs and motioned for me to enter. I walked in, expecting him to follow, but he closed the door behind me. I heard the lock click in the door, and then his footsteps as he walked away down the hall.

diminuendo
Retreat

I tried the handle of the door, though my ears had heard the click. It was locked, as I already knew. The room was dark, with only a pale sliver of moonlight edging around the curtains. I groped along the wall for a light switch and found one to the right of the door. By the light of twin bedside lamps, I saw a delicate, cheerful room, all white and yellow. The bedroom was almost as large as the living, dining, and cooking areas of my own rental home, probably twenty-five feet square. The walls were about twelve feet high and windows stretched along one long expanse from floor to ceiling.

To my right was a king-sized bed, almost medieval in its solidity. Four short posts at the corners were topped by heavily carved finials depicting seed pods, puffed and bursting with emerging life. The head was smothered in white pillows, and a white cotton-eyelet bedspread lay dainty and pristine across the broad masculine expanse and curled seductively around the phallic posts. I had never before thought of a bed as erotic in itself.

I realized with a start that I had used the same bedspread much less effectively in one of my books. I wondered whether my captor could possibly have chosen it deliberately. I dismissed the thought impatiently. I must be careful not to see every action as a deliberate correction of my writing. He was a ruthless kidnapper, not a literary critic, and I had best remember that.

To my left was a sitting area with two sofas, an easy chair, and a wooden rocker. The fireplace hearth stood empty and cold. I suppose he didn't trust me with a fire. The wood floor felt cool beneath my bare feet and I moved to stand on a thick woolen carpet which lay by the bed. I noticed a pair of slippers placed handy to the bedside and slipped them on my feet. They fit.

I walked to the windows and pulled back the drapery. One window was actually a French door and, like the one in the library, it was unlocked. Elated to have found so simple a solution to my imprisonment, I walked onto the balcony, which ran along the whole back side of the house. Eager as I was to depart, my attention was arrested by the view. I looked out over a vast expanse of the Pacific Ocean. The sea was as still as a huge flat rock and lay inky black beneath the sliver of moon. The sight filled me, as the sea always does, with a sense of calm expectancy. I felt its peace invade me, even as my eyes moved along the balcony searching for a way down.

The next room also opened onto the balcony, but my portion of deck was separated from that by a thick glass wall from floor to ceiling. I walked to the railing and found no tree, no drainpipe, nothing to allow me to climb down, just a sheer drop of twenty feet or more. Below lay a garden of rosebushes planted among large sharp rocks. I lifted my eyes back to the horizon and the calm sea bade me accept my fate, at least for the one night.

After several moments, I returned to the room and found a luxurious bathroom through an open archway. The tub was a corner whirlpool, with an array of natural herb bath products along the rim. I decided to accept its tacit invitation and ran a hot, swirling chamomile-scented tub. I removed my remaining clothes: the wool skirt, a heavy-knit cotton sweater, flannel blouse, and bra. Before I stepped into the steaming water, I resigned myself to look in the full-length mirror which filled one wall.

I did have a middle-aged, underexercised body. Two children had sagged my breasts and rounded my belly. I wasn't really overweight—well, maybe ten pounds. My hair curled with rigid correctness, thanks to L'Oréal, and was brown, thanks to Loving Care. The stretch marks, well—I had earned them. I wiped away the dark smudge beneath each eye which was all that remained of my makeup.

I turned my back on the mirror, then twisted around so I could see my buttocks in the glass. They still glowed faintly red and felt warm to my palm. I blushed remembering the strokes in the library. I was still angry—oh yes, very angry—but I felt intimately connected to my captor as I hadn't to any man for a long time. My feelings confused me, but I refused to examine them as I slid into the warm tub. I turned the jets to high speed and let the flow pummel me into a state of relaxed exhaustion. Half an hour later, I crawled naked between the sheets for the first time in many years and fell into a deep and restful slumber.

The next morning I awoke refreshed, not at all confused by the unfamiliar surroundings. I remembered the previous evening clearly. I found a primed coffeemaker and a supply of bran muffins and jam on a tidy kitchen counter tucked into a corner of the room. I turned on the coffeemaker and had a hot shower while it brewed. I scrubbed my face and combed my hair as best I could with my fingers. I couldn't find my watch, which I was certain I had left on the bathroom counter the night before. I had no choice but to dress again in my clothes from the previous day. I felt uncomfortable without underpants but resigned myself to the smallest evil of my current situation. I felt more naked without my makeup than I did without panties.

I took a mug of coffee and a muffin to the balcony, to enjoy with the endless view. The clouds of the evening before had cleared and a strong fall sun shone on the water, now a deep blue. The wind had picked up as well, as it often does when we have sun, and whitecaps skittered along the rocky shoreline.

I sat in a wicker armchair with my feet on a wicker stool and sipped my coffee and munched my muffin. As

I ate, I examined my situation. I had been kidnapped by a deranged fan. He meant to make me live through the fantasies of my books. I shuddered to remember some of my cruder imaginings, then calmed when I remember the real events of the evening before. He had been correct that my fear was far greater than the reality warranted. I compared the chapter from the book to the actual events, item by item.

The heroine of *The Liar* was, as always, a nubile young thing, somewhat sullen and pouty, very sexy. I am none of those things. Far from nubile, I am overly cheerful and optimistic rather than sullen, and pragmatic rather than sexy. The hero of my book, as always, was a handsome, virile older man, commanding the heroine's obedience through sheer force of personality. My captor on the other hand was younger than me, admittedly handsome but not especially virile-looking. He looked trustworthy, even wise, something my heroes never did. I might have hired him as my accountant if he hadn't abducted me. I began to realize that my characters were less interesting than they might have been.

In *The Liar*, the heroine goes to the chateau—it's always a chateau—and begs the hero to tutor her. Expecting great sex, she gets instead a lecture that she's too young and sweet and she really should go home. My abductor had omitted that section; I would absolutely have accepted his offer. The heroine in the book begs and pleads to stay, so the hero decides to show her a taste of what she asks for. That's when he pulls out the whip. She gets scared, as I did, and he threatens her with more strokes of the lash, as the kidnapper did. Then he straps her to the desk.

I had never worked out the actual position of the bodies as he strikes her. If she stayed upright, as I did instinctively, she would have been banged into the edge of the desk with each stroke. Not a happy thought. I also hadn't known, about the trust that grew so quickly between whipper and whippee. In my novel, the man whales away and the heroine cries and screams and gets aroused and has an orgasm. My stomach turned as I imagined what an unrestrained whipping would actually feel like. I realized now that the man must use cautious restraint. I had felt the careful control behind each stroke the night before, and my confidence in the kidnapper's mastery of his art allowed me to relax from my terror and feel the almost-gentle torture of the strokes.

I hated to admit it, but he was right. The whole scene from *The Liar* was wrong. I wanted to pull the book off the store shelves. I did write erotica for money—only for money—but I never meant to write falsely. I had never slipped inside the erotica; I wrote only from my head.

I thought back to the sensations I felt as he whipped me, and then after. In the clear morning light, I forced myself to look honestly. What I saw disturbed me deeply. I had always thought myself conventional—a bit stuffy, perhaps. My on-and-off lovers in the twenty years since my divorce had been the wrong men, but safe. Men who wanted no more of me than I was willing to offer, which often wasn't much. My real self I reserved for my children; no one else touched me deeply. I had been in a sexual coma for twenty years. I felt like a bear awakening ravenous from a long hibernation. My hunger terrified me, a terror deeper even than my captor had elicited the night before. I didn't know what I might agree to, to satisfy the need that oozed from my pores and perfumed the air around me with its heady odor.

I shook my head vigorously, then rose and shook my body from head to foot. If I hoped to shake the need from my soul, I didn't succeed, but I did get my blood stirring. I strode purposefully back into the room and to the door. The handle turned under my hand, and a pair of runners and sturdy cotton socks waited outside the door. I wasn't surprised to find that they fit perfectly. Taking the sneakers as tacit consent to explore my surroundings, I set out.

The doors on the second floor were all locked. There seemed to be six rooms: four at the corners, and two in the center of each longer wall. I assumed they were all bedrooms. As I walked down the stairs, I heard beautiful piano music ascending to meet me. I paused partway down, absorbed by the haunting melody. I walked almost in a trance toward the source of the music, down the stairs and across the vast expanse of marble floor. The music came from a room around the corner from the library; I tried the door but it was locked. The powerful stereo sounded the notes so clearly I could have sworn they came from a grand piano behind that locked door. But no real person played so perfectly, not at home. The recording must be from a famous concert, a perfection achieved only once or twice in a lifetime.

As the notes continued to swirl and build, I drifted around the large central room. I examined the statues that had beckoned to me the evening before and found a Giacometti bronze poised on delicate spindle legs, captured in an instant of joyous movement. Another corner held a plaster cast by Rodin flanked by working sketches and a large photograph of the final statue. Other sculptors I didn't recognize, but the images they trapped were universal and exuded the joy and wonder of the creator. The walls too were hung with precious art, far more than graced our small town museum. All the artwork, from Miro to Gauguin, from Erte to Toulouse-Lautrec, breathed of life and freedom.

At some moment as I wandered through the creative jungle, the music ceased. I mourned its passing briefly, then resolved to ask to hear the recording again later. I caught myself short. I didn't mean to stay here; there would be no later. Shaking myself free of the artistic daze, I walked to the nearest door. The handle turned freely beneath my hand, and I found myself outside in the crisp fall air. I stood on a flagstone terrace which stretched behind the central third of the house. To my left I saw the rocks and rose garden that had prevented me from leaping from the balcony the night before. No need to leap, I thought, if I can walk out the door.

I walked around the house, peering into windows as I passed. I found the music room, which seemed to hold only a magnificent grand piano. The stereo must have been in another room, the sound piped into hidden speakers. When I rounded the corner to the front of the house I saw the porte cochere, but my car was no longer there. I hadn't really expected escape to be so easy. Besides, the car wouldn't get me over a raised drawbridge. I set out resolutely down the driveway, determined to find freedom. Whether I truly still wished to escape, I refused to ask myself.

The driveway led through a beautiful old forest. The trees reached up toward the sky on either side, sometimes meeting over the center of the road in a leafy arch. I was tempted to wander from the drive to explore the woods, but stuck to my original purpose and the road. The drive wasn't paved but finished in a fine pea gravel which crunched beneath my feet. Had I not been forced, I would have loved to walk this way by choice. The road stretched on and on. I walked for several minutes. Watchless, I couldn't mark the passing time and noted the distance only in the muscles of my legs.

Finally I came to the drawbridge. I saw by the light of morning that the bridge itself stretched several hundred yards across the water. The raised center section was only about forty feet long, but at that point the bridge was too high to jump from. No ladder led down the sturdy bridge supports, and it would take a far stronger and more agile woman than I would ever be to scramble down unassisted. I walked back to the beginning of the bridge and along a footpath that led to the water. The current flowed swiftly through the channel. Even if I were strong enough to clamber over the rocks along the shoreline, I couldn't have swum across. The island appeared oblong from the shore I could see and the bridge had been built across the nearest point to shore. Clearly, I would not swim to freedom.

I climbed back up the path to the roadway. I had seen a fork a short distance back and decided to explore that direction. I followed the smaller lane for perhaps a half-mile and came to an ordinary house. Hoping against hope that I would find a sympathetic neighbor, I banged on the door. My knocks sent back only the echo of long abandon, and I eventually gave up my pounding and walked around to the back of the house. A neat lawn, freshly mowed, stretched into the distance, belying my deduction of disuse. Halfway back, the expanse was broken by a low rock wall.

A slanting walkway led past the wall to a small lake. The wooden planks became a small jetty, and I walked to the end and sat down. The lake took me back to my childhood. I'd grown up in a southern town and had spent my happiest hours on a similar jetty, daydreaming my life away beside a similar pond. I'd imagined myself a princess waiting on the wooden dock for my prince to sail to me from over the sea. Other days I had been a forest maiden; a make-believe Robin Hood would join me and we would explore the lake shore together.

I thought back to the paper cutouts I had loved, and the stories I would weave. Sleeping Beauty was my favorite. A friend's mother had taken us to the movie and had bought me the paper dolls. I would dress them and endow them with magical good and evil personalities. Each month I cut the *McCall's* paper doll from my mother's magazine, and for a while became that beautiful, sweet little girl. In reality I was neither beautiful nor sweet, but in my stories I became whoever and whatever I wished.

A wave of nostalgia lapped at my feet, and I stretched my toes to its tickle. What happened, I wondered, as we grew older? Why did reality become so real? The clearest memory of my childhood years was of fantasy, the reality of an anxious youth obscured behind a veil of my own creating. And what harm had I ever done by pretending life was better than it was?

Perhaps that was the call of fiction to me. That I could pretend again and call it art. Yet for five novels, I'd refused to immerse myself in fantasy and had clung instead to clinical descriptions and bogus emotions. I felt at that moment that my erotic writing had been one long faked orgasm, ultimately satisfying no one, least of all me. I ached to sit at my computer and pour out the insights I'd gained that morning. My writing would be real now, genuine, if only I were back home.

I left the wooden jetty and set off around the pond, determined to convince my kidnapper that I'd learned the lesson he'd presented to me and that I was now ready to resume my life. I found a path that led around the pond then over the stream that fed it. I wandered through another small wood and at last through an open meadow that stretched before the main house. I returned eagerly to the scene of my confinement, certain that my captor would listen to the voice of my reason.

pianissimo
Softly He Speaks

As I neared the house, I heard on the wind the music that had enchanted me hours before. The melody was the same, yet the effect subtly altered. Where before the music had uplifted, now it menaced with dread warning. As I opened the front door the tone changed again and the notes drew me inward with a welcoming grandeur. The door to the music room stood open, and I walked forward as one entranced.

The late-afternoon light streamed through the windows to illuminate the figure seated at the grand piano. He seemed as enraptured by the music as I, for my arrival passed unnoticed. My kidnapper's hands skimmed and caressed the keys as if they were a living and beloved beast, one from whom obedience must be coaxed with the utmost patience. On and on he played, and the melody grew and swirled and dipped and spun about us, as elemental as weather. Then, with the caprice of a fall storm, the notes crashed to a halt.

For the first time, I saw his smile, a radiant peace offering, and I sensed that he had known when I entered the room and even when I entered the house. In that moment, he seemed magical, but his words quickly banished the illusion.

"Back so soon?" he asked genially.

I stood dumbfounded; this was my enemy, not my best friend.

"I haven't much choice, have I?" I responded bitterly.

"Not to leave the island, no." My ill will rebounded off his cheerfulness and stuck all the harder to me.

"I want to go home." My insights of the pond were forgotten in my petulance, but when I heard the childishness in my voice, a smile cracked the corner of my mouth.

"You can sleep in the woods or by the pond, if you choose," my kidnapper offered.

"I may do that," I stated flatly. "Last night you said we'd talk today."

"Of course, Chantal. Would you like to talk now, or would you prefer to eat first?"

I was hungry; I hadn't eaten since the bran muffin that morning. Without waiting for my answer, he rose and walked from the room. He led me through the vast central room and to a cozy parlor at the opposite end of the house. Like the music room, it had a lowered ceiling and was surrounded on three sides by windows. Decorated in warm earth colors, the room held plump sofas and chairs and sturdy wooden occasional tables. Motioning me to a chair, my host—no, my kidnapper—told me to make myself comfortable while he found food.

He returned in a few minutes with a platter of sliced fresh fruit, cheeses, and steaming-hot fresh bread. He placed the platter on the coffee table in front of me then left again, to return with a giant pitcher and two tall glasses.

"Water," he explained, waving the pitcher. "I'm a water drinker."

I must have looked skeptical, for he laughed and put one glass down on the coffee table. He poured a glass for me and one for himself.

"Room temperature," I commented with a grimace.

"Cold water is hard on the stomach," he explained. "You'll get used to it."

His comment reminded me of the topic I needed to discuss with him—namely, my imminent departure. He seemed to be in a mellow mood, and I spoke up confidently.

"I believe I've learned your lesson," I began. He smiled patronizingly. Goaded, I carried on more heatedly. "I'm ready to go home."

"Could you explain the lesson, please?" he asked patiently.

"Certainly. You wanted me to realize that my writing doesn't reflect the reality of sadomasochism." He nodded and waited for me to continue. "What you couldn't know, for no one knows but me, is that I won't write any more erotica."

"I knew that was your intent, Chantal," he interrupted me. "That's why it became urgent to abduct you."

"You couldn't have known," I stated flatly.

"You hope to write a great American novel," he explained. That much he might have deduced. What writer doesn't have such hopes? "Your theme is parenting and the tragic but necessary disunity of generations."

My hand, filled with bread and cheese, stopped halfway to my mouth. He could not possibly know this information. I hadn't formulated the thought so clearly even in my own mind. I replaced the bread and cheese carefully on the table.

"Who the hell are you?" I asked. At that moment, I would have believed almost anything he told me.

"You signal your intentions in your writing." The explanation almost fit. But even if he had studied my oeuvre word for word, I couldn't believe he had penetrated so deep into my mind.

"I'm not sure I believe that," I told him honestly.

"It's easier to believe than the truth." His statement was part tease and part confession.

"I don't understand what's going on," I continued, too bewildered to dissemble.

"Are you a Christian?" he asked.

"What?" I couldn't follow his reasoning.

"Are you a Christian?" he persisted.

44

"Not really," I replied, compelled by the earnestness of his question. "If anything, I suppose I might be a Taoist."

"Good." His response baffled me again. "A Christian would be good, but a Taoist is even better."

"I'm not following this conversation very well."

"I wanted to know your position on faith," he explained, though his explanation didn't enlighten me. Seeing my bafflement, he continued. "A Christian understands the concept of faith in a personal God, and I suppose that would do. But a Taoist places faith in the Tao, the universal source. If you're indeed a Taoist, then we'll proceed more quickly."

"You've lost me again," I interrupted. "We were talking about my leaving."

"But you're not ready." He brushed aside my comment. "You must trust me as your conduit to the Tao."

"What?!" I snorted and began to laugh. "I've never heard of a kidnapper-Tao. You're more likely a loony from Riverview."

"Let me show you." He grabbed my hand and pulled me from the sofa. I had to trot to keep up with him as he sped back to the music room.

"Sit," he commanded me and pointed to a cushion by the wall.

I sat on the cushion and he walked to the piano bench. He laid his fingers gently along the keys and we sat silent for several seconds. Slowly, slowly, and so softly I couldn't hear when the sound began, he started to play. He closed his eyes, and the music poured through his body; now a trickle, now a dancing stream, now a waterfall. Soon I closed my eyes as well and let the music flow around and over me. He played on and on. Finally the notes became the familiar and haunting melody he had played for me twice before. I couldn't withstand the strength in his hands, the beauty that held me tight in his grasp. At last the notes died away, and I brushed the tears from my cheeks.

"Who are you?" I whispered.

"Chopin." He gestured to the piano, then held out his hand to me. I stood and moved to stand by his side. He took my hands in his, and I felt heat and beauty flow from him and into my palms and up my arms to my shoulders. I shuddered and the moment broke. He looked at me diffidently and asked, "Do you understand now?"

I shook my head in disbelief. "I don't understand anything."

"I ask you to have faith," he urged me. "Faith in the Tao, faith in God, faith in me, faith in yourself. Find faith somewhere and trust me."

His meaning struck me finally, part blow, part revelation. "My writing can be like your music."

"Yes!" he shouted and jumped to his feet. He held my hands and spun me around. "Yes, yes, yes!"

"That's why you brought me here," I continued, breathless.

"Yes," he agreed, childlike in his eagerness. "So, do you agree, now that you understand?"

I shook my head. I didn't know. I had never really

expected my writing to be great, only readable. I sensed a looming void of effort and uncertainty beneath my feet. What if I tried and failed? What if I disappointed him, and myself? Then a worse possibility occurred to me. What if I didn't try?

I sank back onto the cushion and attempted to corral my skittish thoughts. Writing a true novel, one that would connect to the heart of a reader, was a beloved fantasy; my erotic novels were the reality of my limited skill. But the erotica was fantasy. And this man who played Chopin as if he truly were Chopin? My senses argued for his reality; my mind rebutted that he could only be fantasy.

"Why me?"

"I follow the flow, Chantal." He couched his answer in Taoist terms. "I don't pretend to understand the source. You're my next project."

"Project?" I asked. He nodded. I looked in his eyes and saw in them the next question.

"What if I say no?"

"I'm not sure." He looked truly puzzled. "I guess whatever happened would happen. I suppose you might escape eventually."

He sounded uncertain, as if he hadn't contemplated the possibility of my refusal. The realization frightened me with an intimation of his ruthlessness. I tried to buy time to think.

"I'll tell you my answer in the morning."

"I'm afraid not, Chantal. I must know now."

"Why?"

He shrugged and stared into my eyes. I glimpsed us both for a moment, caught in a relationship beyond our control, he as well as I. The reflection both reassured and frightened me. He seemed more human for the uncertainty, but someone had to remain in control. He might have read the confusion in my eyes, for he seemed to shake himself mentally and I felt the force of his personality reach out toward me as he willed me to accept.

His pressure stiffened my resistance until I thought again of the alternative. I had felt that morning as though I were awakening from a coma. I couldn't return to unconsciousness for another twenty years. I struggled to trust my instincts, which told me that this was the path I was meant to take. An ache to pour beautiful, powerful words from my heart into the heart of the reader began to burn in me, and I realized that I had merely banked that flame for the last three years. If I didn't try, the loss would consume me.

He must have followed the thoughts that churned my brow, for he took my hand and led me from the music room back to the library. He seated me in an armchair in front of the desk, then sat behind the broad marble expanse. He removed a leather folder from the lower right drawer. I hadn't expected a formal contract and stared at the papers in surprise and some apprehension.

"I'll read you the conditions," he offered. "They're quite simple. In layman's terms, you agree to obey me."

"Wait a minute," I interrupted. "I took the 'obey' out of my marriage vows. There's no way I'm going to agree to obey you."

"I'm not your husband, Chantal." His voice remained patient. "I'm not your lover; I'm not your friend."

"Then what are you?"

"I'm your teacher," he explained. "When you went to elementary school, you made a tacit agreement to obey your teacher. Otherwise he or she could not have taught you to read, or to add and subtract. You weren't allowed to make up your own rules; they already existed and you had to follow them."

"I'm not seven."

"But I have knowledge that you want."

"All right, I see your point," I agreed. "But isn't 'obey' a bit strong?"

"No, Chantal." He shook his head. "In fact, I'm adding 'willingly' into the contract here, so that we are absolutely clear."

He opened the drawer and pulled out a quill pen—an actual quill pen—and an inkwell. He dipped the pen in the inkwell and wrote the word "willingly" in bold letters above the "obey." He blew on the page to dry the ink, then pushed the folder and the pen across the desk toward me.

"That's it?" I asked. "I agree to obey you, and that's it?"

"As you pointed out, 'obey' is an all-encompassing word. It is a sufficient explanation of your role."

"And what do you agree to?"

"Read the second page."

I flipped the top page over without signing. His page was considerably longer than mine. He guaranteed that I would come to no physical harm, so long as I obeyed him implicitly. I wouldn't be required to commit any illegal act, nor harm any living thing. He also guaranteed me food and shelter until the contract terminated. Any creative work would remain exclusively my own, free from lien or claim. It was actually a generous contract; the selflessness made me suspicious.

"Why do you do this?"

He smiled and shrugged.

"Where do you get the money to run the island?"

"An endowment," he answered me. "Don't worry. I haven't robbed a bank. I'm not a gangster."

"I want two changes." He looked startled, and I explained. "I want you to guarantee my physical safety, whether or not I obey you."

"All right," he agreed easily. "I've no intention that you come to any harm. The lawyers added that clause in case you tried to swim the channel, which I expressly forbid, by the way."

"I'll add on my page that I won't willfully endanger myself and then you can scratch the 'so long as' clause."

"Agreed. What is the other change?"

"I want to be free to contact my children. I don't want them to worry about me. Also, I need to be available to them if they need me."

"I have a letter for you to sign." He reached back into the drawer. It seemed he had anticipated my demand. "It states that you've taken a retreat at a California monastery, reassures your children of your safety, and gives them an emergency number to contact you."

I'd spoken to my daughters in the past of my whimsical

desire to go on a retreat; I wondered if he somehow knew. He continued to explain.

"If they call, I'll tell them that you've taken a temporary vow of silence. I'll relay any messages. If there is a genuine emergency, I'll send you to your child immediately. You may add all this into the contract if you wish."

I could think of no further objections and nodded to show my agreement. I made the changes to the two pages. As I held the pen poised to sign, I paused and looked at my kidnapper.

"Why do I feel like Faust?" I asked.

He laughed. "Shall I warrant on the contract that I'm not the devil, Chantal?"

His answer reassured me. Before I could think further, I dipped the pen in the inkwell and signed both the contract and the letter to my daughters. He pulled the papers back to his side of the desk and signed with a flourish. I leaned over to try to read his signature; but while artistic, it was illegible.

"What shall I call you?" I asked.

"My mother named me Bran."

I thought of the muffin I'd eaten that morning and smiled. "Was she a healthy eater?"

His laughter rumbled first from his chest, then swelled into a higher pitch of pure hilarity. I hadn't thought I was that funny. After a moment he calmed and answered me, "You might say that. I have the name of a Welsh god, Bendegeit Bran, son of Llyr."

"So you are Welsh," I exclaimed. "I thought I recognized the accent. Wasn't Richard Burton from Wales?"

"Yes, he was," he confirmed. Then he slid the leather folder back into the drawer and his demeanor changed abruptly. "It is time we begin, Chantal. Remove your clothing."

crescendo
Building

"Wait a minute!" I sputtered. Bran stared me in the eye and seemed to dare me to continue. I wavered for an instant. Then my reason reasserted itself and I began again. "I agreed to let you teach me to write. I didn't agree to take off my clothes."

"Our contract says nothing about writing, Chantal," he reminded me. Indeed, I realized, to my horror, that he was correct.

"You have contracted to obey me," he paused, then continued with emphasis. "Willingly."

"What does this have to do with writing?" I wailed.

"You contracted to obey me. If you do not do so willingly, I will punish you. Punishment is not the same as discipline, which you experienced briefly last night. Do you care to learn the difference?"

"You promised not to hurt me." I didn't like my voice but couldn't erase its pleading.

"I promised that you would come to no harm. Pain and harm are very different."

"Shit!" I sat up to the edge of my chair. "I want the contract back."

"Too late." Bran smiled—not the sweet smile of the music room, but a devilish smile of mischief. His voice was stern and commanding as he continued. "Remove your clothing. I will not ask again."

I sat stunned. Shit, shit, shit. My first thoughts were not coherent. Then I remembered the goal, and the way cleared for me. He did make music like an angel. I wanted to write the way he played. I could see no means of escape from the island. And I had signed the damn contract. I reached down and slid off my shoes.

"Stand up!" he commanded.

I stood, and he waved his hand for me to proceed. I focused my eyes on a painting behind his head. It was a Salvador Dalí, one of the *Purgatory* suite. How fitting. As I stared at the image of a spider woman, shunned by society, I began to unbutton my cardigan. I slipped off the sweater, still staring at the painting. Lines stretched to the distant horizon; a red ball floated just beyond her reach.

"Look at me." Bran's words broke my reverie. I swung my eyes from the painting and focused on his chin.

"Look at my eyes." He corrected me and I raised my gaze. "Continue."

My hands moved to the top button of my shirt, then hovered, unable to continue. His mouth curved and he nodded slightly. I undid the first button, and he nodded again. My fingers moved down the front of my blouse, unclasping each button. Finally there were no more and I stood still, clutching the edges together in one hand.

"Remove it." His voice held an infinite patience and kindness.

Somehow I felt foolish to have been so reluctant. I slipped the blouse from my shoulders and let it drop to the floor. I stood before my kidnapper, my tutor, in bra and skirt, waiting. I wanted his voice to coax me on, to make the next step easier. Bran refused to help me. His face became a flat, neutral plane. After a few seconds, he became impatient and opened the top drawer of the desk. The threat was explicit; that drawer held the white whip. I remembered his distinction between discipline and punishment and reached my hands to my back to undo my bra.

My breasts tumbled out and down. They were not pert and sassy like my heroines'. They bore the marks of two pregnancies and breast-feeding. I felt a blush rise to my face; not for the exposure, but for my less-than-perfect body.

"Your breasts are beautiful," he reassured me. I looked into his eyes, startled, and found I believed him. He *did* think my breasts beautiful. He explained further, "Empty beauty doesn't fulfill the senses. Your breasts are full of life and show their utility proudly. That is true beauty."

I stood a bit straighter at his words.

"Show me the stretch marks on your tummy," he prompted.

That wasn't quite as easy. My shoulders sagged an inch, and I remembered my lack of underpants. All that stood between me and total nudity was my skirt. My indecision must have showed in my expression, for he rose from his chair. He circled the desk to stand behind me and unclasped the button of my skirt. Then he slid the zipper down, oh so slowly. As I felt the skirt sag, the hands at my sides clutched the fabric. He placed his hands over mine and loosened my fingers. The final barrier slid over my hips and to the floor.

Bran stood for a moment close behind me, and the heat from his body warmed my skin. When he returned to his seat behind the desk, I felt both bereft at the loss of his warmth and uncomfortably exposed to his gaze. My hands lifted to my breasts and pubic mound, to cover them as best I might. Without speaking, he motioned for me to lower them, and eventually, I did. We stood silent for several moments, my eyes on his face as his gaze roamed my body.

"You have good bones." His prosaic comment brought me back to the moment and my embarrassment. "Place your hands on top of your head."

I stood still for a moment, horrified. I imagined how exposed I would feel with my hands on my head and knew I couldn't do it. He raised one eyebrow, a slight impatience invading his expression. My hands seemed to lift of their own accord. He reached into the top drawer, and my knees began to shake. But instead of the whip, he pulled out a cloth tape measure.

"I need measurements to order your clothes."

His comment broke the tension, and I giggled nervously. He walked to the side wall and switched on a tape recorder. He unwound the tape measure and stood close in front of me. He placed the tape around my neck and called out the measurement for the recorder. He measured my upper arms and then my forearms. As Bran quantified my body, I studied his. I began my inventory at the top, as he had.

His brown hair was vigorously wavy, not tightly curled, but full. He wore it slightly longer than the current fashion. His thick glasses didn't distort his keen brown eyes, which seemed to spark with intensity whatever his task. His face was marked only by wrinkles that radiated from his eyes and suggested a lively sense of humor. He wore another expensive suit—dark navy this time—with a crisp ecru shirt and a swirling, oceanic silk tie. He still looked to me more like a rising businessman than a kidnapper or creative muse.

I could only guess what lay beneath the suit. I imagined sturdy arms, for he had lifted me easily. His stomach was flat, with no hint of indulgence. Before I could reach further in my fantasizing, Bran recaptured my attention abruptly. He held the tape stretched tight between his two hands and flicked it down across my nipples—hard. I flinched and he flicked back up again. I stepped back and he grabbed my hips and pulled me forward.

"Hold still," he ordered and flicked my breasts twice again.

"That hurts!" I protested on a gasp.

"Then pay attention," he commanded. "Your thoughts were wandering. *You* are the subject of investigation, not I."

He flicked the tape across my breasts again and again. An ache began to build in my womb, sharp as the actual pain in my breasts. I moaned softly.

"That's better," he commented. Then he wrapped the tape around my chest and over my nipples, loosely. He called out the measurement to the recorder, then tightened the tape slowly. It pressed my nipples in and in, and I sucked in my breath in a futile attempt to escape the pressure. My lower belly throbbed with an unfulfilled yearning. My hands lowered to his arms and I struggled to loosen his hold. His forearms were stone beneath my hands. The more I pushed him, the tighter he pulled the tape.

"Don't fight me!" he warned and my grip slackened on his arms. Immediately the pressure eased slightly on my nipples, though the ache below continued to build. He tied the tape at that uncomfortable but almost bearable tightness. He raised my arms back to the top of my head and slid the knot around to lie beneath my armpit. The tape pulled my nipples as it slid. I held my breath until at last the sting subsided to a dull-but-persistent pressure.

Bran walked back to the desk and reopened the top drawer. I felt moisture seep from my vagina as my eyes tried to hold his hands back from the drawer. My breasts would not stop throbbing beneath the tape, and my breath quickened. I released a great sigh when he pulled another tape measure from the drawer. He chuckled at my relief and slipped the white whip from the drawer. I caught my lower lip between my teeth and tried not to whimper. He laid the whip on the top of the desk and moved again to stand beside me.

"Keep your eyes and your thoughts on the whip, Chantal," he cautioned needlessly. I could not remove either my gaze or my mind from its dread reality. Bran stretched the tape around my waist and called the measurement to the recorder, then measured my hips. I felt the wetness nestling in my lower mouth and dreaded that he knew.

"Spread your legs," he ordered. I shuffled my feet a few inches apart and he thrust a foot between mine and spread me farther. Kneeling, he began at my right ankle and measured his way up to my upper thigh. Always he touched me only with the tape and held his warm hands aloof from my skin. As he approached my pubic area, I waited breathlessly for him to touch me. When he began again on my left ankle, I sighed, though whether in relief or regret I couldn't say. When he stretched the tape around my left thigh, I again held my breath.

"Is this what you are waiting for?" He placed his hands on my inner thighs. I gasped and shuddered. The ache in my belly became a thundercloud waiting to burst. He slid one hand between my legs and cupped my bottom. With the other, he massaged the crisp hair that curled profusely over my mound. I gazed at the whip that lay patiently waiting on the desk and felt the tight band that would not let my breasts subside. My clitoris swelled in naked need. As I stood helpless with my arms on my head, Bran's one hand warming my bottom as the other gently stroked my pubic hair, the storm gathering in my belly suddenly burst and I was swept up in an orgasm which shook me like a rag doll and left me trembling, barely able to stand. I began to weep.

"You must think I'm pathetic," I whispered.

"I think you're magnificent." Bran kept his hands cupped about me until the final tremors passed, seeming to savor my passion. Then he stood and reached my hands down from my head and untied the tape measure from around my breasts. He gathered me in his arms and held me as I wept. After a few moments, my tears subsided and he handed me a large handkerchief. I blew my nose and walked into the washroom. I used the facilities and washed my hands, then splashed cold water on my face. I found a pink bath towel, which I used to dry my face and then wrapped around me like a sarong. I hoped he wouldn't mind, but frankly, I didn't much care.

When I went back into the library, Bran was seated again behind the desk, and motioned for me to sit in the armchair before him. I lowered myself wearily and gave a great sigh as my bare thighs alighted on the cool leather.

"I'm curious," Bran began. "Why did you describe yourself as pathetic?"

I sighed again. "I knew you would realize that I hadn't had sex in a long time. I had an orgasm over practically nothing."

"You call my careful orchestration 'practically nothing'?" He smiled.

I waved a hand in apology and he continued.

"The ability to reach orgasm is a special gift. You shouldn't be embarrassed." He looked at me askance. "What kind of men have you had sex with, that you would get such a notion?"

"The wrong kind, obviously," I smiled. "And not even too many of them. The last few years, I suppose I buried my sexuality in my books, so that I wouldn't have to deal with the reality of my total lack of opportunity."

"You should have visited Wales," Bran commented.

"But Wales has come to me, instead."

"Let's get back to the topic of your training." Bran pulled a yellow legal pad and a mechanical pencil from a drawer. "First, I want to know what you do and don't like about your body."

"No woman likes her body." I shook my head.

"I can't see why not. For your age and experience, yours is quite nice."

" 'Quite nice?' " I echoed. It had been a while since anyone had described my body as "quite nice."

"What would you like to improve?" he prodded.

"Slimmer hips, flatter tummy, thinner upper arms." I began the litany of almost every North American woman.

"So you agree that you have good legs and nice ankles, wrists, and forearms, and actually quite beautiful hands."

"Thank you." I smiled. I had always been proud of my hands.

"We can fix whatever you want," Bran offered.

"There's a gym and lap pool in the basement. But I want you to be very clear: you need make no improvements to your measurements unless you choose to do so for your own sake. We will eat a healthy diet—interior health is essential—but your appearance is entirely a matter of your own choosing."

I nodded my acceptance. Orgasms and health food—I began to like this place. Bran's next question reminded me of the darker side of my stay, the scarier side.

"Tell me how you masturbate."

"What?" I asked. The question came so swiftly and from such a friendly context, I didn't immediately register its import.

"Tell me how you masturbate," he repeated.

I had never spoken about masturbating to anyone, had never admitted even to doing it. I decided to stick with that story.

"I don't," I explained. I hoped he would take my blush as embarrassment at the topic and not at my lie.

"No one has an orgasm as easily...." I blushed more deeply. Perhaps remembering my tears, Bran modified his statement. "As beautifully as you do without a lot of practice. So tell me how you do it."

"The mechanics?" I asked skeptically.

"That will do for a start. Do you move your finger up and down, or side to side, or around in a circle?"

I couldn't believe we were talking about this. I also couldn't force my mouth to speak. Bran glanced significantly at the whip, which still lay across the desktop between us.

"It's a simple question, Chantal," he stated in a reasonable voice. "I don't think I should have to compel an answer from you."

"Mostly side to side," I looked resolutely into the Dalí painting. "Sometimes in a circle at the end."

"Thank you." There was a touch of irony in his voice. "Tell me what else you do, the mechanics, still."

I spoke to the woman in the painting, not the man sitting across from me. "I lie on my back with one knee out to the side. I dip my finger into my vagina when I start to get wet and bring the moisture up to my clitoris."

"Is it better when you're wet?"

I glanced frowning from the Dalí to Bran. Was he an idiot? Of course it was better. His smirk caught me and held my eyes to his.

"And what do you think about, Chantal, while your finger pleasures you?" Bran's deep hypnotic voice soothed my embarrassment. His eyes became a mirror of my self.

"Sometimes I imagine that I'm on a boat," I began. "I'm lying facedown on the deck in a bikini in the sun, and a man comes up behind me and cuts the strings of the bikini."

"Is he a man you know?" Bran prompted me.

"A little. He isn't a stranger, but he isn't a steady lover either. Just a man I met."

"Is he a real man?"

"Never." For the first time, I wondered why.

"And what does he do next?"

I couldn't tell him the truth so I tried to manufacture a plausible lie. "He rolls me over, and we make love on the deck."

"What does he really do, Chantal?"

I shook my head. "I can't."

Bran looked at the whip.

"Go ahead," I said, giving up. "I can't do it."

"Are you getting moist telling me about your fantasy?" Bran picked up the whip and held it lightly in his hand.

"Yes," I whispered and squirmed in my chair.

"Why haven't you written this fantasy in your books, Chantal?"

"Because it's real," I answered.

"So what is fantasy, my dear, and what is reality?" Bran stood with the whip and walked to my side. He caressed my cheek with the leather thongs. "Answer me."

"I don't know," I whispered.

"That's the right answer, Chantal." Bran continued to stroke the whip along my cheek. "Stand up."

I was so aroused and frightened, I could barely encompass my own emotions. I sat paralyzed.

"Go to your room," he ordered me and dangled the whip lovingly across my shoulder.

I stared at him in disbelief. That was it? I wanted him to touch me again, to relieve the terrible pressure in my loins. Even the sting of the whip would have been welcome at that instant. Any touch, any touch. He turned his back and walked away from me, and I knew that he really did mean for me to leave. I stood on shaky legs and walked out the door. As I crossed the vast expanse of the open central room, I heard the whip crack.

My feet sped across the cold floor. The whip cracked again and again, and I almost felt each blow against my skin. I ran up the stairs, the sound of the whip following me to the doorway of my room. I slammed the door shut and threw myself across the bed, eyes dry and body trembling like the last leaf of fall.

forte
Firmly

I awoke the next morning as if from a long dream. My thoughts were clear and focused, the preceding two days no more than a fevered aberration. I was not the emotional, sensual creature of the evening before. I was a practical, down-to-earth single mother of two nearly grown children. The words "nearly grown" reverberated in my mind and I felt the trembling of a buried awareness. Did I define my life through past responsibilities? I had been primarily a mother for the last twenty-odd years, but was I still?

A slight disturbance in the air ruffled my thoughts. I opened my eyes to find Bran standing by the bed. He was dressed oddly in old-fashioned knee breeches, a cutaway coat and black leather riding boots. I recognized the articles of clothing, and the accuracy of his costume, from the research for one of my books. A sick realization twisted my stomach. He smiled.

"Good morning, Chantal," he greeted me. "Did you sleep well?"

I nodded, unable to speak. He carried a riding crop in one hand and I remembered what the plantation owner had done to the young female slave in my book.

"Would you like to use the washroom before we begin?" he asked mock-solicitously.

Again I nodded my head. With no door, I would not evade Bran by hiding in the washroom. Still, it did contain the item I needed most at the moment: a toilet. The sheets and blankets were tucked tightly into the bed and didn't come free when I tugged. I picked up instead a large feather pillow and held it in front of my body. As I sidled around him and backed into the washroom, Bran chuckled. His laughter was a pleasant low rumble; he seemed genuinely amused by my stratagem. When I could delay no longer, I returned reluctantly to the bedroom. I stood next to the bathroom doorway with my back to the wall and the pillow shielding my front.

"Are you truly frightened or merely apprehensive?" Bran asked, his head cocked to one side.

"I'm pissed off," I rejoined.

"Good," he responded. "You're apprehensive. You needn't be frightened. Remember that I promised not to damage you in any way."

"I'm not a piece of merchandise!" I shouted. "Don't talk of damaging me as if I were one of your precious sculptures."

"Wonderful!" he exclaimed. "I love it. You demonstrate your skill with words even in the midst of your anger. I knew you had potential."

"What the hell are you talking about?"

"You needn't resort to profanity, Chantal. I refer to your use of the subjunctive case, 'if I were.' That was nicely done."

I appreciate a well-turned compliment, and a compliment to my use of language especially, but still I refused to be diverted from our argument by his flattery. Hampered though I was by my near-nakedness, I continued to attack.

"I demand to go home immediately. You have no right to keep me here against my will."

"You're not here against your will, Chantal," he reminded me. "Merely against your whim of the moment. Were you drunk when you signed the contract?"

"No," I had to admit.

"Did I coerce or mislead you as to the nature of the contract?"

I remembered the first evening, when he whipped me. The next night I'd pretended to myself that our contract involved writing, but deep down I had understood its true import.

"No," I admitted again.

"All right, then. I don't want to hear any more quibbling." Bran sounded at that moment like a teacher with a recalcitrant pupil, one he was fast losing patience with. Still I wasn't ready to submit to his will.

"I want to go home," I repeated stubbornly.

"Fine!" he thundered. "You wish to choose death over life."

My knees buckled at his words and I sat abruptly on the floor. Bran rushed to my side and I cringed away from him.

"Chantal," he spoke softly. "Forgive my hasty tongue. I spoke metaphorically. I will keep my promise not to harm you, even at the cost of my own life. You must believe me."

I did.

"Then what did you mean?" I asked.

"You live in a creative void, Chantal. Your former life was a sort of death. By leaving, you choose not to live, not to create."

"I write novels, Bran," I protested. "That's creative. What more do you want from me?"

"So much more that you cannot at the moment imagine the scope of my ambition." He stood and raised me by one elbow. "I'll show you what I mean by death."

"Where are we going?" I asked as he led me, the pillow still clutched to my chest, out the door of my bedroom.

"To death. Metaphorically, of course," he added hastily. He led me down the hall to the staircase on the left of my room. Halfway down the stairs, he pulled aside a large tapestry and opened a hidden door. His hand tightened on my elbow as I tried to pull away. He propped the door open with the edge of the tapestry and dragged me into the chamber. I realized that we must be standing over the library, the scene of my ordeal the night before. The library ceiling had risen only ten feet, rather than the twenty of the central gathering area. This chamber must be tucked between it and the second floor bedroom above.

The room was dim, lit only by the light from the stairway. The inner face of the door had no handle, just a smooth expanse of wood. The room had no windows and the walls were bare of ornament. A sturdy wooden armchair, the room's only furniture, stood solemnly in the center of the chamber. The air was warmer than in the rest of the house, which Bran kept comfortably cool. Even naked, I wasn't chilled. Bran led me to the chair in the center of the room.

"You think you desire a creative death, Chantal, a safe and quiet life with no danger, no overpowering emotions. Let's see what you really want. Bend over."

"I don't want this, Bran," I protested. He twisted one arm behind my back and pulled the pillow from my chest with his other hand.

"I'm tired of your constant protests, Chantal. I'm tired of explaining everything." He bent me over double and shifted my captive arm to his left hand. With his right, I felt him separate my buttocks. I began to squirm in earnest as his finger probed the entrance to my anus. As in a nightmare, I couldn't find voice to protest but only panted and fought to escape him. When his hand withdrew, I relaxed with a sigh. Then I tensed and jerked as he slid a thin straight rod into my rear opening. The end tapered out to a flat disk which rested against the tender skin of my anal mouth. The rod was

71

so slim, I could barely feel it. Yet the violation of my interior filled me with confused emotions. My muscles contracted of their own volition, to expel the invader. At the same time, I felt my vagina flood with moisture.

Bran released my arm and held me bent over by the weight of his elbow on my back. He closed my buttocks with several strips of strong tape, trapping the rod inside my flesh. When he straightened my bent body, I gasped as the rod shifted inside me. He seated me in the chair and strapped my forearms to its wooden arm supports. As he turned to leave the room, I found my voice.

"Tell me what is happening," I pleaded.

He hesitated, then relented.

"All right, Chantal," he sighed. "One more explanation. But don't try my patience too far. No more protests."

I nodded my agreement. Anything to keep him talking, to keep him from leaving me alone in the room.

"You will experience total sensory deprivation. No light, no sound, no smells; only the touch of the chair against your skin and that will become so familiar you will no longer feel it. This is death, or as near as you will wish to come for a long while yet."

"How long must I stay?" I ventured the question in a whisper.

He smiled. "The thermometer will tell me when you have felt the whole range of emotions you're meant to experience in this room."

"What are the emotions I'm meant to feel?" I asked, desperate to prolong his presence.

"No more questions, Chantal." With those words, he turned and walked out the door, leaving me in total darkness and silence. I closed my eyes so I couldn't see the blackness. At first I felt relieved, for the dark and quiet were restful, like a deep sleep. But even in sleep there are sounds, and soon my ears throbbed with the stillness. I began to sing to myself, like a child in a dark closet, hidden safely away, but lonely. My songs grew increasingly childish until I sang "Mary Had a Little Lamb," over and over. When my voice grew hoarse, I tapped my foot against the floor. The steady rhythm lulled me to sleep.

When I awoke, I opened my eyes. The blackness startled me fully awake, and I felt my first moment of panic. I began to sing again and blinked my eyes. After a few moments, I couldn't tell whether my eyes were open or closed. My song rose to a wail. My own voice filled me with a greater dread and I fell silent as abruptly as I had awakened. I rubbed my skin against the wood of the chair, searching for a splinter. I longed for the pain of a prick, anything to focus my awareness. But the wood was like silk, rubbed to a satiny smoothness.

I imagined the other arms that had been strapped to the chair and the other bottoms that had rubbed naked against the seat. I began to feel their presence in the air around me, the ghostly eminence of countless other bodies. The ghosts comforted and calmed me. I wiggled my bottom, to feel the reassurance of the thermometer which had seemed such an invasion. Now I was thankful for its presence—as thankful as I could ever remember

73

being—for it reminded me that I would leave this room, that I was not trapped here forever. It told me, too, that indirectly I controlled the moment of my leaving. My emotions belonged to me, and they regulated the extent of my stay. If I could only experience the right feelings, I would be released.

I remembered one of the poems of the *Tao Te Ching* which spoke of the five colors, the five tones, and the five flavors. The colors blind, the tones deafen, and the flavors jade the palate. To find the Tao, one must avoid the distractions of the senses and focus inward to the true reality. I had never understood that passage, but now I began to see. In the absence of all stimuli, I had only my mind to focus me. The poem calmed me and I began to breathe deeply, no longer frightened of the silence and blackness. My own breathing filled the emptiness with life. I felt an inner stillness descend like a blanket over me. No brilliant insights visited, no images of the path I should take or the future that awaited me. But I felt ready.

Moments or perhaps hours later, I heard a sound not of my own making. The door opened slowly and a thin stream of light from the stairway warmed my eyelids. I opened my eyes slowly and allowed them to adjust to the light. When Bran entered, I smiled a welcome to him, but felt no need for words. He untied my arms and I flexed my fingers. Then I stood and bent over so he could remove the thermometer. He placed it on the seat of the chair and moved back toward the door.

"I'll open the door a little wider, to let in more light."

He spoke softly, yet his words thundered in my ears. "Your eyes will adjust slowly."

I nodded, still unwilling to speak. I squinted in the returning brightness and, after a few moments, walked toward the doorway. Bran held the door open for me and I walked by him and onto the staircase. I noticed in the light that I was still naked, but the awareness didn't bother me now. I saw Bran look at me and I shrugged. He had been careful not to touch me even as he undid the straps that bound my arms and slid the thermometer from my bottom. I was grateful for his restraint, for my sense of touch was as sensitive as my returning eyesight.

"Let's have breakfast." Bran's cheerful words returned an air of normality to the day.

"Could I put on some clothes first?" My voice felt rusty.

"Yes, of course. I like to keep the house cool." Bran motioned for me to return to my room. "Come to the kitchen when you're ready."

I walked up the broad staircase, savoring the marble solid and cool beneath my feet. Each of my senses was heightened by my sojourn in the void. Regaining my room, I went straight to the bath where I submerged into the comfort of a long hot soak. Normalcy seeped into my skin with the smell of jasmine. On my bed, I found a simple unbleached cotton garment, a kind of elongated poet's blouse. The low V-neck reached to my navel, and was secured with a silk tie breast-high. The hem reached below my knees but the sides were slit up to my waist. There was no underwear, no panties or bra, but compared to my nakedness moments before, I felt comfortably clothed in the blouse-dress. I felt a moment's qualm as I realized that the dress had been designed for swift and unblockable access. My fears of the early morning would not die an easy death.

Suppressing my uneasiness, I walked down the stairs toward my fate. The kitchen occupied the space on the opposite side of the entry from the library. When I saw the lowered ceiling, I wondered what secret lay sandwiched above. The kitchen itself was a cheerful white room, rather ordinary for the mansion it served. Plants topped the upper cabinets and yellow flowers dotted the ceramic backsplash. Bran sat at a table tucked into a large bay window and motioned for me to join him. He still wore the costume from plantation days, but the crop had disappeared.

"Sit, Chantal," he invited me. "How do you feel?"

"All right," I answered cautiously. I wasn't eager to discuss my experience. Besides, I was ravenously hungry. I looked around for a sign of food. Bran saw my hungry glance and explained.

"You're going to fast for a while, Chantal."

I groaned, and he laughed.

"Thanks to modern science, you won't go hungry. A lab has invented a product that sends nutrition straight into your bloodstream. Sort of an intravenous fluid, but you can drink it. You gain the benefits of fasting without the hunger."

"What's the catch?" I was sure there must be one.

"Well, the potion tastes foul at first, until your palate adjusts."

"Great!" I wisecracked.

"And it's too expensive for a steady diet."

"Look," I offered. "Why don't I save you some money? I'm sure this house costs a fortune to maintain. I'll just skip the fast. Do you have any toast?"

"You'll come to love fasting, Chantal. I enjoy it so much, I mean to join you."

"You must be nuts."

"Trust me." Bran's smile was both demanding and sympathetic. "Try a sip."

I took the glass he offered and sniffed the contents. It had almost no odor. I took a small sip. Ugh.

"This tastes like water I boiled potatoes in a week ago!" I complained.

"You'll come to love it, Chantal," Bran assured me. He took a long swallow from his own glass and licked his lips. "Yum."

I raised my glass to try again, and he cautioned me.

"Don't try to drink it as fast as I do. Your stomach takes a while to become accustomed to the mixture. Start with tiny sips."

I sipped as he suggested and found the taste less noxious than my first attempt.

"What is this stuff going to do for me?" Skepticism wrinkled my nose.

"Because it goes straight into your bloodstream, your digestive system gets a complete rest. Your intestines will clean themselves naturally over time. Also, the liquid contains no allergens, so if you have hidden allergies, they'll be eliminated."

"So far so good." I took another sip.

"It gets better. You'll drink at least one glass every hour and a half to two hours, so your blood sugar level stays constant. You'll find your energy goes up; you won't feel tired. Also, you can adjust your intake precisely, because each glass contains exactly 150 calories. If you want to lose some weight, you can. You need to drink at least eight glasses a day, though."

"This stuff sounds like every woman's dream. No cooking, plenty of energy, weigh what you want to. Why haven't I heard of it before?"

"The taste and the expense, I imagine. You can buy it at the drugstore. That's where I get our supply."

"Okay," I agreed. By now I'd almost finished the glass. I felt pleasantly satisfied, but not overfull. "I'll give it a try."

"You don't have a choice, Chantal," Bran reminded me. "I'll explain the rest of your routine as we go along."

He rose and waited for me to finish the last sip of my drink. I felt an overpowering reluctance to leave the safety of my chair and the prosaic kitchen. Finally I stood and followed him silently out the door. We returned to my bedroom. The first thing I saw was the white whip spread across my bed.

"How did that get here?" Surprise displaced my instinctive fear. Then I noticed a long black whip which lay along the pillow. Terror, pure and simple, filled me to the extinction of all other emotions.

"No!" I moaned. "Please, no."

Bran picked up the white whip and took my elbow in

his other hand. I pulled back, but his grip was a band of steel on my arm. He pulled me onto the balcony, and for once the sight of the sea failed to calm me. He strapped my hands, spread shoulder width apart, to the balcony railing.

"Do you remember the plantation scene, Chantal?" His voice acquired a Southern drawl.

"Yes," I turned to shout at him. "It was an invention from a talk show. A woman from Detroit made it up. It wasn't one of my own fantasies. I don't want to act it out."

"You'll learn to write from within yourself, Chantal." I wasn't sure whether Bran's words were a reproach, or an encouragement. The ocean breeze blew the cotton dress across my legs and buttocks in gentle mimicry of the coming blows.

"Move your feet back."

"No."

Bran positioned my body as he wanted it, waist bent and hips extended. The wind blew the skirt up and over my back.

"What does the plantation owner do, Chantal?"

I didn't answer him, hoping somehow that if I refused to name it, he wouldn't make the action a reality. I feared the sting of the whip less than I did the words I had written. But I was not to be released so easily.

"He uses the whip as it was truly intended, doesn't he?" Bran stroked the handle of the whip up and down the crack of my bottom. "Let's see how you like the sensation."

Again I felt Bran's fingers caress the fragile opening to my anus. This time they were covered in a fluid grease and slid easily over and into the opening. I gasped as two fingers found their way inside and cursed the ready juice that filled my eager vagina.

"The handle is too big," I protested. "It's bigger than the one in my novels."

"I think not, Chantal." Bran's fingers left my backside, and he brought the whip around before my eyes. I watched appalled as he stretched a condom over the leather.

"You can't really mean to do this, Bran," I begged. "You're just trying to frighten me. I'm scared, okay? I'm scared. Whip me. I don't care if you whip me."

"I'll remember the invitation, my dear." Bran held the whip by the top of the thongs and bounced the handle up and down before my eyes. I tried one last time to move him from his intention.

"I've never done this, Bran." I began to cry as I pleaded. "I'll admit, I've thought about it, but I never really wanted to do this. Please…"

My begging ended on a moan, as I felt the hard tip of the leather phallus press against the doorway to my last virgin territory. One arm held my buttocks steady as the other caressed the handle of the whip up and down the opening. It was too big; it wouldn't fit. I sighed. Then—with a firm thrust—he pushed the tip into me. I tried to arch my back away from the pain, but his arm held me firmly. I heard him tell me to breathe and I began to pant, as in childbirth. The stinging pain eased slightly and a dull throbbing fullness took its place. My womb began to pulse in empty and hungry unison with the ache in my rear opening. Then he eased the phallus another inch inside me, and the pain returned and doubled.

"Stop," I cried. "Stop!"

He removed the handle from my rear, though he continued to hold me fast. I sobbed in relief.

"Have you forgotten last night so quickly, Chantal?" Bran asked.

I remembered his actions of the night before, and a sick horror flooded through me.

"Now I must begin again. You must learn not to tell me to stop."

"Oh, God!" I moaned weakly, even as my vagina flooded afresh. He replaced the handle of the whip against my sore flesh and began to rub again.

"Open yourself to the phallus, Chantal." But I couldn't. He thrust the tip into me again. The pain was worse than the first time. As I fought to breathe, he continued to coax me. "It stings at first, but if you open yourself, the pain will subside and the throbbing will begin sooner."

He began a slow, inexorable pressure against the phallus. I felt the massive leather dildo creeping by slow quarter-inches into me. At last I could squeeze my buttocks no longer and the powerful muscle relaxed. As it did, the muscle in my vagina contracted and I lost control of my thoughts and emotions. My vagina contracted again and again, and I realized dimly that I climaxed. My buttocks stretched of their own accord around the invader and with each renewed pressure, I came to another peak. Finally Bran's hand rested against my skin and the phallus was fully inserted. With the cessation of motion, my senses slowly returned and I became again aware of the ache in my stuffed backside.

"Talk to me, Chantal," Bran commanded.

"What do you want me to say?" I breathed back, exhausted.

"How do you feel?" he prompted.

"Full."

"Are you angry?"

"Not anymore."

"Would you like me to remove the dildo?"

"Yes," I sighed.

Slowly he began to remove the phallus. I felt it slip from me with an aching relief. When the last inch escaped me, I stood to ease my aching back. The thick cotton of my dress slid back down over my buttocks. Bran left for a moment, and I heard a flush as he disposed of the condom. Then he returned and removed the straps from my wrists.

"Tell me how I'm supposed to feel, Bran," I asked him wearily.

"You'll figure that out yourself, Chantal."

"Can't you help me?" I begged.

"I just did."

a tempo
In Time

Bran brought me another glass of the formula, then left me alone to rest. I fell exhausted onto my bed and slept. Later he brought us both another glass. We sat and talked on the balcony as we drank.

"Your day will begin with a form of discipline," Bran began.

"What do you mean by discipline?" I asked apprehensively.

"You know what I mean, Chantal. You behave like a child when you ask me to affirm your thoughts. You tell me what I mean by discipline."

"I imagine you mean to whip me." I felt myself grow both cold and warm at the thought.

"Some days," Bran agreed. "Each day will begin with some method to affirm your awareness of your body."

"An interesting euphemism," I added dryly. He ignored me and continued.

"We're running late today because of your unfortunate reluctance," he admonished. "Are you finished?"

I placed my glass on the table and nodded.

"Good. Come with me, and we'll continue the day."

I rose and followed him out of my room and down the stairs. I was almost eager to see how he meant to stimulate me to write. I might have known by then to expect the unexpected. He led me down another flight of stairs to the basement. The room was vast and open like the main floor and dominated by a long, narrow lap pool. I like swimming and would have enjoyed the pool, but I'm allergic to chlorine.

"Don't worry," Bran answered my thought. "I use an alternative to chlorine. You won't react to the water."

"How did you—?" I began, then stopped as he shrugged. Of course he knew.

"Remove your dress," he ordered me.

I shrugged in my turn. Nudity began to seem less strange to me. I untied the silk ribbon and slipped the dress down over my hips. I walked to the edge of the pool and dipped one toe in the water. It was cool enough to be refreshing, but not cold. I turned back to Bran, a smile of pleasure on my lips. My smile turned to a grimace of dismay; he stood next to a ballet barre, the black whip from the morning in his hand.

"Jesus, Bran," I swore. "Wasn't this morning enough?"

"That was a fantasy we acted out. You'll never know when to expect the pages of your books to come—"

"Back to haunt me," I completed his sentence. He nodded.

"This is your morning discipline. You've told me twice that you would welcome the whip. Don't prove yourself a liar."

"The circumstances were not the same," I countered.

"If you're here in position within ten seconds, you'll get ten strokes. Otherwise twenty."

I stood stunned for an instant, then sprinted to his side. I looked at his face for further direction, but he refused to tell me what position to assume. I remembered the night in the library and stood about three feet from the barre. I bent over and placed my hands on the cool metal.

"Very good, Chantal. Your eagerness is rewarding."

I wondered if he mocked me, for I was anything but eager. However, ten strokes would be better than twenty.

"Let me show you this whip." Bran walked to stand in front of me. He seemed innocently excited, like a child with a favored toy. I gritted my teeth. "This is a real whip, Chantal, not a plaything like the one from your book. See how it's worn from use? Whips are never new. Each tip has been burned in a flame, to harden it. You'll feel the difference right away."

I saw the ends as he held them out to me, and I cringed. The tips were hard and black. They would dig into my flesh like claws.

"Do you enjoy torturing me?" I asked him. "Get it over with."

"As you choose, my dear." Bran smiled and moved behind me. I wondered what on earth had made me speak. I didn't really want him to get it over with, I wanted him to cease to exist. The whip whistled through the air before it landed against my soft bottom. The tips did indeed tease my skin with a fierce sting. I was still a bit sore on the inside from the morning's assault and the ache of the leather reawakened the tenderness. I gasped and clenched the barre tightly. The second stroke came swiftly and I felt my bottom warm beneath the hot thongs.

"Would you like me to stop?" Bran asked.

Just in time, I remembered the lesson of the night before and that morning. If Bran stopped, he would begin again at the beginning. For the first time, I wondered if there were an edge of cruelty to his words. I ground my teeth in frustration and spat out a denial. The next stroke came almost before the word left my mouth and surprised me with its force. I gasped at the very real pain. I had come to trust his restraint and felt both surprised and hurt by the betrayal. The next stroke was lighter and I swallowed my protest.

"Don't grow complacent, Chantal," Bran warned.

By now, my backside felt as though it were on fire. I had counted four strokes and wondered if I could hold still for another six. Before I could decide to lift my hands and run, another smack fanned the blaze. Halfway there. I squeezed my eyes shut and held my breath and waited for the next blow.

"Stop counting, Chantal." Bran sounded amused. "Let yourself go. I won't stop at ten."

"But you promised—" The next stroke cut off my words and I began to despair. Perhaps he would never stop. I would be lacerated to a pulp as I stood, the willing victim of a sadist. As my imagination wandered, the strokes continued to fire my skin, though the worst pain seemed to be in the past. Warmth spread through my body. I felt the familiar seeping of hot juices from my vagina. God, I thought. How could this be? My mind slipped another notch and I began to shake. I felt the crest of a wave begin on a far horizon and then I realized that the strokes had stopped. The wave subsided and I felt strangely cheated. My shoulders sagged and I hung, panting, from the barre.

"How many strokes did you give me?" I gasped, though why the number mattered, I didn't stop to think.

"Ten," Bran replied.

"Why did you stop?" I couldn't believe I would ask such a question.

"Ten was enough," was the enigmatic reply. He placed his cool hand against my hot bottom. "Go have a swim."

"Is that the next part of my routine?"

"For today." He sounded indulgent, like a teacher with a prize pupil who has just scored well on a difficult exam. I walked to the pool and dipped my foot again into the water. I had never swum naked and wondered what the water would feel like against my breasts. I walked to the far end of the pool and down the shallow steps at one side. The lap pool was about 12 feet wide and perhaps 100 feet long. The water stung my hot bottom for a few seconds; then its coolness drained the lingering heat from my skin. When I stood, the water came to just below my breasts. I dipped under the water and emerged smiling and dripping. As I had hoped, the silky slickness felt delicious against my breasts. I swam to the far end of the pool, then turned and swam back again. After two laps I was a bit winded, so I stopped and stood.

"Keep swimming," Bran instructed. He had moved to stand above me at the shallow end of the pool. I might have guessed I would not be left to enjoy myself in peace. I began again, backstroke this time. Each time I reached the end of the pool, Bran would smile and nod for me to go again. When I tired of the back crawl, I did two laps of the sidestroke. I kept alternating strokes until I was truly tired. When I got to Bran, I stood and explained.

"I'm tired."

"Four more laps." His voice did not sound lenient. I set off at a leisurely backstroke and found that I could indeed complete the four laps. He seemed to know my limits better than I did myself. Perhaps we all need a Bran to urge us on. I emerged from the pool and my instructor/coach/tormentor wrapped me in a large soft towel. He dried me gently and put a clean cotton dress on me. I felt like a rag doll, my muscles limp and relaxed from the unaccustomed exercise.

We returned to the kitchen and drank another glass of nourishment. I found it made me thirsty and I gulped down a large glass of water with the formula. So far my routine included Bran's discipline, the fasting, and exercise. I wondered, but almost feared to ask, what came next. My companion must have read my mind again; I became almost accustomed to the invasion.

"Next I'll teach you to make music."

Unfortunately, I'm not musical. Piano lessons had been a trial as a child, and I feared I would disappoint him. Bran led me not to the sunroom with the grand piano, but to the second floor. He opened the door opposite my bedroom, and we entered another music room. This one held two grand pianos, a harp, a cello, a trumpet, and many other instruments I couldn't name immediately. A mellow fire burned in the large fireplace, and plump white sofas and chairs encircled a brilliant oriental rug.

"This is our playroom," Bran announced. "You need not fear discipline, punishment or unexpected fantasies from your books, so long as we're in this room."

"It's wonderful!" I breathed, slightly awed.

"And it's ours." Bran's voice again held the childlike enthusiasm I came to cherish. "You may play with whatever you wish. Don't worry that you'll interrupt me. I concentrate rather well."

My companion walked to a piano and sat at the bench. As he had the day before, he paused for several moments before he began. I curled my bare feet under me on the sofa and prepared to enjoy. The music began as a dull echo and seeped into my bones before it caught my ear. He wove the melody through and around and under me, until it lifted me from the couch and to his side. I placed my hand on his shoulder, and he smiled and motioned with his head for me to explore the room. I walked from instrument to instrument and touched each with a hesitant finger, afraid to hurt them. Then I settled on the sofa once more and surrendered to the music.

My thoughts swelled and swirled with the melody and the creative urge overtook me. I stood and walked around the room, looking for paper and something to write with. Bran's words interrupted my search.

"I can't allow you to write, Chantal." The melody continued to flow from his fingers.

"What do you mean, Bran?" I was more curious than alarmed. "That's why I'm here—to write."

"But not until you're ready," he explained.

"I'm ready now." A tinge of panic edged my voice. When I need to write, I need to write.

"Relax, Chantal. Enjoy the music."

"When can I write?" I asked, frustrated.

"When you're ready." I knew him well enough by now to recognize the finality of Bran's words. I bit back my hasty rejoinder and tried to discover a reason behind his prohibition. So far, I admitted reluctantly, he seemed to lead me in a positive direction. Though I fought his methods, I couldn't gainsay the results. Perhaps my thoughts were influenced by the hypnotic music that flowed effortlessly from his talented hands. I decided for the moment to trust him.

And so the days passed. Again and again Bran pushed me beyond my comfort. He awakened me each morning and sent me to relieve myself. I tried to wake myself before he came, but however early I awoke, he anticipated me. Finally, I gave up and simply slept until I felt his touch on my shoulder. The morning discipline began on the balcony, hands on the railing, eyes glued to the far horizon. He showed me different whips and taught me how they felt. When I relaxed, he brought me back to tension. When I tensed, his strokes relaxed me.

The middle of the day was filled with physical activity. I swam and learned to lift weights. My muscles firmed slowly. For several days, I rode a stationary bicycle furiously. When I asked him, Bran brought me a real bike, and on clear days I rode up and down the driveway and along the path to the pond. I never saw him leave the island and I never saw anyone else arrive; yet we always had whatever we needed.

We continued to drink the formula, and I grew to like the taste. I imagine I lost weight, though there were no scales in the house. For several days my face broke out and I sneezed and had diarrhea as the poisons slowly left my body. Then my skin took on a forgotten healthy glow. The ocean wind didn't allow the pollution from the mainland to approach the island and my lungs grew accustomed to good clean air. The exercise, air, and healthy diet combined to make me feel glad to be in my skin. I enjoyed my body as I hadn't since I was a teenager.

Bran still wouldn't allow me to write. I dampened my frustration by imagining long passages and vivid scenes, as I had when I was a child. Then I'd been too young and the act of writing too physically difficult to be worth the effort. Now the prohibition worked as the physical limitation had then, and deepened my imagination. I would live a scene in my mind, first from one character's point of view, then from another's. Each day I begged Bran to allow me pen and paper, and each day he said I wasn't ready. Each morning I railed and fought him, and each afternoon I found he was correct.

Our sessions in the upstairs music room changed with the passing days. At first I only listened, enthralled by his wondrous talent. Then I began to touch the instruments. He showed me how to blow the trumpet and we laughed at the water buffalo bellow that emerged from the horn. I strummed the cello and the harp and finally drifted to the piano. At first I was afraid to touch the keys, but finally I tried to pick out a little melody. Bran showed me how to place my hands on the keys. He taught me a simple scale, and I practiced it faithfully. The next day he taught me another, and the next day another. My simple do, re, mi became an underpoint to his complicated melodic designs.

Just as the house held no clocks, so, too, it held no calendar. I tried for a few days to keep track of the date, but then I ceased to count. I could tell by the red and golden leaves that winter approached. Bran had abducted me on the seventeenth of September; I thought it must by now be mid-October. In all this time, he had not again confronted me with a passage from my novels, nor pushed me beyond my endurance with the whip. I grew so accustomed to my new environment that at last I began to feel safe.

con forza
Forcefully

The day began with the arrival of dawn, as many of our days did then. Bran's touch aroused me from my slumber and I padded to the washroom. When I returned to the bedroom, I saw that he had laid several whips—some familiar, some new—across the bed. I wondered sleepily what new game he meant to play. He soon enlightened me.

"Today we begin a new era, Chantal," he stated cheerfully. His brightness in the morning sometimes annoyed me. "Choose which whip you wish me to use."

"Choose?" I murmured.

"Yes, my dear. It's become too easy for you to allow me my way with you. You follow my leadership. It's time you took more control of your own progress."

I didn't like his explanation. It was true that I found it relatively easy to comply with his demands, as long as I convinced myself that I had no choice. I was the passive partner and seldom showed more than resigned acceptance of his discipline, though I often came to climax under his hands. Participating would indicate approval, which was harder to admit.

"Do you remember the night you arrived?" Bran interrupted my thoughts. He saw by my expression that I did. "I told you then that we would discuss the notion of consent at some future date."

"And this is the date?"

Bran beamed his approval of my perception. He walked to the sofa and motioned for me to sit next to him.

"Can we have breakfast first?" I asked.

"No." I suppose he was eager to begin. "Mutual consent is an interesting concept, don't you think?"

I settled myself in for a discussion. "Actually, I suppose it is."

"Take your arrival here."

"Your kidnapping me, you mean."

"Yes," he responded impatiently. "Your arrival. You had tacitly consented to the kidnapping, through your books."

"No way!" I argued. "If I write about a serial murderer, that doesn't mean I consent to be murdered. The writer is not the subject. Especially a writer of fiction."

"All right, then, I will grant that the kidnapping was against your consent, but everything since has been consensual."

I snorted my disbelief. "How can you say that?"

"We manufacture consent all the time," he explained. "If a company president wants the workers to produce more product in the same amount of time, he manufactures the consent of the workforce through artificial manipulation."

"Or she," I threw out. But I was interested in his line of reasoning. "Explain what you mean."

"Consent can be gained through incentives like better pay and bonuses. Then we call it bribery."

"Granted, but what does that have to do with sexual consent?"

"Do you think sexual partners don't bribe each other into consent? What do you think flowers and diamond rings are for?"

I saw his point.

"All right," I conceded. "But this isn't exactly a normal sexual relationship."

"How do you know?" he asked. "It's far more normal than you realize."

That observation threw me for a moment. Then I thought of a rejoinder. "But those cases don't involve kidnapping, so they must be consensual."

"I don't believe any relationship is truly consensual, Chantal. Each person brings too many beliefs, too much past history. Can a woman who has never experienced an orgasm genuinely consent to a nonorgasmic relationship? She doesn't know what she's missing, so how can she consent to missing it?"

"Your argument is circular, Bran. Besides, that's a sin of omission. What we do isn't omission, but commission."

"You make my point for me, Chantal," Bran crowed. "At present, yours is an act of omission. You simply allow me to do as I wish with you."

"And you want me to commit the sin of commission?"

"The *act* of commission, my dear, not the sin. There's a great difference. Nothing of what we do is a sin."

"That depends on who you ask."

"True. If you ask St. Augustine, even arousal is a sin. Every man who ever has an erection is a grievous sinner. You can find an extreme for every case. You're single; I'm single. We betray no one; we break no laws. I maintain that what we do is no sin."

"Okay, we aren't sinners. I don't think Taoism recognizes sin particularly, anyway. But that still leaves us a long way from me consenting to your whipping me."

"You're no hypocrite, Chantal." Bran let the simple sentence worm its way into my conscience. He was right. I no longer—perhaps never had—fought the whippings. They aroused me. The morning discipline made my blood thrum and my body pulse. My mind hated that I enjoyed being whipped, but my conscience admitted the truth.

"Shit!" I knew Bran disliked swearing, but no other word could quite express my consternation.

"Which whip would you like me to use this morning, Chantal?"

"Do you have to use the word 'like'?" I complained. He only smiled and moved to the bed. He gathered the whips and brought them to the sofa.

"You enjoy this one, I think." He held up the worn

black leather whip he had used on me the third day of my stay. It was the one he returned to most frequently. "Or how about your white model? A bit puny, but I can make it work."

He continued to tease me with the whips. This one's straps were thin and delicate; this broad one had a special purpose. Did I prefer the thongs short, long, or variegated? Finally he tired of his cajoling and commanded me to choose. I stared at him, not yet ready to take the step to openly consensual participation.

"One last time—I will make life easier for you, Chantal," he offered with a sigh. "You try my patience. For every ten seconds that you don't choose a whip, I'll add five strokes. Beginning now."

Still I stared at him, silent and defiant. Thoughts churned in my brain. How could he know ten seconds without a watch? It was all a game. He would choose for me in the end, anyway. Sometimes ten strokes wasn't enough. Wait. What had I thought? Did I deliberately delay, so that he would stroke me longer? Horrified, I saw the acknowledgment in his eyes. I reached out blindly. When I reopened my eyes, I saw that I had chosen a short, broad whip—more a belt, actually. Bran had never used that one before. My juices began to flow in involuntary anticipation.

"Twenty strokes." Bran's deep tones sounded like the voice of doom. He chuckled. "You have your own way to get what you want, Chantal."

I groaned.

"This whip is different, my dear. I'm not certain you

are quite ready—at least not for twenty strokes—but we'll see."

"Are you trying to frighten me, Bran?"

"No, Chantal. Merely to heighten your experience. We'll go to the basement."

I wondered why we departed from our balcony routine, but didn't ask. He motioned for me to precede him out the door, and I took off for the basement without a backward glance. When I arrived, I was disconcerted to find him already there. He stood in the workout area, in a section he had never allowed me to enter. He called me to his side and motioned me to a narrow leather-covered bench.

"Lie back on the bench, Chantal."

I obeyed him from force of habit and lay on my back on the bench. He pulled me by the shoulders toward the top of the bench. I began to worry when he placed my hands together and fastened them above my head. He had not strapped me in for a whipping since the second day.

"You can't whip me like this, Bran," I ventured. "I'm turned the wrong way."

His smile was no longer sunny and open, but seemed cunning and slightly cruel. I lifted my legs up onto the bench and pulled my knees tight to my chest.

"Nice," he commented, as he smacked my bottom with his bare hand. "But not what I had in mind for today."

He straightened my legs and placed my feet on the floor to either side of the bench. When he pulled my legs open and strapped my feet spread-eagled to the floor, apprehension flowed through my veins like a powerful drug.

"Bran," I cautioned. I had learned over the weeks that silent compliance brought the easiest discipline. But today I was truly frightened, as I hadn't been since the first week. Fear drove the careful lessons from my memory. "Bran, I don't like the look of this."

"Hush, Chantal." His calm words drove my panic nearer to the surface. "I want you to close your eyes."

I shook my head frantically.

"No? All right. You can watch if you want to."

My heart beat frantically as he moved to kneel at the end of the bench, about two feet from my very exposed pubic mound. The realization of what he intended made me dizzy and, as he had suggested, I closed my eyes so I wouldn't see the blow. The fear tasted acrid in my mouth, yet my vagina flowed like a fountain. The first stroke stole my breath. With the second, I found air to cry out. The broad leather strap slapped my aching mound again with a hot crack.

"Oh, God!" I screamed. "Be careful."

He was careful; even in my volcano of sensation, I recognized his care. Each stroke was only just what I could stand—no more, no less. He seemed inside my body, regulating the timing and pressure of each blow to wring the utmost vibration in response. The fourth stroke heated my flesh hotter than the swift inner convulsion that followed it. My vagina throbbed with the aftermath as the tender flesh swelled. With the next stroke, I lost count, and my screaming clitoris arched up to meet the leather. Each following stroke stoked my desire like a probing tongue of fire. I waited breathlessly for the heat and groaned as it passed. Each touch brought a new and stronger pulse within me, until I felt I would burst. I couldn't tell orgasm from lash. After a few moments, the whip became wet with my moisture and brought a new torture. Where the dry whip had only heated me with its pressure, the slick leather stung my unbearably sensitive flesh. I passed a threshold.

I dimly remembered my unconscious connivance to gain more strokes. What had I done? The next blow sent me past the doorway; a creature grew inside my breast. The next stroke brought it screaming from my throat. With each successive stroke, I screamed, in pain, in exaltation, in rapture, in agony, and ultimately, in release. My voice grew hoarse as my lungs exploded, until at last I screamed no more. As breath returned to my aching lungs, I realized that the throbbing in my mount of Venus had begun to subside. The whipping was over.

I pried open my eyes and peered toward the foot of the bench. Bran sat back on his heels, sweat dripping from his forehead.

"God!" I breathed. He smiled and nodded his head in acknowledgment.

largo
Grand Interlude

fortissimo
Lustily

From that day forward, our routine changed. Bran forced me to admit my participation in our activities. He continually tested the barriers in my mind between real and manufactured consent. One morning, I must choose which whip he would use, but was allowed no say in the number of strokes. He would bring me to the point of orgasm, then stop short, no matter how I begged him to continue. The next morning, he would arrive with but one whip, and remind me how I had begged him to continue the day before. His strokes would drive me to and beyond orgasm after orgasm, until I collapsed in exhaustion.

Then, one morning, I awoke to find him sitting on the edge of my bed. Instead of a whip, he carried a tape recorder. When I opened my eyes, he pressed the button on the recorder and I heard first his voice and then my own responding. "Mostly side to side, sometimes in a circle at the end." The tape was of our conversation the second night, just after I signed the contract. I was describing the mechanics of masturbation. He pressed the stop button.

"Show me, Chantal."

"I can't do that." My heart began to beat rapidly and my breathing became shallow.

"Chantal, you can do and enjoy many things you think impossible."

"Let me use the washroom," I temporized. He motioned for me to leave. I delayed as long as I could, then returned reluctantly to the bedroom. I didn't want to do this.

"You're already moist, just thinking about masturbating in front of me, aren't you?"

I had to nod my head, for it was true. Still I couldn't bring myself to walk back to the bed. Finally Bran grew impatient and stood. I knew that once he stated an intention, he wouldn't back down. He never had and he wouldn't start now. I couldn't imagine how he would coerce me to masturbate, but decided I didn't really want to find out. I walked to the bed.

"Lie down in the position you use."

I lay on the bed on my back and pulled the covers up to my chin. Bran laughed and ripped the covers from the bed, so that I lay naked in its center.

"I always do it under the covers," I explained.

"Not today, Chantal, and not tomorrow or the next

day either. Hiding under the covers implies something shameful, and masturbation is neither sin nor shame. You should be proud that you're able to please yourself."

"But it's a private act," I protested.

"Not necessarily. Begin; show me what you do."

"You know from the tape." Moths beat their wings in my stomach as I tried to delay the inevitable.

Bran rewound the tape and I heard my words again. He rewound the tape again and again and played my words over and over, until finally I closed my eyes and began. I spread my knees as I had described and placed my hand against my pubic mound. The tape stopped and I opened my eyes.

"Look at me while you do it," Bran commanded. I groaned but fixed my eyes to his. Slowly my hand began to follow its timeworn path. It found the center of my desire and rubbed the tender bud gently. I dipped my finger into the moist pool below and dragged the wetness to my clitoris. My eyes closed again as my pleasure began to mount.

"Tell me what you're thinking."

"Nothing," I lied. "If you talk to me, nothing will happen. I have to concentrate."

"You can concentrate *and* talk. Tell me."

I kept my finger roving the delicate area, for he would know if I quit, but I separated my mind from the digit's movement. I couldn't reveal my innermost fantasies even to him. I began to spin a false tale that I thought might satisfy him.

"I'm sitting in a room all by myself. The chair is hard

on my bottom." I couldn't think where to take the story. It didn't arouse me at all, but my finger began to. I struggled to continue, mind and body skirmishing for control. "A man comes into the room. He's naked and very beautiful. He walks toward me."

Bran grabbed my hand and flung it from its work. My eyes flew open; he was angry as I had never seen him before.

"You lie, Chantal!" He spit the words from his mouth like a bad taste.

"All right," I apologized, terrified by the wrath in his eyes. The thick veneer of control had slipped and I saw the passionate fury of the man beneath. "You're right. I'll tell you the truth now."

"Too late."

I shrank back to the far side of the bed. Bran reached out a long arm and pulled me to him.

"Please don't hurt me," I pleaded.

"Unlike you, I am faithful to my words." His words cut me deeply, for I knew he was right. He had never been false to me and I betrayed him with my lack of trust. Suddenly, telling him my fantasy seemed a small and natural thing.

"Please give me another chance," I begged.

"Not this time, Chantal. You've used up all your second chances." With those words, he slung me over his shoulder. The remembered discomfort returned and doubled; I was thinner now, and his shoulder dug deeper into my stomach. As I hung naked across his back, he strode down the stairs to the main floor. I wondered briefly if he meant to fling me from the house and banish me to my fate alone. I felt almost relief when he continued down the second flight to the basement. He set me on my feet beside a low table.

"Put this on." He handed me a tiny bikini. I hadn't worn even a two-piece bathing suit in twenty years, but I didn't hesitate a moment to do his bidding. My stomach churned as I recognized the significance of the bikini; it was a prop from the masturbation fantasy I had admitted to him in the library.

"Wait a minute!" I challenged him, indignant enough to lose my fear. "You had this ready. How did you know I would lie to you?"

"I anticipate."

"Then you have as little faith in me as I do in you," I argued. "I won't do this."

"I had faith, Chantal, but you had free will. You chose your path, and now you will follow it."

I glanced at the pool; a raft floated in the center.

"I can't do this, Bran," I tried to explain. "It's a fantasy—nothing more."

"You disappoint me again, Chantal." Bran looked sad as he continued. "The line between fantasy and reality is not only blurred, it doesn't exist. There is no line. Reality is a fantasy and fantasy is reality. You've never had anal intercourse, correct?"

"Yes, and—"

"And you've always been curious." Bran interrupted my objection.

"Only in my mind," I stated firmly. "My body can

imagine how much it would hurt. The mental image arouses me; the physical reality terrifies me."

"The mind is all there is, Chantal. The physical is just a shadow. You broke faith with me before, and you were wrong. You must trust me now. Come."

He led me to the pool and pulled the raft to the edge. When he motioned me to climb on, I steeled myself to trust him, though my body quaked and my heart rebelled. He told me to lie down on my stomach as if I were sunbathing. He pulled my hands above my head and fastened them to rings embedded in the raft.

"Try to fall asleep," he advised me and walked away.

I lay trembling on the raft for what seemed like hours. Finally nervousness exhausted my body and I fell into an uneasy slumber. I was awakened from my troubled dreams by a splash.

"Bran?" I called out, but there was no answer. I felt the back end of the raft dip as he climbed aboard.

"Bran?" I asked again, more urgently.

"I am not Bran," a softly formal Oriental voice replied. "I am your stranger."

I moaned and began to weep. Wetness poured from my vagina in anticipation and dread. Now that I couldn't stop the moment, I didn't know whether I more feared or longed for it.

"Who are you?" I whispered.

"I am a trainer," he replied. "I will be gentle with you."

"I'm not sure I want to do this."

"That is why Bran tied you, to remove the necessity

for consent." His gentle voice sounded wise with the knowledge of centuries. "Often it is harder to admit you want something than it is to submit to the pleasure."

"Can I see your face?"

"No, Chantal," he answered kindly. "Just relax."

A long metal blade slid under my left bra strap. With a razor-sharp slice, the strap dropped to the raft. Twice more he slid the flat of the blade across my skin, only to catch the fabric with a flick. I pressed my unbound breasts to the rough wood.

"Don't move," he cautioned me.

The back of the blade skimmed down my back in a long, smooth motion and then slid under the bikini bottom. I held my breath as the knife twisted up to slice through the elastic and fabric as through it were gossamer. One final slice—and my buttocks sprang apart in release. I squeezed them, but couldn't maintain the tension for many minutes.

When my buttocks relaxed, the man began to massage my body, starting with my feet. The oil was aromatic and slightly sweet; its perfume wafted to my nostrils as he worked. His hands were knowing and as wise as his voice. I felt my muscles relax and my breathing slow as he worked his way up and down my legs. Then he moved to my back. His fingers reached deep into my muscles, and the painful pressure unknotted the tension from my spine and shoulders. Finally he massaged my head and neck, lifting and twisting and kneading my scalp and my temples. My body drifted onto a cloud, detached from earthly reality, in a blissful state of ease.

"Now we will begin." His words awoke a tremor in my breast, but it quickly subsided as he lay his hands on my buttocks. He kneaded the flesh in his powerful hands and found each jangle of tension and stroked it away. When he lifted one limp leg and placed it, knee bent, at my side, I settled into the motion like one asleep. His hands moved to cup my buttocks whole, and I gasped as he parted the mounds. I felt that my bottom would split in two under his relentless pressure. Then his thumbs began to massage the small mouth to my anus, and I moaned.

"Relax," he advised with a low chuckle. I tried to do his bidding, but his thumbs pressed in and in until they were locked together inside me. I panted as he massaged the opening to my back door with the same sureness and strength he had used on the rest of my body. His fingers slid in the slippery oil, and I felt the opening swell and bloom beneath his nimble fingers.

He slid me up then to a near-kneeling position, like a frog. Each leg splayed bent beside my body and my bottom lifted itself, exposed. His hands moved back to my buttocks and again spread the cheeks painfully open. Then he paused and I nearly fainted in the anticipation.

"I am not very large," he explained, as I panted. "And I am wearing two condoms, so you are fully protected. I want you to try to fart."

Anything, I would do anything he asked, if only it would make this easier. I tried to remember how to fart. Nothing came out, but I felt instead a hard insistent pressure inward. I held my breath as the pressure increased. His claim not to be large was false; to my already-sore bottom, he felt huge. As I felt him about to push through the barrier of muscle, I suddenly could bear no more.

"Stop!" I cried out. "Stop! Stop!"

He paused, but did not ease the pressure. When he spoke, his voice held patience and innate politeness. "Bran warned me you might try to stop me, Chantal. I must explain that the worst pain disappears as soon as I am inside. Shall I continue?"

"Yes," I breathed and he thrust hard once. I felt the insistent pressure of his organ through my whole body; pressure but as he had promised, not really pain. Then he pressed farther into me and the pressure built again. My womb felt as full as if his penis lodged there, instead of in my rear. My belly responded to the fullness with a throbbing ache. He continued to press into me until there was no more room anywhere inside me and I felt his testicles brush against my skin. He held me very still and steady then as my breathing returned. We paused for several moments thus, suspended.

"Tell me what you want me to do," he asked.

"Touch me," I answered, for my clitoris ached for its own stimulation. He moved his hand to my front and began to massage my whole vaginal area. His talented fingers wove and dipped and prodded and pulled and swept me to a swift dive over the edge of reason. I felt my orgasm as never before, as it pulsed through my anus and around his organ. His penis began to throb inside me, and I groaned with the aching yet satisfying movement.

He brought me to peak after peak as his penis remained pulsing and steady in my behind.

Finally his hand left me naked once more and moved back to hold my hips steady. He began to move inside me, slowly rocking an inch in, an inch out. With each small movement, I groaned, whether in pleasure or pain I couldn't tell. The raft swayed gently with the motion, heightening my disorientation. The movement deepened and I felt his rod accelerate its motion within me. I grabbed the rings to steady myself and whimpered and panted as the pressure adjusted up and down, in and out. He filled me and then emptied me with a steadily mounting rhythm. My vagina throbbed again with this new motion, and I built toward yet another peak. As my pleasure returned, his motion increased and he swelled inside me. The pressure became exquisite pain. When I felt him explode inside me, I fainted.

When I came to, he was gone. I lay unbound on the raft, alone in the vast basement. I lay bruised but content for long hours as day drifted into evening. I forgot to drink the formula; I didn't need to relieve myself; I didn't even think. I just lay on the raft and absorbed the day.

pesante
Heavy Going

When I returned to my room, I found a desk newly placed beneath the windows. A small, powerful computer—one I had wanted but could never afford—sat on the desktop. The drawers of the desk were filled with writing supplies: pens, pencils, index cards, erasers, rulers, scissors, a stapler, even binders and a hole punch. All the little items I used at home awaited my pleasure. That computer meant more to me than any jewel, for it meant that Bran believed in my readiness to write.

For the next three days, I remained in my room, chained to the keyboard by my desire to create. I didn't write a narrative or poetry. Instead I poured therapeutic words of blood onto the page: words of joy and rage, of sorrow, guilt and hunger. Bran didn't interrupt me, not for morning discipline or exercise or music. Our routine changed in another way as well; I stopped drinking the formula. Food appeared at intervals, simple but delicious meals that arrived hot as if by magic at the table by my door. I knew of their arrival only by the aroma; I never saw or heard their carrier. At the end of three days, I felt drained. The vampire computer had sucked the blood from my body. I fell into an exhausted slumber that night, uncertain whether I had the stamina to continue.

The next morning, Bran again awoke me, as if by cue. He led me silently to the balcony and whipped me firmly. I relished the return to familiar ground. He left me at the computer then, and I found new words for my disjointed song. When food arrived, Bran came as well. I left the keyboard, at first reluctant and then glad to take a break. We ate by the fire, then went down to the basement. I found as I swam that the rote movement freed my thoughts to roam, and they returned again and again to my writing. Images flowed over me as soft as the water. I couldn't wait to get back to my room. I was as eager as a child who has just learned to read and feels the wonder of the printed page for the first time. Bran laughed and shook his head when I explained, but he let me go.

As the days grew shorter, our routine reestablished itself on a new plane. Bran still awoke me each morning, often before sunrise. Some days, he would ask me to masturbate for him. I shared my rambling fantasies freely with him now. Other mornings, he whipped me softly, each stroke a hidden caress. Sometimes we just sat quietly by the fire and talked. We ate breakfast together every day. Then I would work for several hours at my writing. He never asked to see what I worked on, and I never invited him to read my words.

Each afternoon, he brought our lunch and then would supervise me as I exercised. He introduced me to the rigorous beauty of ballet, and I spent many hours stretching and flexing in precise movements at the barre. Some days, I returned to work through the late afternoon; others, I listened to his music. I never tired of the songs that sprang effortlessly from his fingers. I learned the name of the piece he played most often, Chopin's *Fantaisie-Impromptu*. He would improvise, as I had read Chopin did, always returning in the end to the same haunting melody. Our idyllic days passed uncounted until one night it snowed.

Bran arrived the next morning carrying the worn black whip. When we went onto the balcony, I saw that the ground was covered in a thick sifting of sugary white. I shivered in the chill air, for I wore only my flannel smock. I brushed the snow from the railing and cushioned my hands from the cold with cloth from the front of my blouse. Bran lifted the back of the smock, and the cold air raised goose bumps on my bottom.

"Heat me up," I called, laughing.

Bran swung the whip hard, and it cracked smartly across my bottom. The stinging heat warmed me, and I settled in for the coming lashes. A few seconds later, I gasped as icy coldness drenched my skin. Bran had slapped a pack of snow on my exposed rear. Before I could react, the whip cracked again and landed in the midst of my freezing flesh. The heat and cold fought for possession of my skin, until the snow slid from me to the ground. I glanced behind me, to see whether heat or cold would arrive next.

"Don't look!" Bran laughed. "You'll spoil the surprise."

I faced back to the ocean and tensed my buttocks. Anticipation worked its way with me, and I grew as hot and cold inside as my exposed skin. The whip cracked down, followed immediately by the cold of snow. I squealed and wiggled my rear to shake off the snow. Then three strokes from the whip heated me to a fever pitch, both inside and out.

"Finish me, please!" I begged. Bran knew exactly how to bring me to orgasm with the whip, especially with the black whip. I waited for the release I knew lay around the next corner.

"Stand up and face me," he ordered.

I turned to obey, wondering what further torturous pleasure he had in mind. With one hand, he undid the string that held my blouse closed. The other he held behind his back.

"No, please, Bran," I pleaded, laughing.

"Show me your breasts," he commanded.

Shivering in nervous anticipation, I pulled my blouse open to expose my breasts. He brought his hand, full of snow as I had feared, from behind his back.

"Hold still," he cautioned and brought the snow slowly toward me. My nipples rose to frigid peaks, waiting for the unfamiliar and probably painful sensation. I held perfectly still until he touched the ice to the side of one breast. Then I shrank back to the railing involuntarily.

"Come back, Chantal," Bran teased. "Take your medicine."

I straightened slowly, dreading the cold, but relishing the game. He held the snow against my breast and I screamed. When he withdrew his hand, heat flooded my breast, and the skin tingled like a new-lit fire. He brought his hand to my other breast and I closed my eyes, determined not to scream again. But I did. When he withdrew the snow, Bran bent his head and kissed each nipple chastely, the first touch of his lips to my skin in all the months of my captivity. Suddenly I no longer felt the cold.

"Come inside," he invited. "Let's warm up."

My vagina begged for the release of orgasm, but I damped down the need and followed Bran into my bedroom.

"That was fun," he commented enthusiastically as he moved to stand by the fire.

It had been fun, but I wouldn't tell him so. My reluctance and his compulsion formed the basis for our ongoing games. As I moved to stand beside him in the warmth of the fire, questions swirled in my mind. Perhaps the snow reminded me of the passing of time. Perhaps I had reached the end of my self-discovery. I knew only that I needed to talk.

"Bran," I began. I sat on the sofa and patted the seat next to me. "May I go home soon?"

"Do you think you're ready?" he asked.

"I don't know," I answered honestly.

"Then you aren't ready." His reply was final. I

attempted to gather my thoughts, but they wouldn't coalesce into neat bundles.

"What do you get out of our relationship, Bran?" I wanted to know where we were going, but couldn't think of the right questions to ask.

"I'm your teacher, Chantal." Bran seemed surprised by my question.

"But you're a man," I continued. "You have needs, too. Don't you ever want to make love to me?"

"No!" He sounded horrified. "That would be a breach of your trust, Chantal. Do you think of me as a lover?"

Oddly, I realized that I didn't. I was content with our relationship as mentor and trainee. But I did want something more.

"No," I answered him, feeling slightly apologetic. "I don't think of you as my lover, though I do love you."

"Thank you, Chantal." Bran beamed. "I love you as well."

"You must, or you wouldn't take so much trouble with me."

"But not as a lover," he continued, and I nodded my head in agreement.

I smiled and nodded again, wishing I could identify what was missing.

"But you want a lover," Bran answered my question. "A real lover."

"Yes." I realized the truth as I spoke. "I want to make love in some conventional way, with someone I love and who loves me."

"I can bring him to you here if you wish," Bran offered.

"What? How can you know who I'll love, or who will love me? You could bring a man here, but chances are he wouldn't be the right man."

"I can bring the right man here, if that's your choice," Bran repeated.

"Who are you?" I asked, laughing. "Santa Claus?"

Bran shrugged, and I began to wonder in earnest.

"If I don't bring him to the island, you'll meet him when you return to the rest of your life."

"I wish I could be as sure as you are," I commented skeptically.

Bran spoke the words that formed the cornerstone of our relationship, "Trust me."

I shook my head, but deep inside, I did.

"Don't bring him," I answered his earlier question. I wanted my lover to be real, not part of this extended fantasy. "I can wait."

Bran nodded his acceptance of my answer.

"I've gotten lazy lately," he continued. "We'll accelerate your education. The fact that you are thinking of home tells me that I've been remiss."

"Accelerate how?" I asked, not sure I liked the idea. Our days had fallen into a comfortable pattern. I felt as though I'd experienced the emotions of two lifetimes in the last few months. "What do I have left to learn?"

"Wait and see," Bran smiled enigmatically and refused to answer my question. "Let's get started."

I groaned, for I knew each new beginning involved a

measure of fear and pain before the payoff in knowledge and pleasure. Bran grabbed my hand and hauled me to my feet. He pulled off my cotton gown and led me into the hall. When we turned toward the stairs to the left, I thought I might know his destination, the dark room. I began to look forward to the opportunity to meditate in relaxed oblivion. As always, Bran added a twist.

We did indeed go to the dark room sandwiched vertically between the library and my bedroom. This time the room held two high tables. One was thin, about two feet wide of bare smooth wood, with two familiar metal rings. The other held an irregular mound covered by a cloth. Resigned, I moved to the bare table and held out my hands. Bran laughed and boosted me up to lie on my stomach across the wood. He attached my hands to the rings, then strapped my ankles to the table legs with two more leather thongs. I felt trussed for a whipping, and my juices flowed in anticipation.

Bran walked to the other table and removed the cloth. I saw a strange contraption with cogs and a long wooden arm attached to a central core. He flipped a switch and the arm swung out. He flipped the switch off and moved the table closer to me. The next time he turned the machine on the arm patted my bottom gently. A mechanical spanker, I thought, and began to laugh. Bran smiled indulgently at me and turned to adjust the machine. The next blow struck my helpless bottom with a loud *thwack*. I jumped.

"Ow!" I cried, for it hurt.

"Sorry, Chantal," Bran apologized and moved the

machine an inch back. The next smack tingled and left a residual heat but little soreness. Next he moved to my hips and raised one side with his hand. He slid the other hand beneath me; it held a hard object that pressed against my pubic bone. His hand crept along the table until it rested at the opening to my vagina. He slid the object, which felt like a short, thick dildo, into my oozing lower mouth. I sighed and began to move against the hard knob.

"Wait a minute!" Bran cautioned me. He twisted the base of the knob, and I felt a ridge run up my labia and past my clitoris. I couldn't resist the temptation and rubbed myself against the alluring hardness. I sighed in relief; this would be fun. Bran moved to stand by my head and explained my predicament.

"When a trainer whips you, he or she constantly adjusts to your needs. That is the art and the science of whipping. But there is another pleasure that comes from impersonality. This paddle won't adjust to you, Chantal; you must adjust to it."

"Wait a minute," I interrupted. The dildo competed with Bran's words for my attention. "Aren't you going to stay and monitor the machine?"

"No," Bran stated flatly. "The paddle will strike at random intervals, random hardness, and random height. The mechanism is carefully designed so that you can't hear the movement. You'll get no warning, only the sensation of the slap against your skin."

"But—" I began to protest. It was one thing to have Bran, whom I trusted, discipline me. I didn't trust this machine.

"Quiet, Chantal." Bran overrode my sputtering. "If your skin gets too tender, the machine won't know. It may or may not strike you again in the same spot before you are recovered. It is the not knowing that provides the stimulation, and the dildo."

"What about the 'no harm' clause in our contract?" I asked. The dildo tried to persuade me to shut up and get on with it, but I was both indignant and increasingly apprehensive.

"I guarantee that within thirty minutes of leaving this room, you won't be sore," Bran reassured me. Then he turned on the machine and left the room.

I waited in agony for the first blow, but nothing happened. Then, as my buttocks relaxed, the wood smacked my skin. I jumped and grunted, and the dildo shifted beneath me. I had to remain steady to keep its tantalizing pressure in just the right spot. I realized I had forgotten to ask Bran how long I had to stay in the room. Maybe the machine... A smack, half an inch higher and twice as hard, interrupted my thought. I tried again. Maybe the machine was programmed to a certain number of smacks. *Whack!* A soft stroke kissed my skin and left a warm glow in its wake. I wriggled back onto the slippery dildo and decided to count the blows. *Whack!* Another stroke, again light, hit the same spot. The heat intensified. That made four strokes, I thought. *Thwack! Thwack!* The machine struck in swift succession, once high and hard, once low and even harder. The dildo slid from my incautious opening. Ow and double ow. This began to hurt.

122

"Bran!" I yelled. "Stop this machine!"

I didn't know whether he could hear me. No blow came, and I began to hope that he would once again heed my request. I slid my vagina back onto the satisfaction of the hard knob. Even if he insisted on starting the machine again, at least I could ask him how long this would last. *Thwack!* A soft slap patted the center of my bottom. Damn! He must not be able to hear me. For the first time, I realized how truly defenseless I was. The machine would continue, whether I willed it or no.

The next smack knocked me off the dildo. That frustration hurt more than the blow, though it was a hard one. I tried to angle myself back on before the arm could catch me again. *Whack!* The paddle flew; I had not succeeded. I ignored the sting in my rear and fought again to slide onto the knob at my front. I sighed in relief as I succeeded, then clenched my vaginal muscles as the next smack hit my heated rear. I held on and laughed in triumph.

By concentrating hard, I found I could hold fast to the dildo even through the harder strokes. As I focused all my attention on the muscles of my vagina, I reached a new level of stimulation and pleasure. I didn't climax, but found I enjoyed the ride all the more intensely for my efforts. The machine continued to smack my bottom; the heat from the strokes began to penetrate deeper than any whipping. With my vagina adjusting to its new and powerful role, my attention turned to my forgotten-but-not-unstimulated clitoris. As soon as I allowed my focus to waver to the button of joy, I came to a hot and tumultuous climax.

As I shuddered, the machine stroked me especially hard and sent me tumbling over the edge of another peak. In orgasm, my vagina clung hard to the dildo, and my newly rediscovered clitoris rubbed against the hard ridge beneath it. Each stroke of the machine brought a fresh angle of pleasure; my backside shrank from the increasing heat, while my front held hard to the mound of its fulfillment.

Though I grew exhausted from repeated orgasm, still I couldn't relax or the dildo would slip from my grasp and bang painfully against my tender labia. My clitoris cried "Enough!" but the stimulation continued heedlessly. My bottom felt as tender as a raw steak and each new stroke brought tears to my orgasm-exhausted eyes. Finally my body could accept no more. I slid off the dildo and, ignoring the pain, used my vagina to push it clattering to the floor. I withdrew deep into my mind, to a still space far from the machine, till each stroke was only a dim echo in the distance, and I slept.

con anima
With Spirit

I awoke when Bran turned off the machine. With returning consciousness, I became aware of my burning bottom. Bran smoothed on a cool gel which doused the immediate flame. The lingering heat in my muscles would warm me for hours. As Bran promised, the pain disappeared when the machine stopped. The blows had been not hard, but merely continuous.

"How do you feel?" Bran asked as he unstrapped my ankles.

"Stiff." I wasn't really complaining. I waited patiently while he untied my hands, then again when he lifted me to stand on the floor. My unused legs buckled beneath me, and I clung to his arm while the feeling returned. The throb in my legs hurt worse than the heat in my bottom.

"Can you stand now?" Bran asked after a moment.

"I think so." I let go of his arm and took a couple of shaky paces. With each step, more feeling returned. Soon I was as steady as ever. Bran slipped a fresh cotton dress over my head and carefully tied the silk ribbon over my breasts. He held out his elbow for my arm in a courtly gesture from centuries past. I accepted his invitation and we walked slowly, arm in arm, down the stairs.

We went to the salon at the side of the house, a cheerful room with wide sunny windows and soft plump sofas and chairs. I was amazed to see the sun still rising to its peak. I thought I had been in the dark room for many hours. Bran brought a light meal of chicken, carrots, and rice from the kitchen, and we munched in companionable silence for several moments.

"How do you feel?" he asked finally.

"Fine."

"Tell me about it," he prompted.

I thought for a minute, trying to capture the right words to express my insight.

"I feel more in control of myself," I began. Bran nodded thoughtfully, and I continued. "It was all me in there. The machine didn't count. I was the only one. But it wasn't like masturbating because I didn't have physical control."

I paused again and Bran watched my expression carefully. We finished our meal in silence and then I resumed my thoughts.

"The only way I could gain control was through my mind. First I learned to hold myself onto the dildo. That was hard, but once I got the knack, I could do it. I worried that when I had an orgasm I would lose it all, so I fought even harder to control my own response. Finally the orgasm came...." I paused and smiled in recollection.

"And it was the mother of all orgasms, right?"

"Yes!" I replied. "It was incredible. Waiting is a powerful aphrodisiac."

"The best."

"The strange thing was that I didn't lose control at all. If anything, I gained more power through the orgasm. Each time I came, I became more and more powerful, until I felt like one of the pagan goddesses in Olympus."

"You are Aphrodite, my dear."

"Well, I felt like her, anyway."

"What you felt is mastery, Chantal," Bran explained. "By mastering yourself and your response, you mastered the machine and your whole environment."

"I had a Taoist immersion in there." Though I heard Bran's words, I followed my own thought. "I touched the source."

"Tibetan Buddhists would agree with you," Bran agreed, nodding. "Many feel our closest approach to the divine is through orgasm. Though the scientists say it is only a chemical stew."

"Don't spoil my illusion," I half-begged, half-teased.

"I'm happy for you." Bran reached over and ruffled my unruly hair. Since my arrival, it had grown long and shaggy and gray. Though I kept it clean, I couldn't make it neat. I no longer cared; its wild untidiness suited our lifestyle.

"Tell me who you are, Bran." The question rose from my unconscious and startled me more than it did my companion. I hastened to retract. "No, that's okay. It's your own business."

"It's all right, Chantal," Bran reassured me. "I don't mind telling you if you're sure you want to know."

"Well, I'm not sure," I temporized. "Can I ask you questions? Then I can stop when we get as far as I want to go."

"Ask away."

"Are you human?" The bald question seemed gauche as soon as the words left my mouth, yet I had serious doubts as to the answer.

"I'm as human as you are, Chantal." I sighed a great sigh of relief. Then he continued, "But I'm also more than human."

I groaned, because I knew he spoke the truth. I knew he was no madman with delusions of immortality. He was too perfect and too perfectly attuned to my needs. A madman would have been wrapped in his own illusions, not determined to foster mine. I had been afraid of his answer; yet his honesty came as a relief. His keen eyes followed the trail of emotions across my face, searching for clues to my reaction. For once, he seemed unable to read my mind. I tried to smile, to reassure him, but my mouth wouldn't cooperate.

"Are you familiar with the concept of a bodhisattva from Mahayana Buddhism?" he asked. I shook my head and he explained.

"A bodhisattva is a person who has reached enlightenment and gained the right to enter nirvana, but refrains in order to save others." I nodded my understanding.

"Well," he continued, "I'm not a bodhisattva."

I laughed.

"Then why did you tell me about the concept?"

"It's close." He laughed, too. "If I were a Buddhist, I might have become one."

"So what are you?" Our shared laughter made me bold.

"It's easier first to tell you what I'm not. You have many names for my function in your world, but none of them is really accurate. I'm not a fairy godfather or an angel or a devil. I'm not a ghost or a benevolent vampire."

"I know," I replied. "You eat and don't mind daylight. I checked."

Bran's deep rolling laugh warmed the room.

"That shows you the power of fiction, doesn't it? I'm actually classified as a hero, from the days when such creatures existed."

"You mean a Greek hero who becomes a god, like Hercules?"

"Sort of, except I'm Welsh, not Greek. I told you my true name the first time you asked me. I am Bendegeit Bran, Bran the Blessed."

I sat dumbfounded. Bran seemed to take pity on my bewilderment and continued his explanation.

"I was born to human life the son of Llyr."

"Lear?" I interrupted. "Shakespeare's Lear?"

"L-L-Y-R." Bran spelled the name. "Shakespeare based his play on him."

"Isn't *Lear* about daughters?"

"Willie never was too concerned with historical accuracy," Bran laughed.

Willie? I wondered.

Bran continued, "I was considered large and strong for my age. Nutrition and medicine have improved, so now I'm less remarkable. I was a soldier and a leader of men. I was also renowned in my kingdom as a harpist and a poet. When I became king, I tried to lead my people well, watching over them and fighting for them. In the last battle against Matholwch, then king of Ireland, I was mortally wounded. I ordered my men to cut off my head and set it in London, facing the Continent, to protect my people from invaders."

The bloody tale awoke echoes in my mind of similar feats; yet Bran seemed singularly selfless in his devotion to his tribe. No wonder they called him "The Blessed."

"When I reached our heaven, Llyr offered me the choice to remain and serve my people, or to enter heaven and reign at his side. I chose to remain."

"And you've been here ever since?" I asked, aghast. Having watched our degeneration for thousands of years, he must be thoroughly bored and disgusted with humanity.

"No, Chantal," Bran laughed. "I have the gift to appear only when I wish. If I want, I can spend a thousand years in peace before I seek another protégée. But the past few centuries have been most interesting. I find myself drawn to your era."

As Bran talked, his accent deepened. I began to see the ancient hero beneath the man. The patience of the ages sat upon his shoulders, and the wisdom of centuries echoed in his voice. I felt both blessed and mightily confused.

"And I am your latest-chosen protégée?" I asked. "What on earth do you see in me?"

"You're a creative spirit, Chantal. Such people are precious to me, and to the world. When I saw how you wasted your gift, I had to come."

"Because I wrote erotica?"

"Heavens, no!" Bran protested. "Because you wrote mediocre erotica."

"But I'm nothing," I continued to argue.

"Your statement proves only that you aren't ready to leave the island, Chantal. When you truly believe in yourself, then you may resume your life."

"May I ask you some technical questions?" The fantastical conversation had moved beyond my depth. I reached for firmer ground.

"Of course."

"Is time passing now, on the island?"

"Oh, yes, Chantal," he told me. "We're still very much part of the world. I send to Pay and Pack Drugs for our formula. I have a Visa Gold Card. A cursèd nuisance, but there you are. Your daughters' hair will be longer, as yours is, when you return."

"Can you be hurt?"

"I'm as mortal as you, my dear," Bran explained. "If I cut myself, I bleed. I heal quickly, but that's more clean living than immortality. Unfortunately, I have died several times, through my carelessness."

"Then what happens?"

"My body is buried and my spirit returns to our heaven until I find my next project."

"Do you always return in the same body?" I felt like Barbara Walters.

"I happen to like this body." Bran flexed his muscles playfully. "Don't you?"

"Yes," I laughed. "It's a very nice body. What about pain?"

"I feel pain," Bran replied tersely. "Both physical and emotional."

"So the only difference is that you come back again and again?"

"Not really. Several religions believe in reincarnation. If you believe in something, that is what happens. Christians who believe in Heaven go there. Hindus who believe in reincarnation are reincarnated."

"So you could be anyone?"

"I have the gift of awareness, Chantal. I remember every life, even my first mortal one. I also have a few other gifts."

"Such as?" I prompted.

"Money is never a problem. I have a hoard of treasure from the Dark Ages."

"Handy," I commented sardonically.

"Be glad," Bran admonished. "That's what keeps us

safe on this island. I bought it a few years ago with you in mind. That is another gift; I can read souls."

"Whoa!" I backed up on the sofa. "This is getting weird again. You can read my soul?"

"How do you think I found you, my dear?" Bran had a point. "I waited for you to reach the exact point in your life when you would be ready to accept my help. Then I abducted you."

"And you can read my mind?" It wasn't really a question; I knew he could.

"A mind is a bit easier than a soul."

"So when you said I could trust you, you were right?"

"I was right."

We sat in silence for several minutes as I struggled to assimilate all Bran had recounted. He was a Hero, a god, sort of. My conscious mind rebelled, but my unconscious resonated to the reality of what he told me. And I was his protégée, the protégée of a Hero. That was the hardest hurdle of all. I thought of another question.

"Willie?"

"Young Shakespeare?"

"Was he one of your—"

"No," Bran laughed. "Willie was a shake-scene before I ever appeared. He told me to go back."

"He rejected you?"

"I hung around for a few months, trying not to get in his way." Bran shrugged. "He was impolite, brash, and absolutely brilliant."

"Okay." I shook my head in wonder. "So who *have* you taken under your wing? Who that I would recognize?"

"Whose music do I play most often?"

"Chopin," I answered, awed. My voice dropped to a whisper. "You mean you taught Chopin?"

"Nurtured, perhaps. Not taught. He had the will, but his technique was unruly."

"But he is famous for his discipline," I protested. I had read a biography of Chopin while Bran played for me in the early fall afternoons. "It forms the foundation of his genius."

"Exactly!" Bran beamed. "The left hand must maintain a perfect regularity, so that the right may soar to unimagined heights."

"And you taught him that?" I imagine I sounded incredulous, for so I felt. Bran nodded and I continued my questioning. "Who else?"

"Most have been ordinary men and women who have gone on to lead brave-but-ordinary lives. I stayed for a time with a settlement family on the prairie in Saskatchewan. They planted trees. A woman in the early 1900s was about to quit teaching, and I persuaded her to continue. Creativity comes in many forms."

"Have you tutored anyone else famous?"

"The sculptures you see in the main salon…"

"Rodin?" Bran nodded.

"Giacometti?" He nodded again.

"Who else?" I asked, incredulous.

"I prefer to work with artists, but some scientists have attracted my attention."

"Einstein?" I was ready at last to disbelieve him.

"No," he replied, to my relief. "He found his own

134

muse and didn't need my support. When Blaise Pascal decided to follow his father's footsteps as a tax collector, I stayed with him for a few months. Blaise was a remarkable man."

"So is yours the real genius of our age?" I asked, tormented by the thought. Were the heroic men of our times not really great, but merely the vehicle for one man's continuity?

"No, Chantal, no!" Bran exclaimed. "The genius is all within the man himself, or woman. I offer only the opportunity to uncover it. I claim no credit, none at all."

"I'm sorry," I apologized. "You never claimed credit. It's only that I feel so inadequate beside these names. Am I one of the geniuses, or one of the 'brave but ordinary'?"

"You are yourself, Chantal."

"Hmmph."

"Think of the Tao," Bran reminded me. "It flows through you, as surely as it flowed through Pascal or Rodin or Chopin, or Mary in Saskatchewan. I believe true genius lies in the ability to tap into that source. Your synapses don't spark any faster than the next person's; your eyes are no keener; your memory no better."

"Far worse!" I laughed.

"But when you find the source, by whatever name you choose to call it, all is possible. Few bother to look."

"Oh, I'm looking. I only wonder whether I'll ever find anything."

"You already have, my dear."

I thought of Bran's words and realized that he was right. Even in my blindness, I had found him.

poco ritenuto
Slow for a Moment

Bran left me alone for the rest of that day as I struggled to absorb what he had told me. One question tickled at me. Late that afternoon, I left my room to search for my mentor. I found him in the library.

"So you've discovered more questions, Chantal?" Bran smiled at me from behind his desk and motioned for me to sit opposite him.

"I was wondering if you use the same methods with each of us."

"Does the thought of my whipping a naked Chopin horrify you, my dear?" Bran teased me gently. "No, the method must vary with the individual. I helped Chopin rebuild his physical health through a strict regimen, and thus he gained the few years in which he produced his most brilliant work."

"And in the process of becoming healthy, he learned discipline as well?" I asked.

"Yes. Each creative mind has its own bent. I merely follow the natural inclination."

"And my inclination is toward sadomasochism?" I whispered, not well pleased with the obvious answer.

"I wouldn't classify what we do as SM, Chantal. If so, we merely play at it."

What he said was true. His discipline strove to arouse me, not him. "Then how do you describe my talent?"

"You feel deeply, my dear. And on occasion you are able to express your feelings eloquently. Unfortunately, you had buried yourself beneath a blanket of false emoting. I only help uncover your true self."

"Leaving me exposed to the world, like Yeats?"

"Exactly. 'There's more enterprise in walking naked.' He is one of my favorite poets."

"Did you…"

"No," Bran laughed. "Many find their own way. I step in only when the need and my inclination coincide."

"So where do we go from here? Can I go home now?"

"Not yet, Chantal. Are you so eager to leave my protection?"

I thought for a moment and shook my head.

"So, we will begin the next level," Bran rubbed his hands together enthusiastically. My stomach fluttered in dread anticipation. "I believe it is time to enact another scene from your books."

I groaned.

"Remove your dress."

I raised my hand and untied the bow that held the bodice together. When I wriggled my shoulders, the dress slipped down to pool around my waist as I sat in the chair.

"Stand up," he commanded.

I stood and the dress continued its journey to land at my ankles. I stood bare before him. My naked skin felt comfortable to me now, though my naked words did not. Bran opened the top drawer of his desk and removed the white and the black whips. I felt my juices flow as he fitted a condom over the dildo handle of the white whip. I had used that whip so many ways in my books that I could not yet divine his intentions. The uncertainty left me imagining the worst. Bran pushed both whips across the desk toward me, then came to stand by my side.

"I'm Tom, Chantal. Do you remember Tom?"

"Yes," I whispered. Tom was one of the few characters I had created whom I did not like. He took over his own story and became harsher than I had intended. I knew now what Bran would do, and I didn't look forward to the next hour. Though I trusted Bran, I wondered what he meant by the "next level."

"You will address me as 'Master.'" Bran waited for my response.

"Yes, Master." The words were direct from my novel. Bran—the Master, I must remember to call him—sat in the chair I had warmed a moment before.

"Place your foot on the arm of the chair," he directed, turning me to face him.

I raised my leg so that my foot perched on the high arm. He turned out my knee, and my moist cunt spread exposed before him. He reached behind me and picked up the white whip. I knew what was coming. He would force the dildo/handle into my vagina and order me to hold it inside. It would slip from my grasp, and he would punish me with the black whip—really punish me. Not a gentle arousing whipping, but harsh strokes that would leave me sore. I began to cry softly as I waited.

"Are you ready, Chantal?"

I nodded, hoping to get the ordeal over with as quickly as possible. He frowned at my silence. I remembered the character from my novel.

"Yes, Master," I whispered. Bran slid the dildo inside my dripping cavity. The long white thongs caressed my thighs with a whispering tickle. The cool touch of the hard leather made me gasp, and my tears subsided as the welcome pressure filled me.

"Do not allow the dildo to slip," he cautioned, as I had known he would. "If you release it, you will be punished severely. Do you understand?"

"Yes, Master," I replied. When he released his hold on the whip, I felt the shaft begin to slide. I tightened the muscles of my vagina and the sliding stopped. My own efforts aroused me mightily. As I had with the mechanical spanker, I fought to maintain my control. I struggled not to climax, fearing I would lose the dildo in my ecstasy, but the large, hard knob and my own contracted muscles pushed me to the edge of my emotions. My eyes closed and my head tilted back in concentration. Still, I held on to both the dildo and my orgasm. I gripped the Master's shoulders to steady myself.

"You see, Chantal." Bran's words interrupted my concentration. My head dropped and my eyes flew open, but still I maintained a tight grip on the dildo. His voice had changed; he was Bran again, and not the Master. "What you thought was so hard is really quite easy."

He laughed. When I began to chuckle, I felt the whip handle slip. I had to fight harder not to laugh than to hold it in.

"You are the devil, Bran," I protested.

"According to some," he agreed, still laughing. "Hold on tight."

I knew he meant the dildo, and I squeezed my vaginal muscles. The effort brought me again to the edge of a climax. I struggled to control the strong urge for release. Bran lifted my hands from his shoulders and slid out of the chair to stand beside me. He placed my hands on the back of the chair, so that I was bent over in a whipping position. Now the dildo was harder to grip. I truly had to concentrate to keep it from slipping. I lost awareness of Bran's activities until the black whip descended in a *whoosh* across my exposed backside.

The single stroke sent me over the edge and tumbling down the chasm of an enormous orgasm. The dildo in my vagina throbbed as if alive, caught in the rhythm of my climax. The white leather straps stroked my bare inner thighs in gentle imitation of Bran's harsher lashing.

As my muscles convulsed, I realized dimly that I was in no danger of losing the dildo. My spasming vagina held it firm. With the realization came confidence. As Bran continued to stroke my backside I came again and again in pulsing waves of pure emotion. My cries began low and built to a piercing and wordless scream. When the strokes of the whip ceased, I found words.

"Don't stop!" I screamed, though my rear felt as hot as a stovetop. Bran stroked me again, hard, and I screamed wordlessly as a fresh spasm shook my body. He continued to whip me long past our accustomed ten strokes, and I fulfilled my capacity for orgasm. Eventually I found that my reason returned. The strokes of the whip became strokes again; the muscles of my vagina became muscles again; my voice became a voice.

"That's enough," I panted, exultant. I allowed the dildo to slide from my vagina to the floor, and my juices spilled out with it. I turned to face a sweaty and equally jubilant Bran. I grasped his head and pulled it down to mine, kissing him heartily on both cheeks in European fashion. He gathered me in his strong arms and we stood panting, hugging till our breathing returned to normal.

Finally I stepped back out of his arms and asked him cheekily, "So, did I learn my lesson well, Master?"

"That's not the way it was supposed to go," Bran's deep voice was mock-reproachful. "I fear the pupil outstrips the teacher this evening."

"Good," I replied firmly. "It's about time."

"Don't get cocky, Chantal," Bran cautioned me. "Tomorrow is another day."

As he had intended, his words gave me pause. I wondered what had been his original intent that night. Had he meant to frighten me? The scenario from my novel was scary enough, I had to admit. I had known a few moments of uneasiness. But the reality had been far more enjoyable than worrisome. I drifted that night into a deep and contented sleep, little expecting what the morrow would bring.

Bran awoke me in the early hours before dawn. I stumbled to the washroom, then put on my slippers and a warm jacket and joined him on the chilly balcony. My top half felt toasty, though my legs were exposed to the cool, dark breeze.

"Next level." Bran's words were both an invitation and a caution. My senses began to awaken as I nodded sleepy agreement to his unspoken question. He pulled heavy mitts from his pocket and placed them on my hands. Then he motioned for me to bend over and hold onto the balcony railing. He left me standing there, my rear end exposed and freezing, and went back into the bedroom. He returned quickly, again carrying the black and white whips. I wondered with awakening anticipation if he meant to repeat yesterday's exercise. He slipped a condom over the handle of the white whip, and my expectation rose a notch. My moist vagina began to swell eagerly.

"Relax your buttocks," his voice commanded, and I groaned. The contrast between my happy anticipation and the painful reality of the huge protrusion pounding at my rear door brought tears to my eyes. The tears began to fall in earnest as, with no preparation, he pressed the well-greased dildo against my anal mouth. I remembered the words of the Oriental man and tried to relax my freezing buttocks. As I succeeded, I was almost sorry, for he quickly slid the dildo an inch inside me. The pressure was relentless and the pain only too real as the whip handle crept, inch by gasping inch, into my anus.

Finally the journey was complete. Bran gave me no time to relax, but quickly tied the long white leather strands of the whip around my thighs and waist, binding the handle firmly inside me. The dildo shifted as he tied each knot and I jerked and groaned with the unfamiliar movement. From the corner of my eye, I saw him grasp the black whip and cried out a protest.

"No, Bran, you can't!"

My cry ended on a scream as the first stroke lashed my stuffed bottom. The leather straps heated my skin with a welcome sting, but they also landed on the embedded dildo. They forced the stiff leather farther into me in an uneven, jarring motion. Hot tears poured from my eyes onto my frozen cheeks. The handle slid out a little when the strop retreated, and I sighed in relief. The next stroke caught me midsigh and pushed the dildo back in, only to release the pressure again in an instant. It hurt this time—really hurt. Though my vagina felt hot and moist and my rear heated to a warm glow under the repeated strokes, still I didn't come near an orgasm.

After ten strokes, Bran stopped. "Do you want me to keep going?" he asked.

I felt much more pain than pleasure and answered him roughly. "No, damn it! Get that thing out of me."

Bran laid the black whip on a nearby table and bent to untie the white leather straps. As he loosened each knot, the dildo shifted, and I groaned again and again with the discomfort. Finally the knots were all freed and my muscles began to slide the dildo from my bottom. Bran held the whip by the straps to keep it steady, and soon it plopped from my bottom. He took it inside and flushed the condom down the toilet, then returned with my invention to the balcony.

Seeming to sense my anger and frustration, he handed me the imagined and yet all-too-real white whip. I grasped it by the end of the straps and flung it far over the railing to land in the restless sea below. I sent my anger flying with the vanished whip and turned to Bran with a rueful smile. He hugged me wordlessly and led me back into the warm bedroom.

"You were right," I commented as we sat warming ourselves by the briskly burning fire. "I'm not into sado-masochism."

"Now you know for sure," Bran agreed.

"Is that why you did that? To prove to me that I'm not really aroused by pain?"

"Partly. You are no more a masochist than I am a sadist. My pleasure comes from yours. This morning aroused me no more than it did you."

"So you are aroused by whipping me?" I had often wondered.

"No," Bran explained. "I'm aroused by your arousal."

"Don't you get awfully frustrated? Or do you masturbate and relieve yourself?"

"Two thousand years is a long time, Chantal. I lived as Bendegeit Bran about that long ago. I enjoy arousal as a mortal man enjoys orgasm. I don't require the physical release."

"But do you miss it?"

"Think of eating a Popsicle when you were young, Chantal. Today you probably wouldn't enjoy the reality nearly as much as the memory." He gave me a moment to think.

"You've led me off track." Bran continued with his second point. "Everyone has limits. We hadn't reached any of yours until this morning."

I understood his meaning quickly, though I mistrusted the inevitable next step. I spoke flatly. "You mean to make me confront my limits."

"Until you go beyond what is comfortable, you won't know where your limits are, Chantal."

"I don't like the sound of this." I turned away from Bran to face the fire.

"That's because you're afraid, my dear. Fear is an emotion like any other. We'll find the limits to your capacity for each emotion."

"I don't like the sound of this at all!" My hands fisted in my lap. Confronting my limits for pleasure in pain that morning had not been an enjoyable experience. Bran took my fists in his warm hands and unclenched my fingers. He answered as though he read my thoughts, as perhaps he had.

146

"Not every emotion is pleasurable, Chantal. Not every experience ends in orgasm."

His comment broke the tension and I had to laugh as I pictured buying groceries and having a climax, or weeding to orgasm. Unfortunately, Bran was right.

"Have a hot bath and pleasure yourself to exhaustion," he advised. "Don't worry about the inevitable."

"The inevitable?" I questioned. He nodded.

"That's why I'm here, Chantal. To lead you through those experiences you need but can't choose."

When Bran left the room, I began to weep softly as I sat by the fire. I didn't know whether I wept for my sore bottom or for my nervous anticipation of the coming days.

a tempo
Full Speed

The next morning I slept in, then wrote furiously for several hours. My words remained incoherent to anyone but myself, but at last they began to resemble my true emotions. Bran played Chopin that afternoon; the notes drifted up the staircase as I wrote and formed a melodic counterpoint to my turbulent thoughts. He joined me for a simple dinner of sole, roasted potatoes, and Belgian endive. I had acquired a liking for the bitter vegetable and ate two plumply swollen heads.

After dinner Bran asked me to come with him to the library. He was mysterious and playful in his request, and I wondered idly what he planned. The hot dinner must have dulled my wits, else I should have been apprehensive. I followed him through the great chamber and into the library, a lamb led willing to the slaughter. Bran motioned for me to sit in my familiar chair before his desk, then addressed me from his own more imposing seat behind the broad marble expanse.

"We spoke yesterday of exploring your deeper emotions, Chantal."

I thought that he sounded like a psychiatrist. I choked down a chuckle as I imagined the furor a presentation of his methods would create at a medical convention.

"You spoke of that, yes," I agreed reluctantly. "I was somewhat less enthusiastic."

"But you have placed yourself in my hands, and you will obey me."

Bran's comment was neither question nor command, but a simple statement of fact. He continued with what sounded at first like an irrelevant sidetrack.

"It's time you availed yourself of my library, Chantal."

"I've wanted to," I spoke eagerly, distracted from my uneasiness.

"I've made a list for you," Bran interrupted. He reached into a drawer and withdrew a sheet of foolscap. Down the page he had listed about twenty titles. He continued his explanation as I scanned the list. "You're as ill-read in the classics as most of your age."

The list was topped by the sacred books of the major world religions; of them, the only one I had studied was the *Tao Te Ching*. The list named tomes of Christianity, Judaism, Buddhism, Sikhism, Confucianism, Islam, and Hinduism. The task seemed formidable. As if that were not already enough to keep me occupied for several years, the list went on to Greek and Roman philosophers. It seemed I would be reading Plato and Socrates, as well as Marcus Aurelius. In slightly more modern readings, the list of literature included Chaucer, Shakespeare, Pascal, and Milton, with whom I was briefly acquainted from university courses. I must have looked stunned, for Bran commented sympathetically.

"At least I have them in translation for you, Chantal. Pascal read many of the texts in the original Greek and Latin. I added his *Pensées* to the list following his death."

"Is this Bran's World Philosophy 101?" I quipped, feeling eager but overwhelmed.

"More or less," my rigorous tutor chuckled. "We'll discuss them each evening. I've drawn up a schedule which you can meet, with diligent effort."

I understood the wisdom of reading the classics. I had always meant to do so, but had never made the time. Now I had the perfect guide, a man/god who had lived through these times, had perhaps known the very men whose works I would read. The more I thought about it, the more I looked forward to the coming months. Bran reeled in my wandering thoughts with his next words.

"I can see by your eyes that you're eager to begin, Chantal." I nodded like an enthusiastic child. Then his voice took on a harsher note. "What word would you use to describe the opposite of joyful anticipation, my dear?"

I thought for a moment, then murmured my answer. "Dread?"

"Well done," Bran's words almost patted me on the head. "Love and hate are closely aligned emotions, equal in passion, are they not?"

I nodded hesitant agreement, not liking the direction our conversation seemed headed.

"So are anticipation and dread, and for the next two weeks you will experience each with mounting intensity. You can't fully appreciate the one without the other." I swallowed to ease the dryness in my throat. When I didn't comment, Bran continued. "Today is Christmas Day, my dear, and I have a memento for you."

My eyes must have widened at the abrupt change of subject, for Bran smiled as he withdrew a long, flat box from the center drawer of the desk. I didn't remember that drawer with any pleasure. It seemed that only pain-inducing articles were stored there. When Bran pushed the box across the desk toward me, I hesitated to open it. I already felt a good measure of the dread he had promised to inspire. I imagined a new whip, a nasty one with metal tips that would rip my flesh. Then I shook myself; Bran had promised that I'd come to no harm. Whatever the box held, I need not fear injury. With that reassuring thought, I pulled the box to my side of the desktop and untied the ribbon with shaking fingers. Bran smiled encouragement, but somehow I knew from his sympathetic expression that I wouldn't like what I found in the box.

I lifted the lid. The first thing I saw was a large digital kitchen timer. It lay in the center of the box in a crumple of tissue paper. I lifted it out of the carton and placed it on the desk. When I peeled back the tissue paper, I discovered that a sheet of heavy cardboard concealed the remainder of the contents. I sat silent and staring, unwilling to reveal the next layer.

"Lift the cardboard," Bran's voice commanded me.

I blinked several times and swallowed hard. I really didn't want to know what lay beneath. At last, childishly, I looked away. Then, with my eyes still averted, I picked up the cardboard and laid it on the floor beside me.

"Look in the box, Chantal."

Curiosity finally overcame dread. When I turned my head, I hardly knew whether to laugh or cry. Inside, laid neatly in a row, were twelve shining dildos. They looked as if they were made of hard, smooth rubber, like a dog's chew toy. Each was unique and uniquely anatomically correct. Some curved left, some right. Some were bulbous, some slim. The only pattern I could discern was that they grew noticeably larger from left to right. To be sure, the last few were formidably endowed, but the rest looked tantalizingly realistic. My vagina began to drool, imagining the pleasure of sucking each into its moist warmth. The gift seemed more titillating than threatening, and I looked quizzically at the giver.

Bran's stern expression sobered me. Then his words stopped the breath in my throat. "Each day, for twelve days, one dildo will be placed in your anus."

My buttocks tightened in protest, especially as it imagined the last few. Bran's voice continued, inexorable.

"This is a lesson in anticipation—dread, if you prefer. We start at the left and move to the right over the next twelve days. You will report to me here in the library at exactly two o'clock each afternoon."

"I don't like this, Bran," I protested.

"You aren't meant to, Chantal. How do you feel?"

"Scared shitless."

"That reminds me," Bran pulled another box from the drawer, this one clearly labeled 'Fleet Enema.' "You are to give yourself an enema each morning on arising. There are a dozen in the box."

I felt my insides go liquid and doubted I would need the assistance. I took the box as if in a trance. But Bran wasn't quite finished with my mental annihilation.

"Have you taken a moment to wonder what the timer is for?" His voice was both mocking and solicitous. I shook my head, past words.

"Each day the dildo will remain inside you one minute longer, beginning with one minute on the first day and building to twelve minutes by the last."

I started to cry. Bran handed me a box of Kleenex.

"Don't shed too many tears over tomorrow, Chantal," he advised. "The first few days aren't bad."

I felt damned by faint encouragement. What were the last few days going to be like?

His voice continued, though by now I paid scant attention to his words.

"Here's the book you will start reading, Chantal." He placed a volume in my hands. "We'll discuss it tomorrow night. If you read from now till then, taking eight hours out for sleep and a half hour for our session tomorrow afternoon, you can complete your reading in the time allotted."

"How can I read?" I wailed, my emotions overcoming my dignity. "I can't even think!"

"You'll manage, but you must concentrate. If you don't finish the reading, I won't discuss it with you."

At that moment, I didn't care. I stood and left the library without speaking, the book, title unread, beneath my arm. By the time I reached my bedchamber, my natural curiosity reemerged and I glanced at the slim volume. *The Lost Books of the Bible*. In that short glance, I was hooked. I'd always been fascinated by the Gnostic Gospels, those rejected versions of the Old and New Testaments that hadn't made it into our currently accepted Bible.

I opened the flyleaf. The author was a well-respected religious scholar; I had read one of her earlier books. Dread for my bottom forgotten, I moved to a comfortable chair by the fireplace and turned to the introduction. The book included careful translations of each historical document and fragment alongside detailed commentary on their provenance, meaning, and relevance to current Judaic and Christian thought. I absentmindedly threw another log on the fire and turned to the next page. Late that night, I awoke with a start. The book had fallen from my hand as I slept awkwardly curled in the chair. I moved to my bed and crawled beneath the cold covers, wishing I had an alarm clock to rouse me at dawn.

I awoke early, as I had hoped. Perhaps I could now control my waking and sleeping, I thought absently as I picked up the book from the floor. I read as I relieved myself and as I ate hot rice and scrambled eggs for breakfast. The food continued to appear in my room as if by magic when I began to feel hungry. That day I didn't stop to speculate who had prepared and delivered the welcome meal. The book held me enthralled as I

155

read a kinder, less-accusing version of the Garden of Eden. Eve didn't have to be the culprit; she hadn't loosed sin on the world. The woman as evil temptress, so popular with thundering preachers, was only one of several early explanations.

As I read, I wished I had a copy of the King James Bible for comparison. Finally, frustrated by my attempts to remember childhood lessons in Bible studies, I headed to the library to find a copy.

"Right on time." Bran's words halted me at the door. Was it already two o'clock? I had forgotten. In my excitement, I had actually forgotten the ordeal that awaited me. Realization flooded into me, and my bowels turned to liquid. I had forgotten the enema, too.

"May I use the washroom?" I asked, half-nervous, half-defiant.

"Please do," Bran responded politely. His voice followed me into the anteroom. "Tomorrow you must remember the enema, my dear."

Muttering obscenities beneath my breath, I returned to the library. Bran had pulled the box from the drawer and it lay like a curse across the desktop. As I crossed the room, he lifted the first dildo and began to slather cream over the tip and down the sides. He spoke to me impersonally, almost absently.

"Grip the rings and bend over. I won't tie you unless you feel the need."

I shook my head and assumed the position grimly.

"Aren't you going to use a condom?" I asked.

"These dildos have never been used before and will

156

be destroyed when we're done," he explained. "They slide a bit more easily without the condom."

"Yeah," I commented sardonically.

"That's the girl!" Bran cheered me on. "Relax your buttocks. This one isn't particularly difficult."

I felt the cool smooth bulb against my anal mouth and tried to relax. It slid in, but not easily. Nothing is easy in that location. And nothing is small, either. I thought of the coming days, and my buttocks tightened in fear.

"Relax, Chantal," Bran cautioned. He twisted the dildo to a slightly different angle and I gasped. Then he slid it in farther and farther, and I felt my vagina respond to the pressure with a familiar gush of moisture. With arousal, the pain lessened to an almost-pleasurable ache. Finally his hand rested against my buttocks, and the dildo was fully inserted.

"What about the timer?" I panted.

"Drat," he swore mildly. "I forgot. Reach across the desk and turn it to one minute."

"Like hell you forgot!" I sputtered.

Bran chuckled. "If you don't reach the timer, the minute will never be up."

"I can't move," I grunted. Indeed, I felt pinned by the plug in my rear.

"Yes, you can," he admonished, and I found that I could. As I reached across the table, the dildo shifted in my bottom, and what had been a familiar pressure became new. My vagina responded to the movement with its own convulsion. I gasped and moved slowly back to my original position, timer in hand.

"You'll need two hands to set it," Bran explained.

"I'll fall over," I panted, arousal, anger, and even amusement warring in my voice.

"Straighten up first."

"Ugh!" I grunted, as I shifted myself up very slowly. The dildo moved again, though Bran adjusted his position to mine, and again discomfort and arousal vied for my attention. I set the timer, then stood upright, waiting for the minute to pass. Though the pressure was greater that way, still I found I didn't want to make the return slow journey to the desktop. I tried to breathe deeply and watched the seconds tick past. When the buzzer sounded, I heaved a sigh of relief. Then Bran pushed me, gently but with the dildo still inside, back to lean over the desktop. The movement began a tremor inside me and when he swiftly withdrew the slippery shaft, I came to orgasm in a pounding counterrhythm. The muscles of my anus pulsed around the retreating dildo as if trying to hold it inside. A second later, it was gone, but the warm throbbing continued in both vagina and anus for several moments.

In the midst of my climax, Bran spanked me smartly with his hand. Still somewhat dazed, I straightened abruptly and looked at him in reproach.

"That wasn't so bad, was it?" He sounded like a jocular football coach in the middle of a workout.

"I can think of more pleasant ways to have an orgasm!" I rubbed my sore bottom.

"Don't worry about tomorrow," Bran's cheerful reminder aroused the dread he desired. I felt no need to continue this exercise. I didn't particularly like today, though the result had been satisfying. Tomorrow, with a larger dildo and a longer duration, could only be worse. I resolved to get the timer ready in advance from now on. I refused to think beyond tomorrow.

"Did you come here looking for a book?" Bran's question brought me back to the present. "You seemed surprised to see me when you entered."

"I wanted a King James Bible," I answered him sullenly. With the words I remembered my excitement of the morning and my reading, and my voice regained its enthusiasm. "I want to check *The Lost Books* against the ones that were included."

"I applaud your enterprise, Chantal."

"Oh, I love this stuff."

"I know." Bran smiled and handed me the Bible. "We'll talk tonight."

And so day one of my systematic torture—for so I thought of it—was over. The books again distracted my thoughts, and I didn't linger long in anger or any other emotion than the joy of discovery. That night we discussed the lost books and their relation to the stories included in the Bible we know today. Bran hadn't been born when the earliest stories were told, in the first century A.D. As we talked, he told me more of his own human life and I came to envision those long-ago years.

Throughout the ages, his real life had become exaggerated into myth. A mystic at his court had possessed the gift of healing. Over the centuries, the sage's talent had been transformed into a magic caldron that restored the dead to life. Through Arthur's time, the caldron became the Holy Grail and Bran its magical keeper. His height was also remarkable for that age. Most men in Britain were around five feet tall, and his six feet three inches astonished all who saw him. The story was exaggerated as it passed through generations of early Britons. From needing to duck his head for a doorway, he became too large for any ship to hold. Bran told me, too, of his sister, Branwen, who was abused by her suspicious husband. Some stories are eternal.

We passed the evening in enthralled discussion, Bran seeming as eager for my modern perspective as I was for his ancient wisdom. Finally as the moon reached its apex, he packed me off to bed. I held the next volume clutched beneath my elbow as I climbed the stairs, sure I was too exhausted to do more than open the cover that night. Two hours later, I was deep in the philosophy of Islam. I could only barely understand the Koran in English, which wasn't considered a sacred text because of its translation from the original Arabic. The book explained clearly the reverence due the lavishly illustrated text, and I was careful not to allow the book to slip to the floor.

I slept soundly and awoke early to continue my study. I remembered the enema that day, and the brief discomfort was amply rewarded by the relief I felt moments later. Again I felt the urge to go to the library an hour or so after eating lunch. This time, I didn't delude myself with a false request for another book, but went fully prepared for Bran's ministrations. I knew he felt some purpose, some important purpose, would be achieved by this exercise in pain, but for the present it eluded me. My stomach knotted as I approached the door of the library.

"Come in, my dear," Bran greeted me cordially. The box lay open on the desktop, the leftmost dildo missing from its spot. I didn't speak, but walked to the desk and placed my hands on the embedded rings.

"Eager to begin?" Bran teased.

"Eager to finish," I retorted and he laughed. I remembered the timer and let go of the rings to stand in front of the desk. I set the time to two minutes and resumed my position, the timer close to my right hand. I would only need to press the button to start the time once the dildo was inside.

Bran took his time slathering cream on the shaft, a longer, fairly slim model this time with a decided curve to the right. I felt a moment's queasiness as I imagined it snaking its long way inside me. Remembering the lessening of pain when I became aroused the day before, I squeezed the muscles of my vagina trying to start the process myself. My effort worked and I felt a juicy wetness fill me. My breath became shallow in anticipation—and still the devil sat calmly behind his desk.

"You're having so much fun getting ready, Chantal, it seems almost a shame to interrupt you."

"We don't have to do this at all," I reminded him. By then I was both slippery and hot with the need for contact. I began almost, but not quite, to wish for him to begin. He rose from his chair.

"Relax your buttocks," he repeated the familiar instruction as he flipped my dress over my back. I tried.

The shaft resting against the soft lips of my anus felt huge—far too huge to ever enter. Bran had left the box open in front of me and my eyes roamed down the row of waiting dildos. As I saw each a bit larger than its neighbor, I felt an overwhelming dread uncoil in my belly. If this one felt huge, what would the next one do to me? And the twelfth? My mind recoiled and my knees began to shake. At that instant, Bran began a slow, relentless pressure against my anus. I waited for the dual release and pain of entrance, but it didn't come.

"Relax your muscles," Bran murmured, and I realized I had tensed in my fright. I did my best to unclench, and Bran slid the dildo partway in with more haste than finesse. I groaned and he apologized, urging me again to relax. The pressure built in my womb and the muscles in my vagina contracted in a premature spasm. Bran turned the dildo; I remembered its curve as the pressure rotated in my bottom. This time my vagina spasmed in earnest, and I came to a swift climax. Bran seized the opportunity to slide the shaft the rest of the way into me. The rapid movement stole my breath, as even the orgasm had not. I came again.

Bran reached past me to push the button on the timer, for I was beyond coherent action. He twisted the dildo slowly in my sensitive behind as the seconds counted down, and I came three more times in the next two minutes. When the buzzer sounded, I was caught between my desire for another orgasm and the need to end the ache in my bottom. Bran decided the matter for me, pulling the dildo out swiftly. I screamed once with the motion, then collapsed silently onto the desktop. The cold marble penetrated my skin and my awareness, and soon I lifted myself from its icy surface. I pulled my dress back down over me and sat in my chair, ready to argue for the ending of this experiment.

"Go back to your room, Chantal," Bran ordered, his voice weary. "You need to finish your reading for tonight."

Our days continued in a cycle of mental and physical stimulation. As the dildos grew larger, my pain increased, and I came to dread the afternoon with a sickening horror. Though the reading stimulated me and I looked forward to our nights of discussion, still I marked the passing of each hour from dawn to two o'clock. Thus caught in a circle of anticipation and dread, I found my emotions stretched to a fragile, brittle edge.

On the eleventh day, I awoke with my eyes encrusted with dream-tears. I couldn't read, though the text held special meaning. Marcus Aurelius had been Bran's first protégé. His plain common sense appealed to me. But the pages swam in a watery sea before my eyes, and my stomach twisted and heaved. After a few minutes, I gave up. I lay motionless on the bed, awake but paralyzed, waiting for two o'clock. I was crying again as I entered the library.

"Only two more days," Bran said bracingly as he met me at the door. He led me straight to the desk and strapped my hands to the rings. I began to struggle. I couldn't stand one more onslaught on my poor bottom;

I couldn't. Bran moved swiftly to set the timer, then carried the dildo behind me. Holding my hips steady with one arm, he thrust two slippery fingers into my pulsing orifice. His fingers massaged me as the Oriental man's had done, and I felt the worst of my tremors cease. He pressed the dildo against my bottom, and the giant shaft slid inexorably into the slippery doorway.

I groaned as he pressed it farther and farther inside, for once finding no release in pleasure. Each inch brought an answering moan, until finally I wept openly as his hand came to rest against me. Bran pressed the button on the timer, then began to speak. I barely heard his words through the humming in my brain and body.

"Don't focus on what you're feeling now, Chantal." His words tangled in my confused thoughts. "The shaft isn't important; it is the dread that I want you to feel, not the pressure of the dildo. Talk to me."

He began to ask me questions.

"Is this pain anywhere near that of childbirth?"

"No," I whispered, for it was true. The discomfort was more like a dentist removing an anesthetized but root-bound tooth. I didn't like it, but it was bearable.

"Many people feel pain from illness, Chantal. Do you think they wake up each day with dread?"

"No," I answered, remembering my mother's friend who had remained stoically cheerful through a long and ultimately fatal battle with cancer.

"What do they think of?"

"They're glad to be alive, with loved ones," I gasped. "They hold tight to each minute."

"They conquer their dread and much of the pain disappears with it."

"They get drugs," I interrupted.

Bran chuckled. "I want you to concentrate, Chantal. Make the ache disappear."

"I want drugs." A smile tugged at my cheek. I concentrated on Bran's words and felt the pressure ease slightly. I fought to focus my whole being in my brain, as far from my sore bottom as I could reach. It worked, at least a bit.

"Talk to me about Marcus Aurelius," I gasped. Bran's low and soothing voice began to ramble through a long tale of the Roman's youth in the century following the birth of Christ. Bran had worked with him as he mastered the stoic fortitude which marked his years as emperor of Rome. I concentrated on Bran's voice and ignored both the timer and my body. When the buzzer sounded, it startled me and I knew a few moments renewed pain as Bran withdrew the dildo gently.

"Do you understand now?" he asked as I caught my breath.

"Yes," I replied in a whispery but steady voice.

"And you'll be all right tomorrow?"

"Yes." My voice was stronger now and I knew that I would be all right. Though the dread had mastered me briefly, now I had conquered the emotion. I wouldn't think of tomorrow afternoon until the few brief moments arrived. I would focus my concentration away from the ache, and the twelve minutes would pass swiftly. Bran gathered me in his arms and we clung together in exhaustion and triumph.

smorzando
Slowly Fading

Though the Twelve Days of Christmas were past, my schedule of reading continued. Bran left my days free for intense study; my evenings he claimed for rigorous discussion. I achieved in those weeks an understanding of the foundations of thought, both Western and Eastern, that I was to rely on for the rest of my life. Bran was a kind though exacting teacher. He exposed the weaknesses in my reasoning with the same ruthlessness he displayed toward classical authors. He was at once a great respecter of men and their ideas and an aged skeptic who accepted nothing without substantial proof.

I was particularly drawn to certain philosophers. The words of Marcus Aurelius, a devout pagan, captured my situation: "Remember that to change your mind and follow him who sets you right is to be none the less free than you were before." I was struck, too, by the modernity of his thoughts: "The universe is transformation; our life is what our thoughts make it." He might have been a chaos theorist or an existentialist.

One day Bran surprised me with another scene from one of my books, an especially inept rendering of the pleasure of subservience. Neither S nor M of my novel felt the joy and freedom I now embraced. The mechanics didn't even work. As I stood strapped to a scaffold, I began to laugh at the futility of the antics I performed and our session ended in mutual glee at the absurdity of my early literary efforts.

Several weeks later, Bran invited me into the library to discuss my progress, a verbal report card, so to speak. While still excited by the profound thinkers whose minds I probed, I had grown restless for new directions. The near-celibate weeks had also taken their toll and I was, bluntly, horny. Curious to know what Bran planned, I settled into my seat across the desk from my mentor and waited for him to speak.

"Tell me what you've learned, Chantal."

I knew that he didn't mean my specific reading for the day, which we would discuss that night. This was a broader question and one that required a careful answer. I thought for several moments before beginning tentatively.

"I believe the dildos taught me something of the nature and value of time." Bran nodded his encouragement and I continued. "I dreaded each afternoon, and when I couldn't banish the future from my mind, I could no longer enjoy the present. By the twelfth day, I learned to stay within the immediate moment and not worry about the dildo until I walked through the door of this room."

"And how do you feel now about my methods?"

"May I be candid?" I asked. Bran raised an eyebrow, but nodded for me to continue. "It was brutal. I'm still not certain it was necessary to be quite so cruel, but I do admit, reluctantly, that I wasn't damaged and that I did learn something valuable."

"So the end justified the means?"

"I'm not sure," I continued, still thinking. "No, I think not. You presume to know what's best for me. You happen to be right sometimes, but the presumption is still wrong. I got enough of that from my mother. 'I'm doing this for your own good.'"

Bran nodded his agreement. "What would you have done in my case?"

"I have no idea," I had to admit. "I suppose I would just be there in support when genuine trouble came and try to help then."

"I wish I had that luxury, Chantal. At best, tutoring is a rough approximation of life."

"Well, I did learn, and I forgive you."

"Thank you," Bran accepted my words more gravely than I had offered them.

A moment later, he resumed his questioning. "And what did you learn from your discipline this fall, when I whipped you every morning?"

The very topic aroused me. I felt the ache of desire build in my womb.

"That I like being whipped," I responded quickly and enthusiastically.

It was Bran's turn to chuckle. "Aside from that," he probed, "did you learn anything else?"

"When you were gentle, it was fun, and I suppose I learned that some roughhousing is a natural part of sexuality. I was never a tomboy, so the lesson came late."

"What about when I was less gentle?"

My arousal grew and my panties grew moist and hot. I tried to be honest.

"Even talking about whipping arouses me."

"Good!" Bran smiled, then continued more sternly. "Answer the question."

I struggled to order my chaotic thoughts, to make sense of my strong physical attraction to an activity my mind told me was degrading.

"I hate it that I like it so much," I protested.

"But..." Bran prompted.

I called on the wealth of the philosophers I had studied and found in the structure if not the content of their reasoning, a beginning to rationality.

"I think it's because, even when you whip me hard"— I struggled to find the right words—"even then, I'm still the one in control. Does that make any sense?"

"Keep going."

Bran's words neither encouraged nor doubted my reasoning. He left me to flounder through my thoughts alone.

"It's easy to feel in control of yourself when life is easy. I mean, it's fun and all, but it isn't really satisfying."

Bran nodded his approval. "When it's more difficult, like when I have to fight the pain and pull my pleasure out of the center of it, then it feels like I've really accomplished something. It's like 'Wow!'"

Bran smiled, and I apologized ruefully for my awkward explanation. "I'm more articulate on paper."

"Thank goodness for that!" Bran exclaimed, laughing. "But you've caught the kernel of the thought, Chantal. Overcoming adversity through hard work is far more satisfying than easily attained goals."

"Why didn't I say that?" I joked.

"You did, but much more eloquently, my dear," Bran chided me for mocking my own words. "You spoke from your inner feelings; I only reflect those feelings through the filter of intellect."

His words made me brave. For the first time, I asked him to satisfy my needs.

"Will you whip me now, Bran?"

"Remove your dress." His voice became distant and severe and sent a delicious chill through me. I shrugged off my clothing.

I followed him out of the library and into the central chamber. He led me to an elaborate fountain that sprayed noisily in a large bay window overlooking the ocean. A life-size sculpture of a female nude stood in the center of the fountain beneath an overhanging grotto, and the water cascaded over her from the rocks above. A new black whip—one I had never seen before—lay ready on a table next to the pool. The leather thongs hung down from the waist-high table to brush the floor.

"Climb into the fountain and hug the statue," Bran directed me.

I put one toe into the water; it was cold—not icy, but still cold. I looked over my shoulder at Bran, but his back was turned as he picked up the whip. I knew he wouldn't allow me to escape, so I stepped quickly into the ankle-deep pool. The water chilled me to my bones, and I began to shake. By now, Bran had turned back to face me and he motioned impatiently for me to move toward the statue. As I walked, my feet no longer felt cold as they adjusted to the water. I stopped reluctantly about two feet from the chill spray. The statue was marble, and even the light spray chilled me.

The whip caught me by surprise as I stood hesitant and propelled me forward. The yard-long thongs caught my flesh wickedly, and I jumped into the icy spray. Teeth chattering, I moved to embrace the statue. The second stroke caught me before I had settled, and the force drove me into the hard stone. I must hold tight to my stone lover or the whip would crash me against her unmercifully. I found a purchase and nestled my breasts between her cold orbs just before the next stroke hit. I settled in to enjoy the deep heat that I knew the whip would spread through me.

But I had miscalculated. The cold water robbed the whip of its heat, leaving only the pressure and sting of each blow. As hard as I held onto the marble, still I couldn't keep myself from slamming into its surface each time the whip struck. I gave myself over to misery and prayed only for endurance.

The next stroke landed on the back of my thighs. Bran had only ever whipped me across my buttocks, and the lash made me jump in surprise. As my body resettled, my legs parted around the thigh of the statue, and I found the relief I had stopped hoping for. I wiggled my bottom so that my clitoris lay exposed to the smooth, hard muscle of the statue's leg. The next lash drove me into the unrelenting stone, and I gasped with the force of the explosion within me. Each stroke took me near but not quite to orgasm.

Bran varied his targets, moving up and down the back of my body from my shoulders to my calves. With time and repeated strokes, my skin heated to a familiar warmth; but now instead of only my bottom, the whole back of my body glowed. Each stroke tantalized my clitoris with intermittent stimulation; each pause drove me wild. I tried to rub myself against the statue's hard, smooth thigh, but Bran wouldn't allow me to find a rhythm. Each time I mounted toward a peak, his lash would disrupt me and I tumbled to a frustrated ledge, almost but not quite satisfied.

At last the strokes became regular and centered on my buttocks and upper thighs. I moved into the rhythm as into a warm bath and luxuriated in the heat and the hardness and the slippery chill that surrounded me. When a climax became inevitable, I moaned and threw back my head into the spray. With the water beating on my face, I came again and again, and the long black whip snaked around and around my body. I felt primordial, an Eve in Eden, tasting the precious fruit of knowledge. And still the black leather snake tempted me on to yet another and another awakening.

When the whipping ended, I stood draped around the statue, a living addition to the fountain. The water no longer felt cold, but merely refreshing. As my breathing and heart rate returned to normal, I stepped back and beamed my pleasure to my torturer, my whipper, my Master, my emancipator, my friend. He offered me his hand and I stepped from the water into a large, fluffy towel. He wrapped me tight and held me close in his arms for several moments, then dried my puckered skin gently.

"Is this what I'll look like in thirty years?" I asked, laughing.

"You'll be as beautiful then as you are now, Chantal," Bran complimented me. And though I knew he had seen the great beauties of long centuries, I felt in my heart that he spoke the truth. I was beautiful to him in my middle-aged body; I needed no further mirror.

That night I slept soundly, lulled by the aftermath of exhilaration into near coma. As I slept, a wondrous dream invaded my mind. A shadowy man—I couldn't see his face—lay beside me on the bed and gathered me into his arms. He held me close and warm in a loving embrace for long moments, until finally I fell back asleep. The dream began again later, when I felt a soft touch against my innermost self. The man held me still, but now my back was to his chest and his hand rested against my mount of Venus. His fingers teased and slithered and stroked their way inside me and then began to rub against my rock-sensitized labia.

I tried to turn in my dream, but he held me steady against him and I still couldn't see his face. His fingers stroked up and down and around my clitoris, teasing the bud to an aching peak, then leaving it lonely and begging for another caress. I moaned in my sleep and rubbed my bottom against his erection. He felt solid and warm and I yearned to hold him inside me. The weeks and months of stimulation melted away. I longed once again for the natural comfort of simple copulation with a loving man. Still, he wouldn't allow me to turn in his arms.

His fingers grew more insistent and I thrust my mound against him, my longing for the fulfillment of his erect organ lost in the more immediate search for release. The climax came quickly and I arched into him. My hips ground against his, and his erection pulsed in the crack of my bottom. As the convulsion of my vagina slowed, I relaxed, ready to return to sleep, but his finger continued its rhythm without pause. With infinite patience and exquisite timing, he brought me to orgasm again and again.

At first, I continued to try to see him, but he would never allow me to turn. Then I began to feel an overwhelming need to pleasure him, to satisfy him as he did me. Though his penis continued to throb against my skin, he wouldn't allow me to grasp it; nor would he slide it into my eagerly dripping home. At last I ceased to think and gave myself into the pleasure of his talented fingers at the center of my being. We moved from my bed to a ship on the sea, and still his fingers worked magic within me. We drifted for hours through a universe of pleasure until finally I slept dreamless again.

I awoke the next morning to find the sheets damp from the moisture of my orgasms and my clitoris and labia still tender. I looked at my hands in wonder. I had never pleasured myself while asleep before. I smelled my hands; no lingering scent of my essence remained on them. Later, as I soaked in a hot whirlpool, a satisfied cat-in-the-cream smile softened my face. I didn't question the source of my marvelous dream; I only hoped it would come again.

molto agitato
Climax

sempre legato
Together Forever

I moved from the bath to my computer and tried for several hours to capture the essence of my dream into words. I struggled to express the contentment and yearning, the peace and disquiet that the dream awoke in me. For the first time since my arrival on the island, I felt the passage of time. I realized as I wrote that I missed my children. They were adults and I saw them perhaps once a week, but they had been my life for many years. I berated myself for not missing them sooner, then laughed at the accusation.

The words of Marcus Aurelius settled my rambling thoughts: "Time is like a river made up of the events which happen, and its current is strong; no sooner does anything appear than it is swept away, and another comes in its place, and will be swept away, too." I must remember to remain in the present, neither regretting the past nor looking for the future. I would see my children again when I returned to my normal life, and I knew I would return. I wouldn't let longing for their presence obscure the pleasure of my remaining days on the island.

So thinking, I descended the stairs to look for Bran. I found him in the sitting room, gazing silently out the window at the fresh leafy buds that covered the trees with the promise of spring.

"I have a plan." I announced my arrival cheerfully. Bran turned from his contemplation. Suddenly he looked very old to me. His thirty-five mortal years sat like a thin mask over the visage of two thousand years of perception. My plan seemed shallow to me now, useless or even harmful. Bran must have sensed my hesitation for he smiled kindly and held out his hand to me. I sat beside him on the sofa holding his young/old, hard/soft hand and wondered how I would ever bear to live without him.

"You wish to resume your life, Chantal." He read my thoughts easily. I couldn't bear to cause him pain, and I knew that my desire to leave was hurtful to him. Still, his first thought was to comfort me. "Your wish is natural. You're a creature of this world, as I am not. You're my link to the present, and I'm only a tie to the distant past."

"You're far more than that, Bran," I protested, close to tears.

"Tell me your thoughts."

I hesitated for several seconds, then shrugged and began. "I want you to help me plan how I'll live when I return to the regular world. What am I going to do? How am I going to live? What am I going to write? Who will publish it?"

Bran laughed and lifted a hand to stem the spate of questions that tumbled from my mouth.

"Wait a minute, Chantal," he admonished me. "I can't see into the future."

I raised a skeptical eyebrow.

"It's true, my dear," he spoke earnestly. "I can't see the future any more than you can, because it doesn't exist. I know for example that you have the potential to write beautiful books, but whether you create them will be entirely your own choice."

Though I didn't like his answer, I understood the reasoning behind his words. I realized that while I longed for the security of reassurance, still I wasn't willing to give up my free will to obtain it.

I began again. "Let me rephrase my question. You've taught me the value of discipline. I'd like to practice a system of discipline that I can maintain when I return to the real world."

"This island is in the real world, Chantal," Bran reminded me. "There's no reason not to continue as you are now. Describe for me a perfect daily regimen for you on the island."

"You wake me up at dawn and give me a nice gentle whipping. During the course of the day, I read and write. Then in the evening we talk."

"You wouldn't enjoy that schedule for long, my dear."

"Why do you say that?"

"You'll discover the problems for yourself soon enough." Bran's words were final; he wouldn't explain his objections. "We'll try your schedule for a while and see how you like it. Let's eat some lunch."

The discussion was finished. We walked the few steps into the kitchen, where Bran pulled a hot casserole from the oven. I still didn't know whether he cooked or employed a strictly regulated delivery service. I never saw evidence of either possibility, though the food appeared hot and tasty whenever we were hungry. We dug into a mélange of savory chicken, mushrooms, potatoes, and onions, Bran's appetite as hearty as mine. Over lunch we got into an argument over the relative merits of dadaism and impressionism. I favored the older style, while Bran was piqued by the dadaist opportunism of the twentieth century.

I returned after the meal to my writing but found after an hour that I was too exhausted to continue. Instead I moved to the balcony and leafed through a book on Salvador Dalí, determined to find evidence to refute Bran's pro-Dada arguments. Soon I fell asleep over the book and the afternoon passed without my participation. After dinner Bran and I went for a walk around the island in the chilly early-spring twilight. I tried to resume our argument, but hadn't stayed awake long enough to garner new evidence, and the discussion soon petered out.

The following morning, Bran awoke me as requested

and whipped me beautifully to a series of gentle orgasms. I thought I could easily become addicted to such pleasure. I was disappointed that my dream lover hadn't returned, but contented myself with Bran's more impersonal stimulation. I spent the day reading and writing, as I had wished, then enjoyed an interesting discussion with Bran after dinner. He asserted that Johnny Carson had fulfilled the same role on late-night television that the Lares and Penates filled in early Roman households. They were the pagan household gods of the day. He eventually talked me around to his viewpoint, and I went to bed satisfied with the day.

Each morning began with a ritual whipping. The day continued with peaceful reading and arduous writing, culminating in a stimulating discussion. For about a week, I enjoyed the even tempo of my days. Then something went wrong. I felt vaguely dissatisfied for two or three days, then figured out the problem. I was bored. Not only that, I was tired. The sameness exhausted me, and I achieved less and less each day. I thought back to my discussion with Bran. Much as I hated to admit it, he had been right. The routine I had described as perfect fell far short. I decided to ask his help.

"Bran," I interrupted him as he wrote at the marble-topped library desk. He always wrote with a fine quill pen, dipping the tip in a pot of ink every few words. Now he paused, pen in hand, and waited for me to continue.

"Is this a bad time?" I asked.

"Anytime the bills come in is a bad time," he commented

wryly. It was the only truly mundane thing I ever heard him say. We both laughed. "Come on in."

I entered the room and walked to my chair before the desk.

"You were right," I stated baldly. Bran raised his eyebrows at my abrupt capitulation; in our discussions I was prone to argue past the bounds of rationality.

"What was I right about?" he asked mildly.

"This routine"—I held my nose—"it stinks."

Bran smiled at my childish-but-expressive gesture. "Have you analyzed what's wrong with your days?"

"Not really," I admitted sheepishly. "I hoped you'd tell me your idea of an ideal schedule and we could try that."

"I don't think sleeping for three hundred years would appeal to you, my dear."

I saw that I hadn't phrased my request clearly.

"I meant what you think would be the ideal schedule for me," I explained.

"I know that's what you meant, Chantal. Can you see how circular your reasoning becomes?"

I puzzled for a moment, then smiled ruefully. "When you did what you thought was right for me with the twelve dildos, I said you were wrong. No one knows for sure what's right for someone else. I guess I'm old enough to figure it out myself."

"Exactly. Tell me what's missing from your 'perfect regimen.'"

"Surprise!" I exclaimed. "I don't really want every day to be the same. I want only elements of regularity, things I can count on."

"Like meals?" Bran prodded.

"Like a morning whipping," I added enthusiastically.

"That might be a problem," Bran began, his expression worried. I couldn't think of anything problematic; after all, he had introduced me to the habit when I arrived at the island. "Perhaps you're a more addictive personality than I'd accounted for."

"Addictive?" I questioned indignantly. I didn't smoke, hardly drank, had never used drugs, and was far from promiscuous. Promiscuous? Sex? Orgasm? The chain of my thoughts made me pause. Did Bran think I had become addicted to the whippings? Had I?

"All right," I continued, reluctant but determined to show him that I could manage quite well without his morning discipline. "No more whippings."

"It isn't like alcohol, Chantal," Bran laughed. "We can indulge you from time to time, just not every day."

He was right again. I'd always avoided set habits. I hated the thought of actually needing something, or someone, for that matter. It made me feel inadequate inside. That was why I'd never smoked; I couldn't be a slave to a need, especially not a powerful chemical one. I kept thinking.

"The whipping releases endorphins, doesn't it?" Bran nodded and I continued my thought. "And I'm addicted to the high. Just like those women I always laughed at who are addicted to aerobics, only I'm addicted to being whipped."

"I don't think you're actually addicted, Chantal," Bran tried to mitigate my self-disgust.

"Don't ever touch me with a whip again, Bran," I commanded, my voice rising to near-hysteria.

"You're overreacting, Chantal," Bran's flat tones brought me back down. "The whip isn't the problem; neither is your enjoyment of it."

"So what is the problem?" I asked, curious, for I couldn't think of another solution.

"You need a man."

Bran was a man, but I knew what he meant. I thought of my dream visitor, who had come only the one tantalizing, sensual time, and agreed. I *did* need a man. I imagined the missionary position and felt myself grow hot and moist. Plain, ordinary, normal, simple sex—that was what my body craved. The whippings were only a substitute for the real thing.

"Absolutely!" I agreed enthusiastically. I remembered an earlier conversation. "Didn't you promise me once that I would meet the man I would love when I return to the real world?"

"You *will* meet him," Bran agreed. "That much I can manage. But whether you recognize each other, and the course of your relationship, will be entirely up to the two of you."

"You said you could bring him to me here," I reminded him.

"He's been here once."

I was stunned. Bran's words caught my breath and held it for an endless moment. The only man I had met—sort of—on the island, was the Oriental who had introduced me to anal intercourse. I had no objection to a man from the Far East. In fact, I kind of liked the idea. But a trainer in anal intercourse?

"Not Mr. Sung," Bran's voice interrupted my thoughts.

"Then who?" I asked, bewildered.

"He visited you several nights ago. Your request for a daily whipping has kept him away since then."

I must have looked as bewildered as I felt, for Bran prompted me again.

"The dream."

The dream, I thought. How could Bran know my dream? I bridled at the intrusion into my privacy, then calmed as I realized that Bran must have invited the man, even brought him to me.

"Did he dream the same dream?" I asked, not sure whether I wanted more to believe or to disprove. Bran nodded and I struggled to absorb the import of his words. The man I would love came to me in a dream. Okay, that part I could sort of accept. Bran brought him to me. Well, if not Bran, then fate—that, too, I could accept. So what was the problem?

"Can he come again?" I asked, still probing for a weakness.

"Yes."

"Why can't I see his face?"

"I learned a few centuries ago not to tempt the fates beyond their capacity for caprice. He can't see your face, either. You must still find each other by some conventional means."

"Fair enough," I agreed, then thought for another minute. "Holy shit! Is this for real?"

"Reality and fantasy are both illusions, or perhaps delusions. Don't think too hard or you'll lose your capacity for wonder."

"Then why did you have me read the philosophers?" I challenged.

"They're visionaries, Chantal, who create philosophy from their dreams."

"Why do I feel like I'm in about a mile over my head?" I asked, a shaky laugh in my voice.

"Keep treading water," Bran cautioned, laughing, too. "On to more practical matters. What else was missing from your routine, Chantal?"

I switched my thoughts from the clouds back to the earth. I ran days through my mind, from my arrival in the early fall, through the winter, and now into the beginnings of spring. Somewhere around November, I found the answer.

"Exercise."

Bran nodded.

"I should go back to a regular routine in the lap pool and the gym."

Bran nodded again.

"And my dream lover will visit me at night?"

Bran nodded a third and final time, then continued seriously, "You have one lesson yet to learn, Chantal. I will surprise you from time to time, and you'll absorb the final realization."

"Can't you just tell me?"

"You wouldn't believe me."

With those fateful words, Bran left. After several

moments, I arose and left the room to return to my books and computer. Later that afternoon I swam until I could no longer lift my arms. And so my days continued. Bran's parting caution lent a piquancy to my existence. I couldn't determine what the final lesson might be, and I never knew when the instruction would begin.

sempre più animato
Ever Lively

The first night, my phantom lover didn't come, though I waited impatiently. Perhaps I was too disquieted and frightened his spirit away or perhaps he was busy elsewhere; perhaps Bran forgot or chose not to summon him. The second night, I fell asleep easily and was amply rewarded for my lack of effort.

The dream began with a touch, as before, but this time it was not his finger but his tongue that I felt against my labia. While I slept, he had placed my feet on his shoulders with my knees spread open like a feast before him. I dream-awoke to see his silky head above my curly mound and to feel his tongue tease open my eager lips. I gasped when his teeth found the sensitive organ of my desire and tugged gently on the hard, hot bud. I twined my fingers in his hair and stroked his temples as he nuzzled me.

191

After a few moments of comfortable grazing, his tongue probed harder and the juices inside me spilled toward the narrow opening. He scooped a finger inside the soft portal and I moaned at the tender, hard pressure of his touch. He carried my fluids up to his waiting tongue and mingled them with his saliva, then spread the viscous mixture over my swelling flesh. His tongue and lips moved slick and wet against me, stroking and probing each inner recess deftly.

An ache built inside me, both familiar and ever new, and I stilled his roving head and held him steady to my most sensitive marrow. Each tender, rapid flick of his tongue drove me nearer and nearer to the edge of sensation till I tumbled over with an inarticulate cry. My hands released their grip on his head, and I waited for his tongue to relax its fluttering so that I could catch my breath, but he kept going and wouldn't let me rest. The second orgasm shook me with unexpected force, and I arched my pelvis into his greedy face. He caught me beneath the buttocks and held me high, suspended, sucked into him by the powerful force of his strong hands and jaws, and I came again and again.

At last he lowered my whimpering body back to the bed, though he kept his mouth locked onto my aching sexuality. When he at last lifted his head a mere inch, I sighed into the surcease, only to gasp again when he plunged two hard fingers into my steaming opening. His sturdy, thick fingers massaged my inner cavity as surely as his tongue had stroked my outer flesh and I felt yet another orgasm pounding for release. I again arched into him, but this time he pinned me to the bed with his other hand and the restraint drove me wild. Tremors shook my body from forehead to toes, with only a few seconds respite between. He lowered his head back to my throbbing swollen flesh and scooped my vital juices to his tongue with hard, insistent fingers. The more he scooped, the stronger I came, until we seemed locked in an endless cycle of pleasure demanded and supplied.

As before, I fell from the dream somewhere in the midst of fulfillment. My later dreams were troubled by visions of a phantom figure—ever watchful, never seen—that hovered protectively near but would not approach. When I reached for him, he vanished. I couldn't help myself from reaching so he never stayed.

I awoke exhausted and exhilarated; ready to face the day, yet eager to go back to sleep. I compromised by charging down to the basement pool and swimming laps before breakfast. On my way back up the stairs, Bran stopped me with a shout from somewhere on the main floor. I wrapped the towel more snugly around me, for that was all I wore, and followed his voice to the kitchen.

"You're just in time for breakfast," he greeted me as I poked my head around the corner and in the door.

"What are you making?" I asked. Bran wore a huge white cook's apron and had a vast assortment of ingredients spread on the counter before him. He seemed at one moment sure of his efforts and the next puzzled what to make of the haphazard jumble.

"Fun," he answered me mysteriously, leering. He handed me a second long white apron. I dropped the towel to the floor and pulled the loop over my head. I had to fold the fabric several times at the waist to make the apron fit, but at last I tied it securely. Though my bottom waggled open to the occasional breeze, I was certainly protected from spills in front.

"Really, Bran," I tried to sound serious though I felt amazingly silly. "What are you cooking?"

"Genital bread dough," was the bizarre reply.

"What?" I asked, understandably confused.

"Genital bread dough," Bran repeated.

"Is it self-rising?" I asked, getting into the vein of his humor.

Bran roared his approval of my mild pun and handed me a cookbook.

"Find a recipe for pumpernickel," he demanded.

"Pumpernickel?" I asked. Ordinary white bread sounded difficult enough to me. "Do you know how to make bread?"

Bran shook his head.

"But you want to make pumpernickel?"

Bran nodded eagerly, so I searched through the index at the back of the book. To my relief and Bran's dismay, pumpernickel was not among Mrs. Mingener's specialties. The best I could find was a simple white-bread recipe which could be modified for rye, raisin, or cream or hot cross buns. Though the buns sounded inviting —imagine whipping them into shape!—we settled on the simplest recipe: plain white bread.

Bran had found a large metal bowl while I searched for the recipe, and I told him to measure four cups of plain flour into the container. Once the flour was in the bowl, I read further down the instructions and found that we were supposed to sift it, not dump it, and to sift it with salt. I wanted to pour the flour back into the bag and begin again, but Bran impatiently dumped it into the garbage. We found a sifter within ten minutes, a minor miracle. Bran carefully measured the flour and salt into the sifter, then stood waiting for it to trickle through. He was quite pleased when I showed him how to speed the process with the little handle on the side.

The recipe directed us to crumble the yeast into tepid water. We had an argument over the precise meaning of tepid. Bran made me look it up in the giant dictionary in the library. Random House wasn't very helpful: "moderately warm; lukewarm." I remembered heating baby bottles twenty years earlier and testing the temperature on my inner wrist. Bran agreed reluctantly that my method might work, and thus we activated the yeast. We added sugar and butter, then stirred the mixture until the solids turned liquid.

I told Bran to make a well in the center of the flour while I stirred the yeast mixture. He took my words a bit too literally, finding a plastic tube and pushing it down through the flour. I explained that a culinary well was merely a shallow depression. Then I mixed the center portion into a soft batter, leaving a wall of dry flour at the edges. The trouble was that I wasn't sure where the center ended and the edges began. Still, when I was done, the dough looked pretty good. Bran volunteered to knock down the dry walls to cover the soft lump in the middle. I think he's battered a few walls in his day.

Bran decided to take advantage of the twenty minute waiting period and my bare bottom for a random spanking. I was still aroused from the night's phantom pleasure and didn't want to risk missing a return visit. Bran assured me that a little whipping wouldn't keep my dream lover away, and we moved to the library. We didn't have much time left, so Bran got right to work.

"I'm going to let your lover watch us," he offered with enthusiasm, placing my hands on the rings.

I wasn't so sure. Did I want a lover who was attracted to voyeurism? I voiced my objection.

"Don't worry, Chantal," Bran assured me. "He'll think he's me."

Sure enough, when the whip descended with a resounding crack across my bottom, I felt another hand at the control. He seemed unsure how exactly to proceed, and his strokes varied from a little too light to much too light.

"You can hit me a little harder," I commented.

The next stroke was almost too hard, and I heard an indrawn breath to match my own.

"It's all right," I gasped.

The strokes settled into a steadier rhythm, not as smooth as Bran's centuries-old tempo but regular enough to send the adrenaline rushing though my arteries and the fluid gushing to my hot womb. The thought that it was my lover—my future real human lover—who directed the whip sent me spiraling upward into a heady climax. Then the whipping stopped abruptly.

"Don't stop yet," I whimpered, eager for more and more stimulation.

"Bread's ready!" Bran's boyish eagerness filled the room. My more malleable and eager-to-please phantom lover had vanished back into his ordinary life. I hoped he hadn't had a car accident during our daydream. Bran ignored my panting and untied my hands. He led me, only mildly protesting, back to the kitchen. I picked up the cookbook and read the next instruction.

"Mix the dough together and beat well for five minutes," I had to laugh. "At least something is going to be well beaten today!"

When the dough lay springy and smooth in a well-greased bowl, I had to admit it looked pretty good. The eventual product might even be edible. We were instructed to wait forty-five minutes this time, and Bran refused to start another whipping. We went instead to the music room and he played beautiful floury music for me. We had washed our hands, but still I imagined gusts of white fluming from his agile fingertips as they sped over the keys. The music both calmed and invigorated me, and I resolved to hold this morning in my memories forever.

When we returned to the kitchen, I asked Bran why he had said he would make genital bread.

"Watch," he instructed me. He took a fist-sized lump of dough and pounded it down. Then he fashioned a long, thin penis. He laid it carefully on a cookie sheet and grabbed another lump of dough.

"Dig your hands in, Chantal," he invited me.

I grabbed a lump as well and began to pound it down. As I kneaded, I glanced at the inert penis on the cookie sheet, but it wasn't inert anymore. Even as I watched, it began to rise and I understood the joke. The penis swelled and swelled and I laughed till tears ran down my face. I laughed so hard, I started to pee and had to run to the washroom.

When I returned, I had a new inspiration. I fashioned my lump into two attached strips of labia, placing them carefully on the cookie sheet beside the bread-dough penis. They too swelled and swelled. Then Bran added the crowning touch. He drizzled melted butter down the fold in the center of the next pair of labia and, as it swelled, the butter oozed juicily up and over the swollen lips.

I countered with a specialized penis. I hid my dough from Bran's view and rolled a thick strip of apricot jam into the center of the sculpture. I made the model as lifelike as possible, even to the little hole in the end. When I placed it on the cookie sheet, Bran didn't look too impressed; but when the jam oozed from the little hole, he loved it.

We spent an hour or more creating our yeasty genitals. We made buns, of course, lots of buns. Bran made a working pair of breasts that sprang liquid butter from the nipples. I made a penis complete with testicles. As they rose, they gave new meaning to my concept of balls. Finally the bowl of dough was empty. Two cookie sheets were covered with our creations.

We put the sheets into the hot oven and I turned on

the light so we could watch the progress of our creations. The penises swelled to orgasmic proportions and the labia oozed their juices and the breasts got implants, or so they appeared. We watched and laughed and made ribald comments like two giddy teenagers. Then we removed the steaming organs from the heat and took them to the table.

I picked up a hot penis gingerly and licked the tip. I placed it in my mouth and sucked, but it collapsed under the pressure. Bran winced as I bit down. When he picked up a breast and chomped off the nipple, my hand flew to cover my chest. I swear I could feel his teeth. I squirmed as he raised a pair of labia to his lips, and my lower mouth oozed more than his buttery one. It felt strange and almost homosexual to eat breasts and labia, but they tasted just as good. Bran had no difficulty downing a penis. Perhaps there was a lesson there.

Each bite brought fresh laughter as the jam dribbled down our chins, and the butter smothered our lips. We were bread makers par excellence! Through the years, whenever my life has seemed difficult or dreary, I have remembered that magical morning with a smile!

poco a poco crescendo
Slowly Building

That afternoon I went for a long walk around the island. To the west near the house, the Pacific Ocean crashed over craggy rocks, sending spumes of salty spray high into the air. The day was cool though the sun shone optimistic rays from an almost-clear blue sky. Fields of crocuses had bloomed and died, leaving slender graying stalks to mark their passage. Daffodils and tulips gamboled haphazardly through overgrown gardens. It was spring, and the change of seasons lifted my spirits and challenged my expectations.

I continued to my left following the coastline until I found a narrow path to a small beach. The sand was pure black and the cove spectacular. I wondered what freak of nature had brought such inky rocks to pound to gritty fragments on that particular hundred feet of shore. I took off my shoes and strolled, chilled but happy, to the edge of the water. I could see the mainland far in the distance, several miles away. The sight made me weep.

I wept for the lost months of my life, immured on this island, bereft of my children, my friends. At that moment, I even missed my publisher. The ache in my chest suffocated me. I remembered driving and grocery shopping and laundry, and each simple activity seemed an incalculable lost pleasure. I wiped my eyes with the sleeve of my dress as I tried to imagine the events of the world that had passed without my knowledge. I felt at that moment an overwhelming rage at Bran for stealing precious months of my life from me.

At last I couldn't bear to look at the land any longer and I followed the trail back up from the beach to the wider path above. As I walked, my rage died, but it took with it much of my enthusiasm. Though I loved Bran, I couldn't forgive him. Though I wanted to write deeply, I couldn't convince myself that the goal was worth the cost I'd paid. I searched the sides of the path for another trail to the beach, hoping I might find a closer passage across the water. But there was none.

I walked to the top of the drawbridge and stood gazing at the few feet—no more than forty—that sepa rated me from freedom. If only there were some way to cross that gap, to recapture the freedom to blunder through my own mistakes, by myself, to regain control of my life.

"Regrets, Chantal?" Bran's voice in my ear startled

me. I almost fell into the side railing. Bran's hand under my arm held me steady. "You aren't ready yet, you know."

"Who the hell are you, to tell me what I am or am not ready for?"

"I thought you trusted me." Bran sounded upset, but I wasn't swayed by his hurt.

"It sounds more to me like *you* don't trust *me!*" I threw back in his face.

He smiled. The all-knowing smile I'd found so reassuring now seemed complacent and patronizing. I swung my fist into his face and connected jarringly, bone to bone. My hand ached with deep bruises and blood spurted from his nose like a fountain.

"Bran, I'm—"

The apology vanished from my mouth, as suddenly we were in a strange house, the abandoned home I had seen by the pond. The dizzying display of Bran's unleashed power unnerved me, and I screamed in pure terror. Blood still dripping from his broken nose, he held my arm in a grip of iron.

"Never raise your hand in anger." His low, flat voice reverberated through my bowels. "If you wish to leave, we will finish your lessons more speedily."

"No, Bran," I protested. "Anything you say, I'll—"

He cut off my words with a glaring frown and dragged me toward the stairs. I had come to trust the mansion; the unfamiliar house frightened me. I feared anything might happen here. The home was small—a cottage really—and the single door at the top of the stairs opened onto a rough attic. Open beams formed the low ceiling and unfinished plywood, the floor. There were no windows.

I strained against Bran's arm, but might have fought a steel trap with more success. He pulled me inside the room, leaving the door ajar behind us. By the dim light I saw that the room contained a single bed and a chair.

"Look carefully," he commanded. "There will be no light."

I tried frantically to place the locations firmly in my mind.

"What will happen?" I asked, my voice subdued. I didn't know the man who stood beside me, though I'd lived with him intimately for many months. I tried to remember our contract and to convince myself that he wouldn't harm me, but I could no longer believe my old beliefs.

"Learn quickly." The deep voice again echoed through the bottom of my stomach. Then, at the instant his hand left my arm, he was gone. I was left in a darkness blacker than night has been since man found fire. The primeval solitude awakened buried phobias, and I screamed till my voice was hoarse.

When finally my ears told my brain that I had stopped screaming, a feminine voice whispered close beside me, "There, there, sweetheart."

I jumped and landed against a low object. As I fell, I realized that the barrier was the bed. I landed on my back and felt the mattress sag as the creature crawled onto the bed at my side.

"Who are you?" I whispered, terror in my voice.

"Never mind, sweetheart," the voice soothed. It had the silky smoothness of careful modulation, like the alto tones of an exquisitely trained singer. I felt a hand at my breast, teasing open the tie that held my dress closed.

"Don't touch me!" I demanded.

"Relax," the soothing voice murmured, and the hand began to fondle my already-agitated orb. She pinched the right nipple hard, and I gasped and tried to brush her hand away. She calmly released my traitorous breast and strapped my two hands to the bedstead above my head. Then her hand returned to my right breast and I gulped as she kneaded it to an agony of twisting desire. My left breast heaved, beyond my volition, begging for equal rough treatment. She settled her left hand over me, pressing gently at first then harder and harder, until tears trickled from my eyes with the pain and arousal. I begged her to stop; but the more I begged, the more ingeniously she tortured me, until I begged her to continue.

When my begging turned to whimpers and my cunt was as wet as the wide Pacific Ocean, she grasped my dress where the neckline ended and ripped it open to the hem. She parted the cloth, so that I lay fully exposed before her. I hoped she might move her hand to my eager sopping vagina, but she had other plans. She laid an object on my stomach and spoke to me again in that elusive voice.

"What do you think this is, sweetheart?" She rotated the object against me, turning it this way and that, till I grasped its meaning.

"It's a dildo," I whispered.

She lifted the object and placed it again on my stomach, from a different angle.

"And what is this?"

"Another dildo," I answered more quickly, though no less softly.

She rubbed the dildos over and around my breasts and up and behind my neck, and I realized that they were connected. Oh, God, I thought. I wrote about one of those things once—a double-headed dildo.

"Open your mouth!" she commanded, her voice deeper and less sweet.

I opened my lips wide, expecting the dildo to be forced between my jaws. Instead she fell onto me and fastened her mouth over mine. I tried to close my jaw, even a bit, but her voracious mouth wouldn't allow me an instant's peace. I tried to catch her tongue in my teeth and so free myself, but she growled low in her throat and captured my tongue and sucked it almost from its roots. I had heard the expression "devoured by a kiss," but had never experienced the sensation. She stole even my breath, until I was faint from lack of oxygen.

At last I lay quiescent beneath her, and she lifted her mouth from mine and shifted her body upward. I felt the dildo move in her hand down the length of our entwined bodies, and I groaned in fearful anticipation. She slid the hard shaft into me. The ancient power of a captive and gorged vagina brought liquid from my eyes and lower lips. When she raised herself above me, I held my breath in wait for the pain of her descent onto the ungiving shaft that pegged me. I felt instead a gentle rocking motion, more pleasure than pain, as she glided down the ingenious rod that bound us together.

Her breasts hovered over mine and her nipples teased their counterparts cruelly. When she began to rock with the rhythm of the ages, the hard shaft between us moved relentlessly within me. Not malleable like a human penis, it hammered insistently, unfeelingly, wondrously inside my soft cavity. It thrust into me like a man at the peak of orgasm and like the imagined him, I came in a thunder of spasming muscle. I forgot for an instant that a woman rode me, that a substitute filled me, as a second only too-real orgasm swept past my barriers.

"God!" I whispered and lifted my lips to kiss her. She responded to my tentative tenderness with a devouring passion as she recaptured my too-willing mouth in hers. Again she sucked the breath from me and, as I struggled for oxygen, she lifted my right knee up to my shoulder. From the fresh angle, the dildo penetrated farther into my softness until it seemed the walls would be battered down. I came again, moisture flooding both mouths with a sweet furor.

When she lifted my left knee to join its fellow at shoulder height, I whimpered a protest. Surely my body couldn't bend to such a position. But my complaint was soon forgotten as my vagina discovered a new stimulation in that awkward posture. She began a steady rhythm, neither slowing nor speeding up, forcing me to adapt to her pace. As I neared another peak, I tried to move my hips to increase the cadence, but she held me fast to her rhythm, drawing out my climax to an unbearable climb to an unattainable—no, attainable—summit of pounding perfection.

As the height of my passion passed and I began once again to feel the ache in my hard-pressed hipbones, she began a new and faster rhythm that swept my pains beneath the mantle of renewed frenzy. Faster and faster she pounded within me, and the muscles of my vagina squeezed the shaft that speared me with an equally frantic need. We came together, she with a high piercing scream, me with low moaning. Then she released my knees and collapsed across my chest. After a few breathless moments, I eased my frozen limbs back into their normal range of motion and we lay together, still pinned at the pelvis.

At last she eased herself off the dildo, which shifted and lurched painfully within me with her movement. When I protested, she kissed me softly on the mouth and slid the massive playtoy from my clinging netherlips. She lay beside me, whispering softly in a language I couldn't understand, brushing the damp hair from my forehead. When she had soothed me from panting to a drowsy ease, she slid from the bed. Within seconds, I could no longer hear her breathing. I was alone in the chamber once more.

I gave myself over to lazy meanderings, wondering idly who she was. I knew the lesson she taught me. I had never been with a woman, had thought I could never enjoy a woman's touch. I had been wrong. I smiled complacently to think how wrong and drifted into a light slumber.

I don't know how long I slept, but it seemed only an instant. I had been awakened by a new rhythm of breathing in the room. I wanted only to left alone, to absorb the lessons of and recover from my previous visitor. I felt rushed, pressed as I hadn't been through the last months of steady growth. My fuddled senses struggled to identify the observer, for the breathing was now quick and light, then deep and strong. After several moments of puzzled suspense, I realized that two presences beyond mine filled the room.

"I know there are two of you," I stated, emboldened by the success of my previous encounter. "Who are you?"

Heavy footsteps crossed the room to my side. I tried to sit on the edge of the bed, preparatory to standing, but an ungentle hand at my shoulder pushed me back onto the mattress.

"Don't rape me!" I yelled, more threat than plea. "Bran!"

"Like your last visitor?" a low, rough voice chuckled. "Did Gwyneth rape you?"

"This is different!" I argued.

"You won't know until you try it." The lout mouthed the familiar platitude.

"I know, all right," I spat back. "Stop! Bran! Stop!"

A soft, cultured voice spoke from across the room.

"Would you prefer my ministrations, my dear?"

"Yes," I cried, unthinking.

The rough hand left my shoulder, to be replaced by a soft palm.

"Lie back."

Frightened, but not wholly unwilling, I lay back against the mattress. I heard a zipper slide, then the sound of pants dropping to the floor. The rough hands captured mine and pulled them to the top of the bed. Soft hands found my breasts. Then they twisted my nipples between sharp nails. I screamed with the pain, for the wrenching agony brought no compensating pleasure. My vagina dried to a shriveling desert in protest.

"Wrong choice," the pleasant, well-educated, cruel voice taunted me. I began to cry, useless tears of remorse, fear, pain, sorrow, tears for lost hopes, for wasted chances. I felt a slim weight settle over me and those soft, gentle hands parted my knees with an inhuman strength. He plunged into my dry opening, his organ rasping my flesh as it forced through the unwilling doorway. He pumped quickly, two, three, ten times, twelve perhaps, then he came in a feeble burst of impotent acid. He pulled himself from me as quickly as he had entered. The skitter of metal on metal told me he had put his pants back on and closed the zipper.

"Your turn," he spoke lightly to his partner, offering me as though I were a toke of marijuana.

"No way!" I protested, but the soft hands replaced the rough ones at my wrists. Callused fingertips found my bruised breasts and smoothed a soothing cream over their sore flesh. I began to sob again with pain and frustration.

"Hush, now, hush," a low, rough voice accompanied the gentle fingers. My sobs quieted, though I still wept silently. My aching breasts began to respond to the tender massage, and fluid seeped into my sore vagina, bringing balm to my worst hurts.

The rough voice continued, "I'm a gentle man, though I sound a ruffian."

"Are you?" My breath caught between a sob and a hiccup.

"Yes, Chantal, I'm a very gentle man." His calm tones reassured me, and I found the courage to voice my question.

"What are you going to do to me?"

"I'm going to make love to you, Chantal."

"What if I don't want you to?" I asked, desperation tasting septic in my mouth.

"I'm going to anyway," he assured me. "But you'll want me to."

His hands sent calm rivulets of peace through my veins, and with the peace came a pliant renewal of desire. I could believe his words; already the ache of longing built in my womb, the month-old longing for a gentle tender warm human penis inside my ready-made fortress.

"All right," I breathed, trusting the rough man behind the loving hands.

Those hands lifted from my breasts, and I heard again the rasp of a disengaging zipper and the plop of falling pants. I heard, too, the snicker of cruel laughter from the head of the bed.

"Send him away," I begged.

"I'm staying," the aristocratic voice taunted in a lilting tenor.

The bass of my new companion answered more gently, if no less firmly.

"He has to stay, Chantal."

"Why?" I asked.

I felt his shrug in the vibration of the air and in the sniggering laugh of the other man.

"Ignore him," the deep voice urged me as a heavy, solid body settled on the bed beside me.

"Yes," the tenor teased into my ear. "Just ignore me."

I couldn't. Though the rough giant soothed my body with caressing hands, I couldn't banish the other's breathing from my consciousness. Each time I approached a beginning of desire, he would lean toward me and whisper nasty, dirty words into my ear, and my desire would fade into nothingness. The big man moved his head between my legs and stroked me with his broad, flat tongue. Though the sensation was pleasant, it aroused no ardor in me. At last he gave up and, with a regretful sigh, poised himself above me on the bed. He eased himself gently inside me, and I moaned in genuine pleasure as his penis slid home.

He began to rock slowly, in a steady calm rhythm, inviting me to join him in the ultimate joy. But I could find no joy, little pleasure even, beyond the pure physical ease of painlessness, in our joining. I felt sorry, for he seemed a sincere man, and my lack of response made him sad. When he saw that I merely endured his motion, he increased his momentum and came swiftly with a mighty burst of life-giving elixir. At that moment only, I felt at one with him. When he fell onto my chest,

I pulled my hands from the now-silent and limp bastard who held them and ran my fingers over the rough man's face. He kissed my forehead and pulled out of my body. Then he rose from the bed, and both men were gone. I lay silent on my back, staring at the unseen ceiling.

crescendo
Building

I didn't wait long. I recognized the breathing immediately.

"You're a bastard, Bran. Is your nose all right?" I asked wearily.

"It's sore," Bran answered. He sounded as tired as I, but no longer enraged. "You didn't break it."

"Thank goodness at least for that," I sighed. "Bran, I'm really sorry."

"I know, Chantal."

"I never hit anyone before."

"All part of your learning." His voice sounded wryly amused.

"Well, you've repaid me several times over," I added, anger wedging into my voice. "I think it's your turn to apologize."

"Only for the timing." The half-excuse reminded me of my anger by the bridge. Who was he to order my life, to decide the pace and extent of my experiences? I half-rose on the bed to protest further, but fell back exhausted to the mattress. Time enough to argue tomorrow; for now I wanted only to sleep.

"What have you learned, Chantal?" Bran's insistent voice wouldn't let me rest.

"I have no idea, Bran," I answered honestly. "Please go away so I can sleep."

He vanished with my request, and I tumbled into a deep well of unconsciousness. I slept dreamless for many hours, or so I imagined, for I awakened feeling rested and much less sore. Late-afternoon sunlight filtering through the curtains teased open my eyelids. I felt momentarily disoriented, for I was back in my bedroom on my own bed. I wondered whether Bran reminded me again of his power, his control over my body, but decided that he probably meant only kindness. I had slept better in my own bed. I resolved to find him and finish the conversation I had avoided hours before.

I looked first in the library, but he wasn't at his familiar seat behind the massive desk. I smiled softly, remembering the rousing times he'd given me across that marble surface. Though I carried in my chest a residuum of anger, I knew he was no villain—only an immortal man employing ancient methods with a woman anchored firmly in the beliefs and habits of modern life.

I searched each room of the house. In the kitchen, I

thought of the pure fun we had shared only that morning; tears moistened my eyes for the swift passage of that innocent time. The sitting room reminded me of long meals and longer discussions, contented times of mutual respect. The sight of the fountain brought a chill to my skin and a warmth deep within. I hurried past, more eager by the moment to find my difficult and dear companion.

I found him at last by the pond at the end of the island. The house of my horror rose silent behind us, an abandoned cottage once again. Bran sat on the pier, much as I had sat months earlier reliving my sweetest childhood memories. Perhaps similar fantasies filled him, for when I approached he smiled tenderly and held out a welcoming hand.

"Come sit beside me, Chantal," he invited. He wrapped his arm around my shoulder and we sat thus, silent, for several moments.

"I learned that I don't loathe a woman's touch," I resumed our earlier conversation quietly.

"Did you prefer the woman to a man?" Bran asked.

"I certainly preferred her to the two men that followed," I answered with some heat. "But no, I want a kind, normal man, with gentle lips and a talented tongue and a pulsing organ to fill me with life and love."

"And so you learned...?" Bran prompted.

"Not to despise those of other habits. Not that I ever have. But I have more understanding; I have a sense of fellow feeling, having experienced the attraction."

Bran nodded his understanding. We sat in silence for several minutes before I spoke again.

"I find it hard to forgive you for the two men."

"I hadn't wanted to move so quickly, Chantal."

"What did you expect me to gain from being raped?"

"You must tell me."

"I suppose it's a limit, a doorway through which I don't care to pass." I paused in thought. "I don't believe I've ever fantasized being raped; the reality is too awful for too many women."

Bran waited patiently, refusing to prompt me with further questions.

"This morning was the final answer to our debate over consent. I didn't feel the Oriental man raped me, even though he caused me more pain than the thin man in the dark room. The thin man took pleasure in my discomfort and he didn't care about me at all."

"Did the heavy man rape you?"

"I don't know," I answered honestly.

"Think, Chantal," Bran urged. I could see the importance of his question in his eyes. I struggled to sort through my tangle of feelings.

"Yes, he did," I stated finally. "Though I agreed in words, I didn't in my heart want what came. I couldn't respond to him. I hated the thin man's hovering by my head, breathing venom in my ear. I felt sympathy for the heavy man because he tried to be kind to me; but he did rape me, which was an evil thing to do."

"He's not a strong man," Bran explained, though he didn't try to excuse the man's actions. "He falls much under the influence of his friend."

"You wouldn't have done that to me, would you?" I

asked. I felt as though I offered him my heart on a thin golden platter, his to break with the wrong answer.

"No, Chantal, I wouldn't."

"And you would have stopped, anytime over these last months, if I'd truly wanted you to?"

"Yes, I would have."

"So your force, your control, was an illusion."

"Which I used to heighten your pleasure."

I sighed in relief and felt truly at peace with myself and my companion for the first time. He didn't control my life, my actions, my reactions, my soul. I did. At my core, I'd known from the start that he wouldn't hurt me, and the deepest hurt would have been to steal my will. Instead, he had strengthened me by showing me my own power. I embraced him in a fierce hug and gently kissed the awkward white bandage which bridged his sore nose. Thus in harmony we sat together in the warm air, surrounded by calm water and the budding growth of spring. When the sun dropped below the green-tinged trees and the air chilled with the loss of its warmth, we rose and walked back to the house arm in arm.

That night I fell again into a deep slumber, though I'd slept much of the afternoon away. In the early hours of the morning, when the moon dipped back to the far horizon, my dream lover visited me once again. This time the dream was even more vivid and I felt truly awake, for I saw the moon and I saw my lover cross the floor from the window to my bed. His silhouette was backlit by the faint light and I saw that he was a strong man of average height, sturdily built, but still I couldn't see his face. I pulled back the covers and invited him wordlessly into my bed.

He lay beside me, gathered me into his arms and held me quietly for many moments. His gentle strength banished the final remnants of horror from my heart, and bound it up, battered but strongly beating, with loving care. When he tried to place his head between my legs, I held him firm to my chest and then pressed him down to the mattress on his back. I knelt above him to one side and massaged his forehead, neck, and chest. He had a broad, flat, high forehead and I marveled that even that simple surface felt powerful beneath my fingertips. I bent and kissed the throbbing vein that pulsed at each temple. He sighed with pleasure as my hands and lips caressed and eased his taut muscles.

Soon my mouth found his and we joined in a sweet lingering kiss, a kiss of promise and honest pleasure and delight. He grasped my head in two strong hands and pulled me to lie again beside him, and his kiss deepened into my mouth, his tongue darting, then hovering behind my teeth and stroking the roof of my mouth with an agonizing warm rasp. I sank deep into his breath and floated on the waves that lapped through the steamy wetness of my vagina. Each stroke of his tongue aroused me twice: the reality within my hungry lips and teeth, and the imagined memory of his sinuous suckling shaft which teased my lower mouth to desperation.

I forgot my impromptu plan to work my lips and hands slowly down his body, and wrenched my mouth from his to plunge it over his hard organ of desire. He gasped as his penis slid into my hot mouth and the erect shaft swelled to a new firmness. I stroked my tongue up and down the length of his sturdy rod, and he thrust into me once with a convulsive shudder. I squeezed the base of his penis tightly so he couldn't come, then placed my hands on his hipbones to hold him immobile to my ministrations. I moved my mouth up and down along his pulsing shaft, raking the sides gently, oh so gently, with my teeth. The motion drove him wild. I had to press with all my might to hold his hips to the mattress. I wouldn't give him release so soon; I meant to tease him to the frenzy of oblivion, as he had me.

When his organ was as hard as a stone column in my mouth, I ceased my motion and began instead to suck against the sides of his penis in a steady rhythm. The suction of my mouth slurped noisily against his firm flesh, and he moved his hands to twine his fingers in my hair. At last he could restrain no longer and his hips began to pump, my arms now useless to contain their eager momentum. I slid my hands beneath his buttocks and fell into his motion, relaxing my jaw to contain him whole within me. He came at last with a shout and a jet of silky hot fluid that filled my throat. I choked once, then swallowed the warm draft of life, which settled into a nourishing pool in my stomach.

He held my head and stroked my hair as he slid his still pulsing organ from my slack mouth. I licked the last fluid from the shaft, then laid my head on his stomach. His fingers never ceased their tender caresses, and I settled into his warmth and hardness like a kitten into a cozy lap. We lay thus, comfortably content, for long moments. When he raised me up to lie beside him, I snuggled again into his arms, as if into my home, and fell asleep.

I felt him leave my side and struggled to hold him close, but he pushed my sleepy arms aside and pulled me to lie on my back in the center of the bed. I tried to protest that he didn't need to pleasure me, that his joy sufficed for tonight, but I couldn't find my voice. My legs parted naturally to his touch, and I came a little more awake as his head descended between my spread knees.

My center was still tender from my arousal as I suckled him and his tongue shot splinters of electricity from my clitoris to the seat of my consciousness. I came in a swift and powerful orgasm with his first touch. But he wouldn't let me be satisfied with so simple a pleasure. His tongue snaked inside my vagina and sucked out the juice that welled from my pulsing center. His sucking aroused me anew, and I moved my hips with the rhythm of his tongue. He played back my trick at me and pinned my hips to the mattress to still their motion. The restraint fired my desire red hot, and I found the inability to rock with his motion near-intolerable. I pressed and pressed against his iron hands and came in a shattering scream of delight.

Still he wasn't satisfied, but moved his lips to my clitoris and pinched and stretched the hard little bud between the soft cushions. Each motion sent an arrow of fire through my womb and the orgasms that shook me stole the breath from my lungs and the sight from my eyes and the blood from my veins. All air, all redness, all heat, all fire, concentrated within that quarter-inch of agonized flesh, until the essence burst from me in a final flaming shower of light and motion and sound. I collapsed into a panting lassitude as his tongue stroked broadly over my labia, not arousing but calming those heaving shores.

We fell asleep entwined. Skin pressed to skin, each seeking to absorb self and other into a single contented mass.

fortissimo, con forza
Climax

I awoke alone in my bed, but no longer alone in the world. The early hours of the morning remained clear in my mind, lingering as dreams seldom do. The time seemed poised between imagination and reality. I knew my lover existed; I couldn't bear for him not to exist. I yearned to meet him in the daylight, to see his dear face and hear his voice. Was it deep and lilting, like Bran's? Or perhaps a mellow baritone. I couldn't imagine a high male voice swelling from that broad chest, but even were he mute, I knew I would embrace him as my own.

I wondered what color his eyes were. Were they the cloudless guileless blue of the spring sky or the warm bark brown of an oak? I knew his hands were strong and his fingers thick, not slender and artistic like Bran's, but sturdy as those of a master craftsman. His muscles bulged beneath my hands—I smiled remembering—his forearms and triceps and thighs rock solid to my caress. I grew moist and hot wake-dreaming of my phantom lover, soon to be phantom no more. I wondered when and how I would meet him.

The speculation led me to the dilemma of my departure from the island and my resumption of a normal life. A thousand questions presented themselves to my suddenly clear mind. I must find Bran. I showered quickly and donned the clean plain cotton dress that waited as always, neatly folded, on the side table.

I walked first to the library and then through each of the rooms on the main floor, but Bran was nowhere to be found. I went back upstairs and looked into the upper music room, but he wasn't there either. Except for my bedroom, the other doors were locked. No sound emerged from the solid wood doors, though I pressed my ear close to each. The basement was one open expanse, and I saw as I descended the stairs that Bran wasn't in the pool or the gym.

Remembering that I had found him by the lake the day before, I left the house and followed the path through the meadow and into the forest. No familiar smile greeted me from the pier. I began to worry. Bran had never disappeared before. He had left me alone, sometimes for days; but whenever I had sought him out, he was there. He had told me that he could be hurt, and I knew that for the truth by my blow to his poor nose. Perhaps he lay injured, needing my help. I couldn't bear the thought that I wasn't there the one time he needed me. I began to search along the lakefront.

I circled the small body of water, calling Bran's name and poking through bushes to the lake's edge. When I found no trace of his presence, I followed the stream path down to the ocean and walked along the water until I regained the house. By then my stomach remembered my lack of breakfast, and I ducked into the kitchen for a hasty meal. An egg and a potato later, I resumed my ever-more-frantic search.

I tried to remember that Bran was a grown man—far beyond a grown man, in fact. He had powers no person on earth could overcome. Still, I remembered his boyish enthusiasm and lack of trickery. He might have fallen prey to a devious and envious mind. I crisscrossed the forest, losing my way in the sunless depths but progressing slowly through the many acres of tall trees and lush undergrowth. At last I returned to the house, defeated by my aching legs and hunger and a growing sense of my foolishness. Of course nothing was wrong. I was less than sensible in my irrational fears. I made myself a hot lunch of pasta and cheese and calmed the worst of my anxiety. Yet my instincts were uneasy. After lunch I waited impatiently in the library, a book open but unread in my lap.

At last I must have fallen asleep in the chair. When I awakened it was dark; evening had descended upon the house like a smothering blanket as I slept. No lights were lit, for Bran hadn't returned to light them. The house echoed with the empty quiet of unuse. Through the stillness I heard the turning of a doorknob and a creak as the front door swung open. Thinking that Bran had at last returned, I ran eagerly into the hallway, ready to embrace and chide him in one breath.

I stopped short at the library door. It wasn't Bran, but a whole party of men and women who entered the house. They were dressed strangely, like ancient statues, the men in skins and rough boots, their hair hanging past their shoulders in mostly curly locks. The women wore simple garments, not unlike my own save in the fabrics. Theirs were richly brocaded, woven and embroidered in many colors. Both men and women spoke a strange language, guttural and harsh. I couldn't understand a word. When they had all entered, a man stepped forward from the crowd of thirty or so and addressed me clearly in modern English.

"Pardon our speech, Chantal." His voice held the same faint accent as Bran's. "The rest haven't bothered to learn the new tongues, but rely on the ancient Celtic still."

"Who are you?" I asked, though I feared the answer.

"My name is Evnissien. I'm Bran's cousin."

I recognized the name from the books I had read, though Bran had never mentioned the evil man to me. In legend, Evnissien had strewn violence and hatred wherever he walked.

"Oh, I'm not such a bad fellow as all that," he laughed, easily reading my thought.

"Where is Bran?" I asked.

"He's gone, I'm afraid."

My knees began to shake. I clutched the doorjamb for support.

"What happened?" I whispered.

"He had a small accident on the mainland. Unfortunately, it proved temporarily fatal."

The hovering crowd laughed, catching the import if not the exact meaning of his words.

"Oh, my God!" I moaned and sank to the floor.

"Just so," Evnissien sympathized. "He'd bought a trinket for you and was on his way back to the limousine when a car struck him on the sidewalk. A most unfortunate accident."

His snigger told me more than his words. He had engineered the accident. I fastened my mind to the belief that Bran wasn't really dead, for he was immortal. He would come back and deliver me from this callous throng.

"Unfortunately, he won't be able to come back for a few days." Evnissien's words stole my hope of immediate rescue. "His spirit must stay in that body until it's been buried. I'm afraid it will be some time before he can hear your call. Would you like to see what he lost his life over?"

He held out his hand to me. When I didn't rise, he stomped impatiently to my side. He threw the object into my lap and strode back to stand amongst his friends. The trinket was an amulet, an ancient stone carving of an earth goddess threaded with a thong through a circle above the head. I sensed Bran's continuing presence in the cool granite; I held the talisman tight in my palm and raised it to my heart. Evnissien spoke some words in the guttural language to the restless crowd, and they dispersed into the main floor of the house. Then he turned back to me.

"While Bran is away, we shall party." He smiled unpleasantly. "And you shall be our guest of honor."

"No!"

"But of course." His oily voice seeped into my skin. "It's taken me several centuries to capture one of Bran's playthings. You mustn't think I mean to let you escape."

"No!" I screamed and crawled back into the library. I barred the door behind me; but when I swung to face the fire, Evnissien stood beside the mantel, a thin black whip in his left hand. I screamed in pure terror and struggled to reopen the door.

"It won't open," he informed me calmly. "Put your hands by the rings."

I shook my head, unwilling to believe this was really happening. I shook it again, harder, trying to awaken from the evil nightmare, but it was only too real. My tormentor grabbed my arm in his right hand and held me away from his body.

"What does Bran see in you, I wonder?" he mocked.

He began to whip me as I struggled. The lash caught me cruelly wherever it might. The thongs wrapped first around my back and the tips slashed through the fabric across my stomach. The next stroke he aimed lower and the dress shredded across my pelvis, leaving my most sensitive skin exposed to his harsh caress. The third stroke completed the destruction of my garment. The dress dropped to the ground. Needles of fire shot through my breasts.

"What's the matter, Chantal?" Evnissien taunted. "Don't I whip you as well as Bran did? I know you like it."

I shook my head in wordless protest and, stung, he

dragged me to the desk. He wrestled my right hand to the ring by brute force and tied me down. The left was easier, since I couldn't move to ward him away. Once I was strapped to the desk, he didn't care what position I assumed, but whipped me wherever I moved. His strokes were hard but not unbearable. Finally I climbed onto the desk and bore them stoically across my buttocks and back, curled into a fetal position, the amulet clutched tight in my palm. Foul cursing in the guttural tongue poisoned the air as Evnissien swung.

At last he explained his frustration. "Your protector still holds some power, my dear. My arm can't strike you as I would like."

I breathed a silent thanks to Bran who, even in death, kept our contract.

"Ah," Evnissien hissed. "So that's what binds me. No one can break the contract of a god. You'll remain safe from damage, Chantal, though I would gain incalculable pleasure from your destruction."

He paused, then laughed, "But I doubt you will remember this night with any fondness."

He unlashed my hands from the rings and pulled me from the desktop and over his shoulder. He carried me thus, naked, my back and buttocks red from his thrashing, into the pagan throng. One patted me softly on the bottom, and a woman whispered soothingly in my ear as we passed. When Evnissien stood me in the center of the crowd, hands held behind me in one of his, I saw as many glances of sympathy as I did mocking leers. They were not all evil like their leader, only heedless and uncaring. Evnissien spoke some words in their tongue, and the immortals slowly approached me.

My captor stretched me out before him, forcing my arms out straight behind my back, and when I twisted to escape the probing hands, he lifted my arms higher until I stood on tiptoe and couldn't move. I closed my eyes to block out the scene as hands both soft and rough stroked and probed me. Fingers tweaked my breasts and pried open my mouth. I bit one hand, and it slapped my face gently in reproof. The men and women seemed bound even by the intent of Bran's contract, for they hurt me not at all. Or perhaps they were truly gentle creatures and merely curious. Their touch ceased to frighten me. I found myself responding to their caresses.

When the first finger snaked inside my lower mouth, it was to find it moist with the fluid of trepidation. The voice attached to the hand exclaimed, and I found myself freed from Evnissien's hold and lifted by a dozen hands. My eyes flew open as my feet left the ground and I struggled as they carried me across the floor. They set me in a large chair like a throne, one which I had never seen before. The seat was shaped like a U and barely gave purchase to the edge of my bottom. Hands pressed me back into the chair and caressed my forehead and cheeks, while other hands strapped my arms to the arms of the chair. Still I held fast to Bran's talisman. Its presence comforted me even in the chaos of those moments. More hands lashed my legs to the legs of the chair, pulling open my cunt and leaving me exposed to the air and their curious touch.

I understood the meaning of the chair soon enough, for before the strapping was completed, a hand brushed against the hair of my pubis. I closed my eyes so I couldn't see the one who assailed my fortress and threw back my head in fearful anticipation. Hands continued to stroke my skin, my arms, my legs, my stomach, even my hair, while the one hand pressed harder and harder into my curly mound. One long finger poked free of the rest and worked its way through the silky hairs and between my swelling lower lips. Again I heard a gasp of approval at my moist preparedness, though I would have remained as dry as my throat, for my own liking. The hand stroked me gently along the outer labia, ignoring both clitoris and vagina, seeming to delight in the soft, smooth, slick flesh.

I became accustomed to the stroking and began even to enjoy it, but the hand soon withdrew and another took its place. This one was bolder and thrust a hard finger inside me, drawing a gasp from my throat. I heard a murmur of disapproval from the crowd, and the finger began to stroke me gently and expertly. I wriggled on the tiny seat trying to escape the invidious pleasure, but the finger followed me and hands pressed me forward from the sides and back. Several crept under my buttocks and lifted me to the tender probing of the unrelenting finger. Still I kept my eyes squeezed shut in denial of my own stimulation.

When the hand at my front pulled away, I stifled a moan of disappointment. The next touch was feminine; tiny delicate fingers pried open my lips with strong rounded nails. I opened my eyes to see my new assailant and was caught by the wise smile of an old but unwrinkled woman. She held up three fingers before my face, then inserted them into me, twisting and turning and wiggling the digits until I panted with the effort to remain unaroused. She pulled her dripping fingers from me and held them again before my face. Four this time. I shook my head; she couldn't fit four fingers inside me. But she did.

The joined knuckles beat against the opening of my vagina in a steady rhythm and the fingers stroked the inside to a white-hot moistness. I could no longer pretend to be indifferent to her touch, and the hands on my buttocks lifted my undulating pelvis to her service. As I approached an aching orgasm, she withdrew her hand and I groaned in protest. She reached up and touched my cheek with a moist finger, lingering until I opened my clenched eyes. She held up five fingers before my face, and the crowd shifted and held their collective breath in anticipation and approval. My protests went unnoticed by all but one, who placed a gentle hand across my mouth to still my incoherent argument.

The woman flexed her hand playfully before the crowd, who oohed and aahed their encouragement. Mingled fear and hope filled my womb as her fingers soon would. Then she placed her still-wriggling fingers again before my mound and parted my lips with her other hand. The fingers kept moving as they entered me, twisting and turning to find the best angle. The pressure was beyond my endurance, and I cried out into the hand that still caressed my mouth. Another murmur of warning went through the crowd. Then the old woman's hand slid into me—fingers, thumb, knuckles, palm and all—and I felt filled with a delicious wriggling live body.

My hips arched up and I came in an orgasm of intensity. I closed my eyes. The room and all its occupants save the old woman disappeared. The unfamiliar motion within my wondering womb brought me again and again to a crashing summit of catharsis. My soul left my body and flew to Bran's side and I saw him lying on a slab. Though I saw him dead yet, I knew that he lived. He was my guardian spirit, and his talisman would be my eternal reminder. I kissed his forehead, then returned to my own body.

The old woman had eased her hand from my womb and stood before me grinning. The others stood awestruck in a circle around us. I don't know what held them silent, unless it was perhaps the very intensity of my emotion. Evnissien had vanished, banished perhaps by the goodwill of his fellows. All at once a babble of excited voices broke out. I felt a dozen hands release my bonds and lift me to my feet. Arms supported me while my shaky legs regained their feeling. A tall, slender woman brought forward a garment like her own and draped it lovingly around me. She tucked my unresisting hands into the sleeves and knotted the rich gold sash about my waist.

The crowd dispersed into small knots, and I passed from group to group an honored guest. As I approached, the men and women would begin to speak an awkward but understandable English; they could do anything they wished if only they wished it enough. They told me their stories, some singly, some in pairs. The ancient themes echoed down through the ages: sin and treachery, hope and redemption, an ungrateful child, a cruel parent, son fighting brother, religion battling religion. I told them sadly that the stories hadn't changed in the thousands of years since their mortal lives. We sighed collectively for man's recalcitrant unwillingness to learn, until one wise woman turned our thoughts to kind and helpful deeds, of which humanity was equally capable.

Each had a story of a friend in need who had found help, a child sheltered, or a village rebuilt. They told heroic stories of the kindness of great men; I sought through my mind for similar modern tales, but found only too few. Goodness persisted in the small everyday acts of ordinary people, but seemed sadly absent from the grander scale. I pushed the thought from my mind and focused instead on the incredible wealth of history these generous people spread eagerly before me.

At last the moon dipped low to the horizon, and the ancients began to drift away. They left in twos and threes until finally the last was gone. I was still dressed in the brocade gown and held Bran's amulet close in my palm, as I had the whole night. I glanced around the empty main floor of the house, my aloneness pressing against my richly clad shoulders. Tomorrow I must find a way to regain the mainland, but the morning was soon enough to worry about that.

I regained my room to find that I was not alone in the house after all and my night was not yet over. Evnissien waited for me in a chair by the hearth. I didn't feel the same horror and dread he had inspired in me earlier, for the charm and warmth of the other ancients had bolstered my strength. Though they tolerated him, they didn't respect him, and their displeasure had banished him from the room. I knew that in the last resort, I could call them back to me and they would fend him away again. But I hoped to send him from me without need for their assistance.

I knew he read my thoughts, and the realization gave me added strength. He knew I wouldn't cower before him again. Then suddenly I remembered a story I had read of how he had horribly maimed and disfigured a stable of horses in a fit of anger and jealousy. Perhaps he'd planted the memory, for he smiled as I glanced at him in renewed fear. A man who didn't hesitate to destroy a stableful of horses was crueler than I would ever comprehend and vicious enough to frighten any sane creature. Though I strove to banish the fear into a dark corner, it worked on my mind as Evnissien had intended.

When he appeared suddenly at my elbow, I shrank from him, dismayed by the display of his preternatural powers and uncertain now of my ability to master him. Lightning fast, his hands reached for mine and pulled them behind my back.

"Rhiannon dressed you nicely, Chantal." He spoke harshly as he shifted my hands into one of his behind my back. "Too nicely for a whore like you."

His words broke the spell of my terror. I knew I was no whore, and anger banished my fear. His hand paused in front of the sash of my gown as he sensed my new resolve.

"I'm no whore," I stated firmly and bluntly. "Release me."

He couldn't maintain his hold without my unwitting cooperation. His hand released mine.

"Leave me!" I tried, but he wouldn't be vanquished quite so easily. Another memory—an ancient betrayal of my beloved Bran—entered my mind uninvited. But the ruse backfired this time for the betrayal awoke in me only feelings of rage and bitter disgust. Evnissien stepped back several paces from my side; the strength of my emotions had forced him away.

"Begone from me!" I uttered in ancient Celtic, the words springing from some age-old source within me. Perhaps Bran or Rhiannon sent them to me in my moment of need, or perhaps in that instant I proved Jung's theory of the collective unconscious. Whatever the source, the words worked. Evnissien vanished, leaving only the echo of his bitter curses to taint the air of my room.

I opened all the windows wide and let the fresh Pacific breeze clear the air. Then I removed the brocade dress, laid it carefully across a chair, and slipped between the smooth sheets of my bed and slept.

poco a poco diminuendo
Softly, Slowly Ending

I awoke the next morning cold and cramped. I lay on a dusty floor. The brisk ocean wind swept past broken panes to caress my naked flesh to a goose-pimpled firmness. I was in the same room and in the same house, for the morning sun shone in the window at the same angle and with the same intensity. Yet everything was changed. The lovely room was gone. In its place were bare moldy walls and cobwebs in the corners where the wind didn't reach.

I remembered the previous night vividly: Evnissien, the Celtic ancients, my gown, the amulet. I glanced down at my hand and saw the rough stone talisman still clutched in my grip. I sighed in relief, loath to lose every trace of my months of captivity. I sighed, too, for the end of a long and precious dream. Though I was eager to return to reality, still I regretted the passing of this strange half-year. Where the chair had stood, the brocade gown lay in a heap on the floor. Grateful for its warmth, I slipped my arms into its heavy scratchy fabric and knotted the sash about my waist.

The computer was gone, and all the months of work I had done. I knew now why I had begun no concerted project—no novel, no poems even. I had known somehow that I couldn't take the work back with me and so I had honed my craft and dissected my emotions in total privacy. I searched the room for any other remnants of my stay but found none. The whirlpool was now a dented iron tub, the toilet nonfunctioning.

I left my room and headed down the stairs to the main floor. I had to retrace my steps, for the right-hand stairway had collapsed halfway down. The left stairs continued safe to the vast marble floor, unmarred by the neglect the rest of the house could not withstand. The piano was gone—that lovely piano that spelled the melody of our days from Bran's fingers and through my life. I hoped that Bran had somehow been able to take it with him to wherever he went next.

In the library I found one solitary volume: the biography of Chopin that I had read early in my stay. I pick up the tattered book to bring with me, wishing only that more remained. The rest of the house was empty—really empty—no doubt vandalized through the years of any treasures it contained. I left the sad dwelling and resolved to remember it as I had known it that winter and not as it now appeared.

I walked along the driveway, my bare feet cold and bruised by the rough gravel. At the end I found the bridge—not sleek and modern as I remembered, but tattered and broken. The central portion was indeed impassable, not for a shiny drawbridge, but because it had fallen down. I couldn't reach the mainland through the channel, for it was still treacherous with rocks and waves. I walked along the shore until I could go no farther, then cut in to the driveway, determined to find the trail to the black beach. Perhaps I could draw a sign in the sand and attract the attention of the coast guard.

By now my feet were bleeding from small cuts, and I was glad for the cold which numbed them. I passed the entrance to the trail twice before I recognized it. By the time I found the beach, my whole body felt as numb as my feet. The beach was barren and the far shoreline distant, but still I felt this cove offered my best chance for discovery. I found a long broken branch in the trees; it was at least twice my height. I dragged it onto the beach, thinking to erect it as a signal pole. I began to dig a hole with my hands, to plant the pole in, then realized that it would show better with a flag at the top. I remembered a tattered remnant of curtain on the floor by the music-room window and began to trudge slowly back to the house.

I was by now truly hungry. I scrounged in the kitchen for any scraps I might find. There were none, but I did find an old box of matches. I tucked them into the pocket of the brocade gown, alongside my talisman from Bran. Both were to prove vital to my rescue. I found the fabric in the music room; there was more than I had thought. I gathered it all and made my way back to the beach with the awkward bundle. I resolved to erect a flag, then build a fire and wrap myself in the remaining drapery for warmth through the night.

The flag proved both easier and harder to raise than I had expected. The material attached easily enough to the branch, but the heavy pole wouldn't remain upright no matter how deep I dug the hole. I must either stand and support it myself or find a lighter branch. I decided to spend my energy finding a new pole, since I would have to eventually, anyway. Several hundred yards away in the darkest part of the forest, I found a new-fallen tree and pried off a still-willowy branch, closer to eight feet tall this time. The branch stood upright in the sand, and I secured the base with a mound of small rocks. The bravely waving flag raised my spirits.

My next task was to build a fire. I decided to use my former flagpole for the main wood supply. I would build a small blaze and push the log farther and farther into the flames as it burned down. I gathered an armload of kindling and placed ripped shreds of drapery beneath them. I couldn't bring myself to destroy the book on Chopin and hoped the fabric would serve. The fire proved harder to start than I had hoped, for the sea wind blew briskly. The fabric caught flame from the matches, but my meager effort died before the larger log caught.

Buoyed that my method would work, I gathered two armloads of kindling and then another for good measure. I built a berm of sand to block the worst wind and lit the fire again. This time it caught well. Halfway through the second load of kindling, the bigger log began to burn. I felt both relief and an unaccustomed pride. Practical skills had never been my forte and I felt as though I'd accomplished a great feat.

The blaze warmed my feet to an aching awareness of their minor wounds, but still I preferred heat and pain to dull numbness. I wrapped myself in the rest of the drapery and settled in for a long evening. I began to cry as I relaxed at last and remembered the sad fate of my kidnapper. I put my hand in my pocket and held tight to the stone earth goddess and wept tears of loss and futility. About an hour later, I knew I had to get up. My body felt stiff and awkward, and the log no longer flamed brightly. I wrapped some of the fabric around my feet in crude socks, which created their own new pains but at least protected my soles from the pebbles. I gathered another armload of kindling just in case, and also to distract myself from my growing hunger. I pushed the log farther into the fire, then settled back to the sand at its side.

The fire and my memories kept me company through that long night. Every hour I got up and poked a few more twigs into the flame and pushed the log a few inches farther along the fire. The method didn't work perfectly; it spread the blaze too thin, but it would serve for the night. In the morning I would search for an old ax or a saw and cut shorter logs for the following night. I knew I couldn't afford to fall asleep or the fire would die down quickly, extinguishing my beacon and leaving me frozen by morning. My eyelids drooped and my mind drifted and I longed with a physical ache that was stronger even than my hunger for my phantom lover to come and keep me company. No one appeared but my own imaginings. I spent the night mourning Bran.

The air warmed slightly in the early predawn and I at last drifted into a shallow sleep. My dream lover didn't come to me; indeed, he was never to come again. Eventually I accepted that his place in my dreams had been a part of Bran's magic and couldn't continue beyond his death to this life. But I did dream of my lost foe, kidnapper, and friend; we shared a steaming breakfast of pancakes and Vermont maple syrup, with piping-hot coffee.

My eyes fluttered open as I realized that the tantalizing smell was no dream. A man squatted beside me and held out a cup of coffee. I couldn't remember a more welcome sight or smell. I didn't try to speak, but took the cup between near frozen hands and held to the warmth with a shudder of delight. Tears seeped from my eyes. The ordeal, the dream, was finally over.

"How did you get here?" the man asked prosaically. I couldn't answer him, so I countered with a question of my own.

"How did you find me?"

"I saw the light from your fire last night through my telescope," he explained. "I thought you might be a camper. I like to keep an eye on this place, just in case. When I saw your flag this morning, I figured maybe you needed rescuing, so I climbed in my boat and came over."

"Thank you," I sobbed. Tears ran down my face. I wiped my wet cheeks with the back of a dirty hand and wondered for a moment what I must look like. The antique brocade dress was worth a small fortune but must look decidedly odd on the beach, especially combined with rag shoes and months-untrimmed hair. If this was to be the love of my life, he met me at my worst.

"However did you get here?" the man persisted.

I knew I would have to come up with an explanation eventually, but none occurred to me at that moment. I shook my head wordlessly, hoping he wouldn't press an obviously distressed woman. My wish was granted; instead of more questions, I received another mugful of steaming coffee. A few moments later, I tried to stand up, but my leg buckled awkwardly beneath me. The man held me upright by my elbow and took in my bizarre appearance as I shook my legs to restore their circulation.

"What's your name?" he asked as he kicked sand over the already-dying fire.

"Chantal," I replied automatically. Then I remembered.

"No, it's Helen." I corrected. "Helen Trant."

The man looked at me skeptically, and I hastened to explain.

"I'm a writer. Chantal Renaud is my pseudonym." After all the years of careful concealment, I now wanted to shout my true occupation to the world.

"Glad to meet you, Helen." The politeness of careful

training sounded through his words. "My name is Henry James, like the writer. My friends call me Hank."

"I'm awfully glad to meet you, Hank." I began to laugh as I held out my hand to him. He didn't even chuckle, but shook my hand gravely and motioned toward the waiting dinghy. He'd pulled the prow well onto the sand, and I stepped in without getting my feet wet and moved to the back of the boat. He pushed it off the sand and waded into the shallow water before stepping over the gunwale and into the center. He took up the oars and turned us around deftly. Then, with broad, smooth strokes, he began to row us across the expanse of calm water.

As I turned to look back at the island, I felt a crack like a lightning bolt split through me. One-half remained with Bran and my phantom lover in the island of our mutual fantasy; the other half longed to see my children and to read my months of accumulated mail. The tear severed me, and I thought for a moment of plunging into the sea and swimming back to the island, but the impulse soon passed. If I had learned anything in those months, it was not to cling to either past or future. The present had arrived in a small dinghy, and I went with it over the sea.

accelerando
Life Resumes

We arrived at the far shore within minutes, the distance less than it had appeared from the island. Hank rowed in silence, and I gazed at the sea and the sky and the approaching land, lost in my thoughts. We docked at a small pier. Hank climbed out first and helped me ashore.

"My place is just up here," he commented as we walked up the plank which adjusted the dock for the tides.

"Do you live alone?" I asked. Hank looked at me strangely, mistaking my question for more than idle curiosity.

"Yes," he responded gruffly and opened the door to an old wooden beach house. I'd often driven enviously by these houses, which perched on the most picturesque property in miles. Several had been torn down over the years, modern mansions built in their place. I was glad Hank had kept the original exterior, though I saw when I entered that the interior had been remodeled extensively and painstakingly.

"Is this your handiwork?" I asked, awed by the craftsmanship.

"Yes," Hank replied again tersely, this time embarrassed by my mild praise.

"It's beautiful," I breathed, running my hand along the massive cedar mantel. The floors were wood and shone with the patina of ages, polished with care to a gleaming warmth. The house had one main room which served for living, dining, and cooking. A massive antique oak table occupied about a quarter of the space and was covered with a litter of papers.

"Didn't know I'd be rescuing anyone today," Hank apologized, looking at the table.

I smiled and waved a hand in dismissal.

"Would you like some breakfast?" he asked next.

Though the thought of food made me weak with hunger, I was even more eager to reach my own home and a bath and clean, fresh clothes.

"Would you mind calling me a cab?" I asked.

"I'll drive you," Hank offered. I realized belatedly that I had no wallet or money for a cab, anyway. I wondered where my purse was after all these months, and my car. Was it still on the island? I couldn't think how I would get it home. A hundred practicalities hammered at my throbbing, starvation-weakened brain.

"Thank you," I managed to whisper. And then I

fainted. When I came back to awareness, I was sitting on the sofa, another cup of coffee held before my face. Coffee seemed to be Hank's sovereign remedy for distress. I took the cup gratefully and admitted, "Maybe I should have something to eat before we go."

"I've got some bread I baked last night," Hank offered. Tears sprang into my eyes as I remembered Bran's and my morning bread making. Was it only two days ago? Hank must have thought I was losing my mind as I nodded and smiled, accepting his offer of breakfast while tears streamed down my face.

He cleared a space at the table and pulled out a chair for me. I dried my tears and rose from the sofa, smiling my thanks for the courtly gesture. He brought a loaf of bread, a slab of butter, and several jars of homemade jam to the table. He carved us each a healthy slice and we settled in with the simple, delicious food and munched silently. I soon gave up on the adornments and ate my second hefty chunk without butter or jam. He carved slice after slice and watched while I devoured the bread like a starved sailor. I suppose that is what he imagined I was.

Soon I no longer felt light-headed. I wanted to start a conversation but could think of nothing I could say to this kind, plain man, who built his own house and baked his own bread. He probably made the jam, too. I couldn't talk about the news, since I had no idea what had happened in recent months and feared to show my total ignorance. I decided to ask him about himself; it seemed the only safe topic.

"What do you do?" I asked in a pause between bites.

"I'm a carpenter." He didn't elaborate.

"Do you build houses?" I prodded, hoping for a longer reply.

"No, furniture."

"Do you work for a company here in town?" There were several furniture manufacturers in our town, some of excellent quality.

"Just for myself."

Our conversation wasn't heating up very fast. Then Hank surprised me with a question of his own.

"You say you're a writer?"

"Yes, I am," I answered warily. My earlier resolve to be proud of my erotica had faded as the mainland approached.

"What do you write?"

"Adventures," I finessed. I saw a spark flare in his eyes—a spark of humor or disappointment, or perhaps both.

"Ah," he responded, nodding. "Well, shall we be going?"

He rose from the table and pulled back my chair for me. I raised my eyebrows at the unaccustomed courtesy. I thought chivalry had died with the women's movement. Apparently, Hank hadn't heard. I thanked him again for rescuing me, feeding me, and giving me a ride home.

"You don't need to thank me so much," he stated simply, a blush coloring his cheeks. "Next you'll be expecting me to thank you for thanking me."

I chuckled at the unexpected humor; while Hank didn't laugh, he at least smiled. I began to like this man. I gave him my address and he said he knew the area. He drove an old pickup, an impractical vehicle too big to park easily and the devil on gasoline. Still, it got me home without mishap. I began to cry again as we rounded the corner to my house. Poor Hank must have wondered what on earth was wrong with me.

"I've had a long few months," I explained, pulling a tissue from the box on the dash. "I'm okay. Really."

My car sat in the driveway, covered in leaves and dirt as though it hadn't moved in many months. I found my purse tucked under the front seat where I sometimes put it. The house key hid elusively in the bottom of my handbag, but it was there. Hank waited patiently beside me as I fumbled to find the key, then fumbled to place it in the keyhole. Finally he took the key from my hand and unlocked the door.

"Would you like to come in?" I offered halfheartedly. All I wanted was a bath and a clean bed.

"No thanks, Helen," Hank demurred. "You'll be wanting a hot bath and a clean bed, not company."

His words echoing my thoughts reminded me again of Bran, and I burst into fresh tears.

"I'm really not as crazy as this, Hank," I apologized, trying to smile. "Do I dare thank you again?"

"No need," he replied in his short way then turned and walked back to his truck. I waved as he drove away, then stepped into my dusty entryway. A mountain of mail was heaped beneath the slot; I stepped over it, resolving to sort it later. I went straight to the bathroom and filled the tub with plain hot water—no oil, no scent, just steaming clean water.

I lay in the tub till the water cooled, then turned on the shower to a hot spray. I use a water-saver shower-head, but even so I managed to use up every drop of hot water in the tank. I washed the sand and grit from my hair and scrubbed my skin with a washcloth until it glowed pink. Then I tumbled naked into bed.

When I woke up again, it was daylight, but I had no idea of the hour, or even the month and the day. The battery on my wall clock had run down and the hands hung limp at 6:30, without the energy to rise again. There must have been a power failure sometime in the months I was gone; the alarm clock and the stove clock pulsed 12:00. I had another hot shower, I couldn't seem to stay warm enough, and dressed in slacks and a favorite oversized acrylic sweater. Within a few minutes, I had to take both off again for they made my skin itch like a thousand ant bites. Maybe the months of wearing nothing but cotton had made my skin sensitive. I didn't like the constriction of a bra after months of freedom, so I took it off as well. I pulled on jeans and an old cotton sweatshirt and slipped Bran's talisman into the front jean pocket, letting the sweatshirt hang down to cover the bulge. I took the Chopin biography from the deep pocket of the brocade dress and placed it lovingly on the bedside table. I hung the dress in a garment bag in the closet. I would take it in to be dry-cleaned one day soon.

The house had no edible food. The items I had

bought the night Bran kidnapped me had disappeared, and the contents of the refrigerator stank. I checked my wallet and found about thirty dollars and change. Stepping back over the pile of mail, I headed out to my car and breakfast. The car wouldn't start. I didn't know whether to laugh or stomp my foot. I wondered whether Bran would have taken care of these details had he lived to see me home safely. I headed off to walk the mile or so to the nearest strip mall.

As I walked, the asphalt felt confining beneath my feet, the rows of neat houses seemed an imposition. I imagined the land as it had been before the town had taken over and felt for the first time the obscenity of our modern way of life. I chuckled ironically to myself, realizing that hippiedom had finally caught me up. I had watched from the sidelines in my teens and twenties; now I marched with the alternative band.

I looked at the doughnuts in a fast-food shop. In my earlier life, I had waged a constant battle against their seductive lure. Now I couldn't imagine myself eating one. Still, I was awfully hungry. A new little café had sprung up in my absence and by the time I reached it, hunger had overcome my new hippie caution. I ordered the simplest thing I could—eggs and potatoes—and was rewarded with a hearty, simple, and filling meal. I left the eatery half an hour later with my stomach filled and my hopes high.

As I walked along the street, reabsorbing the ambiance of my hometown, I cataloged my immediate concerns. I needed to get my car running; I would have to call a garage and have it towed in and tuned up. Did my phone still work? I doubted that Ma Bell had waited patiently through months of unpaid bills. At least the house still had electricity and gas. As I thought of those ubiquitous bills, I was struck by an anomaly: the rent. Had Bran paid the rent since September? If he hadn't, I would have been evicted long since. Maybe my phone would work after all.

By then I had reached my doorstep. Inside, the pile of mail rose accusingly before me, but I fought it back to a corner of my awareness and plunged through. The phone had a dial tone — miraculous! I hit the first button on the automatic dial. My daughter lifted the receiver before I heard a ring.

"Hello?"

"Danny?"

"Mom!" she screamed. "Oh, wow! Mom's back!"

The last words were shouted away from the phone. I heard my other daughter, Erica, running in the background.

"Mom?" Erica's deeper tones sounded through their extension phone.

"It's me." I tried not to cry.

"I told you she'd be back for my birthday!" Danny crowed.

Oh, dear. I had forgotten to find out the date on my morning ramble.

"Happy birthday, sweetheart," I said enthusiastically.

"It's not for another two days, Mom," Danny corrected me, laughing. "I guess they didn't teach you to be any less absentminded at that monastery."

At least now I knew the date: May 18. I had to get to the library, and fast, and sign out the past months' volumes of some news magazines.

"You've got to come over, Mom," Erica interrupted. "We want to hear everything."

"My car won't start. I guess it sat too long."

"We'll come over there," Erica offered.

"That's great!" Then my tears broke through, and I had to fight to continue. "I really missed you guys."

"We missed you too, Mom," Erica, my rock, answered. I could hear Danny sobbing on her end of the phone.

"Well, get on over here," I ordered, laughing.

"Okay, okay," Erica agreed. "Get off the phone, Danny."

"What if she isn't really there?" Danny wailed. "I can't hang up."

My long absence had created giant holes we would spend months refilling. The realization sank into my heart, and I knew I was really home.

"I'll be here, Danny," I promised, then tried to cheer her with a prosaic comment. "But you have to bring your own food. This place is empty."

"So what else is new?" Danny chuckled. It was a start.

The girls were there within minutes. I waited for them on the front steps. We hugged and kissed and cried for several minutes, then moved inside.

"Mom," Danny chided. "Look at that mail!"

She was always my practical child. She stooped to pick up the pieces on top, then gave up and left the room. Erica and I smiled and stepped over the heap, arm in arm. Danny returned in a few minutes with the laundry basket and loaded up the mound and brought it to the living room. The three of us sorted the mail into stacks, throwing most straight into the recycling bin. I was pleased to see the pile from my publisher grow to a respectable height. We slit open those envelopes first, and Erica totaled the checks with the calculator she carried in her purse.

"Mom, there's fifteen thousand dollars here," she said almost accusingly. "I thought we were poor."

"We were, Erica," I explained as I thought rapidly. Bran must have paid my bills and left my checks to accumulate. He'd left me a financial cushion as his parting gift. I patted the stone goddess in my pocket in thanks. Still, I needed an explanation for my children. I had never lied to them before and hated to begin now. Though I wasn't ready to tell them the whole truth, I resolved to tell each of them the truth in my own time. For now, I would keep my fiction as truthful as possible.

"I was at the monastery," I stumbled over the word, remembering some of Bran's and my activities. I swallowed and continued, "On an endowment. All my expenses were covered. I hadn't realized it, but the endowment must have paid the bills here as well, so my own money accumulated."

"Fifteen thousand dollars?" Erica asked.

"Mom must have spent at least that much in eight months when we lived here, Care," Danny responded, and the familiar nickname almost did me in. As I fought not to jump up and embarrass my children with another burst of emotion, Erica shrugged, accepting Danny's explanation.

"So now, we're not poor anymore," I commented as the realization sank in. "Do you girls need money?"

"Everybody always needs money," Danny laughed.

"But we're fine," Erica assured me. Danny nodded her agreement.

"You don't have to do the co-op program to pay your tuition, Danny," I offered. "I can help you out."

I had always tried to be fair to my children, spending about the same money—what little we had—on each. I remembered Erica's constant struggle to get through university without loans and felt guilty that I hadn't been able to assist her as I could now afford to help Danny.

"I'll give you the same amount I give Danny, Erica," I offered. "I know it's not the same—"

"Mom," Erica interrupted me, exasperated. "Aren't you listening?"

"We don't need your money," Danny repeated. "I like the co-op program."

"And I got two raises while you were gone," Erica added. "We're really fine."

"Congratulations, Care!" I couldn't resist one more hug. "That's wonderful!"

She smiled and hugged me back. "Keep your money, Mom. I'm sure you'll think of some way to spend it."

"So there you go," Danny added. "Enlightenment and a nest egg, all in one. What did you do at the monastery, anyway, besides get in shape and grow your hair? I like the gray."

Both girls looked at me expectantly. I tried to answer as honestly as I could.

"I had time to think about who I am and what I really want from the rest of my life."

Erica nodded and asked simply, "What do you want?"

"To write."

"But you already write, Mom," Danny protested. "What's the difference?"

"I wrote for money before, and I wasn't particularly proud of what I wrote." My thoughts organized as I spoke. "Now I want to write absolutely whatever I want to write; and whatever it is, I intend to claim it as my own and to hell with the rest of the world."

"I told you so." Danny exchanged a meaningful look with her sister. "I knew it."

"You were right," Erica conceded, shaking her head and laughing. "Mom, you've turned into a hippie."

Her words expressed my thoughts as I had walked that morning. I no longer felt in sync with my achiever generation. "You could be right, girls. Maybe I've lost it."

"No way!" they chimed in unison. Following a child-hood ritual, they each licked their right index finger. The two fingers pressed together, then sprang back with a sizzle.

"You've found it, Mom!" Danny jumped from her chair and pulled me out of mine. "Welcome to the nineties!"

"About time," Erica commented as she joined us in the center of the room. "Group hug!"

I have great kids.

sotto voce
Softly

It took me a week to get my life back on track. I got my car towed and tuned. I sent a card of thanks to Hank for rescuing me so kindly. I checked out the last twenty weeks of the biggest news magazine from the library and read diligently every night. I invested some of my nest egg in a new computer to replace the six-year-old relic I had struggled with for years. The hairdresser neatened up my hair, but I left it unpermed and gray. I took the brocade robe to the dry cleaner, who offered me three thousand dollars for it. I declined. I saw Danny and Erica almost every day.

I bought a load of healthy groceries, determined to continue eating as Bran and I had on the island. I even found the formula we had drunk in the local pharmacy as Bran had promised. I bought a box for nostalgia and cried all through the first glass. By the time I finished the box, my body felt energized. I resolved to fast with the liquid for a few days every month.

I even joined a health club. Though I still refused to do aerobics, I found I enjoyed the weights and the exercise bike, just as I had on the island. My only regret was that I couldn't swim; the water was too heavily chlorinated. Danny and Erica had both worked out for years and had tried to drag me along many times. They bought me an exercise outfit of cycling shorts and a giant T-shirt with a barbell across the breasts, an endorsement of my new regimen. The first time I wore it, I felt foolishly youthful. But no one else paid any attention to me, and I prized the clothes as a tangible symbol of Danny and Erica's support of my changed life.

I bought every CD I could find of Chopin's *Fantaisie-Impromptu* and played them over and over for hours. Though no modern pianist matched Bran's fluid submersion in his friend's flawless melodies, I found I liked Arthur Rubinstein's interpretation best. The discipline of his immense technique supported the cascading fountain of notes. Like Bran's playing, the Rubinstein recording shaded Chopin's strict manuscript with the subtleties of the interpreter's emotions and spirit. I recorded the Rubinstein *Fantaisie* over and over on a tape and played it each night as I fell asleep.

I remembered Bran day and night, night and day. I mourned his absence from my life, but I couldn't really grieve. Our months together had been the time they were meant to be. As new daily activities claimed my attention, he remained with me in memory. His wry comments on modern life colored my thoughts like filtered glasses.

I found I viewed many objects and events now as symbolic, or mythic. The story of a celebrity convicted of assaulting his wife reminded me of Branwen's sad tale. The old stories repeated again and again and again through my consciousness, and I recognized finally their importance to my writing. As I relaxed into the flow of history, my sense of my own role as a writer changed. Instead of searching for a plot, I allowed one to find me, and the stories that elbowed through my mind resonated with truth. Characters were no longer the creations of my imagination; they simply were who they were, and I recorded them. My sense of invention dwindled and my powers of observation poked through the cracks. Though my work had no obvious commercial value, I felt I was on the verge of discovery at every moment. Writing excited me almost to ecstasy.

With the unleashing of my captive creativity, my physical needs resurfaced as well. The two aspects to my being were linked. I felt driven to pour out my thoughts on paper and equally driven to share my physical existence with my lover. Bran had promised that I would meet the man I would love, though I might not recognize him. I searched the face of every man I met, wondering if he was the one. The car mechanic, the grocer, the mailman quailed before the intensity of my searching glances. I realized that my own need might keep away the very man I sought, just as it had during the week of his absence from my dreams on the island. I tried to relax my scrutiny—to allow fate to find me—but I wasn't altogether successful.

The phone rang one day as I sat at my computer. I had an answering machine on the line, and I didn't bother to pick up. Several minutes later, the phone rang again. Though I still didn't get up, the ringing interrupted my thoughts. The third time it rang, I jumped from the computer, ready to blast whoever was on the other end of the line. By the time I got to the phone, I heard only a dial tone. I slammed the receiver into the cradle and returned to my work, determined to ignore any further annoyances.

The lack of ringing disrupted me now, as silence stretched through the house like an accusing finger. Shaking my head at my lack of concentration, I went to retrieve the calls. Though the phone had rung three times, I had only one message.

"Hello, Helen." The deep voice spoke hesitantly. I recognized both the tone and the hesitation immediately. It was Hank. My anger dissolved into his placid fluidity. Guilt snatched at me for missing my rescuer's call, or at least so I named the nameless emotion that called to me from his disembodied voice.

"Just wanted to see how you were doing," he continued. "You can reach me at 583-2647, if you want to."

He paused for a moment, and I heard his breathing.

"No need to bother, though, if you're busy," the tape continued, then ended with a click.

I picked up the phone and dialed immediately. How could I have been too busy to talk to Hank?

"Hello," he answered, and I sighed to hear his voice.

"Hi, Hank. It's Helen."

"Oh, hello," he drawled. "I guess you were home, then. I thought somehow maybe you were."

"I'm sorry I didn't answer the phone," I apologized. "I was writing."

"Geez, Helen." Hank's apology made mine sound fake. "I didn't mean to interrupt your writing. You didn't need to call me back right away."

"It's okay, Hank," I assured him. "It's great to hear your voice."

I realized as I spoke the words that they were true. I had missed Hank, though I'd known him only for a few hours.

"And I rang three times," Hank continued to apologize. "I hate talking onto a tape."

"Really, it's okay," I laughed. "How are you?"

"I'm fine, Helen. I always am." Somehow I believed Hank's words; he was a man who would always be fine —not a stoical fine, but a genuine liking-his-fate fine.

"That's good, Hank. I'm fine too." My words sounded inane as soon as I spoke them. I laughed. "Still babbling, but fine."

"How's your writing?" Hank asked after a short pause.

"Really good." It felt as though I spoke with my oldest friend. "I feel like I'm getting into the flow, if you know what I mean."

"I find that with the wood sometimes," Hank replied. "You find the grain and work with it, and the piece comes out the way it was meant to."

"Exactly," I agreed. "Listen—"

"Helen—" Hank spoke at the same time. After a few seconds' argument over who should go first, Hank convinced me to speak.

"I'd like to take you out to dinner sometime," I offered. "It would be great to see you again, and I'd like to do something to thank you for rescuing me."

"Your card was more thanks than I needed. Helen. Why don't you let me make you dinner?"

"That sounds wonderful!" I remembered his home-made bread and jam. "When would you like me to come?"

"How about tonight?"

"I'm going to my daughters' apartment tonight," I explained, then hurried on, so he wouldn't think I was declining the invitation altogether. "What about tomorrow?"

"Terrific!" The enthusiasm in his voice injected me like a hypodermic. "Well, I'll let you get back to your writing. What time would you like me to pick you up?"

"You don't need to pick me up, Hank." Though he seemed the soul of safety, still I wanted my car available if I needed to get away.

"Right." He seemed to sense and accept my caution. "Why don't you come around seven?"

"That sounds great," I agreed. "Can I bring anything?"

"Just yourself," Hank chuckled and I heard an elusive echo under the sound that sent a shiver of anticipation through me.

We hung up and I returned to my computer. My mind felt sharp and clear; the thread that had eluded me spun thin and fine beneath my fingers. I found the tale that needed to be told and the voice that wished to speak it. I worked the rest of the day outlining the story as it came to me, working feverishly as if in a dream, the need to order the next many months of my labor overcoming even the need for food.

I finished at last and stumbled into the kitchen. It was 6:30 P.M., and I was already late for Danny and Erica's dinner. I phoned and apologized. Danny laughed and accepted, though Erica was less forgiving of my lapse. The girls were used to my concentration when writing, though my lack of coordination with the outside world annoyed them occasionally. I took a five-minute shower to wake myself up, and hurried over.

I arrived to the aroma of meatballs and spaghetti sauce. My Sicilian university dorm-mate had given me the recipe years before, and my children loved to make it. Erica opened a bottle of red wine, and we drank a toast to my return. We feasted on pasta shells and sauce, cheese and garlic bread until no one could eat another bite.

As we ate in relative silence, I thought about the novel I had plotted that day. For years, I had never discussed my books with my children, until one day an eighteen-year-old Erica told me she had read my latest manuscript and thought it was pretty good. When I got over the shock of my daughter's reading erotica, I found her approval heartening. Thereafter, we discussed the ins and outs of my plots. At first Danny feigned disinterest, but two years ago, she, too, had begun to read my manuscripts and point out flaws in my reasoning.

After dinner, as we sat over coffee, I told Danny and Erica about the breakthrough in my writing, that my next story had found me. When they asked for details, I found I couldn't tell them. Neither girl understood my reluctance, for I had eagerly shared my other books as they emerged. This one felt too close to me, too fragile. I worried that it wouldn't withstand scrutiny, might crumple in upon itself if examined. The book felt fluid still, like a real life waiting to be born, and I couldn't circumscribe its existence with the rigidity of speech. Rather than face their continued questions, I changed the subject.

"I have a date tomorrow night," I dropped into a stunned silence.

"You have a date?" Danny asked. I might have said I'd seen a cat with three heads. "Not Dr.—"

"No!" I interrupted. The girls had despised my last lover, the English professor. They also knew that I'd sworn off men.

"Sort of a date," I amended.

"What do you mean, sort of?" Erica asked cautiously.

"He's making me dinner. It's pretty informal."

"Mom's got a daa-aate," Danny sang happily.

"You don't need to sound so surprised," I argued, pretending to be affronted. "You girls go on dates."

"But that's different!" Danny continued to tease me. "You're a Mom."

I thought back to my adventures on the island: Bran's whippings and my eventual acknowledgment of my own arousal, the Celtic gods and their different but equally inflaming stimulation. I hadn't felt like a Mom then; I had felt like myself. I still had a distance to go, to merge those two aspects of myself into a working whole.

"Life doesn't stop when you have children," I reminded my offspring, hoping they would do a better job than I had of maintaining their own selves in the midst of parenthood.

"So, tell us about him," Erica urged.

"I don't know much," I admitted. "He's a carpenter, and he lives by the ocean."

"That sounds good," Danny stated. "You love the ocean."

"Don't marry us off," I cautioned, laughing. I thought of my exciting phantom lover and continued, "Hank isn't my dream man."

"Where did you meet him?" Erica asked, a hint of concern and caution in her voice.

"On the beach," I answered truthfully enough.

"So how do you know he's safe?" she continued.

"He seems very kind and honest, Erica." I understood her concern, for I had felt it many times myself. "I'm taking my own car, so I won't be trapped if anything goes wrong."

"Give me his name and address and phone number," my stern eldest demanded.

"Erica!" Danny protested. "You sound just like Mom."

"She's right, Danny," I interceded. "I can't remember his last name, and I know what the house looks like, but I don't know the number. I have the phone number at home."

"Would you let me go out with a guy I knew so little

about, Mom?" Erica's look told me the answer she expected.

"Probably not," I conceded. "But I'm forty-three years old, and—"

Danny interrupted me, infected with her sister's sternness. "As soon as you get to his house tomorrow night, we want you to phone and tell us his full name and address. Right, Erica?"

The two girls nodded and I agreed to their cautious measures, glad I had such loving protectors. I turned the subject then from myself to their concerns. Danny told me how her courses went; she had a strange professor of history, but the rest galloped along smoothly enough. Erica described her new job. She'd majored in journalism and had despaired of finding a real news job. A year before, she'd accepted a position as a gofer at the local press. She'd submitted unsolicited articles doggedly for a year and had been rewarded two weeks ago with a byline.

As I drove home, I thought about what I'd missed of my daughters' lives in the last eight months. I thought about how each of us had changed, and I thought about my writing. I had no idea whether my next novel would even be publishable, let alone great. The difference was that I didn't care; I would write it anyway.

When I got home that night, there was a message from Hank on the answering machine.

"I know you're at your daughters' for dinner. I just called to say good night, and I'm looking forward to seeing you tomorrow."

What a nice man.

rallentando
Slowly

I awoke the next morning, aching for Bran's touch on my shoulder. I wanted him to rouse me, and arouse me. I wanted to be whipped in the worst way—take that as you wish. My children's teasing had reminded me all too vividly how long it had been since I'd had a date. Since the professor, the rituals of courtship had seemed too much bother for the limited gains of occasional companionship and even more occasional intercourse. But the constant sexual stimulation of the last months had aroused my appetites to near-insatiability; the thought that tonight I would be having dinner with a very nice man drove me past endurance.

I decided to try to whip myself. I found a leather belt in the back of my closet. It was a long way from a whip, but it was roughly the right length and shape. No one could hear me in my solitary little house, so at least I would be spared that embarrassment. As I stripped myself naked, I imagined I was being forced to remove each piece as a masterly someone dangled a whip scarily before my eyes. Only the whipper didn't know that I really wanted—more than wanted—the lashing. My pretended hesitation aroused me, and I grew moist as I forced myself to walk naked through each room of my house. Because of the blooming shrubbery, no one could see inside, but still I felt exposed as I passed the undraped openings, and I loved it.

I walked at last into the bathroom and ran hot water and rosemary oil into the tub. Afterward, the whipper would force me into the water. I posed myself against the bathroom counter and paused for a moment to heighten the suspense, then flicked the leather belt across my bottom. Nothing. I hardly felt it, and the location wasn't right anyway. I tried to find a better position for my arm, higher, no lower, no… Nothing worked. I wondered how the ancient martyrs had managed to scourge themselves, because I certainly couldn't do it.

What a bust! My body felt tuned to concert pitch. My nipples throbbed, my vagina throbbed, I throbbed all over, but nothing was happening. I couldn't get any further without masturbating, and I wanted to save that for dessert. I wished then that I owned a dildo. For all my years of writing erotica, I had never bought one. I decided to improvise. I picked up a bottle of shampoo with a knobbed top, and dumped the last dregs of soap down the sink. I rinsed it carefully so no detergent would sting my tender skin. I swirled the knob, bottle attached, in a jar of petroleum jelly. My vagina oozed hot and wet in anticipation.

By then the bathtub was full, so I turned off the water. I lifted my leg onto the edge of the tub, pretending reluctance again. The steam from the waiting bath frothed around me. I tensed in nervous expectation as the hand with the shampoo bottle approached my lower door. I thrust the knob inside me with a swift, smooth motion. It felt like heaven against my tender inner labia, and I rubbed it in and almost out, over and over. My womb tightened, then relaxed again. The stimulation wasn't enough; the knob wasn't very big, and my vagina wanted larger and rougher pleasures.

I gave up. I threw the plastic bottle against the far wall of the bathroom, venting a smidgen of my frustration. I sank into the tub and eased my little finger over my aching clitoris. My finger couldn't press very hard and its gentle ministrations roused me to still greater tension and desire. At last I allowed my strongest, index finger to rub hard against my clitoris and bring me to climax. The waves in my body sent shocks through the bathwater, which sloshed onto the floor with my motion. I kept rubbing, hoping for an elusive second and stronger orgasm. I had never been very successful stimulating myself beyond the first release, and I didn't succeed any better now. Mildly satisfied, I climbed out of the tub and dried myself and the floor.

By the time I arrived at Hank's house promptly at 7:00, I had subdued my needs to a dull roaring. I didn't want to embarrass the shy man by pouncing on him as I walked in the door. He had never even touched me, except to help me into and out of his rowboat. He probably wasn't attracted to me, and I wasn't sure whether I was attracted to him or just desperate. Best let the evening proceed as it would.

Hank may have sensed a difference in my awareness of him, for he seemed changed himself. He was more self-assured than I remembered. When he helped me from my light wrap, his hands lingered at my shoulders for a second longer than necessary—not long enough to make me uncomfortable if I wasn't interested in him, but long enough to catch my attention if I was. The gesture was nicely done.

He looked good that night. His wavy blond hair had been recently cut and painstakingly combed into submission. He must have shaved shortly before I arrived, for his face looked silky smooth. He wore a dark cotton sweater with a plaid cotton shirt underneath. The brown brought out the warmth of his eyes, which I noticed were hazel. He was neither tall nor short, but definitely solid. He might have appeared overweight from a distance, but up close he was reassuringly muscular. His slacks molded slightly to large thighs and I wondered what he looked like walking away. Probably damn good.

I had bought a new raw silk dress for the occasion; silk was the only dressy fabric that didn't irritate my skin. The dress was a size ten, the smallest I'd bought in years. I had mentally thanked Bran from the fitting room. The cut was daring, in a middle-aged sort of way: sleeveless, with a scooped neck and large covered buttons down the front. I think Hank approved. Suddenly shy, I lowered my eyes from the warmth in his and walked briskly into the main room.

"Your house is even more comfortable than I remembered," I commented brightly.

"Thanks." Though my back was turned to Hank, I could hear the smile in his voice. He seemed to absorb my nerves into his large frame, and they couldn't escape out to reinfect me. I relaxed.

"I told my daughters I would phone them when I arrived," I explained. "I hope you don't mind."

"That's sweet," Hank commented.

"Do you think you could just say hello to them?" I asked apologetically. "They worry."

"I think that's great," Hank's hearty approval removed the last of my embarrassment. "The phone's right there."

Hank pointed toward a corner of the kitchen counter. When I dialed, he moved a few feet away to give me privacy.

"Erica?" I asked. "Put Danny on, too. Hank said he would say hello to you."

Erica snorted and I laughed into the mouthpiece. "Now, be nice."

I handed the receiver to Hank.

"Hello," his low voice murmured. I noticed then that his tone changed when he got on the telephone, deepening from a baritone to a bass. I could only imagine the other end of the conversation from his expression, which wasn't very expressive.

"Henry James." Someone had asked his name.

James, James, James. I committed the name to memory. Now they had asked his address.

"267 Bayview Crescent."

Hank smiled at me and shrugged.

"You'll have to ask your mother that," he said next. I couldn't imagine what the question had been and reached to take the phone from him to ask Erica and Danny what on earth they were saying.

" 'Bye," Hank preempted me and replaced the receiver on the cradle.

"What did they ask you?"

"You'll have to ask your daughters that," Hank replied maddeningly. "Would you like a glass of wine?"

"I'd love one." Maybe it would cool my curiosity. He poured us both a large glass and we moved to sit by the fire. The only sittable furnishings were an overstuffed sofa and a rocker. I sat on the sofa, wondering a bit nervously whether he would sit beside me. When he settled on the rocker, I felt a mixture of relief and disappointment. I took a sip of wine to cover my lack of ease.

"This is delicious!" I knew I sounded surprised, which was hardly a compliment, but the wine was really superb. "I bet you made it."

Hank smiled a lazy acknowledgment and lifted his glass toward me.

"Here's to a pleasant dinner, Helen."

I drank the simple toast and proposed my own.

"And friendship. Is it too early to drink to that?"

"Not at all," Hank assured me and leaned forward to click his glass against mine. We both drank deep.

274

"You said you make furniture," I broke the comfortable silence. Hank nodded. "How do you market it?"

"Well," he drawled, clearly reluctant. "I sell some of my designs to Halliwell's."

I raised my eyebrows, impressed. Halliwell's was the top-of-the-line furniture maker in town. I looked more closely at the rocker Hank sat in and recognized the curves.

"That's a James rocker!" I exclaimed. "I read an article about you in *The New Yorker.* They just put your rocker in the Smithsonian. They didn't say you lived here."

Hank shrugged his shoulders sheepishly. I had a hard time reconciling the quiet man in front of me with the renowned designer.

"You have a degree from the Harvard School of Design," I accused.

"Sorry," Hank apologized and we both laughed. I struggled to adjust my grossly mistaken first impressions. Clearly uncomfortable, Hank shifted the focus back to me.

"Tell me about your next book, Chantal."

As he intended, I was diverted by his use of my pseudonym, then remembered that I had blurted it out on the black sand beach. Still, I wasn't sure how to respond to his question. The passage of a day hadn't made me any more comfortable talking about my newly conceived novel. I gazed worried into Hank's kind eyes and decided to tell him the truth.

"I can't really talk about it yet," I apologized. "My daughters wanted to know what it was about last night, and I couldn't tell them either. I feel like I have to keep it inside me, hidden away until it appears on the page, or it will come out distorted."

"It's called privacy, Helen," Hank explained. "I'm sorry I intruded."

"That's okay." I smiled, pleased that he understood so easily. His openness made me want to reciprocate. "You asked me before about my books in general, and I wasn't very forthcoming. I don't mind talking about my work now, if you want to."

"I'd love to hear."

"I write erotica," I stated boldly, and waited, cringing inside, for his response.

"I know." Hank's answer was not what I expected. "I read one of your books once."

"And were never tempted to buy another, I bet," I added wryly.

"Not until last week," he admitted honestly. "I bought them all."

"Oh, dear," I joked. "They aren't very good. I'm afraid you wasted your money."

"Well," Hank spoke slowly, and I could see the impulse for honesty warring with the impulse to be kind. Honesty won, though he did manage to be gentle.

"They are"—he struggled for a word—"mechanical. The sentences are real smooth, but I didn't get a big emotional wallop from the stories."

"I like your words," I agreed earnestly. " 'A big emotional wallop.' That's what I want from the next book, a big emotional wallop."

"If you want it, you'll get it," Hank stated. His assurance

was a tonic to my still-doubting soul, and I basked in the glow.

"How did you get the books so fast?" Two of my novels were out of print.

"I called your publisher, and he sent them by courier. One's a photocopy, but they found the rest in their warehouses."

I thought over his answer for a few minutes. He must have felt some stronger attraction than I did when he rescued me, to have gone to so much trouble and expense. I felt a little intimidated by the assurance and skill with which he pursued me—at least, the writer me. I took another sip of wine, and its warmth chased down my throat and into my stomach. I took another sip. It was exciting to be pursued, I decided. Especially by a man like Hank.

"I think dinner is about ready," Hank broke into my reverie.

We stood and moved to the dining table, which he had cleared of debris. A brace of candles stood in the center with a bouquet of wildflowers in a simple glass vase. Hank lit the candles, then seated me at the end of the table. I was glad to see that his place was set just around the corner from mine and not at the opposite end. First he brought a bowl of steaming soup and placed it before me. It smelled delicious.

"What kind is it?" I was eager to taste it.

"Leek. You'll like it. I made it myself."

I smiled at his self-confidence and dipped my spoon into the thick velvety green liquid.

"You're wrong, Hank," I teased him and was rewarded with a small frown. "I don't like your soup, I love it! This is delicious."

I don't think many people teased Hank—at least, not in recent years. He seemed not to know exactly how to take my comment. He settled at last on a self-conscious smile and I resolved to pull his leg more often. We enjoyed every spoonful of the soup in silence, and then I asked for more.

"Not tonight," Hank's refusal surprised me. "I have a container put aside for you to take home with you."

"You don't need—" I began to protest, then thought better of my words. The soup was really good. "Thanks."

Hank took the bowls to the sink and brought back a large metal pot.

"Rabbit," he announced proudly.

"Rabbit?" I asked skeptically. I had never eaten rabbit before.

"You'll like it," Hank repeated himself, smiling at his own little joke and I smiled, too.

He was right again. The rabbit was even more delicious than the soup. Hank had cooked it with the same dry red wine we drank and a mixture of herbs and spices and prunes. The rabbit tasted both finer and richer than chicken, and I was amazed to find prunes could taste so good. He plucked a bay leaf from his plate and licked it before placing it on the bone platter in the middle of the table.

"Would you like one?" he offered. I thought, Why not? and nodded.

"Be careful not to bite into it," he cautioned as he handed me the large leaf. I sucked the gravy from the rough surface, and my body was flooded with a rush of desire so hot it made me blink. Hank pulled the leaf from my unresisting fingers and placed it in the candle flame.

"Smell," he whispered and held the smoldering scent to my nose. The gesture seemed impossibly sensuous, and the aroma of burning bay aroused me to the point of faintness. I couldn't tell whether Hank was unaware of the effect the leaf had on me, or if he knew only too well and only pretended innocence to heighten my desire by prolonging the suspense. I would have followed—make that dragged—him to the bed that instant had he given me any hint of his own arousal.

Instead he returned to eating his rabbit, my only clue a small-but-persistent smile that wouldn't leave the corner of his mouth. I longed to tease that little smile with my tongue, until he felt as desperately aroused as I did. The hidden desire became a game; I determined to seem as casual as he did and to drive him as crazy as he was driving me. I placed a little bone of the rabbit tenderly in my mouth, drawing it in and out, until I had sucked every morsel of flesh and gravy from it. I fixed my eyes on Hank's and was rewarded when his strayed again and again to my eager lips.

"Time for dessert." After several minutes of my sucking rabbit bones and Hank pretending not to notice, his voice sounded a bit drier. Good.

"Great!" I smiled. The game both cooled and fanned

the fire in me. The fun calmed my most immediate need, and the tension stoked the deeper ache. I placed my hand casually by my place mat, where Hank's fingers could brush it as he placed the dessert plate in front of me, if he wished. His knuckles grazed mine and added another glowing ember to the fire. This was a really good game, and he was an expert player.

When I came back to a sense of the room, Hank sat opposite me, his mild eyes belying his inner pleasure. I knew he knew what was going on; he had lit the kindling with the bay leaf.

"Do you like your pie?" he asked me a moment later. I had taken a bite without registering even what kind it was and had no idea how to reply.

"It's delicious!" I resolved to taste the next bite. The mouthful proved me truthful; the pie was delicious. I tasted apple, but couldn't sort out the other flavors. "What's in it?"

"Apples from the yard." I nodded that I had guessed as much. "And passionberries."

I choked. Score one for Hank. I had never heard of passionberries, but I doubted he had made them up. If that was what he said was in the pie, then that was what I ate.

"It's really good," I managed to squeeze out around the lump in my throat. We ate the pie in meaningful silence. I was thinking about the night ahead, and I would have bet any amount of money that Hank was, too.

il canto marcato
He Sings

I ate the pie slowly, savoring the hot spicy sweetness in my mouth and prolonging the suspense. I was powerfully attracted to Hank. I had hoped to meet the man of my dreams right away, and I wasn't at all sure Hank was that man. Still he was a wonderful human being and the chemistry between us was electrifying. But I had always had a love/hate thing with first times—the suspense was incredibly arousing, the outcome often disappointing.

Hank sat watching me, amused as I dawdled over the last bites of my pie. He had finished several minutes earlier. My game of arousal over the rabbit bones seemed embarrassing in hindsight. Now that the real event approached, every anxiety resurfaced. This time Hank, the patient chef, did nothing to calm my nervousness, but left me to stew. Finally he took pity and spoke.

"Would you like to walk along the beach with our coffee?"

I jumped at the invitation. Hank helped me into my jacket. Again his hands lingered on my shoulders that extra second. His touch calmed me instantly, and reawakened my desire. Clutching hot mugs, we walked down the short stretch of grass toward the black water. The Pacific lived up to its name that night, the water so still we could almost see our reflections. We walked down the pier to the end and stood sipping in silence as the smallest of waves lapped gently against the pylons. After a few minutes, I felt chilly and instinctively moved closer to Hank's side. He put his arm around my shoulder. His solid warmth was as comfortable as an old afghan.

When Hank set his mug on the railing, he pulled me close so that my body followed the movement of his. Then he shifted me in his embrace and held me with both arms. I lifted my head for his kiss, wondering whether his lips would be soft or rough, whether he would touch my lips gently or demand the sweet release of immediate passion. He looked deep into my eyes and perhaps read the lingering questions there, for he turned my head sideways into his chest with his hand and stroked my hair as he held me in a warm embrace.

"Nothing is written in stone, Helen," he murmured in my ear. "We don't need to do anything you aren't ready for."

"My body is ready, Hank." I turned my face to look up into his and smiled ruefully. "Boy, is it ready."

"But your mind isn't sure?" he asked.

I shook my head, then changed my mind. I might never be sure as long as I dangled the hope of meeting my one true lover like a carrot before my eyes. Hank was a warm and solid reality in my arms, not a man to be banished for desire of a phantom. I pulled my arms from beneath his and reach up to cup his face. A hand on each cheek, I pulled his mouth down to meet mine.

"Hank's lips," I breathed into his mouth, "meet Helen's lips."

I pressed my mouth softly against his and the touch awakened every dream, every ember, every fountain of moisture inside me. His lips were both soft and rough, gentle and insistent in perfect balance. Mine parted eagerly, inviting his tongue to explore my first hot moist cavity. Our two organs tangled playfully in greeting, then settled into a soothing, seeking rhythm. My hands moved from his cheeks to the back of his head and twined in his springy curls as the kiss deepened. Hank groaned deep in his throat and pressed me back into the railing and I felt the pulsing of his erection against my abdomen. I pressed against him, my empty womb aching to be filled by the so-near hardness, and he ground his hips into mine until the pressure brought me almost to orgasm.

"Can we go back inside?" I gasped, pulling my lips from his.

"Unbutton your dress," he ordered, brushing aside my request. He meant to have me here, as we stood against the railing of the pier, surrounded by the ocean.

I had never made love out of doors, and the vulnerability of our situation made me pause in fear. Hank parted my jacket, then reached his hands down and began to unbutton my dress from the bottom up. I stood caressing his hair, neither helping nor hindering his work. When he reached my waist, he stopped unbuttoning and moved his hand to grasp the top of my panties and pantyhose. He pulled down, and I wriggled to ease the tight fabric past my hips. He abandoned my left leg at knee height and lifted my right to free it completely. The chill ocean breeze skimmed the bare skin of my exposed thigh.

He moved his hands to his zipper, but I brushed his fingers aside and slid the metal pins slowly apart. I reached inside and pulled out his organ and massaged its substantial length and girth. He sighed beneath my hand and pulled a condom from his pocket.

"Were you a Boy Scout?" I asked in a shaky whisper. He shook his head and I took the condom and peeled off the wrapper. I held it up to the light of the moon to determine which way it unwound, mildly annoyed by the interruption, but thankful for Hank's caution. Thank goodness one of us still had a brain. I rolled the thin latex down the length of his penis, smoothing and stroking as I worked. The movement further aroused us both, and Hank tucked a probing finger into the moisture of my vagina. His finger roused my womb to frenzy and I couldn't wait any longer to feel him inside me. I lifted my right leg and he grasped the knee and held it firm in his hand. He slid his finger from my cunt and I guided his penis toward me. He bent his knees slightly to adjust our heights, then lifted upward as he entered me.

His penis slid inside my empty dripping cave and filled it with light and warmth and pressure. I recognized that pressure with an awestruck delight and burst into ecstatic tears. He pulled back, and I hurried to reassure him.

"It's all right, Hank," I sobbed and held his hips into mine. "It's all right."

When he kissed me, I abandoned myself wholly into his embrace. All fear, all hesitation fled, and I ground my hips against his and drove my tongue frantically into his hot mouth and clutched at his organ with the powerful muscles of my own. As I strove to caress his penis inside me, my own efforts pushed me up and over the first peak of orgasm. The involuntary spasms sped through me, tighter than I could achieve by will, and Hank moaned deep in his throat beneath my kiss.

"Come!" I tore my mouth from his to whisper urgently. "Come now. I'm ready."

"Not yet," he panted. He lifted my knee higher and his penis hammered farther inside me, again and again, until I screamed my release a second time. As my body relaxed, he shifted me hard against the railing and held it tight in his hand, and thrust into me and withdrew, and thrust and withdrew. I was caught between the hard wooden railing and his insistent organ. The restraint loosed the last remnants of my control and I came over and over in deep inexorable pounding waves. I fell through the no-longer-there railing and into the boiling ocean and beneath the waves, and we became part of the sea, my demanding lover and I.

My absorption was so complete, I knew Hank had climaxed only by the eventual slackening of his organ inside me. He withdrew and we groaned in unison, then laughed together weakly.

"Hank," I began, trying to find words.

"Shh!" Hank quieted me and pulled me to rest against his chest. He rocked me gently as we stood, and I absorbed the tranquillity of the sea and of my real and phantom lover like a balm into my soul.

"I love you, Helen," Hank's words were an inevitable benediction. I fought neither their sense nor their timing.

"I love you too, Hank," I whispered back, knowing it was true. We stood thus beneath the rising moon, two boats finally at rest in their own harbor. Then Hank bent and picked up my right shoe and placed it in my hand. He lifted me into his arms without visible effort and I felt supported as I hadn't since early childhood. He carried me back to the house in silence, the other shoe and pantyhose and panties dangling from my bobbing left leg.

"My sweet witch," he murmured in my ear as we crossed the threshold. He placed me on the sofa and I relaxed into the cushions with a contented flop. Hank disappeared into the back of the house and reappeared in a moment with an armload of fluffy blankets and comforters. He laid them out in a thick cushion before the fireplace, then built up the fire to a crackling heap of flaming logs. The setting complete, he sat in the rocking chair and gazed contentedly at my totally relaxed posture.

"Don't tell me you've had enough already, Helen," he teased me.

"I'm insatiable," I tossed back at him, the hot wetness returning to my vagina to confirm my words. "What about you?"

"Men take longer to recover, my dear," he reminded me and I felt contrite. He had satisfied me beyond human expectation only moments earlier, and I didn't want to pressure him. His next words banished my doubts. "Why don't you strip for me? Maybe that will do it."

Ha! He was still as eager as I was. I stood and flicked my shoe in his direction with my foot. Then I rolled the last section of pantyhose and panties down my left calf and flicked them, too. As I walked toward him, I swayed my hips so that the front of my dress, still unbuttoned to the waist, flapped open. When I stood in front of him, I reached down and unzipped his pants. I grasped his bulging organ and squeezed hard, once, twice, three times, then let go and stood again.

"You don't need a strip show, Hank," I drawled. "You're as horny and hard as a bull already."

"But I like it," he argued simply, so I obliged. I had never stripped for a man before and had only watched strippers in brief flashes on television. Had I thought of what I looked like, I would have felt foolish; but the hot approval in Hank's eyes banished all self-consciousness. I had almost nothing left to remove—only the dress—so I made the most of each button. I unhooked the top fastening slowly and flapped the fabric back and forth. The second button offered more scope, for when I slid the fabric, it revealed a glimpse of aching rigid nipple. Only one button remained and I glanced mock-shyly at Hank from beneath my eyelashes. He grinned like a lovesick monkey. I slid the casing from around the button and flipped the fabric open once, then clutched the ends together tightly and turned my back. I let the dress slide down my body and stood naked, but still facing away.

"Turn around!" he commanded and the hint of authority and sternness in his voice thrilled me.

"Or what?" I egged him on.

"Or I'll whip you."

I almost fainted.

I hadn't begun to think how I would explain my love of whipping to Hank. As my phantom lover, he had stroked me in daydreams, and in his unsteady strokes I'd felt the virginity of his effort. I'd never paused to wonder whether he, too, had been aroused by the experience. Now that I'd met Hank in reality, the action seemed foreign to his gentle nature. I had much yet to learn.

"Go to the hutch and open the top left drawer." His command interrupted my thoughts. I walked past the dining table, careful always to keep my back to him, and opened the drawer. Inside was a shiny black case. I lifted it out and placed it on the table. Hank's presence at my back startled me. He whispered in my ear.

"Open it."

I pretended to hesitate; Hank waited me out. My curiosity was no match for his patience, and I lifted the lid. Inside lay a shiny new black whip. Each tip had been carefully flame-hardened.

"Lean over and hold onto the back of the chair."

I obeyed him, all nervous expectation, and hot juice flowed into and through my vagina like a tap. I stood waiting, and waiting, until the anticipation was a thin metal taste in my mouth.

"I can't reach you from this angle," Hank's laughing comment broke the spell. I fought not to laugh with him—to preserve what was left of the mood—and walked slowly to pose, ass poked provokingly outward, behind another chair that offered him more space. His first stroke landed before I had recovered from the surprise of the interruption and sent me farther along the path to climax for my unpreparedness. Hank had been practicing. His strokes landed with a steady rhythm that drove my already-aroused body to an endorphin-assisted orgasm within brief minutes. I thought he would stop then, for I screamed out my release and pleasure, but the next stroke landed before the echo of my scream died.

I settled into the rhythm of the whipping, the white heat of the lash falling with even regularity. I began to pant as I built toward a higher peak. Suddenly the strokes broke their rhythm, and I groaned in frustration. A harder lash choked off my groan and brought me back to the edge. Then a pause, and I slid backward until the next stroke sent me back up toward the peak. Stop and start, up and down, Hank rode my frustration like an unbroken pony. I panted and moaned and finally screamed for release. He stroked me three times, hard, without a pause for even a breath and I came in a crashing symphony of climactic orgasm. Still the strokes continued, gently now and in rhythm with my spasms, until the last quaver was wrung from my satiated womb.

I collapsed against the back of the chair, exhausted. I dimly heard Hank breathing hard by my side. I turned my head to see his grin as he stood panting, the whip dangling from his fingertips.

"You're incredible!" I gasped. He shook his head.

"You're the one who's incredible, Helen."

"So we're both incredible," I agreed with a shaky laugh.

"Come lie down," he offered. We walked side by side to the mound of cushions and I lay gratefully on the soft heap, while Hank threw another log on the fire then stripped off his clothes. His performance was low key but no less arousing than mine had been. I grew excited again watching him.

"You're ready now," I commented, reverting to our earlier conversation. His erection stood sturdy and hard, nestled into the curly black hair of his groin.

"Nothing like a good strip show to get a guy aroused," he teased.

"My strip show was a feeble prelude to your whipping, Hank," I protested.

"Nothing you do is ever feeble, my dear," he complimented, then lay down beside me. We lay on our sides in silence, not touching, absorbing each other's bodies with our eyes. When Hank ran his hand along the length of my side from shoulder to knee, his fingers felt as silky as an extension of his gaze. His hand caressed my skin like that of a blind man, learning as it skimmed. He rolled me onto my back and explored me as thoroughly as Columbus ever explored our eastern coast— even more, for he left no smallest hill or hollow untouched. Each inch of my skin came alive beneath his fingers and I closed my eyes in blissful relaxation.

When his hand lifted my leg and placed it bent and raised alongside me, my labia burbled an eager welcome. A single finger lightly flicked my swollen clitoris, and I gasped as the shock swam upstream through my body. My nipples hardened to pebbles of desire and my lips parted in invitation. His mouth settled its hot wetness against the hot dryness of my right nipple. As his tongue pulled the essence from the marrow of my breast, his finger descended again across my clitoris and flicked it into aching alertness. The dual stimulation continued until I heaved and moaned beneath his touch. His mouth shifted from breast to breast, and his finger from clitoris to vaginal door, each with maddening irregularity and more than compensating dexterity. I rose again and again almost to the peak of desire, but each time he sensed my ultimate arousal and pulled me back.

At last I could wait no longer and pleaded for him to enter me. He rose and I begged him not to leave; then he returned with a box of condoms. I was in no condition to put the safe on this time, so he unrolled it down his penis himself in one smooth motion. Then he turned me onto my back and pulled up my hips to a squat. I moaned in fear and excitement as he rubbed his penis up and down the crack in my rear, pushing hard against the yielding skin. He entered me with a swift thrust, not into my anus but in my vagina, filling it with his rockhard red-hot shaft. The different position put new pressure in unexpected directions, and I groaned in delight. He rode me swiftly and I came within seconds, then again, and again—and then I felt him grow to the final hardness. His explosion matched mine as we pounded together toward home.

When he swiftly withdrew, I cried in alarm for I wanted to hold his warmth inside me. I heard a sizzle and smelled the faint odor of burning latex as the safe melted on the fire. The ripping of another condom wrapper confirmed my suspicion that our intercourse was not yet over. Hank held me firmly with my ass in the air and began to push his penis gently, slowly, calmly, but insistently against my back door. I groaned, half in protest, half in exhaustion, half in anticipation of mixed pain and arousal. Still he pressed, and I could feel that his penis had deflated slightly in the aftermath of climax, and I understood his intention.

I relaxed the muscles of my anus, panting hard. One ungentle thrust of his penis pushed the condom-greased shaft through my portal and wrenched a moan from my throat. He showed me no pity and held my hips in a vise as he pressed inside in one long, smooth stroke. We rested together then, both breathing heavily, but only for a moment. He soon began to stroke his swelling penis up and down inside me, and the pressure filled my backside and womb and pressed against my stomach. He was already larger than the Oriental man had been at climax, and still his penis grew with each stroke. I moaned softly in protest and he laid his chest weightless along my back and wrapped one long arm around my hips to hold me steady.

His other hand found my hungry vagina. He placed two fingers inside, and pressed and wriggled against the other massive hardness at my rear. The dual pressure sent me on a solo journey beyond the horizon. I came in an orgasm so strong I would have collapsed had Hank not held me firm. When his fingers found my clitoris, I lost all reason and sense and I could no longer describe what I felt. I left reality and drifted again in the realm of fantasy with my phantom lover. We traveled to the moon and stars and down into the bowels of the earth. I was both full and empty, filled with satisfaction, emptied of care.

Our mutual and final scream of release returned me to a vague sense of the room and my companion. I felt him withdraw and felt the emptiness of my vacant cavity with an aching, swiftly passing echo of hunger. We collapsed to one side, his fingers still inside me, savoring the lingering pulses that lapped the walls of my vagina. We panted in unison. Slowly our breath calmed, and we fell asleep.

piannississimo
Very, Very Softly

I awoke in the early morning with Hank's arm covering me. He shifted with my awakening and I gently pushed his arm from around my shoulders and rolled to look at him. He lay like a sleeping giant, as solid as the oak trees he relied on for his craft. His hair waved unkempt about his face like a halo, though—thank goodness—he was no angel. He looked unbelievably dear and handsome to me that morning. I couldn't believe I had ever thought him plain. He opened one hazel eye beneath my gaze

"Good morning," he muttered sleepily and closed his eye again.

"Good morning," I chirped back and kissed his nose and both eyes, then his chin and each cheek. As I reached for his one exposed ear, both eyes opened and he smiled.

"That's the nicest wake-up I've ever had," he commented. "Can I keep you instead of an alarm clock?"

"Forever, Hank," I answered seriously and blushed for fear I overstepped the bounds of our one-night-old relationship.

"Sounds good to me," Hank reassured me and reached up to kiss me chastely on the lips. "Are you as hungry as I am?"

I was, and we got up. Hank brought me a huge T-shirt and dressed himself in undershirt and boxers. Thus largely unclad, we rekindled the fire and made breakfast, working in unison by unspoken agreement. He carried the logs and I lit the match to the kindling; he found the bowl and I broke the eggs; he sliced the bread and I buttered; he measured the coffee and I flipped the switch. We carried our food to the table, set our chairs inches apart, and ate elbow bumping elbow.

"Do you think this stage will last long?" I asked, laughing as my elbow cracked his for the third time.

"I doubt it, but it's fun for now. One day soon you'll be off writing and I won't see you for hours on end."

He sounded playfully wry, but his words were true. Writing was a solitary occupation.

"I'll always come back," I promised.

"You have to," Hank stated flatly, the old plain honesty back in his voice. His next words were uttered in the same flat style, and their irony led me to wonder if his speech had ever been as simple as I had thought. "You're addicted to me."

"Oh, I am, am I?" I rose to his bait.

"Yup," he continued, playing the hick to the full. "A little Hank in the morning, a little more Hank every night. That's the ticket."

"You're not so little," I commented as my hand found his penis. His erection and my wetness grew in tandem.

"Why don't you put the dishes in the sink?" Hank prompted smiling.

While I cleared, he rooted in the blankets by the fire. He returned in a minute, flourishing the box of condoms. Then he paused in thought.

"Are you fixed?"

"No," I answered. "Are you?"

"No. Are you on the pill?"

"No."

He shrugged. "Condoms it is."

I sat on the edge of the table and pulled him toward me. Our mouths met in a lingering kiss, then he lifted my knees and tipped me back onto the tabletop. I grunted as my hipbones met the hard surface. Hank walked to the closet and returned with a thick towel. I sat up and he slid the towel under me. I eased back down onto the table.

"So what now?" he asked playfully.

"Take off your gaunchies and get in here!"

"I think I'll have dessert first." Hank pulled up a chair and sat before my spread legs. He pulled me forward to the edge of the table, so that my buttocks lay supported in his hands. I wound my ankles around his shoulders and closed my eyes with a sigh.

"You're quite the sybarite, Chantal," Hank commented to my lazily stretching body.

"What's a sybarite?"

"Never mind." Hank plunged his head into my cunt and attacked me with the ferocity of a starving wolf. My hips rose to meet his lips and my bud of desire stretched to his nimble tongue. He nibbled and teased and worried my lower mouth like a dog with a favorite toy, inflaming me but never settling into an orgasm-inducing rhythm. I twisted and pressed into his face trying to force him to a steady pace. I opened my mouth to scream in frustration. At that instant, his lips grabbed my clitoris—and pulled. The scream turned into one of satisfaction as my body shuddered in climax.

Now his mouth became an instrument of torment as his tongue lashed me to the point of climax then shifted to soothing lapping. I built again and again, but only occasionally did he allow me past the brink, each time more shattering for the delay. As the crest of a tidal wave subsided, he slipped his fingers inside me and I came crashing again at his insistent touch. He laid his head on my stomach and rubbed his knuckle around and around the door to my vagina, and I heaved and bucked beneath him.

"Come inside, Hank," I pleaded. "Please, come inside me." I caressed his head and traced his ear gently. "Please!"

He turned his head to kiss my fingers, then slowly eased his hand from inside me. I grunted as he withdrew, but smiled my encouragement. His fingers shook as he tried to rip open the condom package. I took it from him and laughed as my shaky hands did little better than his. I handed back the safe and he unrolled it swiftly down his smooth shaft. I closed my eyes and reached out my arms to him. He placed his shoulders in my grasp, lifted my hips and entered me on a long sigh.

"Home," I whispered.

Hank took me roughly then, pounding his organ in and out of my grasping cunt until we both came seconds later. Tears oozed from my eyes and I felt a moment of mortal terror at the thought of ever losing this precious man. As the echoes of our orgasm shuddered through our bodies, he pulled me up and held me to his chest as I wept.

"What's wrong, sweetheart?" Hank smoothed my hair as he whispered in my ear. "Did I hurt you?"

I shook my head in fervent denial, but words wouldn't come. He held me for long moments until my sobs died down to hiccups. At last we disengaged and I went to the bathroom to wash my face. When I came back, he sat on the sofa, two cups of coffee steaming on the table before him—Hank's remedy. I smiled and cuddled next to him.

"Tell me what's the matter, Helen," he asked gently, worry clouding his serene eyes.

"Nothing's the matter, Hank," I tried to explain. "It's a big deal, that's all. Making love with you is big—it's huge for me."

"And you're scared?"

"Terrified!" I laughed shakily.

"I'm here forever, Helen," Hank assured me.

"How can you know that so soon?"

Hank smiled. His eyes were no longer troubled, but clear as the Pacific. I let myself float on their surface and felt his serenity invade my heart. I smiled back and began to cry again.

"What now?" Hank asked, half-exasperated.

"I'm so happy!" I sobbed, and we laughed.

"Since you're already crying," Hank paused tantalizingly and pulled me up from the sofa. He led me toward the bedroom door. "Open it."

I turned the knob and the door swung open to reveal a shadowy room. Hank walked past me and pulled back the curtains on a large picture window. The pale light revealed the contents of the room, and my breath caught in my throat. The bed—the exact bed from the island, my bed—stood impossibly between us.

"You made it?" I was stunned.

"I dreamed I made love with my soulmate in this bed."

"You know?" I asked, "About the island?"

He shook his head. "I only know that I had to build this bed." He paused, staring at me in comprehension. "Now I know why."

Hank came to me and took my hand and led me forward. He pushed me onto the white cotton-eyelet cover, down into the white cotton pillows, then lay beside me and pulled me into his arms.

As our bodies met, we both burst into tears. We licked the salt from each other's faces, crying and laughing at the same time. I ripped off his undershirt and he pulled the T-shirt over my head then entered me swiftly.

"The condom!" I cried.

Cursing and laughing, he pulled out of me, reached under the pillow, and produced a strip of safes.

"You'd better hit menopause soon!" he growled and handed me the strip.

I slid the rubber over his straining shaft, then guided it back to its home. For the first time, I lay on my back beneath him, missionary position, and reveled in the ordinariness of our coupling. He lifted my knees high on his back and, eyes locked to mine, began a leisurely stroking. In and out, in and out; the motion was as soothing as the sea. Then his organ grew and the sea became a pounding surf. My neck arched in straining ecstasy and he sank his teeth into the tender skin above my collarbone. I screamed in release as his teeth and tongue assaulted my flesh, and my primitive soul trembled in his strength. Still his organ grew, and its rock-hardness pounded my softness into a pulsing surrender.

I slipped from consciousness into a wave of self-centered fulfillment only to be recalled by Hank's hand pushing insistently at my bottom. He had shifted my knees to his shoulders, and I gasped and strained at the unholy pressure of his huge organ inside me. Then his hand found its purchase, and two hard fingers entered me roughly from the rear.

My fingers dug into his back as I arched my pelvis into his. My teeth bit into the smooth muscle of his shoulder and I felt it blossom beneath my harsh coercion and I heard the breath catch in his throat. His penis swelled and his fingers twisted as I sucked and growled, lost in primeval abandon. Finally the pounding became the beating of a great drum, deafening and thrilling.

Consciousness fled, and we burst together beneath

the surface of our lives. We swam to the center of the universe and stood dancing in moonlight on waves. We spun dizzily and fell headlong into a vast empty space where rocks spoke and the dead lived. Bran embraced us both, and the ethereal melodies of Chopin floated on the wind.

MASQUERADE BOOKS

BOUND TO THE PAST
$6.50/452-6
Anne accepts a research assignment in a Tudor mansion. Upon arriving, she finds herself aroused by James, a descendant of the mansion's owners. Together they uncover the perverse desires of the mansion's long-dead master—desires that bind Anne inexorably to the past—not to mention the bedpost!

SACHI MIZUNO
SHINJUKU NIGHTS
$6.50/493-3
A tour through the lives and libidos of the seductive East. No one is better than Sachi Mizuno at weaving an intricate web of sensual desire, wherein many characters are ensnared and enraptured by the demands of their long-denied carnal natures.

PASSION IN TOKYO
$6.50/454-2
Tokyo—one of Asia's most historic and seductive cities. Come behind the closed doors of its citizens, and witness the many pleasures that await. Lusty men and women from every stratum of Japanese society free themselves of all inhibitions....

MARTINE GLOWINSKI
POINT OF VIEW
$6.50/433-X
With the assistance of her new, unexpectedly kinky lover, she discovers and explores her exhibitionist tendencies—until there is virtually nothing she won't do before the horny audiences her man arranges! Unabashed acting out for the sophisticated voyeur.

RICHARD McGOWAN
A HARLOT OF VENUS
$6.50/425-9
A highly fanciful, epic tale of lust on Mars! Cavortia—the most famous and sought-after courtesan in the cosmopolitan city of Venus—finds love and much more during her adventures with some of the most remarkable characters in recent erotic fiction.

M. ORLANDO
THE ARCHITECTURE OF DESIRE
Introduction by Richard Manton
$6.50/490-9
Two novels in one special volume! In The Hotel Justine, an elite clientele is afforded the opportunity to have any and all desires satisfied. The Villa Sin is inherited by a beautiful woman who soon realizes that the legacy of the ancestral estate includes bizarre erotic ceremonies.

CHET ROTHWELL
KISS ME, KATHERINE
$5.95/410-0
Beautiful Katherine can hardly believe her luck. Not only is she married to the charming and oh-so-agreeable Nelson, she's free to live out all her erotic fantasies with other men. Katherine's desires are more than any one man can handle.

MARCO VASSI
THE STONED APOCALYPSE
$5.95/401-1/mass market
"Marco Vassi is our champion sexual energist."—VLS
During his lifetime, Marco Vassi praised by writers as diverse as Gore Vidal and Norman Mailer, and his reputation was worldwide. The Stoned Apocalypse is Vassi's autobiography; chronicling a cross-country trip on America's erotic byways, it offers a rare glimpse of a generation's sexual imagination.

ROBIN WILDE
TABITHA'S TICKLE
$6.50/468-2
Tabitha's back! The story of this vicious vixen—and her torturously tantalizing cohorts—didn't end with Tabitha's Tease. Once again, men fall under the spell of scrumptious co-eds and find themselves enslaved to demands and desires they never dreamed existed. Think it's a man's world? Guess again. With Tabitha around, no man gets what he wants until she's completely satisfied—and, maybe, not even then....

TABITHA'S TEASE
$5.95/387-2
When poor Robin arrives at The Valentine Academy, he finds himself subject to the torturous teasing of Tabitha—the Academy's most notoriously domineering co-ed. But Tabitha is pledge-mistress of a secret sorority dedicated to enslaving young men. Robin finds himself the utterly helpless (and wildly excited) captive of Tabitha & Company's weird desires! A marathon of ticklish torture!

ERICA BRONTE
PIRATE'S SLAVE
$5.95/376-7
Lovely young Erica is stranded in a country where lust knows no bounds. Desperate to escape, she finds herself trading her firm, luscious body to any and all men willing and able to help her. Her adventure has its ups and downs, ins and outs—all to the undeniable pleasure of lusty Erica!

CHARLES G. WOOD
HELLFIRE
$5.95/358-9
A vicious murderer is running amok in New York's sexual underground—and Nick O'Shay, a virile detective with the NYPD, plunges deep into the case. He soon becomes embroiled in an elusive world of fleshly extremes, hunting a madman seeking to purge America with fire and blood sacrifices. Set in New York's infamous sexual underground.

CLAIRE BAEDER, EDITOR
LA DOMME: A DOMINATRIX ANTHOLOGY
$5.95/366-X
A steamy smorgasbord of female domination! Erotic literature has long been filled with heartstopping portraits of domineering women, and now the most memorable have been brought together in one beautifully brutal volume. A must for all fans of true Woman Power.

MASQUERADE BOOKS

CHARISSE VAN DER LYN
SEX ON THE NET
$5.95/399-6
Electrifying erotica from one of the Internet's hottest and most widely read authors. Encounters of all kinds—straight, lesbian, dominant/submissive and all sorts of extreme passions—are explored in thrilling detail.

STANLEY CARTEN
NAUGHTY MESSAGE
$5.95/333-3
Wesley Arthur discovers a lascivious message on his answering machine. Aroused beyond his wildest dreams by the acts described, Wesley becomes obsessed with tracking down the woman behind the seductive voice. His search takes him through strip clubs, sex parlors and no-tell motels—and finally to his randy reward....

AKBAR DEL PIOMBO
DUKE COSIMO
$4.95/3052-0
A kinky romp played out against the boudoirs, bathrooms and ballrooms of the European nobility, who seem to do nothing all day except each other. The lifestyles of the rich and licentious are revealed in all their glory.

A CRUMBLING FAÇADE
$4.95/3043-1
The return of that incorrigible rogue, Henry Pike, who continues his pursuit of sex, fair or otherwise, in the most elegant homes of the most debauched aristocrats.

CAROLE REMY
FANTASY IMPROMPTU
$6.50/513-1
A mystical, musical journey into the deepest recesses of a woman's soul. Kidnapped and held in a remote island retreat, Chantal—a renowned erotic writer—finds herself catering to every sexual whim of the mysterious and arousing Bran. Bran is determined to bring Chantal to a full embracing of her sensual nature, even while revealing himself to be something far more than human....

BEAUTY OF THE BEAST
$5.95/332-5
A shocking tell-all, written from the point-of-view of a prize-winning reporter. And what reporting she does! All the secrets of an uninhibited tin ageau are revealed, and each lusty tableau is painted in glowing colors.

DAVID AARON CLARK
THE MARQUIS DE SADE'S JULIETTE
$4.95/240-X
The Marquis de Sade's infamous Juliette returns—and emerges as the most perverse and destructive nightstalker modern New York will ever know. One by one, the innocent are drawn in by Juliette's empty promise of immortality, only to fall prey to her strange and deadly lusts.

ANONYMOUS
NADIA
$5.95/267-1
Follow the delicious but neglected Nadia as she works to wring every drop of pleasure out of life—despite an unhappy marriage. A classic title providing a peek into the secret sexual lives of another time and place.

NIGEL McPARR
THE TRANSFORMATION OF EMILY
$6.50/519-0
The shocking story of Emily Johnson, live-in domestic. Without warning, Emily finds herself dismissed by her mistress, and sent to serve at Lilac Row—the home of Charles and Harriet Godwin. In no time, Harriet has Emily doing things she'd never dreamed would be required of her—all involving the erotic discipline Harriet imposes with relish. Little does Emily realize that, as strict and punishing as Harriet Godwin is, nothing could compare to the rigors of her next "position...."

THE STORY OF A VICTORIAN MAID
$5.95/241-8
What were the Victorians really like? Chances are, no one believes they were as stuffy as their Queen, but who would have imagined such unbridled libertines!

TITIAN BERESFORD
CINDERELLA
$6.50/500-X
Beresford triumphs again with this intoxicating tale, filled with castle dungeons and tightly corseted ladies-in-waiting, naughty viscounts and impossibly cruel masturbatrixes—nearly every conceivable method of erotic torture is explored and described in lush, vivid detail.

JUDITH BOSTON
$6.50/525-5
Young Edward would have been lucky to get the stodgy old companion he thought his parents had hired for him. Instead, an exquisite woman arrives at his door, and Edward finds his lewd behavior never goes unpunished by the unflinchingly severe Judith Boston! Together they take the downward path to perversion!

NINA FOXTON
$5.95/443-7
An aristocrat finds herself bored by run-of-the-mill amusements for "ladies of good breeding." Instead of taking tea with proper gentlemen, naughty Nina "milks" them of their most private essences. No man ever says "No" to Nina!

P. N. DEDEAUX
THE NOTHING THINGS
$5.95/404-6
Beta Beta Rho—highly exclusive and widely honored—has taken on a new group of pledges. The five women will be put through the most grueling of ordeals, and punished severely for any shortcomings—much to everyone's delight!

MASQUERADE BOOKS

LYN DAVENPORT

THE GUARDIAN II
$6.50/505-0
The tale of Felicia Brookes—the lovely young woman held in submission by the demanding Sir Rodney Wentworth—continues in this volume of sensual surprises. No sooner has Felicia come to love Rodney than she discovers that she must now accustom herself to the guardianship of the debauched Duke of Smithton. Surely Rodney will rescue her from the domination of this stranger. Won't he?

DOVER ISLAND
$5.95/384-8
Dr. David Kelly has planted the seeds of his dream— a Corporal Punishment Resort. Soon, many people from varied walks of life descend upon this isolated retreat, intent on fulfilling their every desire. Including Marcy Harris, the perfect partner for the lustful Doctor....

THE GUARDIAN
$5.95/371-6
Felicia grew up under the tutelage of the lash—and she learned her lessons well. Sir Rodney Wentworth has long searched for a woman capable of fulfilling his cruel desires, and after learning of Felicia's talents, sends for her. Felicia discovers that the "position" offered her is delightfully different than anything she could have expected!

LIZBETH DUSSEAU

THE APPLICANT
$6.50/501-8
"Adventuresome young women who enjoys being submissive sought by married couple in early forties. Expect no limits." Hilary answers an ad, hoping to find someone who can meet her special needs. The beautiful Liza turns out to be a flawless mistress, and together with her husband, Oliver, she trains Hilary to be the perfect servant.

ANTHONY BOBARZYNSKI

STASI SLUT
$4.95/3050-4
Adina lives in East Germany, where she can only dream about the freedoms of the West. But then she meets a group of ruthless and corrupt STASI agents. They use her body for their own perverse gratification, while she opts to use her talents and attractions in a final bid for total freedom!

JOCELYN JOYCE

PRIVATE LIVES
$4.95/309-0
The lecherous habits of the illustrious make for a sizzling tale of French erotic life. A widow has a craving for a young busboy; he's sleeping with a rich businessman's wife; her husband is minding his sex business elsewhere! Sexual entanglements run through this tale of upper crust lust!

SARAH JACKSON

SANCTUARY
$5.95/318-X
Sanctuary explores both the unspeakable debauchery of court life and the unimaginable privations of monastic solitude, leading the voracious and the virtuous on a collision course that brings history to throbbing life.

THE WILD HEART
$4.95/3007-5
A luxury hotel is the setting for this artful web of sex, desire, and love. A newlywed sees sex as a duty, while her hungry husband tries to awaken her to its tender joys. A Parisian entertains wealthy guests for the love of money. Each episode provides a new variation in this lusty Grand Hotel!

LOUISE BELHAVEL

FRAGRANT ABUSES
$4.95/88-2
The saga of Clara and Iris continues as the now-experienced girls enjoy themselves with a new circle of worldly friends whose imaginations match their own. Perversity follows the lusty ladies around the globe!

SARA H. FRENCH

MASTER OF TIMBERLAND
$5.95/327-9
A tale of sexual slavery at the ultimate paradise resort. One of our bestselling titles, this trek to Timberland has ignited passions the world over—and stands poised to become one of modern erotica's legendary tales.

MARY LOVE

MASTERING MARY SUE
$5.95/351-1
Mary Sue is a rich nymphomaniac whose husband is determined to declare her mentally incompetent and gain control of her fortune. He brings her to a castle where, to Mary Sue's delight, she is unleashed for a veritable sex-fest!

THE BEST OF MARY LOVE
$4.95/3099-7
Mary Love leaves no coupling untried and no extreme unexplored in these scandalous selections from Mastering Mary Sue, Ecstasy on Fire, Vice Park Place, Wanda, and Naughtier at Night.

AMARANTHA KNIGHT

THE DARKER PASSIONS: THE PICTURE OF DORIAN GRAY
$6.50/342-2
Amarantha Knight takes on Oscar Wilde, resulting in a fabulously decadent tale of highly personal changes. One young man finds his most secret desires laid bare by a portrait more revealing than he could have imagined....

THE DARKER PASSIONS READER
$6.50/132-1
The best moments from Knight's phenomenally popular Darker Passions series. Here are the most eerily erotic passages from her acclaimed sexual reworkings of Dracula, Frankenstein, Dr. Jekyll & Mr. Hyde and The Fall of the House of Usher.

THE DARKER PASSIONS: THE FALL OF THE HOUSE OF USHER
$6.50/528-X
The Master and Mistress of the house of Usher indulge in every form of decadence, and initiate their guests into the many pleasures to be found in utter submission.

MASQUERADE BOOKS

THE DARKER PASSIONS: DR. JEKYLL AND MR. HYDE
$4.95/227-2

It is a story of incredible transformations achieved through mysterious experiments. Explore the steamy possibilities of a tale where no one is quite who—or what—they seem. Victorian bedrooms explode with hidden demons!

THE DARKER PASSIONS: FRANKENSTEIN
$5.95/248-5

What if you could create a living human? What shocking acts could it be taught to perform, to desire? Find out what pleasures await those who play God....

THE DARKER PASSIONS: DRACULA
$5.95/326-0

The infamous erotic retelling of the Vampire legend. "Well-written and imaginative, Amarantha Knight gives fresh impetus to this myth, taking us through the sexual and sadistic scenes with details that keep us reading.... A classic in itself has been added to the shelves."
—*Divinity*

....

THE PAUL LITTLE LIBRARY
PECULIAR PASSIONS OF LADY MEG/LOVE SLAVE
$8.95/529-8/Trade paperback

Two classics from modern erotica's most popular author! What are the sexy secrets *Lady Meg* hides? What are the appetites that lurk beneath the the surface of this irresistible vixen? What does it take to be the perfect instrument of pleasure—or go about acquiring a willing *Love Slave* of one's own? Paul Little spares no detail!

THE BEST OF PAUL LITTLE
$6.50/469-0

Known throughout the world for his fantastic portrayals of punishment and pleasure, Little never fails to push readers over the edge of sensual excitement.

ALL THE WAY
$6.95/509-3

Two excruciating novels from Paul Little in one hot volume! *Going All the Way* features an unhappy man who tries to purge himself of the memory of his lover with a series of quirky and uninhibited lovers. *Pushover* tells the story of a serial spanker and his celebrated exploits.

THE DISCIPLINE OF ODETTE
$5.95/334-1

Odette's was sure marriage would rescue her from her family's "corrections." To her horror, she discovers that her beloved has also been raised on discipline. A shocking erotic coupling!

THE PRISONER
$5.95/330-9

Judge Black has built a secret room below a penitentiary, where he sentences the prisoners to hours of exhibition and torment while his friends watch. Judge Black's House of Corrections is equipped with one purpose in mind: to administer his own brand of rough justice!

TEARS OF THE INQUISITION
$4.95/146-2

The incomparable Paul Little delivers a staggering account of pleasure and punishment. "There was a tickling inside her as her nervous system reminded her she was ready for sex. But before her was...the Inquisitor!"

DOUBLE NOVEL
$4.95/86-6

The Metamorphosis of Lisette Joyaux tells the story of a young woman initiated into an incredible world world of lesbian lusts. *The Story of Monique* reveals the twisted sexual rituals that beckon the ripe and willing Monique.

CHINESE JUSTICE AND OTHER STORIES
$4.95/153-5

The story of the excruciating pleasures and delicious punishments inflicted on foreigners under the leaders of the Boxer Rebellion. Each woman is brought before the authorities and grilled, to the delight of their perverse captors.

CAPTIVE MAIDENS
$5.95/440-2

Three beautiful young women find themselves powerless against the debauched landowners of 1824 England. They are banished to a sexual slave colony, and corrupted by every imaginable perversion.

SLAVE ISLAND
$5.95/441-0

A leisure cruise is waylaid by Lord Henry Philbrock, a sadistic genius. The ship's passengers are kidnapped and spirited to his island prison, where the women are trained to accommodate the most bizarre sexual cravings of the rich, the famous, the pampered and the perverted.

....

ALIZARIN LAKE
SEX ON DOCTOR'S ORDERS
$5.95/402-X

Beth, a nubile young nurse, uses her considerable skills to further medical science by offering incomparable and insatiable assistance in the gathering of important specimens. Soon, an assortment of randy characters is lending a hand in this highly erotic work.

THE EROTIC ADVENTURES OF HARRY TEMPLE
$4.95/127-6

Harry Temple's memoirs chronicle his amorous adventures from his initiation at the hands of insatiable sirens, through his stay at a house of hot repute, to his encounters with a chastity-belted nympho!

....

JOHN NORMAN
TARNSMAN OF GOR
$6.95/486-0

This controversial series returns! Tarl Cabot is transported to Gor. He must quickly accustom himself to the ways of this world, including the caste system which exalts some as Priest-Kings or Warriors, and debases others as slaves. A spectacular world unfolds in this first volume of John Norman's Gorean series.

BUY ANY 4 BOOKS & CHOOSE 1 ADDITIONAL BOOK, OF EQUAL OR LESSER VALUE, AS YOUR FREE GIFT

MASQUERADE BOOKS

OUTLAW OF GOR
$6.95/487-9

In this second volume, Tarl Cabot returns to Gor, where he might reclaim both his woman and his role of Warrior. But upon arriving, he discovers that his name, his city and the names of those he loves have become unspeakable. Cabot has become an outlaw, and must discover his new purpose on this strange planet, where danger stalks the outcast, and even simple answers have their price....

PRIEST-KINGS OF GOR
$6.95/488-7

Tarl Cabot searches for the truth about his lovely wife Talena. Does she live, or was she destroyed by the mysterious, all-powerful Priest Kings? Cabot is determined to find out—even while knowing that no one who has approached the mountain stronghold of the Priest-Kings has ever returned alive....

NOMADS OF GOR
$6.95/527-1

Another provocative trip to the barbaric and mysterious world of Gor. Norman's heroic Tarnsman finds his way across this Counter-Earth, pledged to serve the Priest-Kings in their quest for survival. Unfortunately for Cabot, his mission leads him to the savage Wagon People—nomads who may very well kill before surrendering any secrets....

RACHEL PEREZ

AFFINITIES
$4.95/113-6

"Kelsy had a liking for cool upper-class blondes, the long-legged girls from Lake Forest and Winnetka who came into the city to cruise the lesbian bars on Halsted, looking for breathless ecstasies...." A scorching tale of lesbian libidos unleashed, from a writer more than capable of exploring every nuance of female passion in vivid detail.

SYDNEY ST. JAMES

RIVE GAUCHE
$5.95/317-1

The Latin Quarter, Paris, circa 1920. Expatriate bohemians couple with abandon—before eventually abandoning their ambitions amidst the intoxicating temptations waiting to be indulged in every bedroom.

GARDEN OF DELIGHT
$4.95/3058-X

A vivid account of sexual awakening that follows an innocent but insatiably curious young woman's journey from the furtive, forbidden joys of dormitory life to the unabashed carnality of the wild world.

DON WINSLOW

THE FALL OF THE ICE QUEEN
$6.50/520-4

She was the most exquisite of his courtiers: the beautiful, aloof woman who Rahn the Conqueror chose as his Consort. But the regal disregard with which she treated Rahn was not to be endured. It was decided that she would submit to his will, and learn to serve her lord in the fashion he had come to expect. And as so many knew, Rahn's depraved expectations have made his court infamous....

PRIVATE PLEASURES
$6.50/504-2

An assortment of sensual encounters designed to appeal to the most discerning reader. Frantic voyeurs, licentious exhibitionists, and everyday lovers are here displayed in all their wanton glory—proving again that fleshly pleasures have no more apt chronicler than Don Winslow.

THE INSATIABLE MISTRESS OF ROSEDALE
$6.50/494-1

The story of the perfect couple: Edward and Lady Penelope, who reside in beautiful and mysterious Rosedale manor. While Edward is a true connoisseur of sexual perversion, it is Lady Penelope whose mastery of complete sensual pleasure makes their home infamous. Indulging one another's bizarre whims is a way of life for this wicked couple, and none who encounter the extravagances of Rosedale will forget what they've learned....

SECRETS OF CHEATEM MANOR
$6.50/434-8

Edward returns to his late father's estate, to find it being run by the majestic Lady Amanda. Edward can hardly believe his luck—Lady Amanda is assisted by her two beautiful, lonely daughters, Catherine and Prudence. What the randy young man soon comes to realize is the love of discipline that all three beauties share.

KATERINA IN CHARGE
$5.95/409-7

When invited to a country retreat by a mysterious couple, two randy young ladies can hardly resist! But do they have any idea what they're in for? Whatever the case, the imperious Katerina will make her desires known very soon—and demand that they be fulfilled... Sexual innocence subjugated and defiled.

THE MANY PLEASURES OF IRONWOOD
$5.95/310-4

Seven lovely young women are employed by The Ironwood Sportsmen's Club, where their natural talents are put to creative use. A small and exclusive club with seven carefully selected sexual connoisseurs, Ironwood is dedicated to the relentless pursuit of sensual pleasure.

CLAIRE'S GIRLS
$5.95/442-9

You knew when she walked by that she was something special. She was one of Claire's girls, a woman carefully dressed and groomed to fill a role, to capture a look, to fit an image crafted by the sophisticated proprietress of an exclusive escort agency. High-class whores blow the roof off in this blow-by-blow account of life behind the closed doors of a sophisticated brothel.

N. WHALLEN

TAU'TEVU
$6.50/426-7

In a mysterious land, the statuesque and beautiful Vivian learns to subject herself to the hand of a mysterious man. He systematically helps her prove her own strength, and brings to life in her an unimagined sensual fire. But who is this man, who goes only by the name of Orpheo?

MASQUERADE BOOKS

COMPLIANCE
$5.95/356-2
Fourteen stories exploring the pleasures of ultimate release. Characters from all walks of life learn to trust in the skills of others, hoping to experience the thrilling liberation of sexual submission. Here are the many joys to be found in some of the most forbidden sexual practices around....

THE CLASSIC COLLECTION
PROTESTS, PLEASURES, RAPTURES
$5.95/400-3
Invited for an allegedly quiet weekend at a country vicarage, a young woman is stunned to find herself surrounded by shocking acts of sexual sadism. Soon, her curiosity is piqued, and she begins to explore her own capacities for cruelty. The ultimate tale of an extraordinary woman's erotic awakening.

THE YELLOW ROOM
$5.95/378-3
The "yellow room" holds the secrets of lust, lechery, and the lash. There, bare-bottomed, spread-eagled, and open to the world, demure Alice Darvell soon learns to love her lickings. In the second tale, hot heiress Rosa Coote and her lusty servants whip up numerous adventures in punishment and pleasure.

SCHOOL DAYS IN PARIS
$5.95/325-2
The rapturous chronicles of a well-spent youth! Few Universities provide the profound and pleasurable lessons one learns in after-hours study—particularly if one is young and available, and lucky enough to have Paris as a playground. A stimulating look at the pursuits of young adulthood.

MAN WITH A MAID
$4.95/307-4
The adventures of Jack and Alice have delighted readers for eight decades! A classic of its genre, *Man with a Maid* tells an outrageous tale of desire, revenge, and submission. This tale qualifies as one of the world's most popular adult novels—with over 200,000 copies in print!

CONFESSIONS OF A CONCUBINE III: PLEASURE'S PRISONER
$5.95/357-0
Filled with pulse-pounding excitement—including a daring escape from the harem and an encounter with an unspeakable sadist—*Pleasure's Prisoner* adds an unforgettable chapter to this thrilling confessional.

CLASSIC EROTIC BIOGRAPHIES
JENNIFER
$4.95/107-1
The return of one of the Sexual Revolution's most notorious heroines. From the bedroom of a notoriously insatiable dancer to an uninhibited ashram, *Jennifer* traces the exploits of one thoroughly modern woman as she lustfully explores the limits of her own sexuality.

JENNIFER III
$5.95/292-2
The further adventures of erotica's most daring heroine. Jennifer has a photographer's eye for details—particularly of the masculine variety! One by one, her subjects submit to her demands for sensual pleasure, becoming part of her now-infamous gallery of erotic conquests.

RHINOCEROS

KATHLEEN K.
SWEET TALKERS
$6.95/516-6
Kathleen K. ran a phone-sex company in the late 80s, and she opens up her diary for a very thought provoking peek at the life of a phone-sex operator. Transcripts of actual conversations are included.

"If you enjoy eavesdropping on explicit conversations about sex... this book is for you."   —*Spectator*

"Highly recommended."   —*Shiny International*
Trade /$12.95/192-6

THOMAS S. ROCHE
DARK MATTER
$6.95/484-4
"*Dark Matter* is sure to please gender outlaws, body-mod junkies, goth vampires, boys who wish they were dykes, and anybody who's not to sure where the fine line should be drawn between pleasure and pain. It's a handful."   —Pat Califia

"Here is the erotica of the cumming millenium.... You will be deliciously disturbed, but never disappointed."   —Poppy Z. Brite
NOIROTICA: AN ANTHOLOGY OF EROTIC CRIME STORIES
$6.95/390-2
A collection of darkly sexy tales, taking place at the crossroads of the crime and erotic genres. Thomas S. Roche has gathered together some of today's finest writers of sexual fiction, all of whom explore the murky terrain where desire runs irrevocably afoul of the law.

ROMY ROSEN
SPUNK
$6.95/492-5
Casey, a lovely model poised upon the verge of super-celebrity, falls for an insatiable young rock singer—not suspecting that his sexual appetite has led him to experiment with a dangerous new aphrodisiac. Casey becomes an addict, and her craving plunges her into a strange underworld, where the only chance for redemption lies with a shadowy young man with a secret of his own.

BUY ANY 4 BOOKS & CHOOSE 1 ADDITIONAL BOOK, OF EQUAL OR LESSER VALUE, AS YOUR FREE GIFT

MASQUERADE BOOKS

MOLLY WEATHERFIELD
CARRIE'S STORY
$6.95/485-2
"I had been Jonathan's slave for about a year when he told me he wanted to sell me at an auction. I wasn't in any condition to respond when he told me this..." Desire and depravity run rampant in this story of uncompromising mastery and irrevocable submission. A unique piece of erotica that is both thoughtful and hot!

"I was stunned by how well it was written and how intensely foreign I found its sexual world.... And, since this is a world I don't frequent... I thoroughly enjoyed the National Geo tour."   —*bOING bOING*

"Hilarious and harrowing... just when you think things can't get any wilder, they do." —*Black Sheets*

CYBERSEX CONSORTIUM
CYBERSEX: THE PERV'S GUIDE TO FINDING SEX ON THE INTERNET
$6.95/471-2
You've heard the objections: cyberspace is soaked with sex. Okay—so where is it!? Tracking down the good stuff—the real good stuff—can waste an awful lot of expensive time, and frequently leave you high and dry. The Cybersex Consortium presents an easy-to-use guide for those intrepid adults who know what they want. No horny hacker can afford to pass up this map to the kinkiest rest stops on the Info Superhighway.

AMELIA G, EDITOR
BACKSTAGE PASSES
$6.95/438-0
Amelia G, editor of the goth-sex journal *Blue Blood*, has brought together some of today's most irreverent writers, each of whom has outdone themselves with an edgy, antic tale of modern lust. Punks, metalheads, and grunge-trash roam the pages of *Backstage Passes*, and no one knows their ways better...

GERI NETTICK WITH BETH ELLIOT
MIRRORS: PORTRAIT OF A LESBIAN TRANSSEXUAL
$6.95/435-6
The alternately heartbreaking and empowering story of one woman's long road to full selfhood. Born a male, Geri Nettick knew something just didn't fit. And even after coming to terms with her own gender dysphoria—and taking steps to correct it—she still fought to be accepted by the lesbian feminist community to which she felt she belonged. A fascinating, true tale of struggle and discovery.

DAVID MELTZER
UNDER
$6.95/290-6
The story of a 21st century sex professional living at the bottom of the social heap. After surgeries designed to increase his physical allure, corrupt government forces drive the cyber-gigolo underground—where even more bizarre cultures await him.

ORF
$6.95/110-1
He is the ultimate musician-hero—the idol of thousands, the fevered dream of many more. And like many musicians before him, he is misunderstood, misused—and totally out of control. Every last drop of feeling is squeezed from a modern-day troubadour and his lady love.

LAURA ANTONIOU, EDITOR
NO OTHER TRIBUTE
$6.95/294-9
A collection sure to challenge Political Correctness in a way few have before, with tales of women kept in bondage to their lovers by their deepest passions. Love pushes these women beyond acceptable limits, rendering them helpless to deny anything to the men and women they adore. A volume dedicated to all Slaves of Desire.

SOME WOMEN
$6.95/300-7
Over forty essays written by women actively involved in consensual dominance and submission. Professional mistresses, lifestyle leatherdykes, whipmakers, titleholders—women from every conceivable walk of life lay bare their true feelings about explosive issues.

BY HER SUBDUED
$6.95/281-7
These tales all involve women in control—of their lives, their loves, their men. So much in control that they can remorselessly break rules to become powerful goddesses of the men who sacrifice all to worship at their feet.

TRISTAN TAORMINO & DAVID AARON CLARK, EDITORS
RITUAL SEX
$6.95/391-0
While many people believe the body and soul to occupy almost completely independent realms, the many contributors to *Ritual Sex* know—and demonstrate—that the two share more common ground than society feels comfortable acknowledging. From personal memoirs of ecstatic revelation, to fictional quests to reconcile sex and spirit, *Ritual Sex* provides an unprecedented look at private life.

TAMMY JO ECKHART
PUNISHMENT FOR THE CRIME
$6.95/427-5
Peopled by characters of rare depth, these stories explore the true meaning of dominance and submission. From an encounter between two of society's most despised individuals, to the explorations of longtime friends, these tales take you where few others have ever dared....

AMARANTHA KNIGHT, EDITOR
SEDUCTIVE SPECTRES
$6.95/464-X
Breathtaking tours through the erotic supernatural via the macabre imaginations of today's best writers. Never before have ghostly encounters been so alluring, thanks to a cast of otherworldly characters well-acquainted with the pleasures of the flesh.

MASQUERADE BOOKS

SEX MACABRE
$6.95/392-9
Horror tales designed for dark and sexy nights. Amarantha Knight—the woman behind the Darker Passions series—has gathered together erotic stories sure to make your skin crawl, and heart beat faster.

FLESH FANTASTIC
$6.95/352-X
Humans have long toyed with the idea of "playing God": creating life from nothingness, bringing life to the inanimate. Now Amarantha Knight collects stories exploring not only the act of Creation, but the lust that follows....

GARY BOWEN
DIARY OF A VAMPIRE
$6.95/331-7
"Gifted with a darkly sensual vision and a fresh voice, [Bowen] is a writer to watch out for."
—Cecilia Tan
Rafael, a red-blooded male with an insatiable hunger for the same, is the perfect antidote to the effete malcontents haunting bookstores today. The emergence of a bold and brilliant vision, rooted in past and present.

RENÉ MAIZEROY
FLESHLY ATTRACTIONS
$6.95/299-X
Lucien was the son of the wantonly beautiful actress, Marie-Rose Hardanges. When she decides to let a "friend" introduce her son to the pleasures of love, Marie-Rose could not have foretold the excesses that would lead to her own ruin and that of her cherished son.

JEAN STINE
THRILL CITY
$6.95/411-9
Thrill City is the seat of the world's increasing depravity, and this classic novel transports you there with a vivid style you'd be hard pressed to ignore. No writer is better suited to describe the extremes of this modern Babylon.

SEASON OF THE WITCH
$6.95/268-X
"A future in which it is technically possible to transfer the total mind...of a rapist killer into the brain dead but physically living body of his female victim. Remarkable for intense psychological technique. There is eroticism but it is necessary to mark the differences between the sexes and the subtle altering of a man into a woman." —The Science Fiction Critic

GRANT ANTREWS
ROGUES GALLERY
$6.95/522-8
A stirring evocation of dominant/submissive love. Two doctors meet and slowly fall in love. Once Beth reveals her hidden desires to Jim, the two explore the forbidden acts that will come to define their distinctly exotic affair.

MY DARLING DOMINATRIX
$6.95/447-X
When a man and a woman fall in love, it's supposed to be simple and uncomplicated—unless that woman happens to be a dominatrix. Curiosity gives way to desire in this story of one man's awakening to the joys of willing slavery.

JOHN WARREN
THE TORQUEMADA KILLER
$6.95/367-8
Detective Eva Hernandez gets her first "big case": a string of vicious murders taking place within New York's SM community. Eva assembles the evidence, revealing a picture of a world misunderstood and under attack—and gradually comes to understand her own place within it.

THE LOVING DOMINANT
$6.95/218-3
Everything you need to know about an infamous sexual variation—and an unspoken type of love. Warren guides readers through this world and reveals the too-often hidden basis of the D/S relationship: care, trust and love.

LAURA ANTONIOU WRITING AS "SARA ADAMSON"
THE TRAINER
$6.95/249-3
The Marketplace includes not only willing slaves, but the exquisite trainers who take submissives firmly in hand. And now these mentors divulge the desires that led them to become the ultimate figures of authority.

THE SLAVE
$6.95/173-X
The second volume in the "Marketplace" trilogy. One talented submissive longs to join the ranks of those who have proven themselves worthy of entry into the Marketplace. But the delicious price is high....

THE MARKETPLACE
$6.95/3096-2
The volume that introduced the Marketplace to the world—and established it as one of the most popular realms in contemporary SM fiction.

DAVID AARON CLARK
SISTER RADIANCE
$6.95/215-9
Rife with Clark's trademark vivisections of contemporary desires, sacred and profane. The vicissitudes of lust and romance are examined against a backdrop of urban decay in this testament to the allure of the forbidden.

THE WET FOREVER
$6.95/117-9
The story of Janus and Madchen—a small-time hood and a beautiful sex worker on the run from one of the most dangerous men they have ever known—examines themes of loyalty, sacrifice, redemption and obsession amidst Manhattan's sex parlors and underground S/M clubs.

BUY ANY 4 BOOKS & CHOOSE 1 ADDITIONAL BOOK, OF EQUAL OR LESSER VALUE, AS YOUR FREE GIFT

MASQUERADE BOOKS

MICHAEL PERKINS

EVIL COMPANIONS
$6.95/3067-9
Set in New York City during the tumultuous waning years of the Sixties, *Evil Companions* has been hailed as "a frightening classic." A young couple explores the nether reaches of the erotic unconscious in a shocking confrontation with the extremes of passion.

THE SECRET RECORD: MODERN EROTIC LITERATURE
$6.95/3039-3
Michael Perkins surveys the field with authority and unique insight. Updated and revised to include the latest trends, tastes, and developments in this misunderstood and maligned genre.

AN ANTHOLOGY OF CLASSIC ANONYMOUS EROTIC WRITING
$6.95/140-3
Michael Perkins has collected the very best passages from the world's erotic writing. "Anonymous" is one of the most infamous bylines in publishing history—and these steamy excerpts show why! Includes excerpts from some of the most famous titles in the history of erotic literature.

LIESEL KULIG

LOVE IN WARTIME
$6.95/3044-X
Madeleine knew that the handsome SS officer was a dangerous man, but she was just a cabaret singer in Nazi-occupied Paris, trying to survive in a perilous time. When Josef fell in love with her, he discovered that a beautiful woman can sometimes be as dangerous as any warrior.

HELEN HENLEY

ENTER WITH TRUMPETS
$6.95/197-7
Helen Henley was told that women just don't write about sex—much less the taboos she was so interested in exploring. So Henley did it alone, flying in the face of "tradition" by writing this touching tale of arousal and devotion in one couple's kinky relationship.

ALICE JOANOU

BLACK TONGUE
$6.95/258-2
"Joanou has created a series of sumptuous, brooding, dark visions of sexual obsession, and is undoubtedly a name to look out for in the future."
—*Redeemer*
Exploring lust at its most florid and unsparing, *Black Tongue* is a trove of baroque fantasies—each redolent of forbidden passions. Joanou creates some of erotica's most mesmerizing and unforgettable characters.

TOURNIQUET
$6.95/3060-1
A heady collection of stories and effusions from the pen of one our most dazzling young writers. Strange tales abound, from the story of the mysterious and cruel Cybele, to an encounter with the sadistic entertainment of a bizarre after-hours cafe. A complex and riveting series of meditations on desire.

CANNIBAL FLOWER
$4.95/72-6
The provocative debut volume from this acclaimed writer.
"She is waiting in her darkened bedroom, as she has waited throughout history, to seduce the men who are foolish enough to be blinded by her irresistible charms.... She is the goddess of sexuality, and *Cannibal Flower* is her haunting siren song."
—Michael Perkins

PHILIP JOSÉ FARMER

A FEAST UNKNOWN
$6.95/276-0
"Sprawling, brawling, shocking, suspenseful, hilarious..." —Theodore Sturgeon
Farmer's supreme anti-hero returns. "I was conceived and born in 1888." Slowly, Lord Grandrith—armed with the belief that he is the son of Jack the Ripper—tells the story of his remarkable and unbridled life. His story begins with his discovery of the secret of immortality—and progresses to encompass the furthest extremes of human behavior.

THE IMAGE OF THE BEAST
$6.95/166-7
Herald Childe has seen Hell, glimpsed its horror in an act of sexual mutilation. Childe must now find and destroy an inhuman predator through the streets of a polluted and decadent Los Angeles of the future. One clue after another leads Childe to an inescapable realization about the nature of sex and evil....

DANIEL VIAN

ILLUSIONS
$6.95/3074-1
Two tales of danger and desire in Berlin on the eve of WWII. From private homes to lurid cafés, passion is exposed in stark contrast to the brutal violence of the time, as desperate people explore their deepest, darkest sexual desires.

SAMUEL R. DELANY

THE MAD MAN
$8.99/408-9
"Reads like a pornographic reflection of Peter Ackroyd's *Chatterton* or A. S. Byatt's *Possession*.... Delany develops an insightful dichotomy between [his protagonist]'s two worlds: the one of cerebral philosophy and dry academia, the other of heedless, 'impersonal' obsessive sexual extremism. When these worlds finally collide...the novel achieves a surprisingly satisfying resolution...." —*Publishers Weekly*

For his thesis, graduate student John Marr researches the life of Timothy Hasler: a philosopher whose career was cut tragically short over a decade earlier. On another front, Marr finds himself increasingly drawn toward shocking, depraved sexual entanglements with the homeless men of his neighborhood, until it begins to seem that Hasler's death might hold some key to his own life as a gay man in the age of AIDS. Unquestionably the goddess of Delany's most shocking works, *The Mad Man* is one of American erotic literature's most transgressive titles.

MASQUERADE BOOKS

EQUINOX
$6.95/157-8

The Scorpion has sailed the seas in a quest for every possible pleasure. Her crew is a collection of the young, the twisted, the insatiable. A drifter comes into their midst and is taken on a fantastic journey to the darkest, most dangerous sexual extremes—until he is finally a victim to their boundless appetites. An early title that set the way for the author's later explorations of extreme, forbidden sexual behaviors. Long out of print, this disturbing tale is finally available under the author's original title.

ANDREI CODRESCU
THE REPENTANCE OF LORRAINE
$6.95/329-5

"One of our most prodigiously talented and magical writers."
—NYT Book Review

By the acclaimed author of *The Hole in the Flag* and *The Blood Countess*. An aspiring writer, a professor's wife, a secretary, gold anklets, Maoists, Roman harlots—and more—swirl through this spicy tale of a harried quest for a mythic artifact. Written when the author was a young man, this lusty yarn was inspired by the heady days of the Sixties. Includes a new introduction by the author, detailing the events that inspired *Lorraine's* creation. A touching, arousing product from a more innocent time.

TUPPY OWENS
SENSATIONS
$6.95/3081-4

Tuppy Owens tells the unexpurgated story of the making of *Sensations*—the first big-budget sex flick. Originally commissioned to appear in book form after the release of the film in 1975, *Sensations* is finally released under Masquerade's stylish Rhinoceros imprint.

SOPHIE GALLEYMORE BIRD
MANEATER
$6.95/103-9

Through a bizarre act of creation, a man attains the "perfect" lover—by all appearances a beautiful, sensuous woman, but in reality something far darker. Once brought to life she will accept no mate, seeking instead the prey that will sate her hunger for vengeance.

LEOPOLD VON SACHER-MASOCH
VENUS IN FURS
$6.95/3089-X

This classic 19th century novel is the first uncompromising exploration of the dominant/submissive relationship in literature. The alliance of Severin and Wanda epitomizes Sacher-Masoch's dark obsession with a cruel, controlling goddess and the urges that drive the man held in her thrall. This special edition includes the letters exchanged between Sacher-Masoch and Emilie Mataja, an aspiring writer he sought to cast as the avatar of the forbidden desires expressed in his most famous work.

BADBOY

MIKE FORD, EDITOR
BUTCH BOYS
$6.50/523-9

A big volume of tales dedicated to the rough-and-tumble type who can make a man weak at the knees. From bikers to "gymbos," these no-nonsense studs know just what they want and how to go about getting it. Some of today's best erotic writers explore the many possible variations on the age-old fantasy of the dominant man.

WILLIAM J. MANN, EDITOR
GRAVE PASSIONS
$6.50/405-4

A collection of the most chilling tales of passion currently being penned by today's most provocative gay writers. Unnatural transformations, otherworldly encounters, and deathless desires make for a collection sure to keep readers up late at night—for a variety of reasons!

J. A. GUERRA, EDITOR
COME QUICKLY: FOR BOYS ON THE GO
$6.50/413-5

Here are over sixty of the hottest fantasies around—all designed to get you going in less time than it takes to dial 976. Julian Anthony Guerra, the editor behind the phenomenally popular *Men at Work* and *Badboy Fantasies*, has put together this volume especially for you—a busy man on a modern schedule, who still appreciates a little old-fashioned action.

JOHN PRESTON
HUSTLING: A GENTLEMAN'S GUIDE TO THE FINE ART OF HOMOSEXUAL PROSTITUTION
$6.50/517-4

The very first guide to the gay world's most infamous profession. John Preston solicited the advice and opinions of "working boys" from across the country in his effort to produce the ultimate guide to the hustler's world. *Hustling* covers every practical aspect of the business, from clientele and payment options to "specialties," sidelines and drawbacks. No stone is left unturned—and no wrong turn left unadmonished—in this guidebook to the ins and outs of this much-mythologized trade.

"...Unrivaled. For any man even vaguely contemplating going into business this tome has got to be the first port of call."
—*Divinity*

"Fun and highly literary. What more could you expect form such an accomplished activist, author and editor?"
—*Drummer*
Trade $12.95/137-3

MASQUERADE BOOKS

MR. BENSON
$4.95/3041-5

Jamie is an aimless young man lucky enough to encounter Mr. Benson. He is soon led down the path of erotic enlightenment, learning to accept this man as his master. Jamie's incredible adventures never fail to excite—especially when the going gets rough! One of the first runaway bestsellers in gay erotic literature.

TALES FROM THE DARK LORD
$5.95/323-6

A new collection of twelve stunning works from the man *Lambda Book Report* called "the Dark Lord of gay erotica." The relentless ritual of lust and surrender is explored in all its manifestations in this heart-stopping triumph of authority and vision from the Dark Lord!

TALES FROM THE DARK LORD II
$4.95/176-4

The second volume of John Preston's masterful short stories. Includes an interview with the author, and a sexy screenplay written for pornstar Scott O'Hara.

THE ARENA
$4.95/3083-0

There is a place on the edge of fantasy where every desire is indulged with abandon. Men go there to unleash beasts, to let demons roam free, to abolish all limits. At the center of each tale are the men who serve there, who offer themselves for the consummation of any passion, whose own bottomless urges compel their endless subservience.

THE HEIR•THE KING
$4.95/3048-2

The ground-breaking novel *The Heir*, written in the lyric voice of the ancient myths, tells the story of a world where slaves and masters create a new sexual society. This edition also includes a completely original work, *The King*, the story of a soldier who discovers his monarch's most secret desires. A special double volume.

THE MISSION OF ALEX KANE

SWEET DREAMS
$4.95/3062-8

It's the triumphant return of gay action hero Alex Kane! In *Sweet Dreams*, Alex travels to Boston where he takes on a street gang that stalks gay teenagers. Mighty Alex Kane wreaks a fierce and terrible vengeance on those who prey on gay people everywhere!

GOLDEN YEARS
$4.95/3069-5

When evil threatens the plans of a group of older gay men, Kane's got the muscle to take it head on. Along the way, he wins the support—and very specialized attentions—of a cowboy plucked right out of the Old West. But Kane and the Cowboy have a surprise waiting for them....

DEADLY LIES
$4.95/3076-8

Politics is a dirty business and the dirt becomes deadly when a political smear campaign targets gay men. Who better to clean things up than Alex Kane! Alex comes to protect the dreams, and lives, of gay men imperiled by lies and deceit.

STOLEN MOMENTS
$4.95/3098-9

Houston's evolving gay community is victimized by a malicious newspaper editor who is more than willing to sacrifice gays on the altar of circulation. He never counted on Alex Kane, fearless defender of gay dreams and desires.

SECRET DANGER
$4.95/111-X

Homophobia: a pernicious social ill not confined to America's borders. Alex Kane and the faithful Danny are called to a small European country, where a group of gay tourists is being held hostage by ruthless terrorists. Luckily the Mission of Alex Kane stands as firm foreign policy.

LETHAL SILENCE
$4.95/125-X

The Mission of Alex Kane thunders to a conclusion. Chicago becomes the scene of the right-wing's most noxious plan—facilitated by unholy political alliances. Alex and Danny head to the Windy City to take up battle with the mercenaries who would squash gay men underfoot.

MATT TOWNSEND

SOLIDLY BUILT
$6.50/416-X

The tale of the tumultuous relationship between Jeff, young photographer, and Mark, the butch electrician hired to wire Jeff's new home. For Jeff, it's love at first sight. Mark, however, has more than a few hang-ups. Soon, both are forced to reevaluate their outlooks, and are assisted by a variety of hot men....

JAY SHAFFER

SHOOTERS
$5.95/284-1

No mere catalog of random acts, *Shooters* tells the stories of a variety of stunning men and the ways they connect in sexual and non-sexual ways. A virtuoso storyteller, Shaffer always gets his man.

ANIMAL HANDLERS
$4.95/264-7

In Shaffer's world, each and every man finally succumbs to the animal urges deep inside. And if there's any creature that promises a wild time, it's a beast who's been caged for far too long. Shaffer has one of the keenest eyes for the nuances of male passion.

FULL SERVICE
$4.95/150-0

Wild men build up steam until they finally let loose. No nonsense guys bear down hard on each other as they work their way toward release in this finely detailed assortment of masculine fantasies. One of gay erotica's most insightful chroniclers of male passion.

D. V. SADERO

IN THE ALLEY
$4.95/144-6

Hardworking men—from cops to carpenters—bring their own special skills and impressive tools to the most satisfying job of all: capturing and breaking the male sexual beast. Hot, incisive and way over the top

MASQUERADE BOOKS

LARS EIGHNER

WHISPERED IN THE DARK
$5.95/286-8
A volume demonstrating Eighner's unique combination of
strengths: poetic descriptive power, an unfailing ear for
dialogue, and a finely tuned feeling for the nuances of
male passion.

AMERICAN PRELUDE
$4.95/170-5
Eighner is widely recognized as one of our best, most exciting gay writers. He is also one of gay erotica's true
masters—and *American Prelude* shows why. Wonderfully
written, blisteringly hot tales of all-American lust.

B.M.O.C.
$4.95/3077-6
In a college town known as "the Athens of the South-
west," studs of every stripe are up all night—studying,
naturally. Relive university life the way it was supposed to
be, with a cast of handsome honor students majoring in
Human Homosexuality.

DAVID LAURENTS, EDITOR

SOUTHERN COMFORT
$6.50/466-6
Editor David Laurents now unleashes a collection of tales
focusing on the American South—reflecting not only
Southern literary tradition, but the many contributions the
region has made to the iconography of the American Male.

WANDERLUST:
HOMOEROTIC TALES OF TRAVEL
$5.95/395-3
A volume dedicated to the special pleasures of faraway
places. Gay men have always had a special interest in
travel—and not only for the scenic vistas. Wanderlust
celebrates the freedom of the open road, and the allure of
men who stray from the beaten path....

THE BADBOY BOOK OF EROTIC POETRY
$5.95/382-1
Over fifty of today's best poets. Erotic poetry has long been
the problem child of the literary world—highly creative
and provocative, but somehow too frank to be "literature."
Both learned and stimulating, *The Badboy Book of Erotic
Poetry* restores eros to its rightful place of honor in contemporary gay writing.

AARON TRAVIS

BIG SHOTS
$5.95/448-8
Two fierce tales in one electrifying volume. In *Beirut*, Travis
tells the story of ultimate military power and erotic subju-
gation; *Kip*, Travis' hypersexed and sinister take on film
noir, appears in unexpurgated form for the first time.

EXPOSED
$4.95/126-8
A volume of shorter Travis tales, each providing a uniq[ue]
glimpse of the horny gay male in his natural environmer[t]
Cops, college jocks, ancient Romans—even Sherlo[ck]
Holmes and his loyal Watson—cruise these pages, fre[sh]
from the throbbing pen of one of our hottest authors.

BEAST OF BURDEN
$4.95/105-5
Five ferocious tales. Innocents surrender to the brut[al]
sexual mastery of their superiors, as taboos are shatter[ed]
and replaced with the unwritten rules of masculi[ne]
conquest. Intense, extreme—and totally Travis.

IN THE BLOOD
$5.95/283-3
Written when Travis had just begun to explore the tr[ue]
power of the erotic imagination, these stories laid t[he]
groundwork for later masterpieces. Among the ma[ny]
rewarding rarities included in this volume: "In the Bloo[d]
—a heart-pounding descent into sexual vampirism, w[rit-]
ten with the furious erotic power that is Travis' trademark[.]

THE FLESH FABLES
$4.95/243-4
One of Travis' best collections. *The Flesh Fables* includ[es]
"Blue Light," his most famous story, as well as oth[er]
masterpieces that established him as the erotic writer [to]
watch. And watch carefully, because Travis always buries [a]
surprise somewhere beneath his scorching detail....

SLAVES OF THE EMPIRE
$4.95/3054-7
"A wonderful mythic tale. Set against the backdrop [of]
the exotic and powerful Roman Empire, this wonde[r-]
fully written novel explores the timeless questions [of]
light and dark in male sexuality. The locale may b[e]
the ancient world, but these are the slaves an[d]
masters of our time...."   —John Presto[n]

BOB VICKERY

SKIN DEEP
$4.95/265-5
So many varied beauties no one will go away unsatisfie[d]
No tantalizing morsel of manflesh is overlooked—or le[ft]
unexplored! Beauty may be only skin deep, but a hand[ful]
of beautiful skin is a tempting proposition.

JR

FRENCH QUARTER NIGHTS
$5.95/337-6
Sensual snapshots of the many places where men ge[t]
down and dirty—from the steamy French Quarter to th[e]
steam room at the old Everard baths. These are night[s]
you'll wish would go on forever....

TOM BACCHUS

RAHM
$5.95/315-5
The imagination of Tom Bacchus brings to life an extraordi[-]
nary assortment of characters, from the Father of Us All t[o]
the cowpoke next door, the early gay literati to rude
queercore mosh rats. No one is better than Bacchus [at]
staking out sexual territory with a swagger and a sly grin.

MASQUERADE BOOKS

MASQUERADE BOOKS

BEWARE THE GOD WHO SMILES
$5.95/321-X

Two lusty young Americans are transported to ancient Egypt—where they are embroiled in regional warfare and taken as slaves by marauding barbarians. The key to escape from this brutal bondage lies in their own rampant libidos, and urges as old as time itself.

2069 TRILOGY
(This one-volume collection only $6.95)244-2

For the first time, Larry Townsend's early science-fiction trilogy appears in one massive volume! Set in a future world, the 2069 Trilogy includes the tight plotting and shameless male sexual pleasure that established him as one of gay erotica's first masters.

MIND MASTER
$4.95/209-4

Who better to explore the territory of erotic dominance than an author who helped define the genre—and knows that ultimate mastery always transcends the physical.Another unrelenting Townsend tale.

THE LONG LEATHER CORD
$4.95/201-9

Chuck's stepfather never lacks money or clandestine male visitors with whom he enacts intense sexual rituals. As Chuck comes to terms with his own desires, he begins to unravel the mystery behind the stepfather's secret life.

MAN SWORD
$4.95/188-8

The très gai tale of France's King Henri III, who was unimaginably spoiled by his mother—the infamous Catherine de Medici—and groomed from a young age to assume the throne of France. Along the way, he encounters enough sexual schemers and politicos to alter one's picture of history forever!

THE FAUSTUS CONTRACT
$4.95/167-5

Two attractive young men desperately need $1000. Will do anything. Travel OK. Danger OK. Call anytime... Two cocky young schemers want more than they bargained for in this story of lust and its discontents.

THE GAY ADVENTURES OF CAPTAIN GOOSE
$4.95/169-1

Hot young Jerome Gander is sentenced to serve aboard the *H.M.S. Faerigold*—a ship manned by the most hardened, unrepentant criminals. In no time, Gander becomes well-versed in the ways of horny men at sea, and the *Faerigold* becomes the most notorious vessel to ever set sail.

CHAINS
$4.95/158-6

Picking up street punks has always been risky, but in Larry Townsend's classic *Chains*, it sets off a string of events that must be read to be believed.

KISS OF LEATHER
$4.95/161-0

A look at the acts and attitudes of an earlier generation of gay leathermen, Kiss of Leather is full to bursting with the gritty, raw action that has distinguished Townsend's work for years. Sensual pain and pleasure mix in this tightly plotted tale.

RUN, LITTLE LEATHER BOY
$4.95/143-8

One young man's sexual awakening. A chronic underachiev Wayne seems to be going nowhere fast. He finds hims bored with the everyday—and drawn to the mascul intensity of a dark and mysterious sexual underground, whe he soon finds many goals worth pursuing....

RUN NO MORE
$4.95/152-7

The continuation of Larry Townsend's legendary *Run, Li Leather Boy*. This volume follows the further adventures Townsend's leatherclad narrator as he travels every sexu byway available to the S/M male.

THE SCORPIUS EQUATION
$4.95/119-5

The story of a man caught between the demands of tw galactic empires. Our randy hero must match wits—a more—with the incredible forces that rule his world.

THE SEXUAL ADVENTURES OF SHERLOCK HOLMES
$4.95/3097-0

A scandalously sexy take on this legendary sleuth. Study in Scarlet" is transformed to expose Mrs. Hudson a man in drag, the Diogenes Club as an S/M arena, a clues only the redoubtable—and very horny—Sherlo Holmes could piece together. A baffling tale of sex a mystery.

EAT WAVE
.95/159-4

is body was draped in baggy clothes, but there was rdly any doubt that they covered anything less than rfection.... His slacks were cinched tight around a rrow waist, one rise of flesh pushing against the thin oric promised a firm, melon-shaped ass....

ILES DIAMOND AND THE DEMON OF DEATH
.95/251-5

rek Adams' gay gumshoe returns for further adventures. les always find himself in the stickiest situations—with y stud whose path he crosses! His adventures with "The mon of Death" promise another carnal carnival.

HE ADVENTURES OF MILES DIAMOND
.95/118-7

e debut of Miles Diamond—Derek Adams' take on the ssic American archetype of the hardboiled private eye. the Case of the Missing Twin" promises to be a most warding case, packed as it is with randy studs. Miles sets out uncovering all as he tracks down the elusive and lectable Daniel Travis.

KELVIN BELIELE
THE SHOE FITS
.95/223-X

essential and winning volume of tales exploring a world here randy boys can't help but do what comes natu-lly—as often as possible! Sweaty male bodies grapple pleasure, proving the old adage: if the shoe fits, one ight as well slip right in....

JAMES MEDLEY
HE REVOLUTIONARY & OTHER STORIES
.50/417-8

lly, the son of the station chief of the American Embassy Guatemala, is kidnapped and held for ransom. ightened at first, Billy gradually develops an unimagin-ly close relationship with Juan, the revolutionary signed to guard him.

UCK AND BILLY
.95/245-0

oung love is always the sweetest, always the most sorrow-l. Young lust, on the other hand, knows no bounds—and often the hottest of one's life! Huck and Billy explore the sires that course through their young male bodies, deter-ined to plumb the lusty depths of passion.

FLEDERMAUS
LEDERFICTION: TORIES OF MEN AND TORTURE
.95/355-4

fteen blistering paeans to men and their suffering. edermaus unleashes his most thrilling tales of punish-ent in this special volume designed with Badboy readers mind.

VICTOR TERRY
MASTERS
$6.50/418-6

A powerhouse volume of boot-wearing, whip-wielding, bone-crunching bruisers who've got what it takes to make a grown man grovel. Between these covers lurk the most demanding of men—the imperious few to whom so many humbly offer themselves....

SM/SD
$6.50/406-2

Set around a South Dakota town called Prairie, these tales offer compelling evidence that the real rough stuff can still be found where men roam free of the restraints of "polite" society—and take what they want despite all rules.

WHiPs
$4.95/254-X

Connoisseurs of gay writing have known Victor Terry's work for some time. Cruising for a hot man? You'd better be, because one way or another, these WHiPs—officers of the Wyoming Highway Patrol—are gonna pull you over for a little impromptu interrogation....

MAX EXANDER
DEEDS OF THE NIGHT: TALES OF EROS AND PASSION
$5.95/348-1

MAXimum porn! Exander's a writer who's seen it all—and is more than happy to describe every inch of it in pulsating detail. A whirlwind tour of the hypermasculine libido.

LEATHERSEX
$4.95/210-8

Hard-hitting tales from merciless Max Exander. This time he focuses on the leatherclad lust that draws together only the most willing and talented of tops and bottoms—for an all-out orgy of limitless surrender and control....

MANSEX
$4.95/160-8

"Mark was the classic leatherman: a huge, dark stud in chaps, with a big black moustache, hairy chest and enor-mous muscles. Exactly the kind of men Todd liked—strong, hunky, masculine, ready to take control...."

TOM CAFFREY
TALES FROM THE MEN'S ROOM
$5.95/364-3

From shameless cops on the beat to shy studs on stage, Caffrey explores male lust at its most elemental and arous-ing. And if there's a lesson to be learned, it's that the Men's Room is less a place than a state of mind—one that every man finds himself in, day after day....

HITTING HOME
$4.95/222-1

Titillating and compelling, the stories in *Hitting Home* make a strong case for there being only one thing on a man's mind.

MASQUERADE BOOKS

TORSTEN BARRING

GUY TRAYNOR
$6.50/414-3
Some call Guy Traynor a theatrical genius; others say he was a madman. All anyone knows for certain is that his productions were the result of blood, sweat and tears. Never have artists suffered so much for their craft!

PRISONERS OF TORQUEMADA
$5.95/252-3
Another volume sure to push you over the edge. How cruel is the "therapy" practiced at Casa Torquemada? Barring is just the writer to evoke such steamy sexual malevolence.

SHADOWMAN
$4.95/178-0
From spoiled Southern aristocrats to randy youths sowing wild oats at the local picture show, Barring's imagination works overtime in these vignettes of homolust—past, present and future.

PETER THORNWELL
$4.95/149-7
Follow the exploits of Peter Thornwell as he goes from misspent youth to scandalous stardom, all thanks to an insatiable libido and love for the lash.

THE SWITCH
$4.95/3061-X
Sometimes a man needs a good whipping, and *The Switch* certainly makes a case! Packed with hot studs and unrelenting passions.

BERT McKENZIE

FRINGE BENEFITS
$5.95/354-6
From the pen of a widely published short story writer comes a volume of highly immodest tales. Not afraid of getting down and dirty, McKenzie produces some of today's most visceral sextales.

SONNY FORD

REUNION IN FLORENCE
$4.95/3070-9
Captured by Turks, Adrian and Tristan will do anything to save their heads. When Tristan is threatened by a Sultan's jealousy, Adrian begins his quest for the only man alive who can replace Tristan as the object of the Sultan's lust.

ROGER HARMAN

FIRST PERSON
$4.95/179-9
A highly personal collection. Each story takes the form of a confessional—told by men who've got plenty to confess! From the "first time ever" to firsts of different kinds, *First Person* tells truths too hot to be purely fiction.

J. A. GUERRA, ED.

SLOW BURN
$4.95/3042-3
Welcome to the Body Shoppe! Torsos get lean and hard, pecs widen, and stomachs ripple in these sexy stories of the power and perils of physical perfection.

DAVE KINNICK

SORRY I ASKED
$4.95/3090-3
Unexpurgated interviews with gay porn's rank and file personal with the men behind (and under) the "st and discover the hot truth about the porn business.

SEAN MARTIN

SCRAPBOOK
$4.95/224-8
Imagine a book filled with only the best, most remembrances…a book brimming with every hot, encounter its pages can hold… Now you need only up *Scrapbook* to know that such a volume really exists

CARO SOLES & STAN TAL, EDITORS

BIZARRE DREAMS
$4.95/187-X
An anthology of stirring voices dedicated to exploring dark side of human fantasy. *Bizarre Dreams* br together the most talented practitioners of "dark fant the most forbidden sexual realm of all.

CHRISTOPHER MORGAN

STEAM GAUGE
$6.50/473-9
This volume abounds in manly men doing what they best—to, with, or for any hot stud who crosses t paths. Frequently published to acclaim in the gay pr Christopher Morgan puts a fresh, contemporary spin on very oldest of urges.

THE SPORTSMEN
$5.95/385-6
A collection of super-hot stories dedicated to that m popular of boys next door—the all-American athlete. I are enough tales of carnal grand slams, sexy intercepti and highly personal bests to satisfy the hungers of most ardent sports fan. Editor Christopher Morgan gathered those writers who know just the type of guys make up every red-blooded male's starting line-up….

MUSCLE BOUND
$4.95/3028-8
In the New York City bodybuilding scene, country Tommy joins forces with sexy Will Rodriguez in a battle wits and biceps at the hottest gym in town, where weak are bound and crushed by iron-pumping gods.

MICHAEL LOWENTHAL, ED.

THE BADBOY EROTIC LIBRARY VOLUME I
$4.95/190-X
Excerpts from *A Secret Life, Imre, Sins of the Cities of Plain, Teleny* and others demonstrate the uncanny gift portraying sex between men that led to many of the titles being banned upon publication.

THE BADBOY EROTIC LIBRARY VOLUME II
$4.95/211-6
This time, selections are taken from *Mike and Me o Muscle Bound, Men at Work, Badboy Fantasies, o Slowburn.*

MASQUERADE BOOKS

ERIC BOYD

MIKE AND ME
$5.95/419-4

Mike joined the gym squad to bulk up on muscle. Little did he know he'd be turning on every sexy muscle jock in Minnesota! Hard bodies collide in a series of workouts designed to generate a whole lot more than rips and cuts.

MIKE AND THE MARINES
$6.50/497-6

Mike takes on America's most elite corps of studs—running into more than a few good men! Join in on the never-ending sexual escapades of this singularly lustful platoon!

ANONYMOUS

SECRET LIFE
$4.95/3017-2

Meet Master Charles: only eighteen, and quite innocent, until his arrival at the Sir Percival's Royal Academy, where the daily lessons are supplemented with a crash course in pure, sweet sexual heat!

SINS OF THE CITIES OF THE PLAIN
$5.95/322-8

Indulge yourself in the scorching memoirs of young man-about-town Jack Saul. With his shocking dalliances with the lords and "ladies" of British high society, Jack's positively sinful escapades grow wilder with every chapter!

IMRE
$4.95/3019-9

What dark secrets, what fiery passions lay hidden behind strikingly beautiful Lieutenant Imre's emerald eyes? An extraordinary lost classic of fantasy, obsession, gay erotic desire, and romance in a small European town on the eve of WWI.

TELENY
$4.95/3020-2

Often attributed to Oscar Wilde, *Teleny* tells the story of one young man of independent means. He dedicates himself to a succession of forbidden pleasures, but instead finds love and tragedy when he becomes embroiled in a cult devoted to fulfilling only the very darkest of fantasies.

HARD CANDY

KEVIN KILLIAN

ARCTIC SUMMER
$6.95/514-X

Highly acclaimed author Kevin Killian's latest novel examines the many secrets lying beneath the placid exterior of America in the '50s. With the story of Liam Reilly—a young gay man of considerable means and numerous secrets—Killian exposes the contradictions of the American Dream, and the ramifications of the choices one is forced to make when hiding the truth.

STAN LEVENTHAL

BARBIE IN BONDAGE
$6.95/415-1

Widely regarded as one of the most refreshing, clear-eyed interpreters of big city gay male life, Leventhal here provides a series of explorations of love and desire between men. Uncompromising, but gentle and generous, *Barbie in Bondage* is a fitting tribute to the late author's unique talents.

SKYDIVING ON CHRISTOPHER STREET
$6.95/287-6

"Positively addictive."   —Dennis Cooper

Aside from a hateful job, a hateful apartment, a hateful world and an increasingly hateful lover, life seems, well, all right for the protagonist of Stan Leventhal's latest novel. Having already lost most of his friends to AIDS, how could things get any worse? But things soon do, and he's forced to endure much more....

PATRICK MOORE

IOWA
$6.95/423-2

"Moore is the Tennessee Williams of the nineties—profound intimacy freed in a compelling narrative."
          —Karen Finley

"Fresh and shiny and relevant to our time. *Iowa* is full of terrific characters etched in acid-sharp prose, soaked through with just enough ambivalence to make it thoroughly romantic."   —Felice Picano

A stunning novel about one gay man's journey into adulthood, and the roads that bring him home again.

PAUL T. ROGERS

SAUL'S BOOK
$7.95/462-3

Winner of the Editors' Book Award

"Exudes an almost narcotic power.... A masterpiece."   —*Village Voice Literary Supplement*

"A first novel of considerable power... Sinbad the Sailor, thanks to the sympathetic imagination of Paul T. Rogers, speaks to us all."   —*New York Times Book Review*

The story of a Times Square hustler called Sinbad the Sailor and Saul, a brilliant, self-destructive, alcoholic, thoroughly dominating character who may be the only love Sinbad will ever know.

WALTER R. HOLLAND

THE MARCH
$6.95/429-1

A moving testament to the power of friendship during even the worst of times. Beginning on a hot summer night in 1980, *The March* revolves around a circle of young gay men, and the many others their lives touch. Over time, each character changes in unexpected ways; lives and loves come together and fall apart, as society itself is horribly altered by the onslaught of AIDS.

MASQUERADE BOOKS

RED JORDAN AROBATEAU

LUCY AND MICKEY
$6.95/311-2
The story of Mickey—an uncompromising butch—and her long affair with Lucy, the femme she loves. A raw view of pre-Stonewall lesbian life.

"A necessary reminder to all who blissfully—some may say ignorantly—ride the wave of lesbian chic into the mainstream."
—Heather Findlay

DIRTY PICTURES
$5.95/345-7
"Red Jordan Arobateau is the Thomas Wolfe of lesbian literature... She's a natural—raw talent that is seething, passionate, hard, remarkable."
—Lillian Faderman, editor of Chloe Plus Olivia
Dirty Pictures is the story of a lonely butch tending bar—and the femme she finally calls her own.

DONALD VINING

A GAY DIARY
$8.95/451-8
Donald Vining's Diary portrays a long-vanished age and the lifestyle of a gay generation all too frequently forgotten.
"A Gay Diary is, unquestionably, the richest historical document of gay male life in the United States that I have ever encountered.... It illuminates a critical period in gay male American history."
—Body Politic

LARS EIGHNER

GAY COSMOS
$6.95/236-1
A title sure to appeal not only to Eighner's gay fans, but the many converts who first encountered his moving nonfiction work. Praised by the press, Gay Cosmos is an important contribution to the area of Gay and Lesbian Studies.

FELICE PICANO

THE LURE
$6.95/398-8
"The subject matter, plus the authenticity of Picano's research are, combined, explosive. Felice Picano is one hell of a writer."
—Stephen King
After witnessing a brutal murder, Noel is recruited by the police, to assist as a lure for the killer. Undercover, he moves deep into the freneticism of Manhattan's gay highlife—where he gradually becomes aware of the darker forces at work in his life. In addition to the mystery behind his mission, he begins to recognize changes: in his relationships with the men around him, in himself...

AMBIDEXTROUS
$6.95/275-2
"Makes us remember what it feels like to be a child..."
—The Advocate
Picano's first "memoir in the form of a novel" tells all: home life, school face-offs, the ingenuous sophistications of his first sexual steps. In three years' time, he's had his first gay fling—and is on his way to becoming the widely praised writer he is today.

MEN WHO LOVED ME
$6.95/274-4
"Zesty...spiked with adventure and romance... distinguished and humorous portrait of a vanishe[d] age."
—Publishers Week[ly]
In 1966, Picano abandoned New York, determined to fin[d] true love in Europe. Upon returning, he plunges into the city[']s thriving gay community of the 1970s.

WILLIAM TALSMAN

THE GAUDY IMAGE
$6.95/263-9
"To read The Gaudy Image now...it is to see first[-]hand the very issues of identity and positionalit[y] with which gay men were struggling in the decade[s] before Stonewall. For what Talsman is dealing[g] with...is the very question of how we conceiv[e] ourselves gay."
—from the introduction by Michael Bronsk[i]

ROSEBUD

THE ROSEBUD READER
$5.95/319-5
Rosebud has contributed greatly to the burgeoning genre o[f] lesbian erotica—to the point that our authors are among[g] the hottest and most closely watched names in lesbian an[d] gay publishing. Here are the finest moments from Rosebud's contemporary classics.

LESLIE CAMERON

WHISPER OF FANS
$6.50/542-5
"Just looking into her eyes, she felt that she knew a lo[t] about this woman. She could see strength, boldness, o[r] fresh sense of aliveness that rocked her to the core. In turn[,] she felt open, revealed under the woman's gaze—all he[r] secrets already told. No need of shame or artifice...." A[n] fresh tale of passion between women, from one of lesbian[n] erotica's up-and-coming authors.

RACHEL PEREZ

ODD WOMEN
$6.50/526-3
These women are sexy, smart, tough—some even say odd. But who cares, when their combined ass-ets are so sweet! An assortment of Sapphic sirens proves once and for all that comely ladies come best in pairs.

RANDY TUROFF

LUST NEVER SLEEPS
$6.50/475-5
A rich volume of highly erotic, powerfully real fiction from the editor of Lesbian Words. Randy Turoff depicts a circle of modern women connected through the bonds of love, friendship, ambition, and lust with accuracy and compassion. Moving, tough, yet undeniably true, Turoff's stories create a stirring portrait of contemporary lesbian life and community.

MASQUERADE BOOKS

RED JORDAN AROBATEAU

ROUGH TRADE
$6.50/470-4
Famous for her unflinching portrayal of lower-class dyke life and love, Arobateau outdoes herself with these tales of butch/femme affairs and unrelenting passions. Unapologetic and distinctly non-homogenized, *Rough Trade* is a must for all fans of challenging lesbian literature.

BOYS NIGHT OUT
$6.50/463-1
A *Red*-hot volume of short fiction from this lesbian literary sensation. As always, Arobateau takes a good hard look at the lives of everyday women, noting well the struggles and triumphs each woman experiences.

ALISON TYLER

VENUS ONLINE
$6.50/521-2
What's my idea of paradise? Lovely Alexa spends her days in a boring job, not quite living up to her full potential—interested instead in saving her energies for her nocturnal pursuits. At night, Alexa goes online, living out virtual adventures that become more real with each session. Soon Alexa—aka Venus—feels her erotic imagination growing beyond anything she could have imagined.

DARK ROOM: AN ONLINE ADVENTURE
$6.50/455-0
Dani, a successful photographer, can't bring herself to face the death of her lover, Kate. An ambitious journalist, Kate was found mysteriously murdered, leaving her lover with only fond memories of a too-brief relationship. Determined to keep the memory of her lover alive, Dani goes online under Kate's screen alias—and begins to uncover the truth behind the crime that has torn her world apart.

BLUE SKY SIDEWAYS & OTHER STORIES
$5.95/394-5
A variety of women, and their many breathtaking experiences with lovers, friends—and even the occasional sexy stranger. From blossoming young beauties to fearless vixens, Tyler finds the sexy pleasures of everyday life.

DIAL "L" FOR LOVELESS
$5.95/386-4
Meet Katrina Loveless—a private eye talented enough to give Sam Spade a run for his money. In her first case, Katrina investigates a murder implicating a host of society's darlings. Loveless untangles the mess—while working herself into a variety of highly compromising knots with the many lovelies who cross her path!

THE VIRGIN
$5.95/379-1
Veronica answers a personal ad in the "Women Seeking Women" category—and discovers a whole sensual world she never knew existed! And she never dreamed she'd be prized as a virgin all over again, by someone who would deflower her with a passion no man could ever show....

K. T. BUTLER

TOOLS OF THE TRADE
$5.95/420-8
A sparkling mix of lesbian erotica and humor. An encounter with ice cream, cappuccino and chocolate cake; an affair with a complete stranger; a pair of faulty handcuffs; and love on a drafting table. Seventeen tales.

LOVECHILD

GAG
$5.95/369-4
From New York's poetry scene comes this explosive volume of work from one of the bravest, most cutting young writers you'll ever encounter. The poems in *Gag* take on American hypocrisy with uncommon energy, and announce Lovechild as a writer of unforgettable rage.

ELIZABETH OLIVER

PAGAN DREAMS
$5.95/295-7
Cassidy and Samantha plan a vacation at a secluded bed-and-breakfast, hoping for a little personal time alone. Their hostess, however, has different plans. The lovers are plunged into a world of dungeons and pagan rites, as Anastasia steals Samantha for her own.

SUSAN ANDERS

CITY OF WOMEN
$5.95/375-9
Stories dedicated to women and the passions that draw them together. Designed strictly for the sensual pleasure of women, these tales are set to ignite flames of passion from coast to coast.

PINK CHAMPAGNE
$5.95/282-5
Tasty, torrid tales of butch/femme couplings. Tough as nails or soft as silk, these women seek out their antitheses, intent on working out the details of their own personal theory of difference.

ANONYMOUS

LAVENDER ROSE
$4.95/208-6
From the writings of Sappho, Queen of the island Lesbos, to the turn-of-the-century *Black Book of Lesbianism*; from *Tips to Maidens* to *Crimson Hairs*, a recent lesbian saga—here are the great but little-known lesbian writings and revelations.

LAURA ANTONIOU, EDITOR

LEATHERWOMEN
$4.95/3095-4
These fantasies, from the pens of new or emerging authors, break every rule imposed on women's fantasies. The hottest stories from some of today's newest and most outrageous writers make this an unforgettable exploration of the female libido.

BUY ANY 4 BOOKS & CHOOSE 1 ADDITIONAL BOOK, OF EQUAL OR LESSER VALUE, AS YOUR FREE GIFT

MASQUERADE BOOKS

LEATHERWOMEN II
$4.95/229-9

Another groundbreaking volume of writing from women on the edge, sure to ignite libidinal flames in any reader. Leave taboos behind, because these Leatherwomen know no limits....

AARONA GRIFFIN

PASSAGE AND OTHER STORIES
$4.95/3057-1

An S/M romance. Lovely Nina is frightened by her lesbian passions, until she finds herself infatuated with a woman she spots at a local café. One night Nina follows her, and finds herself enmeshed in an endless maze leading to a world where women test the edges of sexuality and power.

VALENTINA CILESCU

MY LADY'S PLEASURE: MISTRESS WITH A MAID, VOLUME I
$5.95/412-7

Claudia Dungarrow, a lovely, powerful, but mysterious professor, attempts to seduce virginal Elizabeth Stanbridge, setting off a chain of events that eventually ruins her career. Claudia vows revenge—and makes her foes pay deliciously....

DARK VENUS: MISTRESS WITH A MAID, VOLUME 2
$6.50/481-X

This thrilling saga of cruel lust continues! *Mistress with a Maid* breathes new life into the conventions of dominance and submission. What emerges is a picture of unremitting desire—whether it be for supreme erotic power or ultimate sexual surrender.

BODY AND SOUL: MISTRESS WITH A MAID 3
$6.50/515-8

The blistering conclusion to lesbian erotica's most unsparing trilogy! Dr. Claudia Dungarrow returns for yet another tour of depravity, subjugating every maiden in sight to her ruthless sexual whims. But, as stunning as Claudia is, she has yet to hold Elizabeth Stanbridge in complete submission. Will she ever?

THE ROSEBUD SUTRA
$4.95/242-6

"Women are hardly ever known in their true light, though they may love others, or become indifferent towards them, may give them delight, or abandon them, or may extract from them all the wealth that they possess." So says *The Rosebud Sutra*—a volume promising women's inner secrets.

MISTRESS MINE
$6.50/502-6

Sophia Cranleigh sits in prison, accused of authoring the "obscene" *Mistress Mine*. What she has done, however, is merely chronicle the events of her life. For Sophia has led no ordinary life, but has slaved and suffered—deliciously—under the hand of the notorious Mistress Malin. The uncensored tale of a life of sensuous suffering, by one of today's hottest lesbian writers.

LINDSAY WELSH

SECOND SIGHT
$6.50/507-7

The debut of Dana Steele—lesbian superhero! During attack by a gang of homophobic youths, Dana is thro onto subway tracks—touching the deadly third r Miraculously, she survives, and finds herself endowed w superhuman powers. Dana decides to devote her powers the protection of her lesbian sisters, no matter how dau ing the danger they face.

NASTY PERSUASIONS
$6.50/436-4

A hot peek into the behind-the-scenes operations of Rou Trade—one of the world's most famous lesbian clubs. Je Slash, Ramone, Cherry and many others as they bring o another to the height of torturous ecstasy—all in t name of keeping Rough Trade the premier name in se entertainment for women.

MILITARY SECRETS
$5.95/397-X

Colonel Candice Sproule heads a highly specialized bo comp. Assisted by three dominatrix sergeants, Col. Spro takes on the talented submissives sent to her by sec military contacts. Then along comes Jesse—whose ple sure in being served matches the Colonel's own. This hor new recruit sets off fireworks in the barracks—a beyond....

ROMANTIC ENCOUNTERS
$5.95/359-7

Beautiful Julie, the most powerful editor of romance nove in the industry, spends her days igniting women's passio through books—and her nights fulfilling those needs wi a variety of licentious lovers. Finally, through a sizzlir series of coincidences, Julie's two worlds come togeth explosively!

THE BEST OF LINDSAY WELSH
$5.95/368-6

A collection of this popular writer's best work. Linds Welsh was one of Rosebud's early bestsellers, and remair one of our most popular writers. This sampler is set to intr duce some of the hottest lesbian erotica to a wid audience.

NECESSARY EVIL
$5.95/277-9

What's a girl to do? When her Mistress proves too syster atic, too by-the-book, one lovely submissive takes th ultimate chance—choosing and creating a Mistress who fulfill her heart's desire. Little did she know how difficult would be—and, in the end, rewarding....

A VICTORIAN ROMANCE
$5.95/365-1

Lust-letters from the road. A young Englishwoman realize her dream—a trip abroad under the guidance of he eccentric maiden aunt. Soon, the young but blossomin Elaine comes to discover her own sexual talents, as a ho blooded Parisian named Madelaine takes her Sapphi education in hand.

A CIRCLE OF FRIENDS
$4.95/250-7

The story of a remarkable group of women. The women air off to explore all the possibilities of lesbian passion, until finally it seems that there is nothing—and no one—they have not dabbled in.

BAD HABITS
$5.95/446-1

What does one do with a poorly trained slave? Break her of her bad habits, of course! The story of the ultimate finishing school, *Bad Habits* was an immediate favorite with women nationwide.

"Talk about passing the wet test!... If you like hot, lesbian erotica, run—don't walk—and pick up a copy of *Bad Habits*." —*Lambda Book Report*

ANNABELLE BARKER
MOROCCO
$6.50/541-7

A luscious young woman stands to inherit a fortune—if she can only withstand the ministrations of her cruel guardian until her twentieth birthday. With two months left, Lila makes a bold bid for freedom, only to find that liberty has its own excruciating and delicious price....

A.L. REINE
DISTANT LOVE & OTHER STORIES
$4.95/3056-3

In the title story, Leah Michaels and her lover, Ranelle, have had four years of blissful, smoldering passion together. When Ranelle is out of town, Leah records an audio "Valentine:" a cassette filled with erotic reminiscences....

A RICHARD KASAK BOOK

SIMON LEVAY
ALBRICK'S GOLD
$12.95/518-2

From the man behind the controversial "gay brain" studies comes a chilling tale of medical experimentation run amok. Roger Cavendish, a diligent researcher into the mysteries of the human mind, and Guy Albrick, a researcher who claims to know the secret to human sexual orientation, find themselves on opposite sides of the battle over experimental surgery. Simon Levay fashions a classic medical thriller from today's cutting-edge science.

SHAR REDNOUR, EDITOR
VIRGIN TERRITORY 2
$12.95/506-9

The follow-up volume to the groundbreaking *Virgin Territory*, including the work of many women inspired by the success of *VT*. Focusing on the many "firsts" of a woman's erotic life, *Virgin Territory 2* provides one of the sole outlets for serious discussion of the myriad possibilities available to and chosen by many contemporary lesbians.

VIRGIN TERRITORY
$12.95/457-7

An anthology of writing by women about their first-time erotic experiences with other women. From the ecstasies of awakening dykes to the sometimes awkward pleasures of sexual experimentation on the edge, each of these true stories reveals a different, radical perspective on one of the most traditional subjects around: virginity.

MICHAEL FORD, EDITOR
ONCE UPON A TIME:
EROTIC FAIRY TALES FOR WOMEN
$12.95/449-6

How relevant to contemporary lesbians are the lessons of these age-old tales? The contributors to *Once Upon a Time*—some of the biggest names in contemporary lesbian literature—retell their favorite fairy tales, adding their own surprising—and sexy—twists. *Once Upon a Time* is sure to be one of contemporary lesbian literature's classic collections.

HAPPILY EVER AFTER:
EROTIC FAIRY TALES FOR MEN
$12.95/450-X

A hefty volume of bedtime stories Mother Goose never thought to write down. Adapting some of childhood's most beloved tales for the adult gay reader, the contributors to *Happily Ever After* dig up the subtext of these hitherto "innocent" diversions—adding some surprises of their own along the way. Some of contemporary gay literature's biggest names are included in this special volume.

MICHAEL BRONSKI, EDITOR
TAKING LIBERTIES: GAY MEN'S ESSAYS
ON POLITICS, CULTURE AND SEX
$12.95/456-9

"Offers undeniable proof of a heady, sophisticated, diverse new culture of gay intellectual debate. I cannot recommend it too highly."—Christopher Bram
A collection of some of the most divergent views on the state of contemporary gay male culture published in recent years. Michael Bronski here presents some of the community's foremost essayists weighing in on such slippery topics as outing, masculine identity, pornography, the pedophile movement, political strategy—and much more.

FLASHPOINT: GAY MALE SEXUAL WRITING
$12.95/424-0

A collection of the most provocative testaments to gay eros. Michael Bronski presents over twenty of the genre's best writers, exploring areas such as Enlightenment, True Life Adventures and more. Accompanied by Bronski's insightful analysis, each story illustrates the many approaches to sexuality used by today's gay writers. *Flashpoint* is sure to be one of the most talked about and influential volumes ever dedicated to the exploration of gay sexuality.

MASQUERADE BOOKS

HEATHER FINDLAY, EDITOR
A MOVEMENT OF EROS: 25 YEARS OF LESBIAN EROTICA
$12.95/421-6

One of the most scintillating overviews of lesbian erotic writing ever published. Heather Findlay has assembled a roster of stellar talents, each represented by their best work. Tracing the course of the genre from its pre-Stonewall roots to its current renaissance, Findlay examines each piece, placing it within the context of lesbian community and politics.

CHARLES HENRI FORD & PARKER TYLER
THE YOUNG AND EVIL
$12.95/431-3

"The Young and Evil creates [its] generation as This Side of Paradise by Fitzgerald created his generation." —Gertrude Stein

Originally published in 1933, The Young and Evil was an immediate sensation due to its unprecedented portrayal of young gay artists living in New York's notorious Greenwich Village. From drag balls to bohemian flats, these characters followed love and art wherever it led them—with a frankness that had the novel banned for many years.

BARRY HOFFMAN, EDITOR
THE BEST OF GAUNTLET
$12.95/363-5

Gauntlet has, with its semi-annual issues, always publishing the widest possible range of opinions, in the interest of challenging public opinion. The most provocative articles have been gathered by editor-in-chief Barry Hoffman, to make The Best of Gauntlet a riveting exploration of American society's limits.

MICHAEL ROWE
WRITING BELOW THE BELT: CONVERSATIONS WITH EROTIC AUTHORS
$19.95/363-5

"An in-depth and enlightening tour of society's love/hate relationship with sex, morality, and censorship." —James White Review

Journalist Michael Rowe interviewed the best erotic writers and presents the collected wisdom in Writing Below the Belt. Rowe speaks frankly with cult favorites such as Pat Califia, crossover success stories like John Preston, and up-and-comers Michael Lowenthal and Will Leber. A chronicle of the insights of this genre's most renowned practitioners.

LARRY TOWNSEND
ASK LARRY
$12.95/289-2

One of the leather community's most respected scribes here presents the best of his advice to leathermen. Starting just before the onslaught of AIDS, Townsend wrote the "Leather Notebook" column for Drummer magazine. Now, readers can avail themselves of Townsend's collected wisdom, as well as the author's contemporary commentary—a careful consideration of the way life has changed in the AIDS era. No man worth his leathers can afford to miss this volume of sage advice.

MICHAEL LASSELL
THE HARD WAY
$12.95/231-0

"Lassell is a master of the necessary word. In an age of tepid and whining verse, his bawdy and bitter sweet songs are like a plunge in cold champagne." —Paul Monette

The first collection of renowned gay writer Michael Lassell's poetry, fiction and essays. As much a chronicle of post-Stonewall gay life as a compendium of a remarkable writer's work.

AMARANTHA KNIGHT, EDITOR
LOVE BITES
$12.95/234-5

A volume of tales dedicated to legend's sexiest demon—the Vampire. Not only the finest collection of erotic horror available—but a virtual who's who of promising new talent. A must-read for fans of both the horror and erotic genres.

RANDY TUROFF, EDITOR
LESBIAN WORDS: STATE OF THE ART
$10.95/340-6

"This is a terrific book that should be on every thinking lesbian's bookshelf." —Nisa Donnelly

One of the widest assortments of lesbian nonfiction writing in one revealing volume. Dorothy Allison, Jewelle Gomez, Judy Grahn, Eileen Myles, Robin Podolsky and many others are represented by some of their best work, looking at not only the current fashionability the media has brought to the lesbian "image," but considerations of the lesbian past via historical inquiry and personal recollections.

ASSOTTO SAINT
SPELLS OF A VOODOO DOLL
$12.95/393-7

"Angelic and brazen."—Jewelle Gomez

A fierce, spellbinding collection of the poetry, lyrics, essays and performance texts of Assotto Saint—one of the most important voices in the renaissance of black gay writing. Saint, aka Yves François Lubin, was the editor of two seminal anthologies: 1991 Lambda Literary Book Award winner, The Road Before Us: 100 Gay Black Poets and Here to Dare: 10 Gay Black Poets. He was also the author of two books of poetry, Stations and Wishing for Wings.

WILLIAM CARNEY
THE REAL THING
$10.95/280-9

"Carney gives us a good look at the mores and lifestyle of the first generation of gay leathermen. A chilling mystery/romance novel as well."—Pat Califia

With a new introduction by Michael Bronski. First published in 1968, this uncompromising story of American leathermen received instant acclaim. Out of print even while its legend grew, The Real Thing returns from exile more than twenty-five years after its initial release. A guaranteed thriller and piece of gay and SM publishing history.

MASQUERADE BOOKS

EURYDICE

f/32
$10.95/350-3

"It's wonderful to see a woman...celebrating her body and her sexuality by creating a fabulous and funny tale."
—Kathy Acker

"With the story of Ela, Eurydice won the National Fiction competition sponsored by Fiction Collective Two and Illinois State University. A funny, disturbing quest for unity, f/32 prompted Frederic Tuten to proclaim "almost any page... redeems us from the anemic writing and banalities we have endured in the past decade...""

CHEA VILLANUEVA

ESSIE'S SONG
$9.95/235-3

"It conjures up the strobe-light confusion and excitement of urban dyke life.... Read about these dykes and you'll love them."
—Rebecca Ripley

Based largely upon her own experience, Villanueva's work is remarkable for its frankness, and delightful in its iconoclasm. Unconcerned with political correctness, this writer has helped expand the boundaries of "serious" lesbian writing.

SAMUEL R. DELANY

THE MOTION OF LIGHT IN WATER
$12.95/133-0

"A very moving, intensely fascinating literary biography from an extraordinary writer....The artist as a young man and a memorable picture of an age."
—William Gibson

Award-winning author Samuel R. Delany's autobiography covers the early years of one of science fiction's most important voices. The Motion of Light in Water follows Delany from his early marriage to the poet Marilyn Hacker, through the publication of his first, groundbreaking work.

THE MAD MAN
$23.95/193-4/hardcover

Delany's fascinating examination of human desire. For his thesis, graduate student John Marr researches the life and work of the brilliant Timothy Hasler: a philosopher whose career was cut tragically short over a decade earlier. Marr soon begins to believe that Hasler's death might hold some key to his own life as a gay man in the age of AIDS.

"What Delany has done here is take the ideas of the Marquis de Sade one step further, by filtering extreme and obsessive sexual behavior through the sieve of post-modern experience...."
—Lambda Book Report

"Delany develops an insightful dichotomy between [his protagonist]'s two worlds: the one of cerebral philosophy and dry academia, the other of heedless, 'impersonal' obsessive sexual extremism. When these worlds finally collide ... the novel achieves a surprisingly satisfying resolution...."
—Publishers Weekly

FELICE PICANO

DRYLAND'S END
$12.95/279-5

The science fiction debut of the highly acclaimed author of Men Who Loved Me and Like People in History. Set five thousand years in the future, Dryland's End takes place in a fabulous techno-empire ruled by intelligent, powerful women. While the Matriarchy has ruled for over two thousand years and altered human society—But is now unraveling. Military rivalries, religious fanaticism and economic competition threaten to destroy the mighty empire.

ROBERT PATRICK

TEMPLE SLAVE
$12.95/191-8

"You must read this book."
—Quentin Crisp

"This is nothing less than the secret history of the most theatrical of theaters, the most bohemian of Americans and the most knowing of queens.... Temple Slave is also one of the best ways to learn what it was like to be fabulous, gay, theatrical and loved in a time at once more and less dangerous to gay life than our own."
—Genre

The story of Greenwich Village and the beginnings of gay theater—told with the dazzling wit and stylistic derring-do for which Robert Patrick is justly famous.

GUILLERMO BOSCH

RAIN
$12.95/232-9

"Rain is a trip..."
—Timothy Leary

An adult fairy tale, Rain takes place in a time when the mysteries of Eros are played out against a background of uncommon deprivation. The tale begins on the 1,537th day of drought—when one man comes to know the true depths of thirst. In a quest to sate his hunger for some knowledge of the wide world, he is taken through a series of extraordinary, unearthly encounters that promise to change not only his life, but the course of civilization around him. An acclaimed tale of passion, and a moving fable for our time.

LAURA ANTONIOU, EDITOR

LOOKING FOR MR. PRESTON
$23.95/288-4

Edited by Laura Antoniou, Looking for Mr. Preston includes work by Lars Eighner, Pat Califia, Michael Bronski, Joan Nestle, and others who contributed interviews, essays and personal reminiscences of John Preston—a man whose career spanned the gay publishing industry. Preston was the author of over twenty books, and edited many more. Ten percent of the proceeds from sale of this book will go to the AIDS Project of Southern Maine, for which Preston served as President of the Board.

BUY ANY 4 BOOKS & CHOOSE 1 ADDITIONAL BOOK, OF EQUAL OR LESSER VALUE, AS YOUR FREE GIFT

MASQUERADE BOOKS

CECILIA TAN, EDITOR
SM VISIONS: THE BEST OF CIRCLET PRESS
$10.95/339-2

"Fabulous books! There's nothing else like them."
—Susie Bright,
Best American Erotica and Herotica 3

Circlet Press, devoted exclusively to the erotic science fiction and fantasy genre, is now represented by the best of its very best: *SM Visions*—sure to be one of the most thrilling and eye-opening rides through the erotic imagination ever published.

RUSS KICK
OUTPOSTS:
A CATALOG OF RARE AND DISTURBING ALTERNATIVE INFORMATION
$18.95/0202-8

A huge, authoritative guide to some of the most bizarre publications available today! Rather than simply summarize the plethora of opinions crowding the American scene, Kick has tracked down and compiled reviews of work penned by political extremists, conspiracy theorists, hallucinogenic pathfinders, sexual explorers, and others. Each review is followed by ordering information for the many readers sure to want these publications for themselves. An essential reference in this age of rapidly proliferating information systems and increasingly extremes political and cultural perspectives. An indispensable guide to every book and magazine you're afraid you might have missed.

LUCY TAYLOR
UNNATURAL ACTS
$12.95/181-0

"A topnotch collection..." —*Science Fiction Chronicle*
Unnatural Acts plunges deep into the dark side of the psyche and brings to life a disturbing vision of erotic horror. Unrelenting angels and hungry gods play with souls and bodies in Taylor's murky cosmos: where heaven and hell are merely differences of perspective; where redemption and damnation lie behind the same shocking acts.

TIM WOODWARD, EDITOR
THE BEST OF SKIN TWO
$12.95/130-6

A groundbreaking journal from the crossroads of sexuality, fashion, and art, *Skin Two* specializes in provocative essays by the finest writers working in the "radical sex" scene. Collected here are the articles and interviews that established the magazine's reputation. Including interviews with cult figures Tim Burton, Clive Barker and Jean Paul Gaultier.

MICHAEL LOWENTHAL, EDITOR
THE BEST OF THE BADBOYS
$12.95/233-7

The very best of the leading Badboys is collected here, in this testament to the artistry that has catapulted these "outlaw" authors to bestselling status. John Preston, Aaron Travis, Larry Townsend, and others are here represented by their most provocative writing.

PAT CALIFIA
SENSUOUS MAGIC
$12.95/458-5

A new classic, destined to grace the shelves of anyone interested in contemporary sexuality.

"*Sensuous Magic* is clear, succinct and engaging even for the reader for whom S/M isn't the sexual behavior of choice.... When she is writing about the dynamics of sex and the technical aspects of it Califia is the Dr. Ruth of the alternative sexuality set...."
—*Lambda Book Report*

"Pat Califia's *Sensuous Magic* is a friendly, nonthreatening, helpful guide and resource... She captures the power of what it means to enter forbidden terrain, and to do so safely with someone else and to explore the healing potential, spiritual aspects and the depth of S/M."
—*Bay Area Reporter*

"Don't take a dangerous trip into the unknown—buy this book and know where you're going!"
—*SKIN TWO*

MICHAEL PERKINS
THE GOOD PARTS: AN UNCENSORED GUIDE TO LITERARY SEXUALITY
$12.95/186-1

Michael Perkins, one of America's only critics to regularly scrutinize sexual literature, presents this unprecedented survey of sex as seen/written about in the pages of over 100 major fiction and nonfiction volumes from the past twenty years.

COMING UP:
THE WORLD'S BEST EROTIC WRITING
$12.95/370-8

Author and critic Michael Perkins has scoured the field of erotic writing to produce this anthology sure to challenge the limits of even the most seasoned reader. Using the same sharp eye and transgressive instinct that have established him as America's leading commentator on sexually explicit fiction, Perkins here presents the cream of the current crop. One of the few available collections drawing on both American and European talent.

DAVID MELTZER
THE AGENCY TRILOGY
$12.95/216-7

"... *The Agency* is clearly Meltzer's paradigm of society; a mindless machine of which we are all 'agents,' including those whom the machine supposedly serves...."
—Norman Spinrad

When first published, *The Agency* explored issues of erotic dominance and submission with an immediacy and frankness previously unheard of in American literature, as well as presented a vision of an America consumed and dehumanized by a lust for power. All three volumes—*The Agency, The Agent, How Many Blocks in the Pile?*—are included in this one special volume, available only from Richard Kasak Books.

MASQUERADE BOOKS

JOHN PRESTON
MY LIFE AS A PORNOGRAPHER AND OTHER INDECENT ACTS
$12.95/135-7
A collection of renowned author and social critic John Preston's essays, focusing on his work as an erotic writer and proponent of gay rights.

"...essential and enlightening... [My Life as a Pornographer] is a bridge from the sexually liberated 1970s to the more cautious 1990s, and Preston has walked much of that way as a standard-bearer to the cause for equal rights...." —*Library Journal*

"*My Life as a Pornographer*...is not pornography, but rather reflections upon the writing and production of it. In a deeply sex-phobic world, Preston has never shied away from a vision of the redemptive potential of the erotic drive. Better than perhaps anyone in our community, Preston knows how physical joy can bridge differences and make us well."
—*Lambda Book Report*

CARO SOLES, EDITOR
MELTDOWN! AN ANTHOLOGY OF EROTIC SCIENCE FICTION AND DARK FANTASY FOR GAY MEN
$12.95/203-5
Editor Caro Soles has put together one of the most explosive collections of gay erotic writing ever published. *Meltdown!* contains the very best examples of the increasingly popular sub-genre of erotic sci-fi/dark fantasy: stories meant to shock and delight, to send a shiver down the spine and start a fire down below.

LARS EIGHNER
ELEMENTS OF AROUSAL
$12.95/230-2
A guideline for success with one of publishing's best kept secrets: the novice-friendly field of gay erotic writing. Eighner details his craft, providing the reader with sage advice. Because that's what *Elements of Arousal* is all about: the application and honing of the writer's craft, which brought Eighner fame with not only the steamy *Bayou Boy*, but the illuminating *Travels with Lizbeth*.

STAN TAL, EDITOR
BIZARRE SEX AND OTHER CRIMES OF PASSION
$12.95/213-2
From the pages of *Bizarre Sex*. Over twenty small masterpieces of erotic shock make this one of the year's most unexpectedly alluring anthologies. This incredible volume, edited by Stan Tal, includes such masters of erotic horror and fantasy as Edward Lee, Lucy Taylor and Nancy Kilpatrick.

MARCO VASSI
A DRIVING PASSION
$12.95/134-9
Marco Vassi was famous not only for his groundbreaking writing, but for the many lectures he gave regarding sexuality and the complex erotic philosophy he had spent much of his life working out. *A Driving Passion* collects the wit and insight Vassi brought to these lectures, and distills the philosophy that made him an underground sensation.

"The most striking figure in present-day American erotic literature. Alone among modern erotic writers, Vassi is working out a philosophy of sexuality."
—Michael Perkins, *The Secret Record*

THE EROTIC COMEDIES
$12.95/136-5
Short stories designed to shock and transform attitudes about sex and sexuality, *The Erotic Comedies* is both entertaining and challenging—and garnered Vassi some of the most lavish praise of his career. Also includes his groundbreaking writings on the Erotic Experience.

"The comparison to [Henry] Miller is high praise indeed.... But reading Vassi's work, the analogy holds—for he shares with Miller an unabashed joy in sensuality, and a questing after experience that is the root of all great literature, erotic or otherwise.... Vassi was, by all accounts, a fearless explorer, someone who jumped headfirst into the world of sex, and wrote about what he found...."
—David L. Ulin, *The Los Angeles Reader*

THE SALINE SOLUTION
$12.95/180-2
"I've always read Marco's work with interest and I have the highest opinion not only of his talent but his intellectual boldness." —Norman Mailer

The story of one couple's spiritual crises during an age of extraordinary freedom. While renowned for his sexual philosophy, Vassi also experienced success in fiction; *The Saline Solution* was one of the high points of his career, while still addressing the issue of sexuality.

THE STONED APOCALYPSE
$12.95/132-2
"...Marco Vassi is our champion sexual energist." —*VLS*

During his lifetime, Marco Vassi was hailed as America's premier erotic writer. *The Stoned Apocalypse* is Vassi's autobiography, financed by his other groundbreaking erotic writing and rife with Vassi's insight into the American character and libido. One of the most vital portraits of "the 60s," this volume is a fitting testament to the writer's talents, and the sexual imagination of his generation.

BUY ANY 4 BOOKS & CHOOSE 1 ADDITIONAL BOOK, OF EQUAL OR LESSER VALUE, AS YOUR FREE GIFT

Gynecocracy

VISCOUNT LADYWOOD

Three Volumes in One

MASQUERADE

THE PARLOR

N.T. MORLEY

"The Parlor is a hot new take on a classic fantasy—or two! For those with dreams of service to a sexy, powerful couple, look no further."
—Carol Queen, Editor, Switch Hitters

MASQUERADE

LUST, INC.

ERICA BRONTE

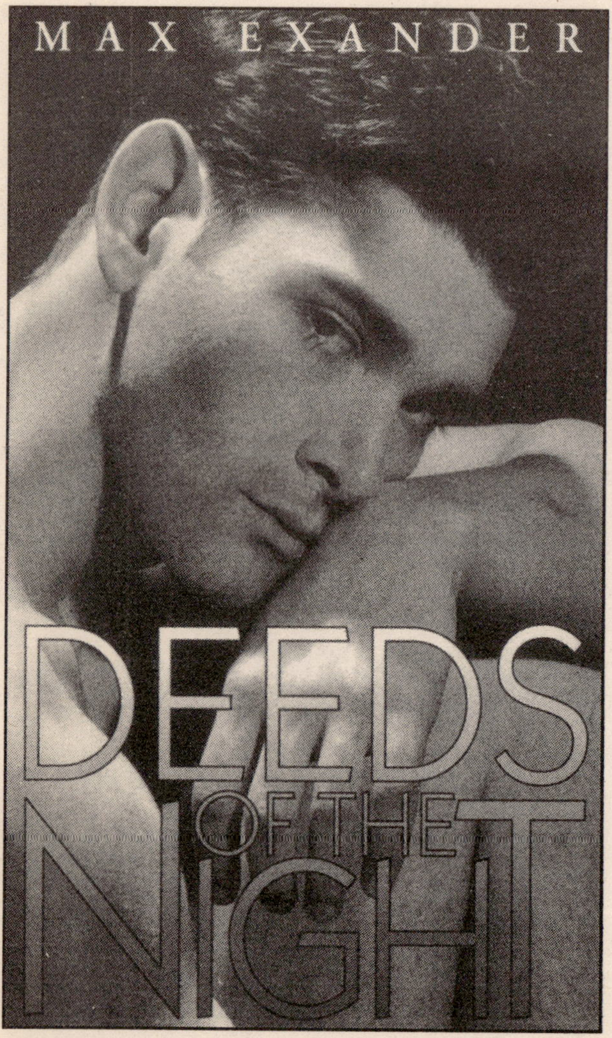
MAX EXANDER
DEEDS OF THE NIGHT

MASQUERADE

TABITHA'S TEASE

ROBIN WILDE

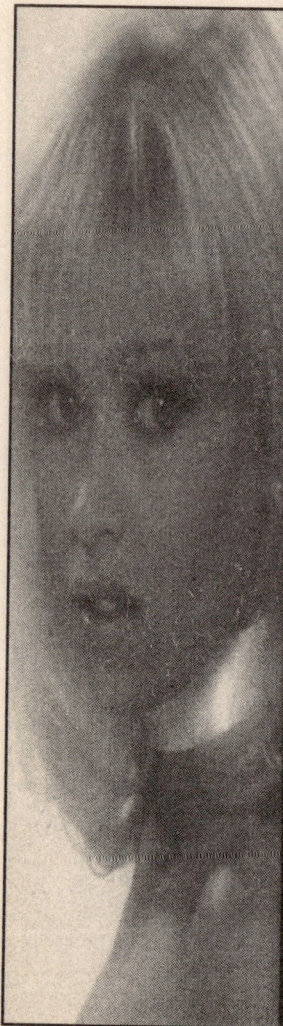

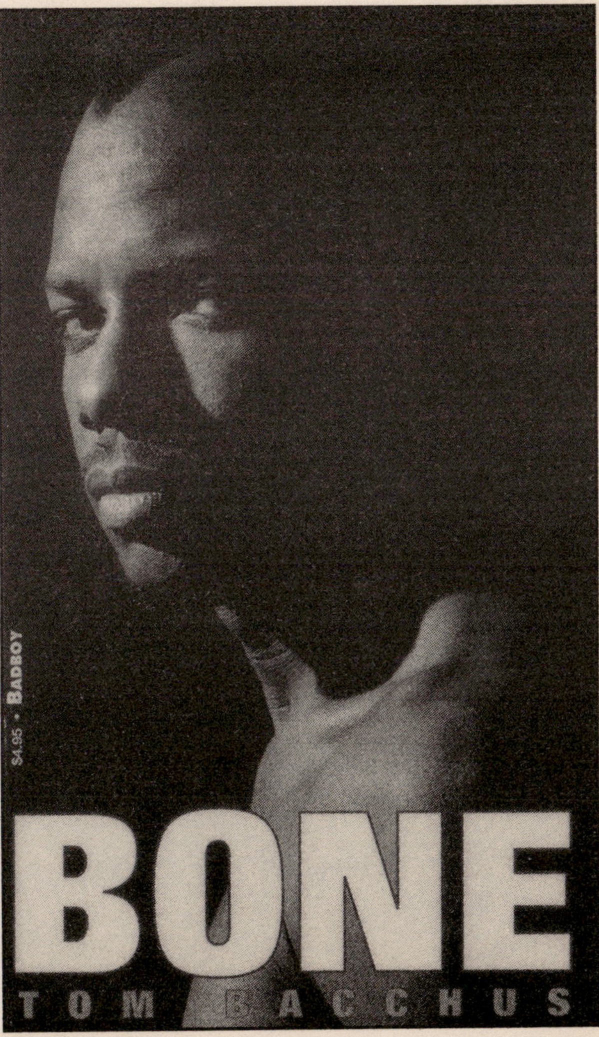

$4.95 • BADBOY
BONE
TOM BACCHUS

MASQUERADE
SCIENCE FICTION

TARNSMAN
OF GOR

INTRODUCTION BY CECILIA TAN

JOHN NORMAN

Man With a Maid

$4.95 (CANADA $5.95) MASQUERADE BOOKS

lustneversleeps

randy turoff

THE SLAVE

S A R A   A D A M S O N

"...perverse SM Erotica, mixing hetero and homosexuality in the tradition of Anne Rice's **Beauty** series."

—*Lambda Book Report*

RHINOCEROS BOOKS

\$6.95 (CANADA \$7.95)

T H E
ARENA

$4.95 (CANADA $5.95) • BADBOY

JOHN PRESTON

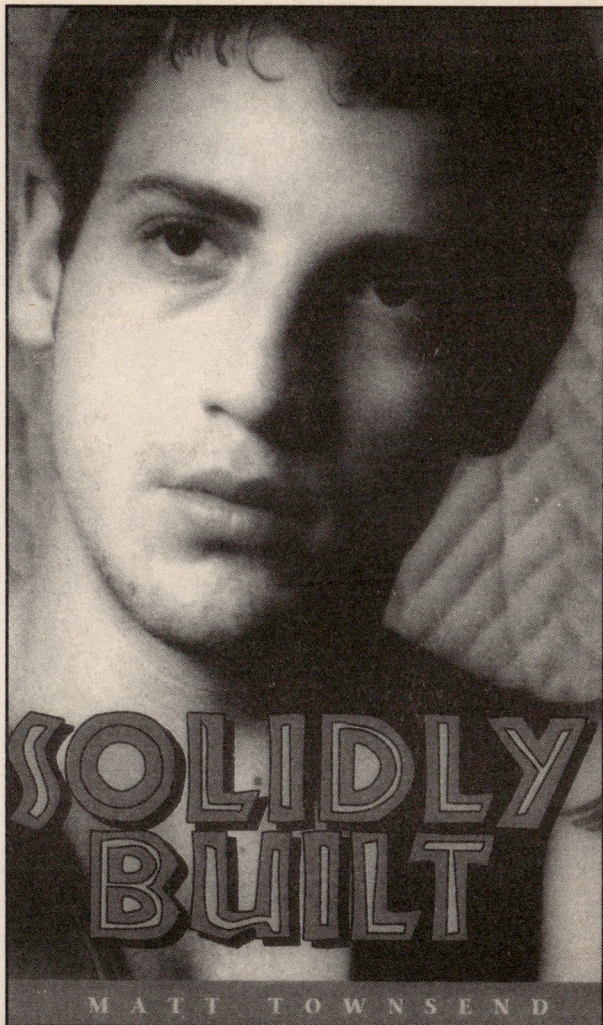

SOLIDLY BUILT

MATT TOWNSEND

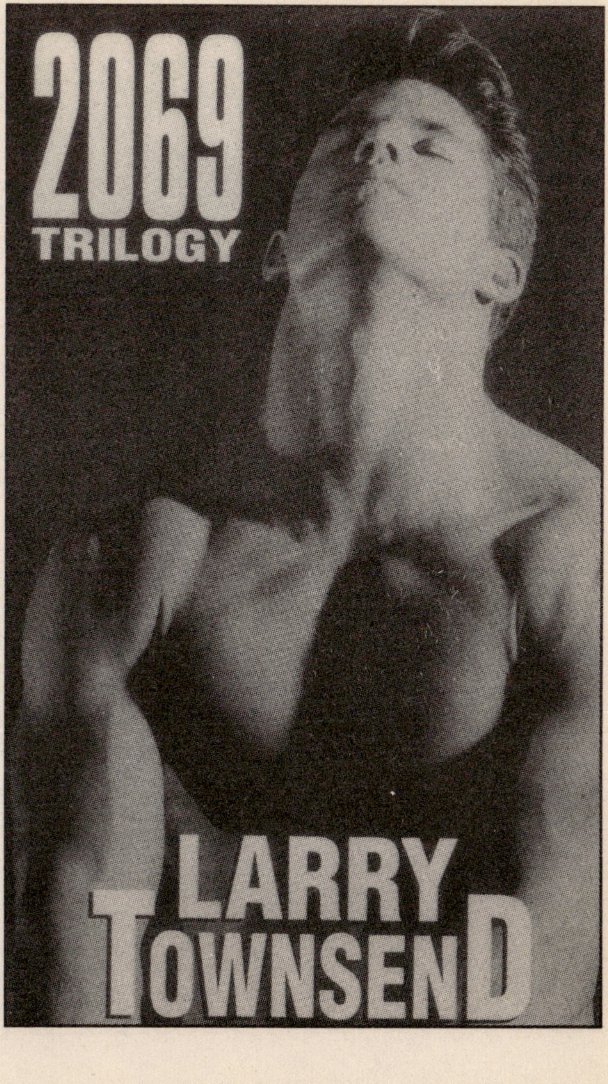
2069
TRILOGY
LARRY
TOWNSEND

BIG SHOTS

"Travis is an extraordinary writer...immediate and intimidating, fevered and anxious."
—Michael Bronski, *The Guide*

AARON TRAVIS

LEATHER AD: S

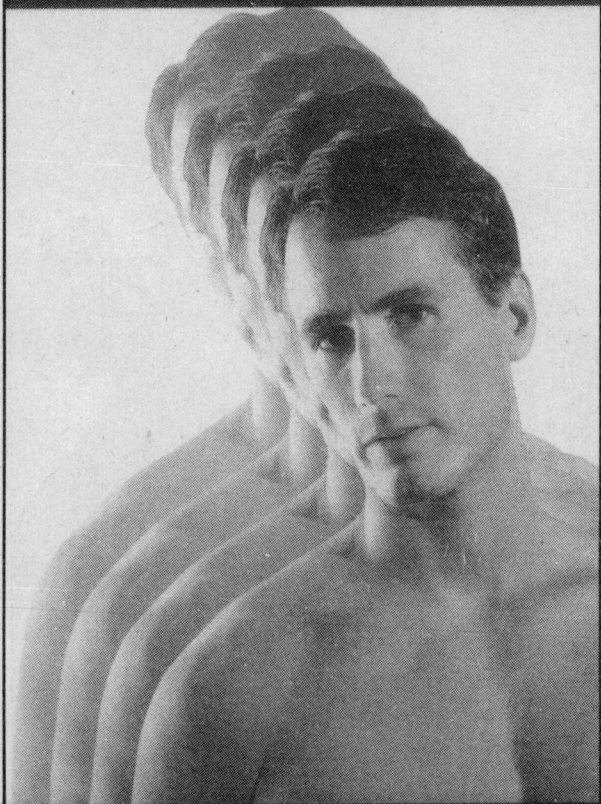

LARRY TOWNSEND

RUN, LITTLE LEATHER BOY

LARRY TOWNSEND

$4.95 · BADBOY

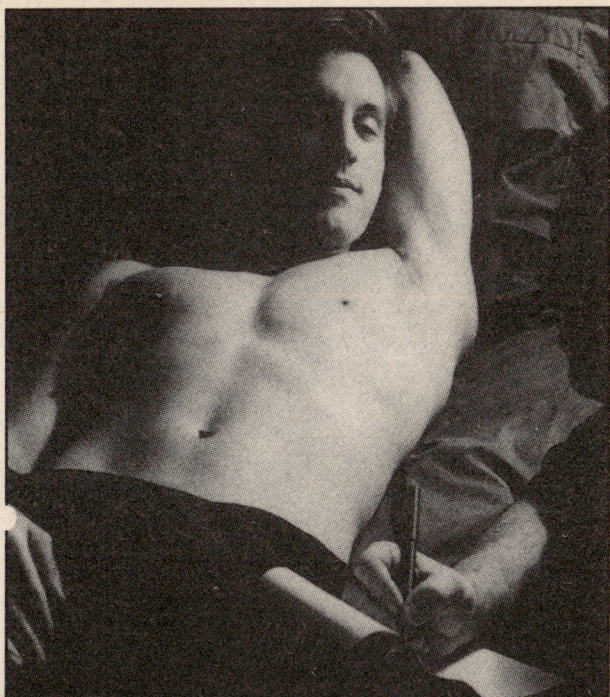

SORRY I ASKED

INTIMATE INTERVIEWS WITH GAY PORN'S RANK AND FILE

DAVE KINNICK

$4.95 (CANADA $5.95) • BADBOY

HARD
Candy
BOOKS

LUCY & MICKEY

A butch trip through life before Stonewall

RED JORDAN AROBATEAU